# BRAND OF COURAGE

He led them through the sweltering jungles, up the endless hills, into a battle they could not possibly win.

He knew it. They knew it. But on they marched, a platoon of ragged, weary men . . . bitter, frightened, brave.

Here is a novel that captures the drive, the brutality, the hate, the vulgarity, the heroism and horror of combat.

*You Tell My Son* is the superb story of a lieutenant who was determined that none of his men should die, even though he knew no man could possibly survive this island hell called war.

THIS IS A REPRINT OF THE HARDCOVER EDITION ORIGINALLY PUBLISHED BY RANDOM HOUSE, INC.

# Other SIGNET Books of the War

**THE SLOT** *by John Clagett*
An explosive novel of a courageous PT boat skipper who fights to win—in war and love. (#S1682—35¢)

**THE SILENT SERVICE** *by William C. Chambliss*
Suspenseful, true stories of submarine warfare in the Pacific, based on the popular TV program.
(#S1658—35¢)

**NEVER SO FEW** *by Tom T. Chamales*
The powerful bestseller about a young American, who finds adventure, wisdom—and love—in the midst of the war in Burma. (#T1645—75¢)

**THE NAKED AND THE DEAD** *by Norman Mailer*
The famous bestseller about fighting men sent on an impossible mission in the Pacific. (#T1549—75¢)

## TO OUR READERS

We welcome your comments about any SIGNET, SIGNET KEY, or MENTOR Book. If your dealer does not have the books you want, you may order them by mail, enclosing the list price plus 5¢ a copy to cover mailing. Send for our free catalog. The New American Library of World Literature, Inc., 501 Madison Ave., New York 22, N. Y.

# YOU
# TELL MY
# SON

Rex K. Pratt

 A SIGNET BOOK

Published by THE NEW AMERICAN LIBRARY

To the forgotten men
of the regular military services,
of whom it was said
*"we shall never forget."*

A clothbound edition of
*You Tell My Son* is
published by Random
House Inc.

FIRST PRINTING, OCTOBER, 1959

*SIGNET BOOKS are published by*
*The New American Library of World Literature, Inc.*
*501 Madison Avenue, New York 22, New York*

PRINTED IN THE UNITED STATES OF AMERICA

# CHAPTER ONE

Huge clouds hung over the island, and the rain which had been falling for five days seemed reluctant to stop. The first rays of the sun were peeking around the edge of the island and painting the landscape. The jungle had become a swamp, with the slimy, sticky mud. The rain sent giant drops of water splashing off the vegetation, while little rivulets of water ran across the jungle floor.

Huddled on a bleak hillside, a platoon of infantry sat in their holes trying to keep the ever-present rain off their rotting bodies. Five days ago they had arrived and dug the foxholes, in rectangular form, around the hill. In the dim light, the four machine gun barrels looked menacing the way they poked out of the earth. The men had placed their shelter halves over their holes in an attempt to keep the rain out, but the holes had long since been saturated. Water was running down the mens' faces, giving them an even fiercer look. The bloodshot eyes, the long beards, and the mud-covered flesh gave the men a uniform appearance. They had once been like all soldiers, immaculate in their uniforms. Now they looked like a band of tramps. The damp climate had rotted their clothing, their equipment, and even their flesh.

On the forward slope of the hill, two men had dug in near the center of the perimeter. First Lieutenant Ernest L. Price and his platoon sergeant, John J. Regeic, shared the hole. Sometime during the night, the wet canteen had slipped under Price's body, and it dug into his side. Although he wanted to sleep, he knew that he would have to wake up soon. Finally he decided to lie there for a few more minutes, and he shifted the canteen. He had long since forgotten how to sleep deeply. The Japanese were very good at sneaking into the perimeter during the night and killing a sleeping man. This had caused Price to learn to sleep with every nerve ready for action. He would wake at the slightest strange noise.

Price tried to remember the dream that he had just finished. Actually, he had dreamed it so often that most of the action was familiar to him; only the setting changed.

It could only happen in a dream, but he had been in Montgomery, Alabama, dressed in civilian clothes. He had been in Sandra's living room, the same one they had been married in. He reasoned that it must have been spring because the mimosas had been in full bloom. Sandra and he had talked about a lot of unimportant things, but the conversation had eventually got around to their remarrying. They had made love. Later, they had talked about her many boy friends, especially an architect. Almost with pride, certainly with no shame, she had admitted having had intercourse with the man. Finally she had told Price that she was pregnant. Even now, when he was awake and realized that it was only a dream, the same sick feeling was in his stomach. The thought of anyone having her made him want to throw up. Price could remember telling her that it did not make any difference to him and that he would marry her and raise the child as if it were his own. Sandra had only laughed at him. Then, as could happen only in a dream, he had been in front of her, dressed in the worn fatigues that he now wore. He had stood there for a moment, and then yelled at her, "You tell my son why I stayed out here until they killed me!"

Price was a big man, standing six feet two inches, and weighing over two hundred pounds. After more than a year in the jungles, he still was ruggedly handsome, even though he had over a month's growth of beard and his eyes were puffed and bloodshot. The biggest change that had come over Price—as well as the others—was the look on his face. The face of a combat soldier is an ever-changing face, for only in battle does it become haunted by the horror that a man faces daily. Only in battle does a face change to reflect the constant fear. Like most of the others in the platoon, Price was a professional soldier, but he changed as the war dragged on. The smile that used to be one of his characteristics had faded after the first shots had been fired at him. After he had dived for the protection of the ground, he had looked up, worried and confused. He had grown used to squinting as he looked for the Japanese soldier who might be hiding in the next tree. Finally, the squint, worry, and confusion had all become a part of his face. He kept his body hunched, out of habit, always ready to throw himself to the ground. Price always gritted his teeth, now. At first, he had done it to calm his momentary fear. Later, it had been to calm his nerves.

Price rose from the bottom of the hole, his shoulders hunched, and wiped his muddy hand across his face, trying to rub the numbness from the skin. Remembering the dream, he wondered if he really did want to die. Finally he had reasoned that if it were not for the desire to get back to Sandra, he might have given up a long time ago. He had always looked on the divorce as a bad dream, and tried not to admit that it had really happened. He could not realize that she really did not love him. He kept telling himself that they would get married again and that everything would be the same.

Price looked at the man beside him. Regeic was about two inches shorter than Price, and had a more athletic build. But the main difference between them was Regeic's large nose. As Price looked at him, he could not help feeling sorry for him. For all practical purposes, he was already dead. He had noth-

6

ing to live for: he had no parents, no wife, no girl, not a person in the world who cared for him. Regeic had been in the army all his working life, and it took the place of a family for him. For the last few months, Regeic had been drinking all the time. It was only a matter of time before he would be an alcoholic. Regeic had lost all the basic human emotions, and all that remained was the shell of a man. During the last year he had forgotten how to love, to hate; he had no pity, no fear. If the platoon stayed in combat much longer, Price thought, Regeic would give up and die.

It had been over a year since the platoon had started the long fight across the Pacific. When they had first come, the Japanese were a far superior army, and the fighting had been vicious. Although the odds were against them, the Americans had fought with courage and determination. A year later, the courage and determination were all used up, and the platoon lived an animal-like life, their only goal being to stay alive long enough to be rotated back to the States.

Before the war, Price had been the platoon sergeant, and Regeic had been a squad leader. When the war came, Colonel Stogner had almost commanded Price to take a commission. When he was promoted, Regeic became the platoon sergeant in his place. They had all come to the Pacific in the same outfit, and many of the men were still alive. Most of the casualties had been in the first weeks of combat. After that, they had learned the lessons of war and it had been the replacements that were killed.

Rain splashed into the bottom of the hole, and the water rose to shoe-top level. Price tried to remember how long they had been living in the mud. It should be five days, he reasoned, but it seemed longer. Mud was everywhere. Morris had described it as being ass-hole deep on a tall Mongolian, and the description seemed perfect. As the sun rose higher, Price wondered if it would get hotter. He even hoped that the rain would stop. He felt depressed and hoped that the sun would at least raise his spirits. Outside the hole, the ground was slippery and the surrounding hills were shining with the dampness. The ground smelled, and the stench rose to the nostrils until it almost made a man vomit. The mens' flesh was rotting away, and that smell, too, was sickening.

The platoon had been fighting for over a month. Two weeks before, the main resistance had been broken and the Japanese had started a slow retreat across the island. The United States Army had been chasing them, but the progress had been slow. A rumor had spread through the division that they were to be relieved by a National Guard division and they had been in no hurry to find the Japanese. They had been through the toughest fighting, and no one wanted to be killed just when they were about to be relieved. When the rain had started, the division had halted, and they were not in a hurry to start again.

7

Every night since the rain had started, the tired men had crawled into their holes. Exhausted from sliding through the mud, they had been able to sleep despite the muck which seeped into their clothing. At first they rose and tried to move about, but moving was torturous in the sea of mud that surrounded them. The mud stuck to their feet in great blobs, making them feel as though they had lead weights attached to their shoes. Insects and bugs attacked them and almost fought among themselves for the privilege of eating their flesh and drinking their blood. Even that did not stop the men from sleeping, since most of them were too tired to raise their arms to slap at the insects.

It had been over two weeks since they had even seen a Japanese soldier, but the men could feel the Japs' presence. They had learned that the Japanese were always there, waiting and watching with a patience that was foreign to the American. For over a year they had sat in holes and felt the fear rise within them at each noise. When a land crab would move, a storm of safeties could be heard being released.

At night, Price would lie in the hole with Regeic, shaking violently. At first, he had tried to convince himself that it was the mud oozing into his clothing which caused it. Now he realized that it was cold fear. Even if the shaking had stopped, he could not have slept. There was always the silence. It was everywhere. The jungle was alive with a stillness that was so intense that you could hear it. It made Price nervous, and he would imagine that the Japs were sneaking up on him. As he shook, he hoped that Regeic had not noticed.

Regeic was having the same trouble, and he also wondered if the man next to him had noticed. Each night he fought with the hunger that was always present. It seemed to him that he had always been hungry. After months of cold food and, even worse, cold coffee, he wondered what a hot meal tasted like. On a hill to the rear, a mess outfit had set up tents, and he was anxious to eat a good meal. There had been a time when he had cursed the powdered eggs, but now he looked forward to them. Thirst bothered him too. He had been able to make a mixture of alcohol and grapefruit juice that tasted fairly good, but every once in a while he would lean back and imagine that a tall glass of cool beer was floating by. Ice water was another thing that he thought about. It had been so long since he had tasted it, that he could not imagine the taste. As he waited for the dawn to break, he wondered if he would ever get enough to drink.

Twenty yards to the right of the hole that Price and Regeic occupied, Morris and Beecraft shared a position. Beecraft, who was short and still a little fat, was asleep and dreaming about his wife Anne. It was not a pleasant dream, since he could not remember what she looked like. Even in his sleep, this bothered him, and he thought that it was ridiculous for a man not to be able to remember what his wife looked like.

She was wearing a black negligee in the dream, and Beecraft made a mental note to buy her one if he ever got back. As he looked at her in the dream, he focused his attention on her eyes in an effort to tell what color they were. What color were they—blue or brown? He tried to see, but he could not tell, and he felt silly. A man should be able to remember what color eyes his wife had.

Morris was awake, sitting in the bottom of the hole, with a poncho drawn tight around his shoulders. He pulled it tighter, trying unsuccessfully to keep the rain out. He, too, was thinking about his wife, whom he worshipped. He chuckled to himself as he thought about her breasts. Each time he thought about them, they seemed to be a little larger. He chuckled, thinking that if he kept enlarging them in his mind they would be bigger than her head.

Choinsky was the only man who looked as if he was enjoying the war. He sat alone in his hole and calmly looked over the rim of it, waiting for the sun to rise. He was a very small man, with beady eyes, and he looked like a weasel. Since his beard was thin, he appeared to be rather young. The other men had often kidded him about his appearance, telling him that he should get a job in the movies. He would make an ideal pimp, they had often said. In an attempt to prove himself as much a man as the rest, he had gone kill-crazy, but his fighting ability was so great that nobody thought of sending him back. He liked to work alone, and often disappeared into the jungle, not returning until he had killed a Jap. He usually kept to himself and seldom spoke to anyone except Bryant. As the sun came up, he peered over the hole with anticipation, his eyes darting endlessly from one side to the other.

The sun was rising higher around the line of trees and green growth. Price saw that Regeic was moving again, and he brought his muddy hand back across his face, slinging the mud and water at the other man.

Regeic sat up with a start, a smile creeping across his face. "Hey," he shouted good-naturedly.

"Grab your socks." Price laughed.

"Balls," Regeic said, using his favorite expression. "The rain is bad enough without you trying to drench me, too."

Price wiped at his face and slung the water at Regeic again. "I had the same dream again and needed some cheering up."

"When are you going to stop dreaming about Sandra?" Regeic said slowly.

"I wish I could," Price said with a sigh.

"Did she tell you to go to hell again?" Regeic asked.

"Again," Price answered with a note of disgust in his voice.

Regeic managed a smile and then wiped at his face. Slowly he reached back for his canteen, and after he had wiped at the top with his muddy hand, he took a long drink. After lowering it, he handed the canteen to Price. "Drink?" he asked.

"Water, or that mixture of yours?" Price asked.

"Same old alcohol and grapefruit juice," Regeic answered, still holding the canteen toward Price.

"It's a little early for me to drink any of that." Price laughed, while he held up a muddy hand.

"You should drink up, Ern. It'll put lead in your pencil."

"It will?" Price asked, in an exaggerated attempt at astonishment.

"I wouldn't lie to you, would I?"

As Regeic raised the canteen to his lips again, Price watched him take a large gulp. "How in the hell can you drink all the time?" he asked good-naturedly.

Regeic took several more drinks. "Easy," was all he said in answer, as he sipped at the canteen.

Price looked at his friend and wondered how to express his thoughts without hurting the man. They had been the best of friends for many years. Regeic had always been a heavy drinker. Even before the war, he had been a man who loved his drinks and his women. He was a man among men. It had been Regeic's strength that Price had relied upon, and now he hated to see him drink himself out of the outfit.

"Can't you find some other way to keep yourself going?" he asked.

"We all crack in different ways," Regeic said, taking another drink.

"I didn't say you'd cracked," Price said apologetically.

"Balls. Don't try to snow me. I know I drink too much and I'm about to crack." He took another drink. "If I hadn't started drinking, I'd of given up a long time ago. The alcohol's all that keeps me going."

Price desperately wanted to ease the tension. "Well," he chuckled, "I'm not but about thirty minutes behind you, so we can at least go to the same nut house."

"We ain't going to no nut house," Regeic said seriously. "We been out here a lot of months too long already, and they ain't never going to take us out of combat until we're all used up. I may get to be an alcoholic, but the Japs will at least have to work hard to kill me."

"You've probably got the right approach," Price conceded. "I've been scared for so long that I wouldn't know what it was like to have my stomach feel normal."

"Yeah," said Regeic, as he slapped at an insect that was crawling down his neck.

Some of the men were rising from their holes and sliding back down the hill toward the mess company. A few were smiling to themselves as they looked forward to the first hot meal that they had been able to eat in over a month. The rain was still coming down, but it was not as heavy as before, and the men hoped that they could keep the coffee hot. Several minutes passed before the first of them came sloshing back, their mess kits bulging with the yellow eggs. Joking with each other, they climbed back into their holes to eat the

10

food. They had lived for so long in the combat zone that they felt naked outside the protection of the earth.

Both Regeic and Price watched as the men left for the food. At length Regeic spoke. "Hungry?" he asked quietly.

"I could eat the ass end out of a rag doll," Price answered.

"Let me see your mess kit," Regeic said, holding out his filthy hand.

Price handed Regeic the mess kit and he disappeared down the hill. It was about five minutes before he returned with both of the mess kits filled with food. He set them in the mud and then climbed into the hole.

"Remember how we used to cuss about these eggs?" Regeic asked.

Price removed the fork from his breast pocket and shoveled a huge mouthful before answering. "Sure taste good."

"The best," Regeic answered, as he gulped at the food.

"Beats the hell out of K-rations." Price laughed as he thought about the food they had been eating during the last month.

They ate their food like starved men, trying to shield it from the rain that was still falling lightly. They did not speak, until they had nearly finished.

Price wiped at the mess kit with a piece of bread, absorbing the last piece of egg. "Do you think it'll stop raining?" he asked Regeic.

"I hope not," Regeic answered.

Price glanced at Regeic over the cup of lukewarm coffee. "If the rain stops we have to move out at 0800."

"I never thought I'd hope it kept raining," Regeic laughed. Then he became serious and added, "We going to have a look at the town first?"

The town was a small village several miles from the hill, and the battalion had orders to take it if the rain let up enough to get there. Price turned to Regeic. "How about getting somebody to wash our gear? We'd better have a look down there."

They both stood in the hole and adjusted their gear. Tenderly, they adjusted the straps so that they would not dig into the already sore shoulders. They fingered their ammunition pouches to be sure they were full, adjusted their helmets, and then picked up their weapons. With difficulty they climbed out of the hole and slipped down the trail.

Just before they reached the edge of the perimeter, the rain stopped suddenly. They slid through the mud in silence until they reached a clear place on the forward slope of the hill, from which they could see the village. Through eyes which were narrowed to slits, Price surveyed the vast expanse of jungle below him. The jungle was bathed by the rays of the sun, which had just come over the line of trees, and he was filled with wonder as the copper rays bounced across the trees. The light blue, almost purple, mist that had clung to

11

the top of the distant mountains began to lift, looking like a giant curtain being drawn across a stage. The contour of the mountains began to take on a dark blue color. To the west, the dark storm clouds hung as though reluctant to leave the island, and a dark patch, where the rain was still falling, could be seen extending to the ground. Directly in front of Price was a long green slope that led to the valley where the village was nestled. To the east, the green sea extended as far as the eye could see, making a man wonder at his smallness.

Awe-struck, the men stood in silence for a long time before either of them spoke. Finally Price said, in a whisper, "Beautiful."

"An ocean of green."

Price took a long breath. "I never saw anything like it."

"Me neither."

"Just like a painting," Price said. He sat down on the ground and leaned back against the trunk of a large twisted tree.

"I wish I was there already," Regeic said, letting out a deep breath and sitting down next to Price.

"Sure does look peaceful," Price said as he fished in his breast pocket for the cigar stub that he had put there the night before. It was water-soaked, and after several attempts to light it, he decided to just chew the end.

Regeic removed his helmet and bit firmly into a plug of chewing tobacco. "Almost like there never was any war out here. I think that I might like to come back out here after the war. I think I could spend the rest of my life right here with a lot of cool beer and a pretty native girl to keep me company."

Price was trying to get the field glasses from their case, but he looked up and mumbled, "Be nice." He leaned back and crossed his legs. The town had been scouted the day before and they had brought back a report that the town was deserted. As he sat there and watched, Price wondered if the scouting patrol had done the job correctly. Men from the National Guard Division had been on the patrol. When they entered the town, the Japs would have stayed in the buildings and hidden if it was possible. As he looked at the rice paddy, Price hoped that there were no Japs in the buildings. The flat rice paddy would be an ideal place to hit the Americans. There would be no cover for them there.

Price lowered the glasses and passed them to Regeic. "You take a look."

Regeic took the glasses and surveyed the buildings. "Sure is quiet," he said, still looking through the glasses. When he came to the church, he surveyed the windows of the steeple very carefully. As he looked for any movement, he reasoned that it would make a good observation post for the Japanese, especially if they had mortars in the town. Satisfied, he

12

lowered the glasses and spat a long stream of tobacco juice.

Price took the glasses and then glanced at the brown juice that was at his feet. "Couldn't you find a nastier habit than chewing tobacco?"

"How about them cigars you smoke," Regeic quipped.

"They aren't as nasty as chewing." Price laughed.

"Everybody to his own," Regeic said, poking at Price's ribs.

"Hell, nothing is as nasty as chewing tobacco," Price said. "Nothing."

Regeic smiled broadly. "You just never looked at the end of one of them chewed-up cigars. Looks like a dog turd."

"Fugg you."

Looking back at the village, Regeic spoke. "How many houses did you count, Ern?"

"Fifteen, maybe sixteen."

"Any movement?"

Price removed his helmet and scratched at his long hair as he surveyed the village. "I didn't see any, but it wouldn't surprise me if it weren't loaded with Japs."

Regeic scratched at his stomach with his long fingers. "You know it was National Guard troops that were on the patrol, don't you?"

"Yeah."

Regeic scratched his chin. "Do you think they looked good?"

"I sure hope so," Price answered slowly.

"You *hope* so," Regeic answered slowly.

"That's right," Price said. "If you can remember that far back, think how good you were when you first came out here. We had a lot more training than these men and we still didn't know how to do things very good."

"I sure hope they did a good job this time," Regeic said. "Except for the rain, we've had a good time of it for the last few weeks. I don't want to stop now that the rain has stopped. Right now, I'd like to get down there and take a good hot bath. I might even shave."

"That, I'd like to see," Price laughed.

"Well, if my guess is right," Regeic said, "the town is probably loaded with Japs. I don't trust anything those National Guardsmen do, not a damn thing. I spent twelve years getting these stripes, and it only took some of them three months to make master sergeant. Why, some of their noncoms ain't even old enough to shave yet. I heard a rumor that they promoted the whole outfit before they called them in."

"I heard the same thing," Price said, scratching a raw place between his legs.

"I wonder what the brass thinks we need them for," Regeic asked. "We can't never win the war with men like them."

"I agree, but they probably hate us too," Price said.

Beecraft and Morris had finished eating and were sitting

13

in their holes cleaning their weapons. Morris looked up from his M-1. "Did you see how tired Price and Regeic looked when they left? I think they've about had it."

Beecraft smiled. "You just haven't looked in the mirror lately. None of us looks too good. I don't know how Regeic and Price make it. They don't have anything at all to go back to. If I had to make decisions like they do, I know I'd crack. Can you imagine how it must be to send men to their death? I don't know how they keep it up."

"It's been hard on Price," Morris said. "I can see a change in him almost every day. Each time a new man gets hit it seems to bother him a little more. Remember how he sat down and cried after Masters was killed?"

"He blamed himself. I think Regeic does, too. That's when he started drinking."

"I guess it was about then that he started hitting the bottle so heavy," Morris said.

Having finished cleaning his weapon, Beecraft relaxed. "He never did complain though," he said, lighting a soggy cigarette. "He's a real soldier; they both are. It must be real hard on Price. Sandra gave him the short end of the stick just before he came out here. I guess that, along with all the men that he's watched get killed, has been more than he could stand."

Morris slapped at an insect. "Well, how'd you feel if your wife left you? Sandra was a real bitch. I don't think she ever really loved him at all."

Beecraft looked very sad for a moment. "I think I'd kill myself if that ever happened to me."

"I know I would," Morris said seriously. "I wouldn't want to live without Roberta."

"Most women would break their necks trying to get a husband like him. As far as I know, he never told a lie in his life, and he always treated her like she was a goddess."

"Sandra was a bitch."

Choinsky glanced at the sky and noticed that the rain was about to stop. He wanted to talk to someone. He glanced around and then saw Bryant. Laboriously, he climbed out of the slippery hole and made his way toward the other man.

"Looks like the rain stopped," he said, trying to smile, as he climbed into the hole.

Bryant had spent a restless night and wanted to be by himself. Annoyed at the interruption, he looked up. "Yeah," he muttered.

Choinsky smiled, his lips twitching nervously. "Looks like we might get a chance at the Japs today."

"I hope not," Bryant said sincerely. He adjusted his helmet.

Choinsky rubbed his slimy hands on his poncho in a futile

14

effort to remove the wet mud that clung to them. "It's been a long time since we saw any real action."

"Yeah."

Choinsky tried to smile again. "Look, I know I'm wet and that I smell like hell, but you can at least talk to me. After all, I came all the way over here in the mud just so we could talk."

"Yeah."

Choinsky realized that something was wrong with Bryant. Usually he talked all the time. Finally he asked, "Something wrong?"

"I don't know."

"Sure you do," Choinsky said, placing his hand on Bryant's back. "You can talk to me."

"I had a dream."

"About a woman?"

Bryant removed his helmet and brushed at the mud in his hair. "No. It was about getting shot. I dreamed that the town was full of Japs, and that they shot me in the balls."

Choinsky laughed. "Hell," he said, slapping Bryant on the back, "we all have dreams, but most of them never come true. I dream about being in bed with a woman all the time, but it never happens."

"Murdock had the same feeling the day he got it," Bryant said flatly.

"Coincidence."

"I hope so."

Choinsky lit a cigarette and then blew the smoke into the air. "Ain't old Choinsky always right?"

"Usually."

"Okay, then smile."

"I don't know," Bryant said slowly. "I can't get rid of the feeling that it's going to happen."

"Hell, cheer up. I heard a rumor that the town was loaded with women. They say that the Japs used it as a rest camp for their officers. They might have left so fast that they left all the women."

"Now I know you're crazy as hell," Bryant said, trying to smile. "What army would ever leave women behind?"

"Hell, they was officers. If they have to, they'll just take some away from the enlisted men. Besides, they heard old Choinsky was coming. I can't wait to get myself one of those Jap whores. It's been so long since I had any that I almost forget what it's like."

"Hell," Bryant laughed, "I'd of already screwed one of the monkeys. The only trouble is, they run too fast for me."

"Don't kid about sex. That's a reverent subject around here."

"I have to kid about it," Bryant laughed. "I'm a married man and I have to be true to my wife."

15

"What your wife don't know, don't hurt her," Choinsky said, poking at Bryant good-naturedly.

"Right."

Choinsky laughed. "For a man that's getting his balls shot off, you're sure interested in sex."

"Lay off that, will you."

Moss and Terry shared the same hole, and they were busy pouring the water out of their canteens and trying to wash off some of the mud. They had managed to get most of it off their flesh, but it still clung to their fingernails.

Rubbing his hands briskly, Moss looked at Terry and smiled. "You ever seen such a mess?"

Terry drew his mouth tight and tried to look very serious. "I can't tell for sure because of the rain, but I think I had a wet dream last night."

"And who didn't?" Moss said.

Terry picked up his M-1 and sighted down the barrel at an imaginary target. "I'd say they'd better send both of us home soon or we're going to dream ourselves to death."

"You know how the army is. They have a good cure for dreaming. They'd feed us saltpeter before they'd send us home."

Terry lowered his weapon. "I think the best thing we could do is request that they never let us go home. I bet we'd be on a boat within a week. Since we all want to go, they'll probably let us rot to death."

"Boy, that's for sure."

"Do you think the National Guard unit will really relieve us?" Terry asked.

"I sure wish they would hurry," Moss said quickly.

Terry shook his head. "Not me. As soon as they get into combat they're going to fall flat on their ass. As soon as the army sees they're not trained too good, they'll come out and tell us that we've just volunteered to stay with them until they get some experience."

"Reminds me of a movie I saw once about some aviators after the first war. There was three of them left after the war. If we stay out here much longer, there won't be enough of us left to have a reunion. About all the ones that were left could do is meet in the old soldiers' home and talk over old times. The rest of us would be busy shoveling coal in hell. Of course, we might be able to talk some too; that is, if the Devil would let us have a coffee break."

Terry lit a cigarette. "I don't know about you, but I'm about fed up with all this crap. I still kid about it a lot, but I don't think I can go through too much more. Sometimes I think I'm about to crack."

"Who don't feel that way?" Moss said. "Think how it was when we first got here. I never will forget when the Japs got after the fleet and it left. That night, when the Japs land-

16

ed troops behind us, I thought I'd crap all over myself."

"I guess that's about right. I was scared pretty bad too. I never will forget how I felt when they started after us. I'll bet I killed a hundred before they ever slowed down. Stacked up the bodies like cordwood."

"I thought there never would be an end to them."

Terry puffed at the cigarette, blowing the blue smoke directly in front of himself. "We sure got a lot of medals, though. It ought to be real impressive when we get back to the States."

Moss laughed. "Hell, most marines get more than us for just going through boot camp."

"They got good press relations."

Price and Regeic were returning to the area, sweat pouring down their bodies in great streams. Each step was more painful to Price as the raw place between his legs became more sensitive. The hot sun was rising fast, and the dampness caused the ground to send clouds of steam toward the sky. Heat waves rose, and gave the ground a moving appearance.

Price brushed aside a wet branch and stepped into the area. As he walked past the first hole, Choinsky looked up at him. "How'd it look down there?"

"Any women in town?" another voice called from across the area.

Price plodded forward, making no attempt to answer the questions. His rash was hurting badly and he wanted to reach his hole and sit down.

It was Regeic who called back over his shoulder and answered. "Didn't see a woman."

Price reached his hole and fell to the ground, his equipment going first. As he relaxed, he knew that Choinsky had asked because he was anxious to fight again. It seemed ridiculous that a man like that could have been such a bad soldier before the war and then turn out so good in combat. If he remembered correctly, Choinsky had been promoted and demoted more times than any man in the army.

After he had relaxed for a few minutes, Price glanced at his watch and rose, standing with his legs apart. In order to be heard, he cupped his hands. "Men," he called, "we move out at 0800. That gives us about fifteen minutes. The CP says that a patrol went in yesterday and that there're no Japs in there. Regeic and I looked just a minute ago and it looks real quiet. The only thing is," Price said, "the National Guard did the patrol." Price scratched at the rash. "Be real careful. The place may be loaded."

Price was speaking mostly for the benefit of the new men. The older ones had been through the same thing over and over. They could be counted on to do the right thing from habit.

"Now," he continued, "if the Japs are there, they'll hit us when we cross the rice paddy. They have a good observation post at a church. If they use it, they'll use artillery or mortars on us. If it happens, run for the village; don't stop. If a man gets hit, leave him there."

Regeic stood up and glanced at Price, to be sure he was through before he spoke. "One thing more, don't try to pick up souvenirs."

Price smiled. "Take care of yourselves. We're due for a trip back home soon and I'd hate to make the trip without you."

The men were nodding their heads. Regeic started to sit down and then remembered something. He stood slowly, and then a broad smile crept across his rugged face. "I doubt if there's any truth to the rumor that the Japs had any women in town, but if you find one save her for the platoon. If we can find enough to go around we can have a party."

The men laughed for a moment and then began to check their equipment. Price turned to Regeic. "You got any of that alcohol left?" he asked.

"Here you go," Regeic said. He passed the canteen to Price.

Price turned up the canteen and took a long drink. He coughed and then spat a mouthful on the ground. "What the hell do you have in here? Antifreeze?" he asked.

"Medical alcohol."

"Did you bother to cut it?" Price spat again.

"I mixed it myself," Regeic answered, pretending to be pulling at a pair of suspenders.

"Will it kill me?"

"It might."

"Thanks," Price said, laughing loudly.

Regeic cut off a large chew of tobacco. "You should be thanking me for saving you from a horrible death. This way, all you'll have is a burning pain in your stomach for a few weeks. After that, you'll die. If I hadn't given it to you the Japs might have killed you."

"There's nothing like a buddy," Price joked.

"Don't worry, Ern, I've been drinking it for weeks and nothing's happened to me yet."

"That's the way it should be. You're a sergeant, and they're supposed to be tougher than officers."

Regeic scratched at his ear. "You shouldn't have a thing to worry about. They say the good die young. If that's true, you should live to be a hundred."

Price reached into the front of his fatigues and pulled out a fresh cigar. He turned it over several times in his hand before he tore off the wrapper and bit the end. Sticking it into his mouth, he asked, "How about a light?"

"One light coming up," Regeic said, reaching into his pocket for the matches.

Price held the cigar in his mouth while Regeic lighted it. "Thanks."

18

A smile played across Regeic's face, and then he gave the man next to him a friendly shove. "I still say that cigar looks like a dog turd."

Price removed the cigar from his mouth and looked at it as he rolled it in his fingers. At last he spoke. "You might be right at that," he said, knocking the ashes from the cigar.

"Ain't old Regeic always right?"

"I'd say that you're right about two per cent of the time," Price said, returning the shove that Regeic had given him.

Price took another large drink from the canteen and then handed it back to Regeic. Regeic took two large drinks and then replaced the canteen in its pouch. The liquid almost evaporated in Price's throat, and he began to wonder if Regeic might not have been telling the truth when he said it might kill him.

"Regeic? You did drink some of that last night, didn't you?"

"Yeah, why?"

"Just wondering."

They sat in silence. At length, Regeic turned to Price. "You ain't got any answers from those letters you wrote to Sandra, have you?"

Price had not wanted to think about Sandra after his dream, and for a moment he thought about telling Regeic that it was none of his business. Finally he answered, "Not yet. I tried to explain to her how important it was for her to write, but she probably doesn't care."

"Did you tell her about your dreams?"

"Yeah, only I left out the part about where she was getting screwed by that guy. I figured that might make her mad."

"I know it ain't none of my business, but I think you're a damn fool for wanting her back."

"I know that, but I can't help hoping that we can get together again."

Regeic placed his hands on the ground, and then eased himself down to the side of the foxhole. A serious look came over his weather-beaten face. "Like I said, it ain't none of my business, but she's going to hurt you again. If you'll remember back to when she left you the first time, it took a long time for you to get over it."

"I know that. The only thing is, I have to try. Your trouble is that you don't know what it means to love a woman."

"What do you mean I don't know what it means to love a woman? I'll bet I've had more women than you."

"I'm talking about a different kind of love. I'm sure that you've been in bed with your share of women. When you really love a woman it's a different kind of love. Morris and Beecraft, they know. They have a woman back in the States that they love, and it keeps them going. Me, I love Sandra, and have a son I want to see."

Regeic smiled. "The others may know, but what about that Bryant? He just got off of his honeymoon before we came out here. I'll bet he ain't slept with his wife for more than fifteen nights at the most."

"I feel sorry for him," Price said solemnly.

"I don't." Regeic smiled. "If I had a wife that looked as good as his I'd of gone AWOL instead of coming out here."

"Yeah, but you don't have a wife. You just never fell in love."

"Hell, I've had lots of women in my life."

"Sure," Price said, "but they've all been whores."

"That may be true, but I'll bet I know more about women than you do."

"That's a bet," said Price.

Morris was still cleaning his weapon, sitting with his legs crossed. After a few minutes, he pointed his weapon at Price and Regeic, whom he had been watching for some time. "They're sure living it up over there," he said to Beecraft.

"They should be," Beecraft said. "Me," he said, pointing to his chest with a dirty finger, "I got a wife back in the States to worry about. I worry about getting killed all the time. I want to see my wife at least once more. If I was like them I could relax and not worry so much."

Morris turned his attention to Beecraft. "You know better than that. We're lucky, you said so yourself. We kid ourselves a lot about the way they're supposed to henpeck us, but I wouldn't trade her for a hundred other women. Look at Price. He hasn't been happy since Sandra left him."

"I was just kidding. They don't have a person in the world that cares whether they get back or not. I don't know how they make out at all. Price knows what it was like."

Beecraft got a faraway look on his face. "I wonder what my wife is doing right now?"

"No telling," Morris mumbled. He tried to think about his wife and what she might be doing. What day was it in the States? he wondered. The international date line always confused him. It was summer, and he wondered if she might have gone to Myrtle Beach.

Across half the world, the afternoon sun was burning down on Myrtle Beach. Morris had been right; his wife was sunning herself on the hot sand. Roberta was on her stomach, letting the warm sunlight dance across her tanned back. Waves pounded on the beach. The calm of the beach was a scene which was directly opposite from the horror of the war in which her husband was participating.

Every few minutes Roberta would glance around and look at the men on the beach. It had taken her several months to make up her mind to let one of them pick her up. She had started several times, but had decided that it would be wrong.

Now she was here, and she reasoned that she would have a night of fun and no one would be the wiser.

Roberta was not beautiful, but she was attractive, and she was fully conscious of the fact. She had long brown hair, which she wore piled on her head. She was on her stomach because her husband had always told her that the prettiest part of a woman was her back. Her body was still firm and she had a deep tan from the top of her neck to her feet. She lay on the ground with one of her long legs raised.

Several of the men who were walking down the beach passed her, and she was conscious of their stares. After three groups had passed and none had made a serious pass at her, she became annoyed and wondered what she would have to do to attract more attention. Almost before the last of the third group had passed, she reached to her back and unsnapped the halter. Carefully she placed the straps on either side of her body and relaxed again

Several minutes passed before she saw a man coming toward her. He was walking slowly, dragging his feet through the surf. The man was tall and muscular, and reminded Roberta of a Greek god. He walked along as though he saw nothing, and Roberta wondered how she could get him to make a pass at her.

She waited until the man was almost upon her. Then, pretending to be asleep, she rolled over onto her back. Opening her eyes wide, she pretended to be startled, and placed a protective hand on each breast. Then she rolled over again.

As soon as Roberta was back on her stomach, she looked up at the man. "I . . . I . . . I . . ." She stammered, trying to sound as innocent as possible. "What I mean to say is . . . all I can do is . . . apologize. I must have embarrassed you. I was asleep."

"It did scare me a little," the man said, looking down at his feet.

"You will accept my apology?" she asked sweetly.

"It was an accident," the man said, still looking at his feet.

"I did embarrass you, didn't I?" she asked.

"No, ma'am."

"My goodness," she said. At the same time, she was thinking about the man. Damn, he's just a boy. I believe he really was embarrassed. She was beginning to think that she would have to show him how. "I really did embarrass you," she said.

"No, ma'am. I was startled just a little. That's all."

While he spoke, Roberta reached under her body and started placing her breast into the halter, being sure that she exposed much more of her flesh than was required. When it was in place, she made several clumsy attempts to fasten it. Finally she partially rolled over and asked him to help.

She noticed that he was shaking badly, and it took him several minutes to get the hooks done. When he was finished, he spoke so quietly that the noise of the waves almost drowned out his voice. "There you are."

Roberta stood slowly, making sure that the big man watched her. She faced him, and a smile spread across her pretty face. Then, as he stood, his mouth open, she adjusted the halter from the bottom where a small portion of her breast was showing. "Would you like to sit down?" she asked him.

As they lowered themselves to the blanket, he extended his big hand. "I'm Mac Lantrip."

"Roberta Morris," she answered.

Mac withdrew his hand and then grinned. "I'm sure glad to meet you, Roberta. I've been wandering around town for two days hoping that I'd meet someone nice. I met a lot of girls but I wanted someone nice like you to go out with. You see," he paused, "I'm going overseas as soon as my leave is finished."

"Oh," she said sympathetically, "I'm sorry to hear that."

"Do you live here?" Lantrip asked.

"No, I live in Florence," Roberta said quietly.

Lantrip was looking at Roberta's long legs. He began to smile. "Isn't that near here?"

"Just a few miles," she answered. Things were progressing well, she thought. He was shy and a little scared but if she led him on she could have him easily and he would treat her better than her husband did. It would probably be his first time. "Where is your home?"

"Paris, Texas," he answered. Lantrip let his eyes wander from her tanned legs, up her flat stomach, and then to her bosom. When his eyes rested there, he remembered how her breasts had looked when she had rolled over. He had left a girl in a motel room just that morning, but Roberta looked better to him than the other girl had. He realized that she thought he was shy, and he was pleased with himself. The same technique had been working for him since he was old enough to go out with women.

"Do you know where they're sending you?" Roberta asked.

"Pacific."

Roberta wondered whether she should tell him she was married. She finally decided that even if he turned out to be one of those people who didn't like to go out with married women, she could lead him on. "My husband is out there."

"He been there long?"

"Almost since the first," she answered. Then she decided to make the first real step. "If he doesn't get home soon I don't know what I'm going to do. I get so lonesome that I could die."

"Oh."

Roberta was disappointed. She had hoped that he would ask her out when she gave him an opening. Then she decided that he was really timid. "Would you like to have dinner with me?" she asked.

"Well, I don't know if I should," he said, knowing that he had already made her want to go to bed with him.

"I'll pay the bill," she said. "I know how it is when you're in the army."

"It's not that," he said. "I might see your husband and then I'd feel like a heel."

"I'm just lonesome. I'll write him and tell him all about it. He won't mind at all."

"Well," Lantrip said slowly, "I guess it'd be all right."

Roberta looked at the man for a moment, and little shivers of anticipation ran through her. "I'll have to change first," she said. "Are your clothes in the bathhouse?"

Lantrip nodded his head, and ran down the beach. She thought about calling the whole thing off and leaving before it was too late to stop, but decided against it. A few moments later he reappeared, buttoning his shirt as he walked.

They walked to the motel in silence. When they reached her cabin, Roberta took out her key and unlocked the door. She noticed that Lantrip looked very scared. Roberta had decided that she would have him before they ate, but she was still undecided about how to do it.

They stood there for what seemed like a long time. Finally, with a sweep of her arm, she indicated a chair. "Have a seat."

Without paying much attention to him, but knowing that he was watching, Roberta began to rummage through her suitcase, which was on a stand at the end of the bed. Realizing that he was watching every move, she slowly took out her black lace panties and placed them on the bed. Next came the bra and slip.

Intentionally forgetting to lay out a dress, she walked to his chair. As she walked, she made a fuss over the hooks on the back of her halter. Finally she stopped, her back to him. "I never could do these things. Would you mind helping me again?"

When he had undone the hooks, he sat back in the chair. Holding the halter to her, she went to the bed and bent over for the things she had laid out. When she bent down to pick them up, she held the front of her suit to her breast, but not too tightly.

Roberta took a quick shower and then walked to the door in her slip. "I forgot to get a dress," she said. She walked across the room toward the closet. She was reaching for the dress when he approached her.

Hearing the movement behind her, Roberta let a smile play across her lips for a fleeting minute, while she waited for Lantrip. When several seconds had passed and he still had not touched her, she turned and smiled at him. Casually, she held her dress in front of her body, being careful not to hide herself completely. "You have seen a woman in a slip before?" she asked.

"Of course," he said.

Roberta smiled. His voice had betrayed his inexperience, and she decided that she would have to make the advances. She moved forward until her body was barely touching his and remained there for a moment, studying the frightened expression on his face. "You aren't afraid of me, are you?"

"Why would I be afraid of you?" Lantrip asked in his most innocent voice.

"You just looked a little scared," she answered, moving closer still and increasing the pressure with her body. Now she was firmly against him. She locked her arms around his neck and kissed him passionately. While still in the embrace, she began to walk forward, backing him to the bed. Without releasing the pressure, she forced his body down until they were both on the bed, rolling across the bedspread in a tight embrace. Lantrip was still acting as though he were a little boy caught stealing candy. She fondled his neck and ears and continued the long kiss.

"I shouldn't be doing this," she said, trying to sound coy. "My husband is out there fighting." Lantrip kissed the back of her neck, and she wondered when he would get on with it.

"Oh, Mac, I shouldn't . . . I shouldn't," she gasped.

He kissed her again, very tenderly. Slowly he pushed her back against the bed and held her tightly in his arms.

"Mac . . . please don't."

She was more than ready for him and she looked at him through half-closed eyes. Lantrip was not as rough as her husband. He was very gentle, almost too gentle. The more she looked at the man next to her, the more she wished that he was her husband. Lantrip's hands were all over her body, loving and caressing her. Suddenly, she realized that she did not want him to do it to her. She wanted her husband.

Roberta thought about leaving, but Lantrip seemed to have ten hands, and they were everywhere at once. She started to leave, but little darts of pleasure were shooting through her. She tightened for a moment and then fell into his arms. She felt his naked chest and then realized for the first time that she was naked. When had he taken off her clothes? she wondered.

"Say something," she pleaded. "Please say something and make it right."

His hands worked faster and she became more excited. She seemed to be falling now, and everything seemed light. Even the pressure of his chest against her seemed light.

"Make it right. Please say something to me," she pleaded.

He continued to kiss her and his large hands ran over her body. His lips were finding her eyes, arms, neck. As her passion mounted she dug her fingers into his back. "Now, now," she sobbed. "Please tell me something, anything, just talk to me." She was shaking violently now and passion seemed to be filling her like a balloon which was about to explode. "Please say something."

"Shut up," Lantrip shouted savagely.

Crushed and filled with a sense of guilt, Roberta placed her arms around his neck and held on as the world shook. It seemed to her that the blood was flowing out of her body and that she was growing lighter. Her body felt like a feather and she was floating toward a light.

She opened her eyes quickly and looked into the face of the man above her. It wasn't her husband. She remembered where she was and closed her eyes, too tired to move, ashamed of what she was doing.

Something in the back of her mind kept bothering Roberta. She tried desperately to remember what it was. Then, suddenly, she knew. Had he used anything? She started to ask him, but fell back, too exhausted to care.

The high roof of the Dallas depot echoed the hurrying footsteps of the crowd below. On the floor were groups of people—two, three, four—large groups, and small ones. Long lines of people waited for the trains that would carry them to their destinations. Almost every group of people was centered around a man in uniform. A wife kissed her husband, while tears streamed down her face; a grizzled master sergeant, with a sleeve full of hash marks, wept as he knelt on the floor with his son.

Edward Ruffin stood, shifting his weight from one foot to the other. His ill-fitting uniform looked out of place on him. He stood only five four, his sensitive face almost beardless.

Martha, his high-school sweetheart, stood beside him, aware of the perspiration on their hands. As they stood silently, Edward felt self-conscious, since this was the first time he had ever held hands with a girl in front of his parents. He felt like dropping her hand each time his mother's glance fell upon them, but he held it tighter in the realization that this might be the last time he would be with her. As they waited for the train, he thought about their romance. They had gone together all through high school, and he had already made up his mind to marry her when he got back.

Edward felt a tugging on his loose khakis. It was his little brother. "Gee, Ed, I wish I was old enough to go with you and kill some of those mean old Japs."

"No, you don't," Edward said. "You have to stay home and take care of Mother and Daddy for me. You're the oldest boy in the family now." As he spoke, Edward noticed that his mother was close to tears. He wondered what he should say to her.

"Now you be a good boy and behave yourself," his mother was saying. "You keep right on going to church, too. What is it they call it in the army?"

"Chapel," Edward said, trying to keep his voice normal.

"That's it," his mother said. "You be sure and keep going regularly."

"I will, Mother," he said.

"You'll meet the right people there," his mother continued.

There was a moment of silence and Edward felt that he should say something, but his mind was blank. He merely stared at his feet and thought how relieved he would be when the train left the station. When he looked up from the floor his father was fidgeting with his wallet. He noticed that his father had managed a smile even though he must be on the point of breaking down. Finally, he removed a twenty-dollar bill from his wallet and pressed it into his son's hand.

"This should get you to California," his father said, the smile that looked like one in a toothpaste ad still on his face.

"I have enough, Dad," Edward protested.

"Take it, you might need it," his father insisted, with a note of urgency in his voice.

Realizing that his father was trying to do one last thing for him, Edward took the bill and stuck it into his pocket.

Edward's little brother was pulling at his trouser leg again. "Bring me a Jap sword, a real one."

"Sure, Tommy, sure."

"You will promise me that you won't start drinking, won't you?" his mother was saying. It was clear to Edward that she was talking now to keep from crying harder.

"You know that I don't drink, Mom."

"I guess I'm just acting like a mother," she said, while she played with the latch of her purse.

Edward's father realized that the situation was about to get out of hand and he placed his arm around Mrs. Ruffin. "Now, Mother," he said.

Mrs. Ruffin opened her purse and pulled out a small package which she handed to Edward. "It's a Bible. I thought you might like to have it with you."

Edward placed the package in the pocket of his shirt. "I think that's wonderful of you," he said. As he buttoned the flap he wished that it was time for the train to leave. He loved his parents but the tension was almost more than he could stand.

The monotone of the station caller's voice rang through the station like the voice of doom. The echo seemed to be endless. Edward fought with the lump in his throat. He placed his arm around his mother and then kissed her. When she stepped back, she stared at his face as though she were trying to memorize its features. He reached forward and shook his father's hand. Then, after the two men looked at each other, they kissed also.

Edward's father caught the look that had passed between his son and Martha and knew that the two wanted to be alone. He placed his arm around his wife and spoke tenderly.

26

"Don't you think that we should leave the young people alone for a minute?"

Mrs. Ruffin nodded, tears streaming down her face.

Mr. Ruffin began to guide his wife and Tommy away from them and looked over his shoulder. "We'll meet you at the car, Martha." As they walked away, Edward heard his mother's sobs grow louder, a sound which he told himself he would never forget.

As his family went through the door, Edward led Martha to a deserted bench. He walked with her, holding her arm tightly, and he wondered what he was doing there. He remembered how he had been in basic training and how the others had kidded him constantly. He had gone to chapel every Sunday and had been the butt of a lot of jokes. They reached the bench, but neither of them spoke. They stood for some minutes looking at the floor.

Then, Edward spoke. "You don't want to change your mind about waiting for me? If you do, I'll understand."

Martha looked up with tears in her eyes. "Oh, no, no . . . I love you."

"Are you sure?"

"I'd wait if it took ten years."

"Thanks," was all he could say.

Martha looked straight into his eyes. "Are you scared?"

"A little."

"Kiss me," Martha said.

They stood in a tight embrace until the caller interrupted them. Then they parted, and for one terrible minute stood looking into each other's eyes, afraid to let the next minutes pass. In desperation, Edward tore himself away and ran for the gate without looking back.

In Montgomery, Alabama, Sandra Price stood at the door of her home. The glare from the street light cast eerie shadows through the large mimosas, and the man who had his arms around her was barely visible.

"I enjoyed the movie," she was saying to the handsome man.

"Me, too," he said, kissing her on the forehead.

He pulled her tighter and placed his lips on hers. "Not tonight," Sandra said, pulling away.

The man looked into her face, and she turned her head to the side. "Your folks are asleep. We can go in the front room like we did last night; they won't know about it."

"I'm sorry," she said. "I got a letter from Ernest this morning and it's got me upset."

"I'm sorry," he said, kissing her forehead.

Sandra looked back at the man and knew that he wanted to go back into the living room as they had the night before. They had made love for a long time and she had enjoyed

27

herself. Tonight, however, she was worried about the letter from her ex-husband. "I even thought about calling you and breaking our date," she said.

"I'm glad you didn't," Andy said.

"So am I," Sandra said.

"Did he write you the same old crap," the man beside her said.

Andy was caressing her back now and he let his hand reach around to her breast.

"He wants me to come back to him again."

Still caressing her, Andy whispered in her ear, "Why don't you forget about him?"

His hand was on her breast now, but there was no sensation. When he reached for the button, she removed his hand. "Please, not tonight. Will you call me tomorrow?"

"Are you going to be a little more loving?"

Sandra was disgusted with him. All the men she went out with were the same. They all thought that a divorcée was fair game, and she spent the greater part of most of her dates trying to fight them off, only to finally give in. "I promise."

Andy kissed her and quickly left her at the door. "See you tomorrow," he called over his shoulder, as he bounded down the steps.

Sandra entered the house and slowly found her way up the stairs until she came to the first door. She opened the door to her son's room and noted with satisfaction that he was sleeping soundly. The little boy looked exactly like his father.

As she made her way to her room, she realized that she had never really loved her husband. She had been taken with the uniform and had rushed into the marriage. Later, the horrible realization that she could not stand being away from her parents made the marriage more difficult. She thought about the mess that she had made out of her life. His too, she thought, but he was a man and should be able to get over it. She decided to write him the next day and tell him to go to hell.

## CHAPTER TWO

Private Sterner lay in the partially burned-out hut with the fifteen other replacements. Outside, the rain continued to come down, and the depressing effects of the dismal weather seemed to permeate him. For two days they had been slipping and sliding through the mud, trying to make their way to the front. Sterner had been on the move since they had reached the island and he had not even had the energy to ask the other men their names. At night he had fallen in his tracks when the sergeant had told them to halt. The rain and the insects had made his life a living nightmare.

Occasionally, he would wake at the sound of a lone explosion, but the front seemed quiet. Cold from the rain, Sterner woke up and glanced at his watch. It was three o'clock.

Somebody opened the door, and a driving rain followed him, keen as a knife. A figure wrapped in a poncho and carrying a submachine gun shouted at them. "Everybody outside."

Sterner thought that the man had not sounded as brutal as the sergeants back in the States. Even so, all the men began to stir, and soon they were making their way outside. It was the same routine. The sergeant never explained anything to them and they followed him like so many sheep.

The rain swept the sleep from his eyes, and Sterner fell in with the others in a loose column. The rain was driving hard, chilling them to the bone. No one spoke as they moved forward. The night was pitch black. The only sounds were the sloshing of the men's feet and the clatter of metal equipment as it banged together. Soon, word was whispered from the front of the column: "The Japs have broken through our line."

Ahead of them a flare burst overhead. A machine gun rattled, and there were isolated cracks of rifles in the distance. They kept marching forward, as far as the place where the flare had come from, and then turned right. They marched for another hour and then the column halted. "Dig in," the word was passed.

Sterner teamed up with a tall man. Together, they dug in, in the wet mud. At last they fell into the shallow hole and waited. There was no sound now, only the uneven breathing of the men.

Hours passed. In the east it was getting light, but the rain was still falling. Sterner was getting soaked by the water which was rapidly rising in the hole. His eyes were tired from staring into the quiet jungle, waiting for the Japs to come, and thinking that each shadow was a lurking Jap.

Sterner was thinking about all the confusion, and was trying to convince himself that the sergeant who had brought them was not lost. Still, all the moving, then the stopping, were beginning to panic him. He was shocked when a deep voice spoke from behind him. "Are you the new men?"

"Yes, sir," he answered.

"Don't sir me," the voice said, as if the speaker did not care if he spoke or not. "You two men come with me."

They walked in silence for a long time, trying to keep the rain out of their clothes. The rain was stopping and the heat was beginning to be more than he could bear. They climbed up the slope of a hill, past a machine gun, and then stopped. All around him men were making ready to move again. They were the filthiest men Sterner had ever seen. Most of them sat around cleaning their weapons.

The sergeant who had brought them stopped at the

first hole. "New men," was all he said, and then he left the same way he had come.

Confused, Sterner looked into the blank face of the man with whom he had arrived. Finally he walked over to the hole nearest him and looked into the bearded face of a man who looked more animal than human. "Where is the platoon leader?" he asked.

"Wouldn't bother him," the man said quietly. Then he went back to cleaning his weapon.

"How about the sergeant?" Sterner asked.

"Wouldn't bother him either," the man said, without looking up.

Sterner was becoming desperate. He was confused and wanted someone to at least explain things to him. So far, he didn't even know what outfit this was or what he was supposed to do, much less where he was. "Where should I dig in?"

"Wouldn't."

Sterner felt the anger rising, but he felt a healthy respect for these front-line veterans. "What in the name of hell should I do then?" he asked.

"Just take it easy."

Disgusted, he sank to the damp ground and cursed to himself. For two days he had been herded around like an animal. No one had told him anything. Now he was assigned to an organization, but the men around him didn't seem to care whether he was there or not.

The hot sun burned down on the men, sending sweat streaming down their tired bodies. Bryant walked slowly, wiping his forehead. There was a sharp burning pain in his feet and he remembered how they had looked yesterday when he had taken his shoes off. There had been a large raw place between his toes. Even the men's bodies were not immune to the slow festering of everything in the jungle. As the heat became worse, the sweat ran faster, making each step torture. Bryant thought about the designer of fatigues and cursed to himself. He remembered the dream that he had had last night and a sick feeling started growing in his groin. The pain that he was feeling was something like what he had felt when someone had once made as if to hit him in the groin. Of course dreams meant nothing. It was all a matter of luck. Some men had had premonitions which had come true; others had had premonitions which had not come true.

Price walked with his feet as far apart as he could place them, favoring the raw place between his legs. When his legs rubbed together with each step he took, a streak of pain went running through his body. He fought a terrible urge to scratch himself, knowing that if he did it would only get worse. As he walked, he tried to think about how pleasant the shade of the buildings was going to be. He even tried to think about a cold beer.

As the men moved forward in a weaving line, his thoughts of a beer were interrupted by a call from the back of the column. It was the high-pitched voice of Coit. "Hey, Price, I gotta piss."

I have to do everything but tuck them in bed, Price cursed to himself. He turned his head over his shoulder and yelled, "Tie a string around it!"

The sight of a military unit advancing had always filled Price with a pride that he could not explain, even to himself. The same feeling surged through his mind as the battalion emerged from the brush like so many ants from a disturbed ant hill. They moved for another thirty minutes, sweating profusely. The entire island seemed to be full of moving men. Without any command, the advance stopped and the tired men fell to the ground, taking a break.

Price motioned to Regeic, and together they found the shade of a small tree. The two men tossed their equipment to the ground and sat, loud grunts of tiredness coming from their puffed jaws. Regeic sat with his head almost between his legs, while Price used his helmet as a pillow.

When they were both settled, Price wiped at his forehead with his dirty hand. "Damn, it's hot. How'd you like to find a case of beer down there?"

"You're dreaming," Regeic laughed. "Even if we found some they'd come up with some regulation that said we couldn't drink it. It'd be nice, though. The Japs make better beer than the people in the States, a lot better."

"I sure could stand one," Price said wistfully. He licked his lips.

Regeic laughed quietly and then reached for his canteen. After he had removed it from the pouch he placed it to his lips and took a long drink. When he took it down he wiped his mouth with his dirty hand and then handed it to Price.

Price accepted the canteen and took a long drink. He gulped at the liquid and then smiled at Regeic. "Damn your soul, you're going to make an alcoholic out of me yet."

"You're already one," Regeic laughed. "A regular member of the funnel gang. I'll bet one thing, though. If the rest of the army drinks as much as we do, half of the fleet must be bringing medical alcohol over here."

Price turned his head slightly and tried to make it comfortable on the steel helmet. "If I didn't drink I'd lose my mind."

"Right."

Price lazily reached for a soggy cigar that he had in his breast pocket. He placed it in his mouth and then scratched at the rash.

Regeic reached over with a light. "Want another drink?"

31

Price took another long drink. When he was through, he shook the canteen before giving it back to Regeic. "I'm sorry about drinking so much of your stuff," he apologized.

Regeic drained the canteen. "Lots more where this came from."

"Say," Price said, raising himself to a sitting position, "didn't we get two replacements right before we pulled out?"

"I think so."

"New men?"

"Probably."

"You get their names?"

"Not yet."

Price looked back to see if he could locate the new men, but they weren't in sight.

They sat in silence for a few minutes. Regeic broke the silence. "Be some joke if the Japs are in that town. They're probably just waiting for us to start across that rice paddy."

"Some joke."

"They'll knock the hell out of us."

"That isn't funny," Price said. "It would be hell, though, if the Guard had to come and get us out of it."

"They'd never let us forget it," Regeic said, as he stretched out on the ground.

Price chewed on the cigar. "I'd never forgive them for coming if the town did have some women in it."

Suddenly the break was over and the battalion began to move toward the rice paddy. As they entered it, the smell of the human manure was overpowering, and some of them began to be sick. They had been in fields fertilized this way before, but none of them could get used to the idea of walking through the brown juice, and when it entered their shoes their stomachs tightened.

Price walked through the rice paddy, cursing the stench that rose from the ground. The morning calm was shattered with a loud explosion that sent his nerves skyrocketing. The first shell landed a hundred yards to his right, in the area that had been occupied by the first platoon. Forgetting his instructions to the platoon, Price dived for the ground, and was immediately sick as the brown slush entered his mouth. The second shell was closer as it sent a shower of hot, hissing steel and manure over him. Another shell fell and the ground shook. To his left, he heard a man thrashing on the ground and screaming in a high-pitched voice. More shells exploded and then they came so fast that there was one continual roar. The ground shook and rumbled. Price's raw nerve ends tingled, shooting their electric messages of fear to his numbed brain. There was an acid taste in his mouth and his stomach tightened and was cramped with the certain fact of death. The air was filled with death, and the smell of manure, urine, vomit, death, and blood was all around him.

With each blast, the equipment that he wore bounced against his body. He wanted to crawl into the ground. Fighting the fear that seemed to hold him on the ground, Price rose and ran. A hundred yards loomed in front of him, and he knew that he would never make it alive.

The rice paddy was a forest of rising fountains of smoke, as though the earth had opened in a thousand places. Within seconds, screams of the wounded could be heard in every direction. The battalion lay like a many-limbed animal, withering under the murderous fire. As more shells landed, the noise drowned out the screams of the wounded.

To his right, Price saw one of the men who had been sent to the platoon that morning. He was on his back. The man's arm was stuck straight up in the air, his fingers slowly moving as if he were trying to get a grip on the air. Price felt callous as he remembered that he did not even know the man's name. Norstad, one of the old-timers, was lying on the ground, his face pressed into the earth as though he had found a passage that he could look through to the other side of the world.

As Price ran, the clods rained down his neck. Dead men were all around him. His head roared with a buzzing that drowned out the terrible explosions. He heard a voice calling his name, but he continued to run. Seventy yards more. He noticed that others were running toward the town, some of them without weapons. As he ran, he heard another voice, this time in his own mind. It was the voice of the colonel the day they left the States. They were supposed to be noble defenders of their country, going out to fight a war to punish the Japs. Now, he was just a man running through hell, trying to stay alive. Survival was his only thought and he did not give a damn about anything else.

The explosions continued to come and he heard his name called again. It had sounded like Regeic, but he could not see him. Captain James ran past him and stumbled, eyes open wide, mouth hanging open, fear written on his face. The captain's arms dangled at his side like a rag doll's. For one terrible minute, the captain looked at Price and then fell to the ground. To his right, Price saw a man reach into the air with both hands and then spin all the way around before he fell.

Price continued to run, stumbling over the bodies of dead and wounded. He did not hesitate at the holes but ran around them, running straight toward the bamboo houses at the edge of the village.

The first house was bamboo and had a thatched roof. When he reached it, Price heard someone call his name. He started to look toward the caller when his knees buckled under him and he fell to the ground, gasping for breath.

Blasts were sending the foul-smelling showers of earth and manure over Regeic as he stumbled forward. Close to him, men were doubling up and hitting the ground, some writhing with pain, others dead. As he ran, a blast shook the earth under him. The concussion lifted him from his feet and sent him to the ground. Regeic realized there was a sharp pain in his left arm and he called to Price. At once, he realized how ridiculous his action had been. Price could be dead already, he thought. Regeic climbed to his feet and began to run forward again. He saw Captain James stumble and fall forward to his face. Another man came staggering past him with both hands shot away. When Regeic saw the bamboo house in front of him he plunged to the ground. Price was coming up, too, and Regeic called to him. Regeic saw that there was a look of terror on Price's face as Price turned his head to see who had called his name. Then Price fell to the ground, gasping for breath.

After he had fallen to the ground, Price looked up at the man who had called him. "Regeic," he managed to say, while still trying to get his wind back. Regeic just looked at Price and then felt his bleeding arm. Cautiously Price inched his way toward his friend. When he reached him, he gently pulled back the rotten material and examined the wound. Although it was bleeding badly, the wound turned out to be very slight, and Price applied sulfa powder and a compress. While he worked, Regeic said nothing.

While Price was bandaging the wound, other men were reaching the house and falling to the ground. Each man would arrive with his eyes wide with the horror that he had just run through. The question that was written on their faces was, How did I make it? Over his shoulder, Price could see that the shells were still exploding, giving the earth the appearance of erupting. Through some miracle, men were still making it through the holocaust. Some stumbled and fell, others disappeared into a cloud of dust. The ground shook, and the din was tremendous, as the explosives shook the earth.

The barrage stopped with a terrible suddenness, and the silence seemed intense to the men. It was several minutes before Price realized that it was over. Almost as if he were in shock, Price began to count the men around him. Twelve men were missing, but it was possible that some of them were with another outfit. There were about five men around him whom he had never seen. All of the older men were there, so that meant that the missing ones were replacements. It seemed to him that it was that way all the time lately. Nearly all the older men had given up trying to know the replacements. Their reasoning was that an infantryman needed no friends. It was much easier to witness the death of a stranger than that of a friend.

The edge of the village was a scene of mass confusion. Men were collecting themselves in little groups, with an officer or N.C.O., and spreading out along the village. There seemed to be a complete lack of any co-ordinated effort to take any action.

Price was stretched out on the ground, still trying to recover from the shock of the sudden attack. "Collect the men," he gasped out, to Regeic. "We can't stay here all day, so I'm going to see if I can find the CP and get some dope." He gulped hard for air. "If the Japs are going to put up a fight for the town, they'll attack any minute. Get the men dug in."

Regeic, too, was having a hard time getting his breath, but he managed a weak "Okay."

Price crouched, as he went down the line of exhausted men. The heat, added to the running he had been forced to do, had sapped nearly all his strength, and his knees felt as if they would give way. Twice he had stopped to rest, but each drop of sweat that rolled from his forehead seemed to make him feel weaker. Price was used to seeing men who had given all they could until their minds had gone, but there seemed to be more than usual this time. The men sat on the ground, staring off into space, their lips quivering, their eyes wide with horror. It was apparent that the whole battalion was used up. He realized that he, too, would be in the same condition. Everywhere men milled around in confusion.

As Price continued to search for the Command Post, other men joined him, mostly noncoms. As they continued to look, Price began to wonder if he was the only officer left. That would leave him in command. Finally, half-hidden under a bush, they found Captain Van Zee.

Sterner, the new replacement, lay on the ground, unable to control his shaking. He had been in combat less than half a day, and he felt like a front-line veteran. No one had spoken to him and he was desperately lonesome. When he had emerged from the rice paddy, he looked around for the other replacement who had come with him. The other men around him joked and looked very casual, as if they cared for nothing, and Sterner wondered if he would ever get like them.

Sterner did not understand. He thought that the men around him were casual, but their nerves were at the breaking point.

They had been in combat for so long that they had developed a sixth sense for any hard combat that was about to happen. When a fight was about to develop, the air grew charged with excitement. It was only during the periods of quiet that a feeling of comradeship grew, and even the oldest jokes brought down a gale of laughter. It was then that they were aware of their relationship, of belonging together. Lately, however, these moments had been fewer.

After so many months of combat, they were hardly aware of the fear that was always with them, making their lives a nightmare. The men would never admit what was happening inside them, except to their closest friends. They did not want the others to think they were cowards. When the fear seemed to be more than they could stand, they cursed, or they acted casual, knowing that the others would not think it was a sign of fear.

When the fighting got hard no one wanted to be the first to hit the ground. They all waited until the last minute, wanting someone else to be the first. They would do almost anything to keep the others from knowing that they were afraid. When a man was killed, they acted casual, referred to it as though an animal had been killed. They pretended that they did not care, but it was a futile attempt to deceive themselves.

However, the feeling could not be shaken off, and it would not be too long before they would give way to it. When a man openly admitted his fear he was all used up. With them, the mounting fear grew worse with each dead body they saw, with each moan from a wounded man, with each close call that almost ended their lives.

Their fear was worse at times like this, when they waited for the fighting to start. When the fighting started they could forget some of the fear in an attempt to survive. The only thing that controlled the fear was hope—futile, groundless hope which was based on rumors that they would be sent home.

Beecraft and Morris lay on the ground looking down the dusty street that stretched in front of them. They waited for the attack that they knew would come, shaking with fear.

"Morris?" Beecraft heard himself say in a high, unnatural tone of voice.

"Yeah?"

"Think the Japs will attack?" Beecraft sounded worried.

"If they don't," Morris answered, "they're crazy as hell. We're so shot up that we couldn't fight a troop of Boy Scouts. Half the men are shell-shocked."

Regeic's eyes were bloodshot and he looked as though he had not been to sleep for several days. He felt terribly afraid and wanted to talk to someone. "You'd better not let the medics hear you say that. There ain't no such thing as shell-shocked. They call it combat fatigue now."

A flake of dried manure was bothering Beecraft and he pulled at it. The flake was stuck fast and it almost brought tears to his eyes as it came free. When it was gone, he pointed to a man who was sitting on the ground shaking violently. "I know there isn't anything called shell shock, and you know it, but does he?"

Morris and Regeic looked in the direction that Beecraft had pointed. The man was staring straight forward. A look of terror was in his eyes and his ashen skin was drawn so tight that it looked as if it would split.

"What do they do with a man like him?" Morris asked.

"Section eight," Regeic commented quietly. "They send them back to the hospital and lock the door."

Bryant came sliding over to the men. "Horrible, ain't it?" He squatted on the ground and smiled at the other men, making an effort to hide his fear. "I remember when I was a kid," he said. "There was a man in town who had been in the first war. He used to hang around a corner and had a lot of trouble controlling his bladder. Used to piss all over himself. All of us kids used to laugh at him a lot. Sometimes we'd make a loud noise just to see him piss his pants."

"Any of you whoremongers got a drink?" Regeic asked. No one answered, and Regeic licked his lips. "Looks like I'm going to have to start my own distillery if the Japs didn't leave us something to drink."

Morris moved closer to Regeic and examined the bandage on Regeic's left arm. "I'd say that you'll probably get all the drinks you can take when you're lying up in some hospital. I think you may have gotten the million-dollar wound."

"I wouldn't go back across that rice paddy for two trips to the States," Regeic answered, as he looked at the bandage himself. The arm was swelling and the bandage hurt a little.

Beecraft looked up the road, wondering why it was so quiet. He had expected to see the Japs counterattacking any time. Nothing seemed to be moving. "I wonder why they haven't shot at us before this," he said.

Regeic spat, and then turned his attention to the village. "The town looks deserted to me. I'll bet they ran out of ammunition. It might be that the navy has shot the hell out of them. Besides, this side of the island is only a small part of the operation. From what I've heard, they're giving us hell on the other side of the mountains. They may have left just enough men in town to slow us down."

"I hope they didn't leave anybody in there," Beecraft said.

"It wouldn't make me feel bad if I never saw another Jap," Regeic answered.

The hot breeze carried the smell of burnt powder to the men from the rice paddy. The street looked deserted and reminded Regeic of a ghost town. He stared down the empty street and slowly chewed on a plug of tobacco. Down the street a curtain flapped slowly in the breeze, the only movement on the entire street. A strange feeling of homesickness overtook him, as he stared into the emptiness. He was reminded of all the times he had stood on a corner and looked in at the houses, wondering what kind of people lived in them. The feeling had always been bad when he had

37

been alone on the post. Nothing can be as lonely as a deserted barracks. Regeic tried to get rid of the feeling, but with each flap of the curtains he felt more alone.

The quiet of the town was taking its toll on all the men. Bryant paled and his lips trembled. "They're going to blow our asses off," he whispered.

All the men nodded in agreement. They stood up and looked down the street, wondering who would be the next to die. They were ragged and tired. Months of fighting had made their eyes bloodshot, their bodies gaunt, uniforms ragged. And sweat ran down their manure-covered bodies.

"You know what it's going to be like?" Regeic asked. "Just like Buna. House to house, room to room. Every time we run them out the back, they'll come in the front. There'll probably be a Jap in every pantry and two in every crack in the wall." Regeic looked down the street and wondered who would be the next to die.

Beecraft laughed. "I'll bet the Japs'll have everything in the town booby-trapped."

"They always do," Morris said. "I heard a story about a sergeant who stopped a man from picking up a sword that one of his troops found on a path. Just to prove to the man that it was wired, he tied a string to it and jumped in a hole. He thought he would pull the string and set it off. The only trouble was, the hole had a mine in it. Blew him all to hell . . ."

"Bastards," Choinsky muttered.

"You troops are just scared of dying." Regeic laughed nervously.

"You ain't?" Bryant asked.

"Hell, no," Regeic answered casually.

Sterner, the new man, listened to the men and wondered how they could be so calm. Finally, he decided that they must be crazy.

The group looked up and saw that Price was moving along the line of men at a fast pace. He was bent low and he had an angry look on his face. Surely he picked his way among the groups of men, and finally sat down next to Regeic.

When he was settled, he threw his helmet to the ground, where it landed with a dull thud. They were all waiting for him to speak, but he was apparently in no hurry. He wiped the perspiration from his forehead and then lit a cigar. When he had examined it, turning it around in his fingers, he spoke.

"Captain Van Zee is the battalion commander," he announced. "He wants to go on in and take the town. I kept trying to tell him that we should wait for some help, but he won't listen."

Regeic smiled. "You know damn well that he's right. If we don't get out of here before night, the Japs will cut us to pieces. It may mean that a few more of us will get it be-

38

fore we can be relieved, but at least it'll help win the war."

"I'm tired of winning the war," Price said.

Regeic only smiled. "Hell, that's what we came out here for, isn't it?"

"You win the war; I'm tired," Price said, as he picked up his helmet.

"Besides," Regeic continued, "if we break, the Japs would be able to split the island in half. You don't think the Guard would be able to stop them, do you?"

Realizing that as the platoon leader he should do what he could to keep the platoon going, Price knew that he should not have been so cynical. "I know all that," he conceded. "I was just bitching. I'll stay out here and fight until it rots off if they tell me to."

"That's what I thought," Regeic laughed. "What time do we start?"

"Five minutes."

While the platoon waited for the order to move, the minutes ticked by. Morris stared down the street, obsessed with the attack to come. He could not forget the fear and his fatigue. He remembered back to the time in the States when they had all thought they were about to become heroes. Even though they were professional soldiers, war to them was taking a town or an island. Two hours later the world would know about them, and he had imagined how proud his wife would be when she told people that her husband was out there. He had imagined the pride that he would have in wearing his medals. If he had been killed, it would have been a hero's death.

At first, he had been casual about it, even to himself. He tried to convince himself that he couldn't live forever, anyway. He had even thought with pride that all real men die with their boots on. Live fast, die young, and leave a beautiful corpse.

Now he realized that it was all a lie. There was no glory. If he got killed, his wife would be deeply grieved. He thought about all the men he had seen killed. His mind went back to the sergeant he had seen almost cut in half by a machine gun. For hours he had lain on the ground and his blood had slowly seeped away while he stared into the air. Now Morris only wanted to go home. He did not want to become a hero and he wondered why he had to be out there. Most of them would be killed before the war was over.

The curtain flapped in the silent street, and he could not help but wonder who would be next. It might be Price, it might be Regeic. It could be Beecraft. Worse still, it might be him. Someone had to die, but who? Over and over, he asked himself, who, who, until he thought he would scream.

Regeic looked around. "Anybody got a drink?"

Sterner immediately pulled his canteen from its pouch.

Cautiously, he crept toward Regeic and offered it to him.

"What's the canteen for?" he asked.

"Didn't you ask for a drink?" Sterner answered.

"I don't want *that*," Regeic answered.

The other men roared with laughter. Sterner felt like crying and almost broke into tears. He wondered if the men would ever accept him. Finally, he crawled a few paces from the others and sat with his head resting on his knees.

The others did not speak until Sterner had moved away. "If we find any," Price said, "you guys remember that rank has its privileges. I want the first drink."

"Sure."

Several yards to the right of the group of men, Terry and Moss were talking. "Do you think the Japs have any women in town like they say?" Terry was smiling.

"Is that all you ever think about?" Moss asked.

"Yeah, I think about my wife."

"Yeah, hell. I'll bet all you think about is screwing. What the hell color are her eyes?"

"You mean you don't think I know what color my wife's eyes are?"

"Can you remember?"

"If you know so much about the color of her eyes, you tell me."

"I asked you first."

"Blue."

"Hell."

"Well, I think they are anyway."

Regeic turned to Price and poked him in the ribs. "If I had a wife that looked as good as his, I'd remember what the hell she looked like."

Beecraft laughed. "I thought you always said that they all looked alike in the dark?"

"They are," Regeic answered. "But with her, who'd need the dark." Regeic seemed to be remembering her, as he spoke. "The best I can remember, her nipples always stuck out a mile or so."

As Regeic talked, Price became disturbed. All of them had passed the breaking point, and if Terry heard Regeic there probably would be a fight. Price wanted to change the subject before it got out of hand. "I thought you were in love with that girl down in Texas," he said.

"Hell, no," Regeic snapped.

Price laughed. "She was about the only thing you talked about when were were in Camp Maxie. I'll bet you spent more time in that college in Commerce than the rest of the outfit put together."

"Sure I did, but that don't mean that I loved her," Regeic answered.

Price scratched his long hair. "You sure acted like it."

"You know better than that," Regeic answered.

Beecraft looked up and asked Regeic, "How about the kid?"

Regeic hesitated a minute before answering. "That's her problem, not mine."

"He is your son," Morris said. "Don't you ever wonder about him?"

"No."

Choinsky slid his helmet low over his eyes, walked over to Regeic's side and placed his arm around the other man. "Regeic and me are two no-good bastards. Nobody ever gave a damn about us and we never gave a damn about anybody. Matter of fact, we're so damn no good that our own mothers don't like us too good."

Price looked up from the ground and laughed. "None of us are much good. We've lived like animals so long that we don't even remember what it's like to be a human being. Didn't you ever notice that all we ever talk about is sex? On top of that, every other word is a cuss word. I guess we're a sorry lot compared to what we were when we first came out here."

Morris laughed. "After the war, nobody's going to believe that Americans could get like us."

"I cuss because I like to," Choinsky announced.

"If you ask me," Beecraft said, "the reason we cuss so much is that we're trying to prove to everybody else that we're not scared. I remember once a minister said that people cuss to hide their own weaknesses. That's probably the real reason."

"Fear," Choinsky said lightly, as if he had never even thought about being afraid.

"Yeah," Beecraft said. "You're probably the only man here that ain't got enough sense to be afraid of anything. To tell you the truth, I don't want to go into that damn town at all. Not one little bit."

Price was trying to think of a comment that might relieve the crawling fear which was eating at his stomach. His mind was a blank and he glanced at his watch in an attempt to relieve the tension. He saw that it was almost time to move out. "You men collect your nerves and get ready to move on out."

Wearily, almost as if they were going for a stroll, the men rose from the ground and began to move down the street. Choinsky took the lead as he always did, machine gun held in a ready position.

The men split up and began to move down both sides of the street, some of them taking a last drink from their canteens as they walked. Choinsky walked boldly down the center of the street, but the others moved cautiously, taking advantage of all the cover they could find. When they came to a house, they would enter it carefully, expecting to meet a Jap with each step. As they moved forward, the only movement was the flapping of the curtain in the distance.

The silence was terrible and there was no sound but the movement of their feet. They moved in silence with a sureness that came from experience. Suddenly, Choinsky stopped in the center of the street and held up his right hand as a signal for the others to stop. For a moment, the platoon froze in their tracks and then leaped for cover. As they crouched behind the meager cover they could find, the men looked desperately in the direction in which Choinsky seemed to be looking, but there was no movement. Choinsky stood quietly in the center of the street and calmly took out a cigarette. After he had lit the match, he casually threw it to the ground.

Price was crouched at the corner of a bamboo house. His eyes were mere slits as he searched the houses in front of him for any sign of movement. As he carefully searched, he could not help feeling as if there was a Japanese rifle pointed at his heart. After he had convinced himself that there was no movement in front of him, he felt like yelling at Choinsky.

Choinsky continued to look at the window where he had detected some movement. Something moved again. Deliberately, Choinsky raised his submachine gun, like a man in a shooting gallery. In the second before he fired, there was a storm of clicks as the other men released their safeties. Choinsky fired at the window, and then all the others opened fire. Chips flew from the window as the slugs tore into the walls. Nothing moved as the roar became louder. All over town, other men fired. Choinsky had set off a chain reaction.

As suddenly as it had started, the firing ceased. Choinsky pulled a grenade from his pocket and began to inch forward. Then he stopped. A cat jumped from the window and ran around the corner of the house. A snicker sounded, and then another. Soon, the whole platoon was in tears, from laughing so hard.

Price felt the tears roll down his cheeks as he laughed. A cat had scared the entire platoon and had set off a hurricane of fire all over town. He laughed for what seemed to be a long time. The incident had been the thing they had needed to break the tension. For a brief moment, they had been just a group of men walking down a lonely street, and the war seemed far away. "Okay, you cat killers, let's move," Price called, as soon as he could control his laughter.

The street seemed to be alive with rising steam. The heat waves that rose distorted the vision of the men, and it seemed to be even hotter than before. Sweat was running from their bodies. Price scratched at his rash. Regeic scratched at his head. Bryant was conscious of the smell that rose from the manure which had dried on his face. They plodded past several more houses, sweating and cursing. Gradually, the bamboo houses gave way to the better built ones. Each man had the feeling that he was going to die. If the Japs were in town, this would be the section. Somewhere in the distance, several shots rang out. The men halted for a moment, but continued after they realized that the shots were far to their right.

Choinsky still walked down the center of the street, his gun resting on his hip ready for instant action. As he walked, there was no evidence that he had ever even thought of being afraid. Price had long ago given up trying to control the man. He seemed to live a charmed life and preferred to operate by himself. Choinsky seemed to enjoy the killing and could always be counted on to know where the Japs were. He seemed to have a sixth sense about them and was rarely wrong.

They approached a frame house and Choinsky stopped and held up his hand again. He held up two fingers to Price, which was his way of calling for two men. Price and Regeic walked toward Choinsky quickly. The house was long and had a wide porch that extended around the entire structure. The paint had been worn away, and it looked as if the house had not been repaired for several years. By the time the two men had reached Choinsky, he was crouched at the bottom of the steps. They came to his side and dropped to the ground.

"I'm going in," Choinsky said. "You two guys wait here, just in case."

Price had no idea what Choinsky had in mind, but his experience had taught him not to question the man, in a situation like this. He looked at Regeic with a questioning look, only to find the same expression on his face.

The three of them walked up the steps as quietly as they could. Choinsky entered and the other two men waited at the door. Choinsky dropped to the floor and began to crawl into the front room on his stomach. He crawled until he was in the center of the room, where he stopped. Suddenly, he yelled at the top of his voice, "Hey, you Jap bastards!!!!!" Boards and splinters flew from the wall as the blast of a machine gun tore through the wall. Choinsky screamed as if he had been hit. Both Price and Regeic started to enter the room, but Choinsky waved them back with a smile on his face. A second blast came through the wall. Quickly, Choinsky crawled across the floor and disappeared out the back window.

Price and Regeic stood rooted to the porch, wondering what to do next, when the blast of an American grenade sounded in the house. It was followed by the chattering of Choinsky's machine gun. The two men dashed into the house and ran toward the door that led into the room where the Japs had been. The door flew open and Price almost fired a burst into Choinsky, who stood there with a smile on his face. Price's jaw muscles twitched as they usually did when he was mad. "Damn you. I almost shot you. When in the name of hell are you going to learn not to surprise a man like that?"

Choinsky was coiled, ready to fire. "How about you, Ern. You came running in here like a madman. For all you know, the whole house may be full of Japs. There might be one getting ready to shoot you in the back right now."

Price felt like a small child who had been reprimanded by his mother. He felt a little relieved as he noticed that some of the other men had entered the house and were already searching the rooms.

Choinsky was still smiling, his lips twisted. "Come on in and see what I got myself," he said, waving his weapon.

Price entered the room, with his weapon ready. Three men were on the floor. One of them lay with his hand clutching his head, as if he had made a last effort to keep his brains from coming out of the hole in the top of it. His brains, which looked strangely like spaghetti, were all over his face and the floor. The second Jap was lying on his back, his stomach riddled with holes. Several of the cuts were large enough for his intestines to poke through. The third man was riddled with shrapnel. One hand was gone and the other hung by a thin piece of flesh. His face was blasted away.

Price looked at the dead men, and the thought passed through his mind that it might be he on the floor instead of a Jap. His stomach was turning over, partly from fear, and partly from the sickening sight that was in front of him. He thought about a drink and wished that he had one. The thought of himself lying on the floor passed through his mind again and he wanted to vomit.

The quiet of the room was disturbed when the Jap with the stomach wound moaned softly. His hand moved slightly, fingering his intestines as though he could not believe they were his. The Jap's eyes opened slowly and he stared into the vicious face of Choinsky, who was standing over him. Slowly, deliberately, Choinsky sent his shoe flying into the head of the Jap. He kicked him again and again.

Horrified by the action in front of them, both Price and Regeic grabbed Choinsky and began to pull him away from the Jap, who was now dead. "You didn't have to do that," Price yelled. "You killed him the first time."

"He's a Jap," Choinsky said.

"You could of shot him," Regeic said.

"Do you think they would treat us any different?" Choinsky answered as he pulled himself from their grip.

"No."

"So I kicked the hell out of him." Choinsky was glaring now, his shifty eyes dancing. "Isn't that what they sent us out here to do, kill Japs?"

"I guess so," Price conceded. "But we're still human beings."

"Look, Ern, I fight this war the best damn way I can," Choinsky said. "If I don't do it to suit you, why don't you have me transferred to some other outfit?"

"You know I wouldn't do that," Price answered. "I wouldn't trade you for a dozen men, you know that. I guess I've gotten sentimental in my old age. You're right."

"How in the name of hell did you manage to get these Japs so fast?" Regeic asked.

"I just crawled in the back window. They weren't expecting me to come in that way."

"One of these days," Price said, "you're going to get your ass shot off doing something crazy like this."

"Not me, I've got a charmed life."

"I hope that your luck doesn't run out," Price said, walking out of the room.

"Hey, Ern," Choinsky called. "Don't them brains smell like hell? Look like spaghetti too."

"Yeah," Price mumbled, fighting the vomit which threatened to come all the way up this time. He swallowed hard several times before he felt sure he would not be sick.

"You look sick," Choinsky chuckled.

"I'd feel a lot better if you'd keep your fuggin' mouth shut," Price said.

Just as he entered the next room, Price saw that Lockworth was reaching for a samurai sword in the far corner. Price's warning cry came too late, and the explosion sounded as he threw himself to the floor.

Almost before the blast had been expended, Price was running toward the injured man. Regeic followed, and when they reached him, Lockworth was lying face down on the floor. Gently they rolled him over. His face, chest, and stomach were torn open and both of his hands were blasted off.

Price turned to Regeic. "Can you fix a tourniquet?" Price knew from the long look which Regeic gave him that Lockworth was going to die and that nothing they could do would save his life.

After hesitating for a moment, Regeic answered, "Okay." He opened his first-aid pouch and began to work rapidly.

While Regeic worked, Lockworth opened his eyes slightly. Blood began to trickle from his mouth and made a sickening gurgling sound. Gasping for breath, the man talked slowly, sounding pathetic. "My wife, my poor wife," he gasped. Tears began to stream down his face. "What's she going to do? She always depended on me so much. My poor wife."

Price was seized with sympathy and he wanted desperately to make the man feel that he would live. "You'll be all right. You'll make it fine. Regeic and me'll have you fixed up in no time at all. I'll bet you're home with your wife before you know what happened." The man gasped once and then his head rolled back. He was dead.

Regeic assumed an almost hurt look. "Why does it always have to be the good ones that get it? He never hurt anyone. I'll bet he was trying to get that sword for his kid. He told me last night that his kid had written him and asked him to bring one home."

Price's stomach was acting up again and he thought he might be sick. One by one, his men were getting killed, and there was nothing he could do except lead them to another place where more of them would die. Lockworth had been a quiet sort of man who had never attracted much notice. He had been drafted and had been a replacement several months ago. Most of the time he had kept to himself. He had been well liked in the outfit, and Price knew that what he was going to say might make some of the men mad.

"How many times do I have to tell you dumb bastards to keep your hands off of things. Look at Lockworth. He didn't have to die. How do you think his wife is going to feel when she gets the word that he's dead. Do you think his kid will think that the sword was worth it? Hell no, he won't. Take a good look." Price saw that Bryant wasn't looking. "You, too," he said to Bryant. "All of you take a good look at him and then see if you can't do like I tell you."

Silently, the platoon left the house. On the steps, Regeic caught Price's arm. "You've been jumping at everybody this morning. What's the matter?"

Price removed his helmet and wiped the sweat from his forehead with his sleeve. "This is my platoon. Most of the men are friends of mine. Do you think that I like to see them get killed? I'm supposed to get them through this war, and damn it all to hell, I'm going to do it. I must have told them a thousand times not to pick up things. I hated to say what I just did, but it might have made an impression on some of them."

"You didn't have to be so rough about it. He had a lot of friends in the platoon."

"Dammit, Regeic, you know better than that. Being a platoon leader isn't the most pleasant job in the world, but that's what the Army made me. Don't you think I'd rather be a private and just follow orders than be responsible for getting men killed? It's too much responsibility for one man, at least for me. I've dreamed about some of them at night. They almost haunt me sometimes, and I wish it was me that had got killed instead of them. Much more of this and I'm going off my rocker, I'll be crazy as hell. When that happens, you'll have to make the decisions and you'll know how it feels."

"I know, Ern. What we need is a good leave in the States."

"Regeic, I'm not sure that anything can make me forget this."

"Me, either."

Morris came out of the house after Price. His feet ached and he felt exhausted. His rifle hung loosely from his right hand. His prime concern was to get away from the body of Lockworth. Morris had been standing close to the man when he had died, and remembering that his last thoughts were of his wife made him feel like crying. Morris could see himself in Lockworth's place on the floor and he knew that he too would be thinking about his wife at such a time. He realized more fully than ever before that his wife meant everything in the world to him. Morris couldn't help worrying about what she would do if he were killed. As he tried to imagine how it would be for her if he died, his thoughts became confused. The only thing that he was certain of was that he had to survive to be with her again.

Beecraft ran after Morris. They had been good friends for many years and he knew that the look on his friend's face meant that he was thinking about Roberta. Beecraft knew that Morris was deeply in love with his wife, almost too much for his own good. He too loved his wife, but she was almost a memory now and didn't seem too close. He caught up with Morris and made a comment about the weather.

Regeic left the house after Beecraft and fell in just behind Price. Why was it, he wondered, that they always thought about their wives just before they died. He supposed that it was because the men placed their wives and sweethearts on a pedestal. Their memories played tricks on them and women became goddesses. For the first time, Regeic realized that he had missed one of the better things in life. He compared himself with Price and even conceded that Price was better off because he at least had someone to remember.

The platoon split into two columns and began to move through the sun-drenched street. As he walked, Price looked at his shoes and noted that they were cracked and run over. They were only a few weeks old and he wondered if he would be able to get a new pair soon. One thing for sure, he thought, I don't want to die with dirty feet. As he thought about it, that seemed a little silly to him.

From another part of the town, the sound of rifles and grenades sounded. A Nambu answered with several bursts. The firing became more intense, and Price dropped to the ground. He looked around and saw that the whole platoon was taking cover. There seemed to be no immediate danger to them, so Price rose. "Keep moving, men," he shouted. As the platoon started down the street again, Price removed his canteen from its pouch and took a long drink of the lukewarm water. It almost made him sick.

Choinsky walked ahead of the platoon. He reached the next house and stopped. He walked to the side of the house and placed his ear against the side of the wall. Choinsky heard a whimpering sound. At first, he thought it might be an animal, but then he decided that it sounded like a man warning someone else to be quiet. He signaled for the rest of the men to stop. Then slowly, deliberately, he unhooked a grenade from his pack straps and eased out the pin. He held it for a moment and then tossed it through the window.

Even before the explosion, the men were firing at the house and Price was running toward the door. The house shook with the blast and Price reached the opening right behind Choinsky. They entered almost at the same time. The room was dark, but a shadow moved and both of the men fired at the same time. He ran toward the spot where the shadow had fallen and fired another burst at it.

When he approached the body, his stomach tightened and his face fell. It was a woman. Not three feet away lay the torn body of her child and next to it lay her husband. They were all dead. Choinsky knew that the sound he had heard must have been the baby and the other one must have been the father trying to get it to be quiet.

"My God," Price whispered.

Choinsky was alarmed by his own feelings and tried to keep up his false front. He forced out an insanely brutal laugh.

"Damn you," Price spat.

"What the hell's the matter with you?" Choinsky asked. "Haven't you got any feelings at all?"

"Sure, it's bad that they got killed, but there's nothing we can do about it now. Hell, how did we know they were civilians. Do you think I'd shoot a kid?"

Price gritted his teeth and turned on his heel. "All right, we had to kill them, it couldn't be helped. That's no sign that you can laugh about it."

"I didn't mean nothing by it. I felt bad, too."

Price's face reddened with anger. "Then by God, why don't you try and act like it. You're the best man that I've got out here, but damn if I can stand much more of your attitude."

"That's what we came out here for. I thought you said that this morning."

"Yeah, but only a crazy man would laugh about killing a kid."

Regeic had been standing in the doorway and listening. He walked to Price and led him from the room. "Don't let it get you down, Ern. It couldn't be helped, just one of those things that happen. We all feel bad about it, but we have a war to fight and some of the things that happen aren't too pleasant."

They entered the street again. Bryant called to Price, "What'd you get in there?"

"Nothing," Price muttered. "Let's get moving."

But the word was passed from man to man that a child had been killed. Although all the men had seen most of the horrors of war, this was the first time any of them had directly killed a child and they were shocked. Shame began to build even in these battle-weary men as they continued to move from house to house.

The child's death was very deeply felt by Price. For months, he had almost been able to keep his emotions suppressed. Now, the shame of what he was doing there began to fill him. It seemed almost as though he held himself responsible for all the brutal acts of the war.

He plodded forward, thinking that his entire life had been useless. As he looked back over all the years, he could not remember a single decent act. He looked upon himself as the shell of a man devoid of all emotions. All of the old gods were dead and nothing was there to take their place. As he thought, he knew that there had to be something more to life than the killing and dying. Something more than the filth and the dirt. Suddenly, Price wished desperately that he had something to hold on to. He wanted to believe in the powers of a Supreme Being but, as he tried, his mind refused to accept the thoughts. Very little mattered to him any more. About the only thing that was important was survival. Long ago, Reverend Simpson had told him that he should always live so he would be prepared to meet God, but Price wasn't so sure now that there was a heaven. He heard himself speaking to himself. "We'll all be in hell before this day is done."

Regeic's voice broke into his chain of thought. "Huh?" "What?"

"I thought you were talking to me," Regeic said.

"Just thinking out loud," Price muttered.

Regeic pulled his steel helmet low over his face. "Scared?"

Price kept scanning the empty street, alert for any movement that would indicate the presence of the Japanese. The hair on the back of his neck was almost standing straight up. He knew that he was so scared he wanted to run. Finally, he answered Regeic's question. "No."

"I'm scared too," Regeic said. "Almost as scared as you."

"I said I wasn't."

"I could say the same thing, but there's no use in both of us lying."

Price walked down the street, watching the shadows that the late afternoon sun was casting. Each shadow could hide a Jap. Every door, every window, every crack could be a strong-point. With each step, Price could imagine the terrible black snout of a Nambu pointed at his chest. He pictured the little man behind it as smiling, his little eyes squinting through his steel-rimmed spectacles. Sweat was running down Price's body and the rash between his legs itched. In other parts of the village, shots could be heard. Each shot sounded the alarm that sent the acid juices flowing in his veins. What was that . . . click the safety off. No, it was only a bush. Panic began to rise in his mind and he found himself wanting to throw his weapon down and run. He kept telling himself to last just one more day, then the National Guard would take over.

The platoon had slowed down and Price was becoming so tired that he was going to have to stop. Over his shoulder, he saw that the heat had had its effect on the other men. They were visibly tired, their eyes red, their bodies sagging.

Connors stopped to relieve himself against the side of a building. Price was about to shout at him, when a sound very much like a sledge hammer hitting a rock caused him to fall to the ground. Smoke drifted from a second-story window across the street and the sound of a machine gun reached him again. Connors sagged for a moment and then fell into the puddle he had just made.

For a second, Price was paralyzed with fear. Bullets kicked up the dust around him and he struggled with himself before he had the courage to rise and run for the protection of a doorway. He fired as he ran. Others were in the house. "Johnson, Petras, Young," he called, before triggering another burst at the window. The three men looked at him. "Get in there, we'll cover you."

Almost before they had reached the street, he knew that he had made an error. The men would probably die! Suddenly, he wished that he did not have to make decisions where one error could kill a man.

Johnson ran as fast as his tired legs would carry him. Before he had gone a dozen steps, he jerked erect. A large red hole was visible in his chest. He staggered for a moment. Petras and Young reached the house and flattened themselves on either side of the door. They watched Johnson stumble past them and enter the house. The look on his face told them that he knew he would die, and they knew that he would detonate a grenade.

There was a terrible explosion. Young and Petras pulled the pins from their grenades and threw them through the door. After the explosions, they entered the room, their guns blazing.

As soon as Petras and Young moved, the other men began to run out into the street, firing at the windows as they came. The machine gun answered and men began to fall in the street.

Price's former wife, Sandra, lay in the darkness of her room, unable to sleep. A slight breeze fluttered the lace curtains, but the night was hot, and beads of perspiration ran down her body. Her thoughts kept running to the island with the strange-sounding name, and she could not seem to get the picture of Ernest out of her mind. Sandra knew that she really did not love him, but you couldn't live with a man and not feel something for him, especially after you had borne him a son. She felt a little sympathy, and wondered what his life was like.

Sandra's mind went back to that afternoon, just before her date had come for her. Her son had been sitting on the floor in the living room. He was in the middle of a group of toy soldiers and was playing soldier. Just like a child can, he had looked up and asked her where his daddy was. It was a question that she had been expecting, but not wanting to have to answer. Now that it had been asked, she could not find a good answer. She had thought for a long time before answering. Finally, she had explained to him that his daddy was out fighting in the war.

Just as she had feared, he had asked the other question. "When is Daddy coming home?" It had been a painful experience. The only thing she could tell him was that his daddy would be home when the war was over.

The last letter that Ernest had sent her was the one in which he had asked her to remarry him. She thought about answering it. Over the radio, they were always saying that people should write to the servicemen, especially if they were overseas. Sandra had tried to place herself in his position. She knew that he had loved her very deeply, but that had been a long time ago. He must certainly be over it by now. The only reason he might have had for writing the letters was that he wanted her to feel sorry for him. She reasoned that he could not possibly be in love with her any more. It couldn't really make much difference to him, she thought. Finally, she decided to write him and tell him not to bother her again.

The more she thought about him, the madder she got. She was the one who had all the responsibilities of raising their son. All he had to do was send her the money. She had to solve all of the problems. She remembered how soft the army life had been. She could not remember him ever having to work too hard. Right now, she thought, he might be out there on some island paradise—surrounded by beautiful girls, having a real ball.

In Myrtle Beach, Lantrip was standing beside the bed. Roberta was asleep, her back to him. She was still naked, and the curve of her back was visible to him. At that moment, she looked like a pin-up picture. He lit a cigarette and sat back on the bed, being careful not to disturb her. He listened to her breathing and then leaned back on the bed.

He remembered how she had cried and he wondered why.

51

He remembered how she had gone out of her way to pick him up and bring him here. She had reacted as if she had not been loved in a long time, desperate and passionate right up to the final moment. Then he thought back. Just when the act was coming to a conclusion, she had called him James. He wondered if that was her husband. She's probably crazy as hell, he thought. Some women are like that. Her husband could be dead, or even worse, he might be at the same place I'm going to, Lantrip thought. It'd really be something if we get in the same outfit.

Then his thoughts shifted to the war. He was already scared. He had always been tough, the toughest boy in school. He had often heard others talk about their fears, but he had never admitted that he felt the same way.

Roberta felt the presence of the man beside her. She wanted to get up and run, but she was afraid that Lantrip might make love to her again if he thought she was awake. She heard him move, then heard the scratch of a match. The room glowed and she felt him sit back down on the bed. Why don't you go to sleep, she wanted to scream. This had been the first time she had ever done anything like this and she felt sick. For some time, she prayed that there would be some way for her to go back in time and blot out the ugly act. She had slept with several men before she had been married, but this was different. When she remembered how full of love James's letters had been, she felt worse. All he ever wrote about was how much he wanted to get back to her. And now she had done this.

Time and time again, she went over the letters in her mind. Remorse swept over her. Suddenly, she felt as though she needed a bath. She felt filthy. She realized that she would never be able to forget what she had done. If I get pregnant, she thought, what will I do? For the next few minutes, she imagined that she could already feel a child moving in her stomach.

# CHAPTER THREE

The platoon ran across the street, trying to dodge the hail of lead which the Japanese were firing at them. The piercing chatter of the machine gun was punctuated by the flicking of dirt at the men's feet as the deadly messengers of death sprayed among them. In rapid order, more than a dozen men were down. Some of them simply collapsed. Others were forced backward or were spun around with terrific force. Cooper, one of the new men, had his rifle shot from his hands. He looked at Price for one terrible minute and then dropped to the ground, bullets ripping into his body.

The men were only halfway across the street when the sound of machine gun fire faltered and then failed. They broke ranks and began running for the protection of the house which they had just left. They were cursing and gasping for breath as they leaped for cover. Bullets plunked against the side of the house. As soon as most of them were safely inside the house, the Japanese gunners began to spray those still left in the street.

Sterner turned, just as he started to enter the house. Every nerve in his body was jumping and he wanted to run desperately. For some reason which he could not explain, he turned and peered into the window from which the machine gun was chattering. He thought he saw a figure move in the window. The figure was exactly in his gun sight. He squeezed the trigger and felt the weapon recoil. As he hammered out the bullets, he forgot the terrific fear that had almost made him run. His only thought was to kill the man in the window. The figure slumped and fell forward. His head appeared near the window sill for a moment and then disappeared, as if someone had pulled him back.

Now that he had got the man, his knees felt as if they'd give way, and he almost collapsed before he could get into the house. After he was in, he sank to the floor, gasping for breath. He was proud that he had hit the Jap, that he had not failed the other men. The rest of the platoon must have seen what he did and he waited for them to congratulate him. Now they might accept him as a member of the platoon.

While he gasped for breath, a man approached him. He walked hunched over and looked very old. "Better get some water. We'll be back out there in a minute."

Sterner was surprised that the man did not say anything about the Jap he had hit. Trying to sound casual, he mentioned the incident. "I hit one of the Japs."

The man did not say anything. Finally he growled, "You might get yourself killed."

Sterner felt deflated. They had not even noticed him.

Price removed his helmet, so he wouldn't present a good target, and looked over the edge of the shuttered window. His face became red as he saw the carnage in the street. Enraged, he emptied his weapon into the window. While the weapon bucked, he cursed and shouted. He knew that he had made another mistake and that it had cost the lives of a dozen men. He felt a wave of remorse as he thought of Petras and Young, who had entered the house. They were surely dead. He cursed himself for not stationing some men with automatic weapons in this house. They could have kept the Japs down while the rest of them attacked. Even a new lieutenant out of O.C.S. would not have made that mistake.

Regeic studied Price's troubled face and knew what was running through his mind. Price's jaw muscles always jumped when he was mad or worried. They were jerking violently now. Price had talked about the burden of leadership before. After so long, the weight of having to make decisions that sent men to their death would bother anyone. Each time you made a mistake, men died, and there was no way to get their lives back. Price had been one of the best platoon leaders that the war had seen, but Regeic began to wonder how much longer he could take it?

The Japanese machine gun continued to fire at them, and down the street a violent fire fight seemed to be going on. Dust and smoke seemed to be rising as high as the clouds, as if trying to escape the holocaust below. Price peered out of the window and surveyed the ugly pockmarks which their bullets had made on the house across the street. The familiar sick feeling returned to his stomach. "It's insane," he muttered.

Regeic spoke. His voice seemed to be coming from very far away. "Ern, we can't stay here. We've got to get those Japs."

Slowly, Price collected himself enough to speak. His voice sounded very weak. "I can't order them out there again. I've already lost too many men."

It was a familiar pattern. Often, the plans that are laid out, back at headquarters, go awry. It is at those times that the American soldier's capacity to think for himself pays off. Little units, cut off and without communication, do the best they can and keep moving forward. "Use your head, Ern," Regeic said. "If we don't clean this town out before dark, they're going to clobber us good as soon as it gets dark. We're committed to take the town and that's what we've got to do."

"I know that," Price answered, wiping the cold sweat from his forehead. "I thought you'd understand. I can't order another attack, I just can't." He paused for a moment and swallowed hard. "I've already killed a lot of men. Do you think I can send any more out there to die?"

"I've seen you do it before," Regeic said quietly.

The machine gun chattered again.

"That was a long time ago. I can't do it again."

Regeic placed his big hand on Price's shoulder and noticed that it was trembling. "You know that war never was meant to be any fun."

Suddenly, Price began to shake with violent laughter. It sounded strange in contrast to the chattering machine gun. His laughter rose above the sound of the slugs as they slammed into the walls. Regeic was afraid Price had lost his mind. He shook his friend as hard as he could. "Ern, have you lost your mind?"

"I just thought of something funny."

"Here?"

"Yeah, here," Price answered, the tears streaming down his face. "Did you ever hear of a bunch of rats fighting for a chance to get at the cat?"

"That your idea of something funny?" Regeic snapped.

"Don't you remember that song, 'Bring on Your Goddamned Cat'?"

"It don't seem so funny now."

54

The machine gun chattered again and Price waited for it to stop before he answered. "No, but the whole thing is silly. When we started at them, I'll bet the Japs in there were scared as hell, just like we were. Right now, I'll bet they're crapping in their pants, waiting for us to come back. If I could get over there and talk to them, I'll bet they'd be glad as hell to come out and forget the whole thing, if we would, too. Here we sit, neither one of us really wants to get killed, but here we sit, doing our best to kill each other. It just doesn't make any sense."

The machine gun chattered again and Regeic glanced out into the street. "I never thought about it that way before. You just ain't supposed to think that way. It's unpatriotic. We're professional soldiers and our way of life is death; it's our business. Ever since we came out here, I've gotten up each morning and made up my mind how I'm going to die. Every night I go to sleep ready to die. If you think about it, you'll remember that dying is what we spend most of our lives learning to do."

"You may be right, but I don't think we're supposed to be different from other men. I know that I'm not too anxious to get killed. For my part, I'd like to spend the rest of my life back in some stateside bar."

"Sure, so would I, but by now you must have found out that the only way out is to get yourself killed. We're the only trained troops out here. They ain't never going to let us get out of here in one piece. As soon as this outfit is shot all to hell, the ones of us that are left will have to fill up the Guard units."

"You're probably right. We'll have to get ourselves killed to get out of it."

"That's what I've been trying to say."

"Hell, Regeic, you've said things that I've tried to put into words for a long time. You must have heard someone else say it. I know that you'd never be able to say it by yourself."

"No, I've just had a lot of time to think about it."

The machine gun sent slugs into the house again. "If we try that house again, you won't have to think about it much longer."

"We'll take it this time," Regeic said. "You want me to get someone at the window with a BAR?"

"I can't do it. I can't send the men out there again."

"Sure you can. If you don't, I will."

Reluctantly, Price spoke. "Get the men."

Morris and Beecraft were fighting for their breath, as the Nambu slammed its slugs into the wall which gave them protection. It was several minutes before they lit cigarettes. Morris let the cigarette dangle from his lips without lighting it. "As they say in the movies, here we go."

Beecraft lit the cigarette. "Can't you be a little more serious about it? If you ask me, there won't be too many of us left tomorrow. As soon as we try to take that house again, they'll kill all of us."

"We aren't more than fifteen now. They got at least twelve in the streets."

Beecraft looked around the room, squinting through the smoke in his eyes. The sweat from his fingers was making the cigarette soggy. He threw it away. "I wonder who they got out there in the street."

"Connors got it first. He was taking a leak. Ain't that a hell of a time to get killed?"

"I don't guess it makes much difference what you're doing when you get yourself killed. It's so final that I don't care how or when I get killed."

Morris scratched at the rash which was starting at the corner of his mouth. Soon he had the scab off and his mouth was bleeding. Lately his thoughts had only been about getting killed. Besides Roberta, it was about all he ever thought of. "If it wasn't for wanting to get back to Roberta, I think I'd give up and let them kill me. That's really the only thing that keeps me going. If it wasn't for her, I'd want to get wounded real bad just so I could get out of here."

"I guess hell can't be much worse."

"If I get hit out there," Morris said, trying to choose the right words, "will you promise me that you'll see to it that Roberta gets taken care of? I wouldn't want her to have too rough a time of it. She's always been dependent upon me and I don't know what she'd do."

Beecraft felt very close to Morris and looked his friend straight in the eye. "Of course I would. If I get it, you'd do the same thing for me, wouldn't you?"

"Sure. Are you thinking that we might all get killed too?"

"It's been going on for too long now. Back at headquarters they're drinking beer. To them, we're just a bunch of little pins on a map. We fight our way from one mess to another and get out of it just in time to make the next one. It's always the same thing, over and over. One of these days we're going to run out of luck and get killed. Besides, I've fought until there's nothing left to give. All of us are in the same shape. We're not half the soldiers that we used to be. Right now, I wouldn't give you ten cents for our chances."

"Price might not make us try again," Morris said.

"He has to. He'll lead us over there or kill us trying. We'll all go out there, too, even if it kills us."

Choinsky sat by himself. He was shaking with fear, and he hoped that none of the others noticed. For a long time he had fought with the fear that seemed to be eating at his insides and he had never admitted that he felt it. Time after time, he had taken chances and come through without a scratch. After so long, he had been able to convince himself

56

that he was invincible. Suddenly, out in the street, all his confidence was gone, like a bowstring that had snapped. He was scared, terribly afraid. Instead of going first, he wanted to run, run clear back to the beach. Choinsky stared at his hands. They were shaking badly and he hoped that none of the men would see it.

Bryant noticed that Choinsky had a pained expression on his face. Since this was not at all like Choinsky, Bryant approached him. "What's the matter?"

"Nothing."

Bryant saw that Choinsky's hands were trembling, and he wondered for a moment if Choinsky had at last gone off his rocker. He dismissed the idea, however, since he had never seen Choinsky show any kind of fear. "I'm still a little shook about the dream I had. Every time I think about getting my nuts shot out I want to be sick."

Choinsky started to speak, but the best he could do was to mumble a few words that did not make any sense.

Price adjusted his helmet and turned his head to the right. Regeic was lying on the floor, his face sallow, his lips twitching. Choinsky was sitting on the floor, and his hands, which were shaking violently, held the submachine gun so hard that his knuckles were white. Both Moss and Terry were peering over the window and looking out into the street. The skin on their faces seemed to be drawn so tightly that it looked as though it would split at any minute. Beecraft looked as though he was praying, while the sweat and manure on Morris' face looked like drops of blood against the white flesh.

The machine gun continued to chatter, and there were sounds of fighting in the distance, but a calm seemed to be in the house. It seemed strange that there could be so much silence in the house with all that noise just outside the door. Price glanced at the two men at the window and was pleased to see them sighting down the barrel of the BAR.

Price let out a piercing cry, which sent the men dashing from the house and out into the street. Two hundred steps, twenty seconds—that was all it would take. They ran, and the next few seconds seemed like hours to them.

Price puffed hard and was dimly aware of the whistling sound his breathing was making. He knew that men were running around him, but he concentrated all his efforts on making it to the door. He felt the dust bite into his face and knew the sweat was pouring off him, but he continued to run. He had covered only half the distance when he became aware of the machine gun. It seemed to be firing directly into his face. As he placed one foot in front of another, he kept telling himself that this would be the last time he would have to face a Jap machine gun. He told himself that he had to survive.

He looked up again and realized he had almost reached

57

the door. All around him men were running. Some of them fell in the street.

Price did not slow down as he came to the door. He plunged in. The bodies of Petras and Young were on the floor. There was a door to the right. He kicked at the door and entered, firing. He was aware of Regeic at his side. They both fired until the clips were empty. Calmly, they saw that the room had been deserted, and they jammed fresh clips into their weapons.

Together, they entered the front room. Most of the men had made it and were now huddled at the bottom of the stairs. "Get away from there," he shouted. "The Japs will start rolling grenades down here any minute."

The men had just started to scatter when the first came bouncing and smoking down the steps. Price leaped, head first, for the cover that the stairwell provided. He landed in a heap, Regeic and Choinsky landing on top of him. Both Terry and Moss leaped through the doorway.

The explosion shattered the room and sent wood splinters and shrapnel bouncing off the walls. Showers of plaster came off the ceiling.

Quickly Choinsky turned over and began firing his submachine gun through the ceiling. Price could feel the vibrations as the gun fired. As the plaster fell from the ceiling, Price felt a hot shell casing tumble down his back. Almost before the clip was empty, Regeic squirmed from the floor and ran for the stairs. Price rose and followed. He saw that Choinsky was shaking so violently that he could not fit the clip into his weapon. Several more of the men were firing through the ceiling at the spot where a Japanese soldier would have to stand to throw a grenade.

Both Regeic and Price had grenades in their hands. They removed the pins before they were halfway up the stairs. Both of them threw the grenades at the same time and then stopped to wait for the explosion. As the report sounded, they rounded the corner, firing as they went.

Two Japs were on the floor, and Price and Regeic were relieved to see that the hall was deserted. Price jumped over the bodies and placed himself so he could shoot down the hall if there was any movement. Soon he heard the others coming up the stairs.

The hallway had two doors on each side. As the others reached the head of the stairs, he shouted, "Cover those doors."

Suddenly Price was aware of the quiet in the house. His nerves began to tingle. Instead of his usual caution, he walked to the first door on the right and kicked it open. At the same time, he threw his body flat against the wall on the right side of the door.

The consequences of his recklessness were frightful. A machine gun barked and slugs tore through the opening. The bullets ricocheted off the walls in the corridor and swept several men away, as though they were dominoes. A scream sounded down the hall.

Only a split second after his foot had hit the door, Price knew that he had made a mistake. He fumbled furiously, trying to get another grenade from his belt. Haltingly, he pulled the pin and threw it into the room. The explosion echoed so violently down the hall that Price's first reaction was to clamp his hands over his ears. Paying no attention to what was going on behind his back, Price leaped into the room, firing blindly into the semidarkness. Regeic was at his side again. Two Japs were trying desperately to get the machine gun pointed at the Americans, but the slugs from Price's gun tore into them and the force smashed them against the wall. One of them made a sound like a stone falling, and a scream was choked off as he died. There was a movement in the corner and they both fired. A very high scream greeted them. Suddenly there was a noise behind them. They both spun and fired.

Moss and Terry froze for a moment and then they fell. Price and Regeic exchanged pained looks, horror in their eyes. In a split second they had reached the two men and were kneeling beside them. They shouted at them, as though their shouts could bring the two men back to life. "Oh, my God," Price moaned. "We killed them."

"They shouldn't have come in here like that," Regeic said. He sounded as if he was trying to convince himself that what he said was true.

"I should have looked before I pulled the trigger," said Price.

"You know better than that. So did they. If you always looked first you wouldn't live too long out here."

Price's stomach was acting up again and his head began to swim. He sat back on his heels. "Damn, I've about had the course. This is about all I can take."

Regeic spoke in a very weak voice. "What are we going to tell their wives, Ern? What will we tell them?"

"I don't know," Price said with an unsteady voice.

"I'll never be able to just walk up and tell them that I killed their husbands, not ever."

"We might not live that long."

"I almost hope I don't."

Price started to speak but heard a movement in the far corner. He turned and almost fired, but something seemed to keep his finger frozen on the trigger. The person in the corner was a woman.

"What in the name of hell!" Regeic whispered.

They rose together and walked over to the corner, guns held at ready. When they bent over the body, the woman looked terrified and tried to roll away from them.

The woman was dressed only in a pair of baggy trousers.

59

Her chest was naked and she had a long gash that ran all the way from the nipple of her left breast to the center of her stomach. The raw wound was almost an inch wide and was bleeding badly. Thoughtfully Price bent over her. He couldn't help thinking she would have been rather pretty if she was cleaned up. His gaze swept over her pale face, rested on her heavy eyelids, and finally stopped at her breast. For a moment he was tempted to close his hand around the uninjured breast.

"Does it hurt?" Price asked tenderly. Blood ran down her body. He realized that his question was ridiculous, since she could not understand him. Finally he looked up at Regeic. "She's going to die."

"Can't we do something for her?"

"No."

"We ought to try."

Price shuddered at the thought that had entered his mind. He had never killed a woman before. "She's a Jap. If we leave her she'll try to kill us."

"Damn if I'll do it," Regeic said.

Price looked at her for a long moment and then raised his weapon. He started to pull the trigger when she slumped forward. He bent over her. She was already dead.

"Let's get out of here," Regeic said.

"Sure."

The rest of the men were still waiting for them in the hall. Regeic and Price searched the room across the hall and found it empty.

Suddenly there was a noise. It sounded like the moan of a teakettle and seemed to be coming from the roof. There was something horrible about the noise, and Price felt his nerves going. He narrowed his eyes until they were nearly slits, trying somehow to shut out the noise. His brain kept sending messages to his body, messages that his body refused to obey. Then, as if he were another person watching his own actions, he was aware of his helplessness. Sweat ran down his face and trickled off his nose. He could feel his emotions go from shame to hate, over and over again. He could hear Choinsky shouting at him from a great distance, but he could not make out the words. There was a crash, and he was conscious of Choinsky running down the hall.

Price clamped his hands over his ears, and then he roared with laughter. He felt himself lose all control of his actions. He doubled over with laughter. He laughed like an insane man and still knew that there was nothing funny. Every time he straightened up he could see Regeic's startled face watching him. Price was afraid he had lost his mind, but he could not help himself.

Regeic watched Price for a moment and was horrified. Then he, too, began to feel himself going. His body shook and his knees began to turn to water. Morris had been watching the scene, and he motioned to Beecraft to follow him. Together, they reached the two men and shook them violently. "Have you lost your minds?"

Several minutes passed before Price was able to speak. Finally he explained, "I lost control of myself."

He glanced at Regeic. He, too, had begun to regain control of himself. Price rubbed his hand across his face in an effort to restore some feeling to it. He felt ashamed of his actions as he looked at the other men.

The noise came again and Price felt his body jerk again. The events of the day had almost been too much for him and he knew that he was through as a combat soldier. He was frozen to the spot.

Morris looked into Price's frightened face. "Let's get in there and see what it is."

Price knew that they were waiting for him to make the decision, but his mind refused to let him act. "Where is Choinsky?" he asked, stalling for time.

"Let's get in there," Beecraft said.

"Where is Choinsky?" Price screamed at the top of his voice.

"Ern . . ."

"Didn't you hear me?"

"He ran," Morris said.

"Choinsky?"

"Yeah, he ran."

Price did not speak. He was terribly ashamed of the way he had acted. He tried to twist the facts, but the simple truth could not be ignored. He had lost his nerve. He had been scared before, but this was the worst. He looked at the door through which the sounds had come, but knew that he would not give the order to go in there. He could not make the decision. He was not sure he could ever make another decision. He thought about Choinsky running and knew that if Choinsky had broken, the rest of them could not be far behind.

Morris grasped the situation at once and made the decision for Price. He pushed Price away and walked up to the door. He raised his rifle and pumped the entire clip through it. When he heard no answering fire, he kicked at the door. It did not move. He shoved another clip into his M-1 and fired at the lock. Morris kicked at the door again and this time it swung open. He held his weapon at ready but did not fire. Instead, his jaw dropped and his eyes opened in amazement.

Price struggled with his nerves, and after a few agonizing seconds which seemed like hours, he walked to the door and looked into the room. Crowded together on straw mats, half a dozen women were trying to crowd into the corner. Each face registered horror. Price was the first man to enter the room. The blood seemed to be leaving the women's faces as they huddled closer together.

Shakily, Price walked to the first woman and stopped directly at her feet. Once he realized it was a woman who had made him act like a coward, he felt disgusted with himself. Then he felt very tired. It took all his energy to raise his weapon.

Beecraft realized that Price might shoot the women and he rushed forward to place his hand on Price's weapon. "Don't lose your head, Ern. We're all on edge a little."

"Yeah."

"Are you all right?"

"I think so; how is Regeic?"

Regeic's voice came booming in through the door, his rich bass voice echoing down the hall. "I'm all right."

Morris came in and looked at the ragged women. "What in the name of hell can we do with them?"

"They're Japs," Price said acidly.

"You mean shoot women?" Beecraft asked.

"Can you think of any better way?"

"No," Beecraft answered, with a shrug of his shoulders.

Morris clamped his lips together until the pressure was almost enough to bruise them. Beecraft watched through squinted eyes, while Price raised his weapon. . . . The submachine gun was pointed directly at the stomach of the first woman, and Price took a final look into the faces of the women before he fingered the trigger. Suddenly they all looked like ordinary women and he was ashamed that he had wanted to kill them. He was still a human being. Even the war couldn't change that. Something inside him rebelled at shooting women. As he lowered the weapon, Price smiled a little, knowing that all the decency had not left him.

"You'd better do something with them," Beecraft said. "If the other men see them, there'll be the damndest rape you ever saw."

"That's for sure," Price commented. "Get two men on the door downstairs and have Wheatley search the other room."

"Hey!" Morris yelled. He had discovered a large stack of beer bottles, wrapped in straw and stacked like bombs. He had already knocked the top off one of the bottles and was pouring the beer down his throat. Much of it splashed down his face and uniform.

"This room's empty," Wheatley called from across the hall.

Price let his glance go from the beer to the women and a serious frown came across his face. He had a handful of survivors who were almost out of their minds, a house full of women, and all they could drink. Normally, this would be a simple problem, but this time the platoon was supposed to be taking the town. If there was any delay he would never get the men out of the house.

Regeic realized that Price had a serious problem on his hands. He searched his own mind desperately for a solution,

62

but there seemed to be no answer. He thought about tying up the women, but there was no rope. So that was out. Finally, he gave up and just stared at the closest woman.

Morris was standing next to Price now and had an open bottle in his hands. "Are you going to kill the women?"

Price looked directly into Morris' troubled face and then at the women. Little beads of perspiration were forming on his face and all the blood was draining out of his cheeks. He rubbed his hands briskly over his bearded face in an attempt to start the circulation. Price's hand moved toward his weapon and then he relaxed. He knew that he could not kill them. They would probably try to kill every man in the platoon if they got the chance, but he did not have the guts to pull the trigger. Price knew that he had to make a decision, but the ability to give the order was not in him.

Beecraft spoke from the door. "Choinsky came back. Wheatley's with him."

Price turned and faced Beecraft. At that minute he welcomed the opportunity to have something else to occupy his mind. He rubbed his face again. "How is he?"

Beecraft walked toward Price and began leading him from the room. "You'd better come see for yourself."

As he rounded the corner, Price called back to Regeic, "Watch the women." He walked down the hall and found Choinsky sitting on the floor with his back propped against the wall. His legs were spread out at a forty-five-degree angle and his arms hung loosely at his sides. Choinsky's skin seemed tight and his lips were trembling violently. Probably the worst thing about him was the look on his face. His little eyes seemed to mirror the horror that he had seen over the months. Price waved his hand in front of Choinsky's eyes but there was no reaction. If it had not been for the irregular breathing, Price thought, you wouldn't be able to tell if he was alive. Price removed the ammunition from Choinsky's pouches and stuck them in his own empty pouches.

"How long has he been this way?" Price asked Wheatley, who was standing near Choinsky, a troubled look on his face.

"He just wandered in a few minutes ago and sat down. He hasn't moved a muscle since then."

"Cracked for sure."

"Yeah."

"I'd have bet everything I had that he would have been the last one to go," Price said.

"Me, too."

Price saw Bryant and one of the replacements standing near the head of the stairs. "How about relieving Wheatley and watching Choinsky for a minute? If he tries to get out again, hit him."

All the way back down the hall, Price was trying to make some decision about the women. He knew that he would have to have one as soon as he entered the room.

Regeic accepted another beer from Morris, who had already finished several. The warm beer felt good as it ran down his dry throat. Remembering his action in the hall, he was a little ashamed, but he reasoned that after a few more beers he would be as good as new. Of course he knew that a few drinks wouldn't do him any good at all. He had reached the limit, and his nerves would be gone soon. He took another big drink and saw that Morris was back with two more bottles. Regeic moved back against the door and leaned against the frame. For the first time since he had been wounded, he examined his arm and noticed that the bleeding had stopped. The shock was wearing off and he could feel the wound beginning to throb.

The women had no way of knowing what was going to be done with them, but they looked as though they expected to be killed. They had been very frightened at first, but now they seemed to be a little more relaxed. Just like these slant-eyed bastards, Regeic thought, they never get too excited. The women were talking in low whispers, and Regeic had the feeling that they were making fun of him. He took another long drink and cursed them viciously. The only thing he accomplished by the swearing was that they stopped talking for a moment. He shouted at them again several times, but it had no effect upon them.

Regeic looked from the group to the woman directly in front of him. He guessed that she could not be more than twenty, but it was hard to tell about the Japanese. The woman had a round face and a very small nose. Her eyes were more moonshaped than slanted. He glanced from her face to her figure, looking her over several times. Suddenly she seemed desirable to him and he thought it strange that he had not considered her in that way before. Women had been the only topic for discussion for months, and now that they had some, they only thought about them as Japs. The problem of what to do with the Japs seemed terribly simple to him at that moment, and he wished he was alone with one of them.

Morris interrupted Regeic's thoughts by approaching him. "Are you thinking the same thing I am?"

"You mean the women?"

"Yeah."

Regeic hooked his right thumb through his trousers. "Price won't like it. He wants to get on to the next house. He wants to get rid of the women."

"We ain't got enough men for that. Besides, Price ain't in such good shape himself. Both of you almost went to pieces, and he doesn't want to have to make a decision."

Regeic looked at the floor. "I guess I did make a horse's ass out of myself."

"I wouldn't feel too bad. We've all been out here too long. A man can't take but so much."

Regeic finished the bottle and tossed it on the floor, where it made a loud clanking sound. He surveyed the women for a few minutes and then gestured toward the woman he had looked at before. "Come here," he ordered. A look of fear shot across her face as she stared up at him. He yelled at her again, but she continued to sit on the floor and stare at him. Finally he realized that she did not understand English and he felt ridiculous. He took a long step and roughly grabbed the woman's arm. With a tremendous effort, he jerked her to her feet and shoved her out of the door and into the room across the hall.

Almost as soon as Price had entered the room, he noticed that Regeic and one of the women were missing. He glared at Morris fiercely. "Where did he take her?" he demanded.

"Across the hall."

"Get them."

"Ern—"

"I said get them."

Morris started to go, and then turned. "Ern, I never crossed you in my life, have I? Well, this is the first time. Why the hell should we have to kill the women? The Japs brought them out here so they could have something to screw, and we might as well get some of it for ourselves. They killed most of your men, anyway. We ain't got enough men to get any further. As far as I'm concerned, I'd just as soon die in here as out in the street."

For a moment Price was tempted to hit Morris. Then he looked at the women and he wanted to run. There was too much to decide. The platoon should be moving on through the town but he really did not have enough men left. Years of training told him that he should move on a little further before it got dark. Then, there were the women. Right now there was no way to get them back to the rear, and if they were left there and could find any weapons, they might kill some Americans. Finally Price spoke. "We've got to go."

Beecraft looked at him. "Why, Ern? If we move, we'll all get killed. Choinsky can't move and both you and Regeic are in bad shape."

"We've got to go," Price repeated.

"Ern, dammit, I don't know whether you realize it or not, but you've only got ten men left and one of them is cracked. If we get out of this house, they'll cut us to pieces."

"I've got a full platoon and they're the best men in the army. If we don't move on out, Colonel Stogner will raise hell with us."

Beecraft looked at Price and wondered if he had lost his head again. "Don't you remember, Colonel Stogner is dead?"

Price remembered that the colonel had been killed back in the field. He realized that he must have really been tired

to have made the remark that he had. "Yeah, I guess he is."
"Do you still want to go on?"

Price still did not want to make a decision. Guiltily he decided to stay. "You make any decision you want, and I'll back you. In the meantime, I'm going to have a little fun and relaxation." He looked around and located a Japanese woman who didn't look too dirty. Roughly he jerked her to her feet and dragged her from the room, stopping for some beer on the way out.

As soon as they reached the door, the woman tried to break free, but Price had expected this and he gripped her arm tighter. He walked down the hall until he found a door, which he savagely kicked open. He half pushed and half slung the woman through the doorway. As he was placing his weapon against the wall, she tried to escape a second time. In one leap, he was at her side, sending the palm of his hand against her face with enough force to knock her to the floor. He was upon her instantly, panting with excitement. The woman tried to defend herself by beating her small hands on his chest and face but it was no help. When she screamed, he covered her mouth with his filthy hand. Finally, he ripped her clothes from her body and fell on her like a wild animal.

Later, she moved a little and Price was ashamed of himself for raping her. He had satisfied his lust, and now that the first biting sting of his passion was over, he felt dirty. Over and over, he kept telling himself that she was only a Jap and that it did not matter. He kept telling himself that she was no better than a soldier and that she was lucky that he had not killed her. At the same time, he knew that this was another human being and that he had been wrong.

Price banged a beer bottle against the wall and took a large drink. Drinking on an empty stomach had always made him drunk, and he knew that he was already feeling very little pain. After several drinks, Price smiled and tried to give the woman a drink.

The woman looked up at him and Price thought he read pain and hurt in her expression. Looking at her, he felt even more ashamed of himself. He almost wished that he had killed the women. He knew that he wouldn't feel any worse if he had. The more he looked at her, the more depressed he became. In one day he had killed two of his own men and a woman, he had raped a woman, and he had gone to pieces.

Suddenly, as he looked at the Japanese woman, he thought about Sandra. He thought of all the times he and Sandra had stayed in bed together, their desire satisfied for the moment, but knowing that it would rise again. He fought with the memory and wished desperately that he could forget her. He had already lost control of himself once, and if he did it again, he might not recover quickly enough. He had to hold on for the rest of the night. The Japs would be back

66

in town for sure and he would have to be at his best to keep from getting killed. If he could survive the night, the war would be over for him and he would be on his way back to the States.

Price felt as if he needed only one thing to make him feel like a human being. He wanted someone to love him in the same way that Sandra had before they had been divorced. He wished he could tell this Japanese woman how desperately he wanted her to be tender and sweet to him. Suddenly, he was very tired and he felt a million years old.

With great tenderness he placed his arms around the woman and very gently pulled her to him. Her eyes revealed fear and reminded him of a small animal that had been caught in a trap. Once again, she beat her hands on his chest. "I'm not going to hurt you. Please stop struggling, please," he pleaded. The woman continued to fight until she was exhausted.

Price kissed her trembling lips, but she did not respond. He continued to kiss her, and after a while he noticed that her lips had stopped trembling and she seemed to be relaxing a little.

The door flew open and Regeic, who was very drunk, stuck his head through. "Ern, old boy, this is the life."

"Can't you see I'm busy? Get the hell out of here!"

"Some business you've got here."

"Get out!" Price screamed.

"Come on, Ern, let's have a party."

Reluctantly, Price rose from the floor and made his way to the door, where he gently began to push his friend back into the hall. Regeic looked as though he would pass out any minute, and he stumbled drunkenly as he was forced backward. "Come back and see me tomorrow," Price said good-naturedly.

Regeic grinned. "That's no way for an old buddy to treat old Regeic. Let's have a party." Regeic stumbled backwards until he hit the opposite wall. "Them mean old Japs are going to come back and kill the hell out of us tonight. Let's have a party and die drunk."

"I wish to hell you'd leave me alone. If I get the chance I'm gonna screw myself to death before they get here."

"You old whoremonger," Regeic laughed loudly.

"What about you?"

"To hell with me. How about you and me changing women?"

"I like the one I've got. Now why in the name of hell don't you get the hell out of here and leave me alone?"

Price gave Regeic a shove, ran back into the room, and slammed the door before Regeic could regain his balance. Regeic returned to the door, but after a few minutes of banging on it, he left, and there was quiet again.

Price walked back to the woman and sat on the floor next

67

to her. This time, she did not seem so afraid. Gently he held her face in his hands and looked into her eyes. When he finally slid his hand down her naked back, she held her face up to him as if she wanted to be kissed. She moaned softly as he caressed her, and for a brief moment the war seemed far away.

Bryant sat on the steps with a cigarette dangling from his lips. The smoke curled upward and made his eyes water. He removed the cigarette and placed it on the edge of the stairs. He had just taken his place on guard. Otis and Dalzel were with him. Another man came down the stairs and sat next to him. All three of them had been in the outfit only a short time, and Bryant wished that some of the more experienced men were there with him. He knew that these men thought the old-timers were no good, and he wished there was some way for him to explain what the months of fighting had done to them. He wanted to tell them that they were scared, too, but he knew they would not believe him.

He thought about his wife, Pat, and wished that he could see her for just a moment. Although she had not spent too much time with him before they had left the States, she had been very sweet, more like a mother than a wife. He wanted to laugh a little about the way she worried about him getting his feet wet, and wondered how she would feel if she knew how he had been living? He could not think of any good reason for remembering things like that when there should be something important about her to remember. He tried to think about the Japs, who would be trying to take the town back, but his thoughts seemed to stay with his wife. Realizing how lightly he was taking it when he was so close to dying, he was forced to laugh.

When he laughed, the three other men looked at him as if they wondered whether he was going to crack up, too. They had not learned to understand that his laughter was a device which he used to hide his fear. He shot a warning glance at them, and nobody spoke.

Bryant's thoughts went back to the woman he had just raped. The word sounded hard and he had trouble realizing that it fitted the act he had committed. He wondered how he could degenerate to such a thing. She had struggled almost to the last, but he had forced himself upon her. As he thought about it, he remembered how the colonel had always said, "If rape is inevitable, lean back and enjoy it." Now, the remark seemed to make more sense to him. Once again he chuckled to himself. That seemed like a million years ago. He wondered how his wife would feel if she heard about it. He knew that she would never understand. He tried to justify the act to himself, then he tried to feel bad about it. The only thing he was sure about was that he felt better for having done it. He had tried to tell himself that he had imagined

68

it was Pat the whole time, but he knew better. This might be his last night on earth and he had a right to enjoy whatever pleasure he could find.

Dalzel stood up and walked toward the door. Bryant stiffened and whispered, "Keep your ass still. You want to get us killed?"

Dalzel shot a look at Bryant which indicated that he wanted to talk back, but he remained silent. Bryant took another puff of the cigarette and tried to forget about the present. What would Pat do if he got killed? He wasn't sure that he really loved her but, on the other hand, he thought about her all the time. Maybe he did love her; he could not be sure. If he did, why couldn't he remember what she looked like when she smiled? As he thought about it, he realized that he really did love her. He admitted that he had just been away too long. At that moment, the most important thing in the world to him was that he wanted to tell her that he loved her.

Bryant was suddenly brought back to the present. The first indication that there were people in the street was a scraping sound. It might be the National Guard unit coming to relieve them, but it was probably the Japs. The others had not heard. Bryant took another puff from the cigarette and listened for the sound to be repeated. "Somebody is out there," he whispered. "It could be the Guard coming to relieve us, so don't shoot until you're sure." He turned to Sterner. "Go upstairs and tell Price I heard something."

"Who the hell is Price?"

"The lieutenant. How long have you been in the platoon?"

"A day."

"Christ," Bryant muttered, as the man backed up the stairs. As he listened for the sound again, the minutes ticked by very slowly. They must be right outside by this time.

Finally a voice spoke. It spoke English. "Any G.I.'s in there?"

Bryant thought about the voice. It sounded enough like an American, but you could never be sure. "Say Lilly lollipop," he said.

Silence followed, and Dalzel became irritated. "Are you crazy?" he said to Bryant. Before Bryant could stop the man, Dalzel rose and made for the front door. There was a shot, then a scream.

Realizing that the voice must belong to a Jap, Bryant anticipated the grenade which would be coming through the door soon. He moved behind the stairwell and called for Otis to come back with him.

There was a clunking sound, and then something rolled through the door. The explosion that followed shook the room. Bryant knew that the Japs would be pouring through the door any minute. He raised his weapon and waited. The Japs started through the door at the same time. They were

69

running in a crablike formation, bent over very low. He fired blindly into the mass and heard Otis emptying his clip. He heard the pinging sound which meant that his rifle was empty, and he quickly jammed another clip into the weapon. He pumped several more shots into the rushing Japs and did not stop until they were all down. No more Japs came in. He pulled a grenade from his pocket and waited. Upstairs, he heard the sound of moving men. "Stay up there," he called. Above him, he heard the sound of a submachine gun. An American grenade sounded in the street and he knew that the men were firing out the windows into the street.

"Get up here." It was Price who gave the order, but his voice sounded weak and unnatural, as though he were in great pain.

Bryant was on the first step when the Japs began to rush through the door again. He threw the grenade and ducked. Otis fell at his feet at the same time. The grenade landed in the midst of the Japs and as soon as the explosion sounded, Bryant began to back up the stairs, firing as he went. The Japs were firing at him and the slugs sounded very loud as they hit the wall around him. As he retreated, he wondered why they did not hit him. Suddenly his body was filled with pain everywhere at once and he knew that he had been hit, but could not tell where. Then he knew. He grabbed for his groin and felt the mass of torn flesh. Bryant forced his eyes open, but he could not see through the wall of gray that seemed to be in front of him. The pain became unbearable and he screamed until he thought his lungs would burst. He was conscious of running and being unable to stop his legs. He was barely conscious of shots and voices. He heard his own voice telling someone to kill him.

It was dark outside when Price woke. The Japanese woman slept at his side, and even in the dark he could see that she was smiling. Price sat on the floor and wondered how he could ever have considered killing the woman. He watched her for some time, and he could not help but remember the times he had seen Sandra in the same position. Almost as though she knew that he had moved, the woman shifted her position in order to be next to him.

The Japanese woman was almost as dirty as Price, and as he looked at her he thought about Sandra and wanted to move. For the first time, he was aware that the woman smelled like fish. Her hair had been saturated with some kind of oil. When Price looked at the rotting flesh of his own body, he wondered how the woman had been able to stand him, especially with the dried manure all over him. The more he looked at the woman, the more he wondered how he had been able to have anything to do with her. He became disgusted with himself and he wanted to get away from the woman. He rose to a kneeling position. The woman opened her eyes. For a long moment, he looked into her eyes. She seemed to be pleading with him not to leave her alone.

She wanted to be kissed again, and put her face up to his. Almost as though he had no control over himself, Price placed both of his hands on her face and shoved her as hard as he could. The woman hit the floor, uttering a little cry.

He wanted to help her to her feet, but before he could do that there was a shot, and then a scream, from downstairs. A second of quiet followed and then he heard the shattering explosion of a Japanese grenade. He grabbed his trousers and struggled into them as he ran for the door. He saw Regeic running down the hall. Price had reached the door and had bent down for his weapon, when there was a sharp jab at his back. His knees buckled. When he hit the floor, he rolled over on his back and tried to look through the haze which was forming in front of his eyes. He saw the woman bending over him with a bayonet raised. Savagely he kicked out with both feet. When his feet tore into her stomach she screamed and fell to the floor. Quickly he reached for the weapon and fired a burst into the woman's face. He staggered from the room and tried to make his way down the hall. Each step sent shock waves through his body.

When he reached Regeic's side, he was forced to hold onto the wall for support. His head was spinning and his back felt as if it must be on fire.

Regeic was looking over the railing. "Bryant's down there."

Calling to Bryant took all the strength that Price could muster. "Get up here!"

There was an explosion. Bryant came into view as he backed up the stairs, firing as he came. Bullets were hitting the walls all around him, smashing into them with terrific force. Price yelled encouragement to him and it looked as though Bryant would reach safety. Suddenly Bryant screamed and grabbed his groin. Then he dropped his weapon and raced up the stairs, screaming like a madman. He ran wildly, screaming fiercely as he came. He ran past the men at the head of the stairs and bounced from wall to wall until he reached the end of the hall, where he fell. Once on the floor, he clutched at his wound and screamed.

Price watched Bryant flop around on the floor. After several seconds he gasped, "My God!" Quickly he turned to Regeic. "Start throwing grenades down the stairs." Then he ran toward Bryant, who was still on the floor screaming.

The first grenade exploded just as Price knelt beside Bryant. Trying to ignore his own pain, Price pinned the other man to the floor. He looked down at Bryant's face and knew that the pain must be unbearable. Bryant no longer looked human. All the color had drained out of his face and his features were distorted with pain.

"Bryant!" Price said urgently.

71

"My balls!" the man screamed.

"Bryant!!!"

"Oh my God, my balls!" Cold sweat was running down the other man's face.

"Bryant, listen to me. Can you hear me?"

"Oh, Christ," Bryant screamed.

"You'll . . ."

"Kill me," Bryant suddenly pleaded.

"Just take it easy."

"Kill me."

"You'll be all right."

Price could not hold the man any longer. Bryant tore himself from Price's grasp and rolled to the other wall. Then he rolled back toward Price, his hands still clutching the wound.

Bryant continued to scream and plead with Price to kill him. It was all so horrible that Price wanted to run and never come back. He had heard about men getting hit like this, but it was the first time he had come face to face with it. It was the one thing they all dreaded most. In an effort to hide their fear, they had even joked about it. Price wanted to help Bryant, and for one long moment he even considered shooting him. Finally he realized that he could not pull the trigger. Bryant screamed until Price wanted to tell him to shut up. The screams were tearing his nerves apart. In desperation, Price sent his fist smashing into Bryant's face. Bryant jerked once and then was quiet.

Bryant's screams were still ringing in his ears as Price walked down the hall. When he passed Choinsky he stopped and looked at him. Choinsky was staring blankly into space, unaware that he was in the middle of a war. He had obviously lost his mind. All of Price's men were dead. The entire platoon was gone—shot both mentally and physically.

When Price reached the head of the stairs, Regeic was still throwing grenades down the stairwell. Wheatley was bending over a box of Japanese grenades and was passing them to Regeic. Price's back was hurting badly and he was finally forced to lean against the wall for support. "Where are Morris and Beecraft?"

Regeic threw another grenade and then quickly indicated the front room where Moss and Terry were lying dead. "In there," he said, before cracking another grenade on his helmet.

Price watched as another grenade tumbled down the stairs. "Hold up a minute. They may not still be down there."

Wheatley was very drunk and he half straightened, with a grenade still in his hands. "Would you like for me to go down there and see?"

"You'd get yourself killed," Price said.

"I'll be all right."

"You'll be all right. Hell! You're drunk."

"Yeah."

72

"You stay here," Price commanded. "If we stop throwing the grenades, the Japs will be up here soon enough. If they don't come they must have given up on us."

"To hell with it," Wheatley said. "I might as well die right now as any time. That's what the Army brought me out here to do." Before they could grab him, Wheatley was staggering down the stairs.

He had nearly disappeared around the curve of the stairs when the shot rang out. The blast of the machine gun almost tore him in two. The force slammed him back against the wall. He stiffened and then slid down the wall. He was in a sitting position when the next blast tore into him, and he slumped forward. Just before his head disappeared from view, his eyes had opened for a second, as if he had seen death face to face.

Price and Regeic both threw a grenade at the same time. The two explosions shook the house. Both men continued to throw grenades at regular intervals and soon it became apparent that the supply of grenades would soon be exhausted.

Price turned to Regeic. "Regeic, I think I'm hit real bad. That Jap bitch stabbed me in the back when the first shot was fired. I don't think I'm gonna live. Take Choinsky and get in the room right across from Morris." He threw another grenade and waited for the report before he continued. "Get in there and don't come out until you hear my submachine gun. That's an order," he said, as Regeic hesitated.

As soon as Regeic had pulled Choinsky into the room, Price crawled to the corner at the top of the stairs. There was no light there, and if the Japs rushed up the stairs too fast they would rush right past him. The pain in his back was agonizing now and he gritted his teeth. Two things could ruin his plan. The Japs might throw a grenade first and then come up the stairs. If that happened, he had very little chance of living. Then there was his own condition. His head was spinning badly and he might pass out any minute.

The minutes ticked by very slowly and each second seemed to be reluctant to pass. Still there was no sign of the Japanese. Each time there was a noise, he readied his weapon, but no one appeared. Each time his nerves would jump as though hot coals had been poured into his blood stream. Price was resigned to the fact that he would either die from the wound or the Japs would get him. He had always been afraid to die before, but now that he was sitting in the dark and waiting, there was no fear, hardly any emotion at all. He realized that if he died, Regeic would also be killed and then no one would ever know what had happened to his platoon. That would make his life a tremendous nothing.

At first, he only heard their voices. Then there was the heavy trampling sound of many feet pounding up the stairs. He clicked off the safety, and it sounded terribly loud. The Japanese soldiers were chattering in their monkeylike voices as they came running up the stairs. He could almost imagine that they were talking about the Americans and how they had run out of ammunition. Their heads appeared first, and then their bodies, as they spilled out into the hall. He thought there must be at least ten, possibly twelve.

The Japs bunched together as they entered the hall and started for the doors. Price jerked on the trigger and a scream arose from the mass as the slugs tore into them. It was too dark to see all the way down the hall, but he could imagine that some of them were swept the entire length of the hall. He fired until the weapon was empty. Quickly he jerked the clip from the weapon and jammed another into it. Then he heard firing from the other rooms and knew that Morris or Beecraft had come out. So had Regeic. He was afraid to fire down the hall again, so he looked over the stairs, determined to prevent any more of the Japs from coming up.

"Put a slug in all the bodies," he heard Regeic saying. "They might be playing possum."

"Get back in the rooms," Price called. "More of them might try it again."

Price sat in the same place for almost an hour, and there was no more movement downstairs. The only sound was the creaking of the house. The pain had become so great that Price had stuck the sling of his weapon into his mouth and had clamped his teeth down on it.

Finally Regeic came out of the room and made his way to the head of the stairs, where he knelt beside Price. Regeic knew that Price was in pain. He tenderly removed his fatigue jacket in order to look at the wound. Reluctantly Price lay face down on the floor so Regeic could work on the wound.

Regeic was looking at the ugly wound which was right over Price's kidney, when the others came down the hall. He could not tell how bad it was, but the gash looked deep and was still bleeding heavily. He removed the first aid pouch and went to work.

"If the Japs come back," Morris said, "we'll hear them in time."

"They better not," Regeic said. "I ain't got but one more clip."

Beecraft banged his helmet on the floor. "Did you ever know of them giving up until they were all dead?"

"No," said Regeic.

"All right then, they'll be back."

Price bit tighter on the strap, as Regeic bandaged the wound. "My last clip is in my gun," he said to Regeic.

"Mine too," Beecraft said.

"I got two," Sterner said.

"How about grenades?" Regeic asked.

"Looks like we got two Jap grenades," Morris answered.

"Well," Regeic said, "the only thing we've got to fight with now is our bayonets and a lot of beer. I think I might as well

74

be drunk as hell when they kill me. How about one of you going and getting some of the bottles for us? Why don't you go?" he said to Sterner.

"Bring it all out here," Morris called after him. "We might as well sit right here and drink it all."

"Sure thing."

Price's head was swimming and he was barely conscious, as they waited for Sterner to come back. There were several loud clanks when Sterner dropped some of the bottles. He cursed several times, but soon he appeared with his fatigue jacket full of bottles.

"How many Japs do you think we got?" Morris asked, opening and passing around the bottles.

Price sat up again and felt the wound with his hand. Then he took a large drink of the liquid. Some of the beer trickled down his chest and it felt cool. "A whole hell of a lot. Look at all the bodies in the hall and there ain't no telling how many we got with the grenades."

Beecraft gulped at his bottle of beer. "Morris and the kid and I must have killed a hundred out in the street. We got three grenades in a big bunch before they could scatter. I know they had a company out there, maybe more."

"You know"—Regeic laughed—"I'm surprised that we got any of them. We were all either shacked up or drunk as hell when they hit. I'm surprised that they didn't shoot the hell out of us."

Price fought off the pain and laughed with Regeic. "Hell, they almost did get me. That Japanese bitch stabbed the hell out of me."

"Does it hurt bad?" Regeic asked.

"Just like the very hell. I think she cut out my kidney."

"I think you'll make it, though," Regeic said sympathetically.

"Well," Price lied, "the beer makes me feel a little better at least."

"Can we do anything to help?" Morris asked.

Price threw his empty bottle down the stairs. "Yeah. How about another bottle of beer?" Morris handed him another bottle of beer and Price drank it all without taking the bottle from his lips.

"Want me to light you a cigar?" Regeic asked.

"What the hell do you guys think I am," Price asked, "an invalid?"

Regeic fumbled in Price's pockets until he found a cigar. He lit it and handed it to Price. "Here you go, the condemned man's last request."

Price laughed. "They ain't yet made that Jap that can kill me. Go to hell!"

"I probably will." Regeic laughed. "Tonight we probably all will have to make the trip. I'll bet they got a first sergeant down there that's just waiting for us. He probably has the

75

supply sergeant standing by to issue us our shovels so we can go right to work on the coal."

They all laughed except Sterner. He could not understand these strange men yet. He was beginning to understand the fear they lived with, because he, too, felt as though he were going to die, but he could not understand how they could be so calm in the face of death. He sat with the same bottle of beer that he had started with, not wanting to be drunk when the Japanese came back. There was a long period of silence.

Morris was the first to break the silence. He sounded very drunk. "This the worst yet. You know we're prob'ly the only ones that've survived outta the whole outfit? A lifetime of makin' friends an' they're all gone, dead. It's not fair," he said bitterly. "This whole war's crazy as hell. They've made an animal outta me. Most us just raped some women and didn't even think anythin' 'bout it. This the craziest damn thing ever heard of."

It seemed to Price that Morris was about to go to pieces, and he remembered how he himself had felt earlier. He wanted to say something, but he was afraid that anything he said might be the wrong thing.

The others tried to ignore Morris. They left it to Beecraft to try to quiet him. Morris began to cry like a baby.

Regeic began to laugh, and Price turned to him. "Have you gone off your rocker?"

"I thought about something funny."

"Just what in the name of hell is so funny?"

Regeic laughed again. "I was just wondering how you're going to be able to explain that wound to the doctors?"

"Hell, I'll just tell them I fell out of bed and cut my back on a beer bottle."

"Who would believe that?"

"Only a damn fool."

They laughed for a long time and then drank for a long time, waiting for the Japs and discussing the old days, remembering their recruit days and retelling old stories. Always, though, they waited for the Japanese to come. One by one, they passed out, until only Sterner was awake.

Sterner had listened to the others as they talked. Several times he left them to see how Choinsky and Bryant were, but neither of them moved. They were breathing, but Bryant looked as though he might not last the night.

It was during the conversation that Sterner had realized that the thing that made these men different was that they were professionals who lived by deeds and not words. Sterner looked down at the drunk men around him and was proud of the fact that he was there with them. They had not accepted him as one of them, but he knew they would in time. For the first time he realized that these men had been together for a long time and that many of their friends had been killed. To them, a friend meant that they would have one more death to mourn. For the first time he realized the meaning of something he had heard—"An infantryman needs no friends." These men would only accept a man when he had proved himself.

He looked at Price and wondered if he would live. From the way the others had talked about him, Price was the kind of man who commanded respect. When he could not command respect, he demanded it and was prepared to fight a man to prove his right to it. He was a man among men.

Sterner then looked at Regeic—tough, dependable, and a good soldier. Here was a man who was in love with the army. It was his life. Regeic could always be counted on to bear more than his share of any task and still do an excellent job. He was the backbone of the army.

Morris and Beecraft were very much alike, except that Morris was the more aggressive. Neither of them were born leaders, like Price and Regeic, but they were dependable and did their job well. Both of them were married and gave the army its most stable personnel.

Sterner felt pride for having the privilege of serving with these men, but he wondered if he could ever measure up to their brand of courage. He heard a creaking sound downstairs and wondered if he would ever see the morning arrive.

## CHAPTER FOUR

The last thing Price could remember, except for a vague sense of moving back, was drinking the beer and waiting for the Japanese to come and kill him and his few remaining men. There had been times when he had dreamed about Sandra again, but he could make no sense of it.

One dreamlike experience kept coming back to him. He remembered the hay ride he had taken with Sandra. It had been sponsored by Maxwell Field. Hand in hand, they had walked to the line of waiting, hay-filled wagons. He could still remember how her hand had trembled as they had approached the last wagon. He had taken her in his arms and they had looked into each other's eyes for a long moment before he gently lifted her into the wagon. He had climbed in behind her and they had settled into the hay together.

The night was beautiful. A large yellow moon and a vast sky of twinkling stars were overhead. There was a cool breeze blowing. Hardly a word passed between them as they sat on the shore of the lake and sang songs and ate hot dogs.

When he stood in front of her door later that night she told him that she had enjoyed herself. She had said it in such a way as to leave no doubt that she meant it. Price had meant to go, but she had persuaded him to come in. They were sitting on the floor.

"Penny for your thoughts," she had whispered.

"I wasn't thinking about anything."

"Yes you were."

"All right. I was thinking about how my wife would look sitting here."

She had looked very shocked. "You told me you weren't married."

"I'm not."

"You said your wife."

"I was thinking about the one that I'll have some day."

"Ohooooo," she had cooed.

She was on her stomach and he started rubbing her back. He had seen the piece of hay on the hem of her skirt and had reached to pull it off. She didn't move, so he massaged the back of her leg. Then he bent and kissed the back of her knees. She turned over, slowly and openly.

For Bryant, the days in the hospital dragged on endlessly. The heat was more than he could stand and the sweat poured from his body. Vaguely, there seemed to be something he should remember, but the shots they kept giving him kept him from thinking straight. Someone was talking to him, but the words seemed to be coming from a great distance. He fought with the dope, and things seemed to clear a little. "He's coming around," he heard the voice say. He tried to open his eyes, but he did not seem to have the strength for even that. He tried several more times and finally the haze cleared enough for him to see the man bending over him.

"Well," the man was saying, "it's good to see you awake. You had me worried for a while there."

Bryant stared up into the man's ruddy face and decided that he was a doctor. That meant that he had been wounded, but he could not remember where.

"We'll have you out of here in no time at all," the doctor was saying.

Why in the name of hell doesn't he tell me where I got hit and how bad it is, Bryant wondered. The doctor looked worried, as though he had something important to say and did not quite know how to go about it.

"Bryant, we had to remove your testicles." The words rang out like a sledge hammer.

It was several long agonizing seconds before Bryant realized it was not a dream. Suddenly he remembered the stairs and the pain. He wished that he had been killed. Then he heard a whispering voice and it was filled with horror. For a moment he did not recognize it as his own. "Oh, my God, not my balls!" Bryant searched the face of the doctor for some sign of hope but all he saw was sympathy.

"You're lucky to be alive. Only six more made it. You should consider yourself very lucky."

"Piss on the others," Bryant screamed. "Piss on you too.

I'd rather be dead than like this," he cried out. At that moment he did not care about the others. The only thing in his mind was the brutal fact that he was castrated. The thought bore down on his brain like a lead weight.

If there was pain, Bryant did not feel it then. The only thing he was conscious of was the sickening fact. He raved and cursed like a maniac. He tried to jump out the window, but the doctor and an orderly held him to the bed. Quickly there were more men at his bed. They held him while a shot was administered. He fought them and screamed until the shot took effect. A giant spiral seemed to be in front of his eyes and he seemed to be falling.

When Bryant woke up, his body seemed to be very tired. The first thing he noticed was the large man sitting at the side of his bed. The man was looking at Bryant and he was smiling.

"How are you doing?" the man asked.

Bryant found himself afraid to answer. He remembered all the jokes about a castrated man's voice changing. He could not bring himself to speak for fear that his voice would sound like a woman's.

"Can I get you anything?"

Bryant looked at the man's face and imagined that he saw contempt mirrored there. He knows, Bryant thought, he knows what they did to me. He thinks I'm a queer. Ashamed to face the man any more, Bryant turned over and buried his face in his pillow. The next thing he knew, he was crying into the pillow, and he knew that it was because he was becoming more of a woman than a man.

Mentally, Bryant knew he was all fouled up. Between sobs, the only thing he could think of was the jokes. He knew that his voice would change. He also thought he would start walking like a woman. He worried about the fact that he might want to wear women's clothes. His whiskers might stop growing. Worst of all, he was afraid that he would return to the States and become a queer.

Then, the worst thought of all occurred. What about his wife, how would she take it? A lifetime without sex would probably be more than she could take. He wanted to scream.

Price lay in the hospital fighting the sticky heat. He could not remember much about the morning that the National Guard had come into the town and taken them out. He could remember that they had been terribly upset when they had found them drunk. The only thing that saved them was the fact that all the other outfits had bogged down at the same time. He barely remembered Regeic helping him down the stairs into a waiting jeep. That had been two weeks ago and most of that time had been spent recovering from the fever.

Price had been afraid that he would die when he first arrived and for the first weeks he had thought that he could not last from one day to the next. After a while, he got used to the routine. He was amazed at the difference that little things made to him. For instance, the toilet. The bed sheets were another thing that he could not get used to. He found himself almost feeling like a human. Even during the day, when the heat was the worst, he would pull the sheets up over him just so he could feel them.

The ward nurse, Betty, also made a difference to him. She was always cheerful and, better than that, she was pretty. Price guessed that she must be about thirty. Although she was a little plump, she was pretty. Price especially liked the way she always wore a ribbon in her hair. He had tried to get fresh with her but it had done him no good.

One day, as usual, she came into the room without knocking. She was wearing slacks and a khaki shirt. Her uniform was always the same, he noticed, as she swayed up to the bed. She never seemed to be wearing anything under the shirt. He had come to look forward to her visits, just so he could watch her breasts bounce when she walked across the room. She sat on the edge of his bed. She was very happy and she smelled clean and fresh.

"How is my lover today?" she asked. There was a slight trace of a laugh in her voice.

"Now just where in the name of heaven could I find a woman to love out here?" he asked. "It's been so long since I saw a woman that I wouldn't know what to say."

She tried to make her voice sound hurt. "Don't I qualify as a woman?"

"Let me see," he said, moving his hand toward her.

"Oh, no you don't," she said. Then she laughed and tossed her head back. "Let's get you turned over and let me have a look at those bandages."

Price turned on his stomach, and she pulled the sheet off him. He couldn't get used to her seeing him without any clothes.

"Can't you ever wear the pajamas we gave you?" she asked.

"Don't you like these?"

"Khaki shorts look like hell."

"I like to wear them."

He started to speak, but she was working on the bandages. Gently she began to remove the old bandage. Several times the tape hurt as it tore loose, but she was very gentle.

"You were a mess when they brought you in here," she said absently.

"Isn't everybody?" he asked over his shoulder.

"Not like you were. I don't know where you had been, but you were covered with manure. And you had enough mud on you to sink the Navy. I don't think you could have looked worse if you'd tried."

"How did I act?"

80

"What do you mean?"

"Did I act out of my head or anything?"

"No worse than the rest."

"That's a relief. I thought I was about to crack up out there. As often as I've cursed the ones that did, I'd hate to do the same thing."

She had finished placing a new bandage on his wound. Now she was massaging his muscles. "I wouldn't say that they're cowards. We get them all the time. Some of them wet the bed. Some of them vomit. I've seen men who screamed all the time. Part of them even get paralyzed when there isn't anything wrong with them. Your friend Choinsky just stares into space."

Price interrupted her. "How is he?"

"Fine."

Price was going to ask her some more about Choinsky, but her hands continued to massage him and he didn't want to spoil his enjoyment.

"I think about one out of every twenty men who go into combat suffer some kind of mental disturbance. I think it's terrible that you men think of them as cowards. It happens all the time."

"There is a good reason why we hate them. In combat, a man who goes to pieces places his whole outfit in danger. If he becomes a babbling idiot and just sits there, it leaves one gun less. If he starts screaming at the wrong time, he draws fire, and a lot of people can get killed. If nothing else happens, he ruins the morale of the outfit."

"I know," she said softly. "You men think they're just faking so they can get back to the rear. Some may be faking, but most of them are really sick. I'll always remember a man they bought in here with a paralyzed arm. There wasn't a thing wrong with it, but he couldn't feel a pin when we stuck it in him. He wasn't faking."

"Like hell."

Betty leaned close to him. "You said you almost cracked. Were you faking?"

"No, but that was different. There wasn't any fighting going on then." Then Price remembered that he did not know whether there were any Japs in the room when he had lost his head. "Besides, I'd been out there a long time when it happened."

"That's it," she said, still rubbing his back. "No one can say how or when a man will crack up. One thing I do know, it's no disgrace."

Price looked back over his shoulder. "Do you think I might do it again?"

"I doubt it. At least not if you don't have to go through too many more bad experiences."

"Yeah," he said. He wondered how she knew what had happened to him.

81

"I think you did a very brave thing."

"What do you mean by that?"

"I don't know of many men who would charge a squad of Japanese soldiers with nothing but a bayonet. It was even braver for you to keep fighting after you were wounded."

Price almost laughed, but he wondered where she had heard that story. "Where did you hear about it?"

"Sergeant Regeic. He told me about it. I don't guess anybody else has told you, but you've gotten a Silver Star for it."

So Regeic had saved him the trouble of explaining the wound after all. That meant that the others had gone along with the story. "I didn't do too much. When he's fighting, a man will do a lot of strange things."

"I think you're being modest."

"Don't get too impressed with me."

"I'll bet that wasn't your first decoration, was it?"

"No."

"What else have you done?"

"Let's not talk about all that. You're making my back feel too good for me to play at being a hero."

Finally she patted his back and told him to roll over. He stayed on his stomach, not too anxious to turn over at that moment.

"You can pull the sheet up first."

"How did you know?"

"I've been around you men for a long time."

"You're sure you wouldn't like to get in here with me?" Price laughed.

"Not while I'm on duty. Besides, you'd be a lousy lover."

"How do you know?"

"I saw you when they brought you in."

Price felt the blood rush to his face and he knew that he was blushing for the first time in several years.

Regeic had just come from the psycho ward. This was the section of the hospital where all the nurses were big men. His visit had been like a nightmare. As soon as he had entered the ward, he could hear the gibbering, crying, or screaming men and it had frightened him. It had been a very rough visit. The men dragged their slippers across the floor when they walked and it sounded like sandpaper being dragged across a rough surface. One of the men had thought that he was Christ, and he had lashed out often in sermons about sin. One boy just sat in the corner and wept. A man masturbated while he sat up in his bed. Still another man had run to the screen and rubbed his face against it until the orderlies had carried him away.

The doctor had been with Choinsky when Regeic had entered the ward. He had slipped in and sat on the next bed while the doctor had talked to Choinsky. All through the conversation, Choinsky had talked in low tones and had stared straight off into space while his hands shook violently.

"We can have a lot of talks," the doctor was saying.

"Why?" Choinsky asked.

The doctor had gasped and then groped for an answer. Then he asked Choinsky, "Do you mind?"

"No."

"Then it shouldn't make much difference to you," the doctor said sympathetically.

"Not much, I guess."

Abruptly the doctor glanced at his watch and left. Then the big orderly gave Choinsky a shot. Before it had time to take effect, Regeic tried to speak to Choinsky. But Choinsky just stared straight ahead and did not seem to know anyone. Then he turned to the orderly and asked him why he was there. The orderly smiled at him without answering. In a few minutes Choinsky was asleep.

When Regeic left the ward he knew he would never come back. The place depressed him. The feeling was even worse when he realized he had almost cracked up too. Then he began to wonder if he would have remained sane if the Japs had come back.

Now that he had seen Choinsky, Regeic headed down the corridors to find Price. He had tried to see him several times before, but Price was not conscious and Regeic had been told to come back. That morning, they had told Regeic that Price would be leaving the hospital the next day.

Regeic cleared with the ward nurse and found out that Price could have visitors. He found the room and entered without knocking. Price was asleep. "Wake up," Regeic shouted. Price stirred in his sleep. Regeic approached the bed and slapped Price's rear.

Price jumped erect in the bed. "You scared the hell out of me," he sputtered.

"What's the matter?" Regeic laughed. "Do you still think you're out in the jungle?"

"You'd better believe it. Every time someone walks up behind me, I want to turn around and shoot. Of course it makes you feel a little silly when you realize that you don't have a gun."

"I'm the same way."

Price laughed lightly. "I'm glad someone else has the same trouble."

"I guess we're all a little psycho."

There was a long period of silence. Then Price spoke. "How is Choinsky?"

"Just like he was in the house. He just sits there and stares straight ahead. He didn't even know me."

"God, that's terrible."

"Yeah."

"How about Bryant?"

"He won't see anyone, won't even talk. They told me that

he's going to be flown back to the States soon. The doc's been trying to explain to him that it don't necessarily mean he can't play around any more—just that he can't have any kids."

"Yeah?"

"Yeah. But Bryant don't believe him."

Price thought about what had happened to Bryant and felt almost sick to his stomach. "I hope that it never happens to me."

"I guess he must feel real bad. I'd almost rather die."

"He wanted me to kill him that night. I don't think I'll ever forget the way he screamed."

"It was horrible, all right."

"Well, at least it's back to the States for all of us. We won't have to go through any more of this crap."

Regeic had hoped Price would not bring up the subject of going back to the States. "I'm not going back," he said bluntly.

Price was visibly shaken. "Not going back?"

"That's right, not going back. Beecraft and Morris aren't going, either."

"What in the name of hell happened?"

"Morris and Beecraft got drunk and volunteered to stay with the National Guard outfit. When I heard about it I decided to stay too. They were asking for volunteers to help fill up the ranks. Don't ask me what made them do it because I can't think of a damn thing. I did because I wanted to be with them."

"Don't try to snow me. You wouldn't go home if they tried to make you."

"Like hell! If I got the chance I'd get out of the damn army today."

"I've heard you say that every day for twelve years. You're more in love with the army that most people are with their wives."

"You're staying, too," Regeic said.

"Like hell! I didn't volunteer for anything."

"We told the CO you'd want to go along with us."

"You did what?" Price screamed.

"Volunteered for you. Are you going to court-martial me?"

"I should."

"We knew you'd want to stay."

"I'll bet you did. You drunk bastards fouled yourselves up and couldn't stand to see me live through the war!"

"We were drunk when we gave your name to the CO."

"Well, what can we do to get out of it?"

"Not a thing. The colonel over there would let you go, but the general was pushing the program. They want all the combat experience they can get."

"It sounds like you no-good bastards really got me into it."

"Yeah."

"Regeic, do you really think you can live through much more?"

"I don't know, Ern."

"I sure as hell don't think *I* can. Are you sure you no-good bastards can't get me out of this? For all I care you can stay here until you rot, but I want to go home."

"I don't see how."

"By God, I'll tell them you had no business giving them my name. If I didn't like you bastards, I'd turn you in."

"If we'd been able to stay sober, we wouldn't be in this mess. Morris and Beecraft feel worse than hell about it. They want to get back to their wives."

"How long do we have to stay?"

"Couple of months, that's all."

"Well, I don't know of anything to do but go out and get drunk as hell."

"Where in the name of hell can you do that?"

"They've got a recreation hall downstairs."

"Can we get anything to drink?"

"They've got a bar for the officers."

"I ain't no officer, Ern."

"You'll be my guest."

"Hell, I don't know about that."

"You just meet me here at seven. I'll take care of the rest."

Regeic left the room, and Price tried to grasp what he had just said. After looking forward to returning to the States for over a year, he felt trapped.

Now all Price could think of doing was to get drunk. It seemed too much of an effort to think his way out of the situation.

He looked at the yellow walls and wondered what the huge house had been used for before the war. It must have belonged to some rich planter. The longer he stared at the wall, the more he thought about the coming night and the drinks that he would have. The doctor wouldn't like it and Betty would be terribly mad at him, but he didn't care what they thought. If he was going back to the front, it wouldn't make too much difference anyway. Absently he unwrapped the cellophane from a fresh cigar and lit it. When he had it lit, he propped himself up on his pillow and began to blow smoke rings at the ceiling.

Betty suddenly appeared at the door and made her way toward his bed. "My, aren't we comfortable!" she said.

"I don't know about 'we,'" he said. Nurses always said "we," and it had gotten on his nerves. "I'm having a ball."

"You look like a real gentleman of leisure. I wouldn't be surprised if you're not up and around soon."

He looked her straight in the eye. "I wouldn't be surprised either."

Betty caught the twinkle in his eye. "I'm going to have to warn you. You stay in bed until the doctor tells you to get up. He'd really raise hell with you if he found out you'd been up."

"Well, you don't think you can keep me here too much longer, do you?"

"Look," she said. "You be a good boy and mind the nurse."

"You'd keep me from enjoying anything if you had the chance. I think you're just a Jap spy, trying to ruin my morale."

"Is that any way to talk to me?"

Price watched her walk from the room and noticed that she swung her hips almost like Sandra. "I might see you sooner than tomorrow," he said.

"I'd better not hear about you getting out of bed."

"Yes, ma'am," he called after her.

Price and Regeic reached the bottom of the stairs and halted at a heavy wooden door. The sounds of laughing and a group of male voices singing "Roll Me Over" came through the door. They stood there for a minute. "Sounds like a real party," Price commented. Price opened the door, and they entered the smoky room. At first, they could not see through the thick haze of cigarette smoke that floated around the room. There were about two dozen men in the room and about half of them were standing around a piano singing. The others sat in pairs at tables cluttered with bottles and glasses. They found their way to a table across the room from the piano and sat down.

A waiter came over to the table and scowled at Regeic. "We don't allow enlisted men in here."

Price rose to his feet and stood on his toes to emphasize his height. "Look, sonny, he came in here with me, and by God, you'll serve him anything he wants. Understand?" The waiter seemed about to argue with him. Price gritted his teeth and spoke very deliberately. "We want two drinks. A bottle of bourbon, if you have it. And I'll give you just about another thirty seconds to bring it."

"Y-y-yes, sir. But all we have is beer," said the waiter.

"Then bring that."

Regeic looked around nervously. "I knew that I shouldn't have come in here." He looked around the room again. "I'll get you in trouble."

Price grinned and patted Regeic on the shoulder. "We've been friends for a long time. I don't intend to let a little thing like the army get in the way of that. Hell, you drunken bastards went and fixed it so I'd get killed and I'll be damned if we can't enjoy ourselves before we go back."

The waiter came back to the table and placed two beer bottles in front of them. Price looked at the bottles for a minute and then turned to the man. "Bring us a dozen more."

"A dozen, sir?"

"Yeah, and hurry. I've been looking forward to a cold beer for a long time, sonny. It's been so long since I could enjoy a cold beer that I've almost forgotten what it's like to drink one."

"You can say that again," commented Regeic.

"It's fifty cents a bottle," the waiter said.

"I don't care if it's ten dollars a bottle." Price laughed. "What good is all that crap?" he said, throwing a large roll of bills on the table. "I've been saving it for longer than you've been in the army. There wasn't any place to spend it where I was, and there won't be any place to spend it where I'm going."

The waiter took several of the bills. "I'll bring your change," he said.

"Keep it. I thought I told you that I wouldn't have any use for it."

Price and Regeic picked up the bottles and drained the contents without taking them from their lips. The waiter had brought the other bottles. Then they repeated the process. After the second bottle, Price laughed. "We'll be stewed real quick if we keep this up."

Regeic wiped his mouth on his sleeve. "I'll bet I can make it through the first ten before you can."

Price looked at the money on the table and then he decided to do something he had always wanted to do. He unwrapped a cigar and stuck it in his mouth. Then he struck a match and used it to light a bill. When the bill was flaming, he lit the cigar. "I've always wanted to do that."

Regeic reached for a bill and did the same thing. "Me, too. This is great."

An officer had been watching them from across the room. He walked over to their table. He sat down without any invitation and offered his hand to Price. "I'm Dr. Hoffman."

Price glared at him. "Go to hell. Can't you see this is a private party?"

The doctor acted as if he hadn't heard Price. "Should you be throwing your money around like that?"

"Why not?" Price said. "What the hell is it good for. I won't be able to take it to hell with me."

"You could send it home."

"Who to?"

"Your wife."

"Don't have one."

"How about your parents?"

"Do you send your money home?" Price asked.

"Yes."

"Why? So they can put up a nice tombstone for you and have it carved real nice? They could put 'died in the defense of his country' and all that other junk on it."

87

"They can always use it. Besides that, it will be there waiting for me when I get home."

"Look," Price said. "I want you to understand something. I'm still dead sober. There may be a lot of things I don't know, but there is one thing that I'll bet on. When you get to heaven and spend all your time walking around the clouds, or if you come to hell with me, all the money in the world won't be any help to you. It won't buy you a damn thing. That's why I'm going to spend every cent I can."

"You're really a pessimist."

"You bet your ass. You've probably got it made, but me and old Regeic here, we can't live through it. We're as good as dead already. You don't know it, but we came out here with a lot of good men, and they're all dead. We're two miserable bastards who have all the medals in the book. If I tried to put them all on I don't think there would be room. So we have medals. But we're damn sick of getting shot at. They ought to make you rear echelon bastards go get shot at for a while."

"I think you've had too much to drink."

"And I think you'd better get over to where you came from before I get up and knock the hell out of you." Price rose to his feet. "I think I told you this was a private party. Just Regeic and me. We don't need any of you shoe clerks to help us have a wake."

The doctor rose and moved across the room without saying another word. Price sat down again. His face was still red. Tiny beads of sweat rolled down his cheeks. He drained another bottle.

Someone was singing, and the piano plunked out a tune. Price began to hum the melody to himself. All at once the room began to sway.

"Look at them," Price said. "Look at the kids, Regeic, old buddy buddy. They just don't understand what life is all about. They think that you can live forever. They still don't know what it means to know that you're going to die."

"Here's to the ones that are already dead."

"Here's to our joining them," Price said, clinking his glass against Regeic's. Then Price began to sing loudly.

"You're drunk," he heard a throaty voice saying.

It seemed to be his wife. "Look, Sandra . . ." Then he stopped and stared into the face that belonged to the nurse. It wasn't Sandra. He looked down at the floor. He was embarrassed.

"Are you too drunk to even remember my name?" she asked.

Price took another large drink and then cleared his throat with a loud noise. All the beer had taken its effect and Price knew that he was in a bad mood. He tried to sound casual. "Regeic, old buddy, buddy, this is my friend, mother and nurse, old Betty. Just old Betty."

Regeic hardly looked up at the woman and then returned to his drinking.

Price looked up at Betty and tried to see her, but she appeared as a pale shape only. He thought about apologizing for his actions, but instead he decided to ignore her. His face felt numb, felt like a mask. He wiped at it with his hand. Betty continued to look at him, and at last he slammed the bottle down on the table. "Why don't you get the hell away from me," he shouted. Then he walked from the room.

Price stopped to light a cigar as he left the hospital and headed for the beach. He was staggering, and he kept telling himself that he should not have drunk so much. Then he violently shook his head from side to side and told himself that he didn't care what she thought anyway. Then he thought of Sandra and swore. He wished that he had been nicer to the nurse. His head was growing heavier as he stumbled toward the ocean. When he reached it, he quickly stripped off all his clothes and fell into the water face first.

As he staggered to his feet, he heard Betty's voice screaming in his ear. Her hands clutched at him. "Have you lost your mind? Get out of there. You're not in any condition . . ." He flung himself from her grasp and stared into her face.

"You put your hands on me again and, by God, I'll drown you."

She reached for him again. "Price," she almost cried.

"What the hell do you want? Is there something special about me? I'm drunk."

She stood looking at him. "Please," she pleaded.

He turned and ran out into the water and swam until he was exhausted. Coming in, he could see that she was still on the beach waiting for him. Suddenly he felt sick and fell back into the water and vomited. He could feel his body heaving as the tide carried him away from the shore. Suddenly he felt himself being pulled back. Struggling for breath, he lay on the ground feeling more sober. Her horrified face was right above his, crying. "What is the matter with you? What are you trying to do?"

He was overcome with shame when he realized that he was naked. The taste of vomit was in his mouth. "I thought you had gone," he screamed. "Get the hell away from me."

"I didn't want to see you get hurt."

Suddenly she was quite beautiful and desirable to him. Before she could move he had pulled her down to him, thrown himself on top of her, and pressed his knee between her legs. She fought back desperately. His hands found the front of her blouse and with one jerk ripped the buttons off, bringing her breasts into view. For a minute he stared and then began to rip at the buttons on her slacks.

"For God's sake, do I have to scream?"

He placed a hand over her mouth and jerked at the slacks until they came loose. For a minute they rolled on the ground as he struggled with her slacks. Finally they were off and she was naked under him. He raised his body and was about to come down when he thought about the Japanese girl. Have I gone out of my mind, he wondered.

He rolled away from her and said, "I'm sorry."

"You scared me to death for a minute. I thought you were going to kill yourself."

He felt ashamed. "I shouldn't have treated you that way."

"You still want me?" she asked, making no attempt to cover her nakedness.

"Yes."

"One hundred dollars," she said, matter-of-factly.

Disgusted, he once again rolled over her. A whore, he thought.

Price lay on his bed, remembering the night he had spent on the beach with Betty. He kept thinking that she was nothing but a whore, and fitted into place with all the rest. He bitterly remembered them all and cursed to himself. He wondered if he would ever find a woman whom he could love. Somberly he reflected on how much he wanted her to be different, someone he could take back to the jungle in his thoughts, someone who would be sweet and wonderful to remember.

"Ern?" It was Betty, sticking her head around the corner.

He looked up and felt sick to his stomach. "Get out of here," he said harshly.

"Can I talk to you for a minute?" She almost whispered, sounding like a little girl.

"No."

"Ern, I've got to."

He looked at her impatiently. "What is it?"

"Can I come in?"

"It looks like you're already in," he answered, as she crossed the room and sat on the bed.

"I brought your money back."

"Keep it."

She looked as if she would cry. "You make me sound so cheap."

"And?"

"And I want to give it back. Will you take it?"

"You probably need it more than me."

She looked him squarely in the eyes. "Ern, I don't want you to think that about me. I did it because you raped me, or at least tried, and I wanted to get back at you. Do you understand that?"

"No."

"It's true. I would have gladly given in to you if that's what you wanted. I wouldn't have even come out there if you hadn't been so drunk. I was afraid that you'd kill yourself, and you almost did."

Price looked her in the eye and thought that she was either a good liar, or she was telling the truth. "I'm sorry that I made you believe that I thought less of you. Really I didn't want you to think that at all," he lied.

"I wish I could believe that, I really do. I don't think there was a thing wrong with me wanting you."

"I just never thought about it that way before. You must have had a rough time."

"A little."

"I'm crazy as hell for making a career out of the army, where I'm paid to be a killer, but you're just as crazy. All you do is patch men up enough for them to go back out there and get the hell shot out of themselves. If you were normal you'd be back in the States raising babies and going to bridge parties."

"You sound bitter."

"I am. If I was your daddy I'd spank the living hell out of you. He ought to have his fanny kicked for letting you come out here where there are too many men."

"I told you, or at least I tried to tell you, I'm a big girl now."

"So?"

"So I know what I'm doing. I've been through the mill. Right after I graduated from nursing school, I got married and then divorced. You think I don't know what life is all about?"

Price hesitated and then he decided to ask her what had happened. As soon as he had asked the question, he wished that he had not.

Her tone of voice indicated that she was not mad but wanted to talk about it. "I thought my husband was the most wonderful man in the world. We had a wonderful life together, and I still believe that he loved me more than a husband should. I was in love with him. I still am, for that matter. He was a salesman and had to go out of town a lot. One night, I let an intern take me home. We got drunk and the next thing I knew, my husband was standing at the door of our bedroom shouting at the other man. To make a long story short, he divorced me and got custody of our child. The war came, and here I am." Betty was silent for a minute. "Do you know how much I want to be with my child?"

"I think so."

"You couldn't. A man wouldn't understand."

Price looked at her for a long time. "I think I would."

"I slipped just once, and it ruined everything. It made a bad mess of my husband's life, my son's and mine." She looked very sad. "I know exactly how old my son is. Six years, three months and five days. I guess it sounds silly to you, but I keep track of it by marking it down on a calendar. If the judge had known how much I loved my boy, they would never have taken him away from me. They shouldn't

91

ever take a child away from his mother, not ever."

Betty looked as if she might cry. "His name is Johnny. He has beautiful brown hair and blue eyes just like his father has. I know that I was a fool to ever let myself get so fouled up that I'd lose my son. At the time, I thought I didn't care too much, but I was wrong. He was a wonderful man and never mistreated me. Well, I'm independent as hell now, and look at me. I did manage to keep my son for a few weeks but they came and got him. They said I wasn't a fit mother for him, and I suppose they were right."

"It's a rough life for a lot of people."

"Is that all the sympathy you can muster?"

"It may sound a little funny to you, but I don't think I'm capable of any kind of emotion at all. All the feeling that I ever had got used up out in the jungle. I'm not a man any more. Just the shell of a man. I don't think I believe in any of the things that it takes to be classified as a human being."

"You'll be all right after you've been out of the jungle for a while."

"That's the trouble, I've got to go back out there. I'm scared as all hell. When they first sent me I was scared too, but it was different then. I didn't know what to expect. Now I know, and I'm even scared to think about it."

Betty bent over him and ran her hand through his hair. For a minute, she said nothing. Then her voice was almost a whisper and very sympathetic. "Is it really bad out there?"

At first, Price did not know how to answer. He could still see the dead men in the jungle. He could almost hear the screams of the wounded and dying. "It's a little bad."

Then he decided to tell her. "It's not the sounds of the dying that's so rough. I don't think it's really seeing them that's bad. In fact, I'm not sure I can explain it in words; it's more like something that you can feel. The first dead man I saw was a Jap and it bothered me, especially when I thought about him as being alive just a few minutes before that. After I saw more of them, I got to the point where I thought about them as something like a fallen tree on the road.

"The worst part comes when it's one of the men you know. You might be in the same hole with him and he suddenly falls. Other people look at him and pass just like you'd passed the others. The only difference is, you know that this man used to be alive. One minute you were talking to him, and the next he was dead. That's when you realize for the first time that it could be you there on the ground. After that, it's almost impossible to explain how you feel. It's a fear of being wiped out, of suddenly ceasing to exist."

Tears welled up in her eyes. "You shouldn't think about it that way."

"What other way is there to think?"

"I know it sounds a little silly coming from me," she said, as she wiped a tear from her eye, "but did you ever pray?"

"That's one of the things I don't believe in any more."

"What makes you so bitter?"

"I'm still in love with a woman. I was married once and have a son. The bad part is that I don't know why my wife left me. All of a sudden, she just up and left. She took my son with her."

"I'm sorry."

"I think you mean that."

"I do."

Price fought off the desire to reach out and hug her. Instead, he took her hand and held it gently. "I should hate you for what you did last night, but I don't. I wish I could have met you a long time ago. We might have made a good life then."

She seemed to be looking into the past. "Yes," she whispered. Betty turned away and looked out into the yard, where the hot wind was blowing the green growth. She wished she could leave the island. Torn bodies, gangrene, stink, and death seemed to be crushing her flat, leaving her no time for anything else. Everything in her life was being squeezed out.

Part of her world was filled with men who had self-inflicted wounds. Whenever the lines stabilized themselves, some of the men shot themselves just to get out of it. Some of them held their weapons so close that the powder burns would be severe. At times, they would let trucks roll over their feet. Each time, it meant dishonorable discharge, but it was a way out.

Men who had been wounded, often wept with joy when they found out that the wound was severe enough to keep them off the line.

She remembered that she had been proud to be a nurse. It had been a source of pride to know that she was saving the lives of the men the people in the States were reading about. She had even seen them force a man back to the rear for attention, only to have him run away to get back to the fighting.

Price sat quietly. He realized that she must be thinking about the things she had seen. "It gets you down, doesn't it?"

"No, I'm fine."

"You ought to get a transfer back to the States. They don't have any right to make a woman stay out here in all of this."

"No, I want to stay," she lied. "These men need me."

"There must be a lot of nurses."

"Not out here."

"Do you think you'll ever get used to it?"

"I think I may."

"If it's anything like the rest of the army you'll never get used to it. If you do, you have to cease being a human being."

She looked at him. "I wonder what makes it so hard."

"I don't know really. All I know is that a man can do al-

93

most anything, even be a hero if he can get clean and be rested before the time comes for him to go into action. The army wears you down until you can't stand any more and then sends you back. When you can't go any further, they throw you back into the grinding machine again. Suddenly, one day you wake up and find out that you've used all of your energy just keeping alive."

"I think you've said everything I've been thinking. Every day I have to look at the horrible results of the slaughter and it's beginning to wear on me. It's almost like water dripping on a rock, wearing it away a little at a time. Just last week, they brought a man in here who had been hit with a phosphorous grenade. He was burned so bad that he looked like a piece of crisp bacon. He lived for three days and never was out of pain. We had trouble finding a place big enough to give him a shot of morphine. It almost makes you want to run."

"I guess it gets real rough."

"Sometimes I think I may lose my mind."

"I'm sorry for you."

"You're just like me. We both need a lot of affection to remind us there is some good left in the world. I guess that's the reason I did what I did last night. It may be wrong, but it is the one way I can forget for a while."

"I think I understand. You weren't very affectionate, though, and it hurt my feelings."

"You were too drunk to know the difference."

"I'm sorry."

"Forget it." She offered him the money again. "Please take it back. I wouldn't feel right with it. Please."

"All right." He winked at her.

Betty smiled and walked from the room.

It was the evening before Price was to be discharged from the hospital. Betty and he sat in their favorite spot on the beach, looking out over the water. It was a bright night and the moon hung like a bright yellow lantern over the water, sending its reflections skipping over the surface. The waves pounded on the beach and then disappeared in the sand. Price was sitting silently, his head propped on his hands, fighting the melancholy that was rising fast. He wanted to see his friends again, and he felt as though the sentimental attachment he had for them should overshadow his regret over leaving the hospital, but it did not. The present always seemed to overshadow the past, and today seemed to always be giving way to tomorrow.

He looked out at the waves, which were pounding themselves to death on the shore. To him, the sea seemed very sad. He thought about all the other men who had sat on some shore and watched the waves and thought the same thoughts. He thought about all the others who would come after him. As he watched the waves, he knew that nothing ever changed.

Betty had been watching him as he looked at the sea, and she was filled with a sense of sadness that seemed to be floating from him. She wanted to mother him, but she knew that his very nature would cause him to protest. "You've got to stop thinking about going back," she said softly.

"Tomorrow is not too far off," he said bitterly. "I have to think about it, whether I like it or not."

They sat for a long time, not speaking and not moving. Finally Betty pointed at the waves and spoke quietly. "Look at them." Then she pointed up at the thousand twinkling stars. "They make you realize how small all of us really are, don't they. It makes you feel unimportant when you realize that we're no more than a grain of sand in the universe. Not really important to the running of the world at all."

Price glanced at the twinkling stars and reflected on his importance. Her idea was probably sound, but he could not help feeling that his living or dying must be important. "I wish tomorrow would never come. I'd like to stay here with you forever, just like this."

"Sometimes," she was saying, "I get the craziest feeling."

"What feeling is that?"

"Sometimes I think that the human race may survive in spite of all the attempts we make to destroy ourselves."

"You might be right, but I doubt it." Then Price looked back at the stars. "Let's not worry about the world. Look at those stars. This is the most beautiful night I believe I've ever seen. Let's just sit here and enjoy it and pretend that tomorrow won't ever come for either of us."

"Well," she said brightly, "there must be some good left in a man who can enjoy a beautiful moon."

"It's the company. Let's not talk so much."

"May I ask you a question?" Betty said.

"Let's enjoy the night."

"Just one question?"

"Oh . . . all right."

She turned to face him. "Do you think you will make it now? What I'm trying to say is, has our knowing each other made any difference?"

"Yes."

"Ern?"

"Uh huh."

"Are you really worried?"

"About what?"

Betty sat on the ground beside him and began to fondle his earlobe. "About Moss and Terry and the Jap women. About you getting killed, and all those things."

Her gentle touch felt good to Price and he wanted to relax and enjoy the quiet. "Yes, I can't help remembering."

"Can't you think about it as a nasty job that someone

95

has to do? It's really what you trained for all your life."

"I used to try to think about it that way, but lately all I can do is be afraid that I'll be killed."

"Ernest, the thing for you to do is to think about today, take just one thing at a time. Don't worry about tomorrow. Think about how a cigarette tastes, or how a drink smells. That's the only way to keep on living. Once you start worrying about the future you may crack up."

"I wish I was meeting you here for the first time tonight."

"You have to take one thing at a time." She ran her hand through his hair.

"I'll try."

"As I remember our first romantic encounter," she said, "we could have both done a little better."

Price thought about the time he had spent in the hospital, and how he had thought of Betty as a whore that first night they were together. Each night since, they had met and walked along the beach together. Each night she came to be more of a part of him. For the first time in many years, he was at ease with a woman. With her help, he had discovered something worth-while in life. Price's fatalism had even lessened a little and he found himself thinking about Sandra a little less each day. He even realized that he might be falling in love with his nurse and thought that it would be an impossible romance. All that could result would be more heartache.

"You know, I really don't know too much about you," Price said quietly.

"Well, I don't know too much about you either. Perhaps it is best that way."

"Maybe."

"Besides, why would you want to know any more about me?"

"I was thinking that after the war we might be able to find each other. Then we'd have time to do things right."

Betty stopped stroking his neck and smiled. "I'd been thinking the same thing."

"Things need time to develop," Price said.

"Things?"

"Yes, things."

"Like what?"

"Things like me and you. I suppose what I'm trying to say is love."

"Oh, Ern, I'd hoped that you'd say that."

A lone, dark cloud passed overhead. For a moment, the stars seemed to be fighting to keep their light, and then they went out like so many matches.

Betty rose to her feet and looked down at Price. "You wait here, I'll be right back."

"Where are you going?"

"Back to the hospital."

"You are coming back, aren't you?"

"You just wait, I won't be very long."

"Please don't go. Let's not waste any more time than we have to."

"I've got a surprise for you."

"Can't it wait?"

"It could, but I think after you see it, you won't mind if I stay gone for a few minutes."

"Don't go."

"I'll be right back," she said.

Betty walked down the path. She looked beautiful, with the moon shining down on her, as she walked through the growth. Several times Price glanced at his watch. The luminous dial shone brightly, and he could remember all the times he had wondered if the glow was too bright when he had been on guard at night. The minutes slowly dragged by, and he began to convince himself that she was not coming back. It was just like being in the jungle, wondering if you were all alone. As he waited, he let the thought come into his mind that they might have been happy together if he could have met her at some other time. She had gotten off on the wrong path. A divorce could do that to a person. After Sandra had left him, he had gone out with every woman he could find, in a futile attempt to find what he had lost. It had always seemed cheap to him and he realized that Betty was just doing the same thing. Price rationalized that she was no worse than he, but he knew that he did not believe that. A woman was supposed to be better than a man.

Betty came down the path wearing a dress that had a flowing skirt. She looked almost like a magazine picture coming to life. She looked very feminine as the wind blew the dress against her body. At that moment, she was the most beautiful woman in the world.

"Like me?" she asked.

Price took her hand as she came to him. He kissed her gently on the cheek and stood looking into her face for a long moment. "You're beautiful."

"I knew you'd like me. It's your last night and I wanted it to be just right. You deserve better than a girl in a pair of G.I. slacks and a shirt."

"I'll always remember you just like you are tonight. When the war is over I'll find you some way."

He took her hand and they walked out on a narrow neck of sand. When they were almost to the water's edge, they sat down on the sand and faced the water together. Price placed his arm around her shoulder. "Why?"

"What?"

"I was wondering why there had to be a war."

"I'd like to think that it was all arranged so we could meet. It's strange how things happen. It took a war to bring us together."

97

"That's a pretty thought."

Betty traced the outline of his lips with her finger. "It's what I want to believe."

Price kissed her first on the cheek and then on the mouth. He kissed her for a long minute and then whispered. "Where will we meet again?"

"Somewhere out there," she said, pointing out into the far horizon.

"I mean seriously."

"Oh. I'm afraid after the war you wouldn't want to say that you knew me."

"I would. Do you think you could find the Baker Hotel in Dallas?"

"I think I could." She kissed him lightly on the ear.

Price smiled. "Tomorrow I'll give you my home address. If you'll give me yours we can write to each other after the war and arrange it."

Betty hugged him tightly. "Tomorrow."

Price kissed her again and pressed her to his body. They kissed again. "Be sweet and tender," she whispered.

While he kissed her, he worked at her dress until it was off. They sank to the ground together and neither of them spoke as their busy hands fought to free themselves of their clothes.

When the first rays of the sun hit him, Price stirred restlessly. Her head was resting on his chest and her rumpled hair was reflecting the sun's rays. She had said that she could not go to sleep on a night like this. Then she had slowly closed her eyes. The expression on her face indicated that she was happy she had given him something precious that he could take back to the war with him.

She moved slightly in his arms and he smiled to himself. Then she threw her head back as though she had seen something horrible. He stroked her forehead and she relaxed again.

He reached behind her and pulled her close to him while he whispered her name.

Betty opened her eyes slowly. "It's getting light. We'd better be going."

"You're beautiful," he said as he looked at her naked body.

Betty blushed but made no attempt to cover herself.

"Do you mind me looking at you like this?"

"Not if that's what you want to do," she answered. Then she took his hand and placed it against her breast. "Did I make you happy?"

"More than I have ever been."

"More than Sandra?"

"More than Sandra."

"I used to be a nice girl. Really, I haven't always been like this. I guess it was being lonesome that made me get this

98

way. I've been so lonesome that I thought I would die of it. I think you might understand how it is. When you need love, you can go out of your mind if you don't get it.

"When I got divorced, that was all that I had left—lonesomeness and heartbreak. I made up my mind that it wasn't going to be that way. Can you understand that?"

"Yes."

"I hoped you would. It's very important to me that you understand. I don't care about other people, but I wanted you to understand."

Price took her into his arms again.

# CHAPTER FIVE

The National Guard division was quartered in a camp by the ocean, a gigantic city built of tents with streets that were paved with stones painted white. Each tent had its side rolled to the exact height of the next, giving a picture of uniformity to the area. For more than a month, the division had been there training. Replacements were streaming in from the States, and there was an air of urgency as the officers and noncommissioned officers fought the heat to train the men.

To the regulars who had been assigned to the National Guard division, the men of the National Guard division seemed to be very little more than basic trainees wearing stripes. A standing joke among them was that none of the first sergeants was old enough to shave. Jokingly, they referred to the division as the Boy Scout division.

In the tent which had a flagpole in front of it, the commanding officer of the National Guard division, Colonel Thomas, sat behind his field desk. He was a short man, barely over five feet tall, and appeared even fatter than he was, with his stomach protruding over the top of the desk. He held his hands tightly clasped over his stomach as he talked to the adjutant who stood in front of the desk.

The adjutant had worked for the colonel before the war and had been next in line for the presidency of the colonel's company. They had been discussing the regulars who had been assigned to the division, and the colonel was frowning. "Why in the hell they had to assign them to my outfit," he grumbled, "is more than I can guess. They'll ruin the outfit. I've got the best damn outfit that they ever had in the army, and I hate to see it ruined. I'll bet I've got more college graduates in the ranks than any other division."

"I imagine that's right," the adjutant said.

"Take a look at these records," the colonel said, handing the folder that was marked PRICE, ERNEST L. to the adjutant. He continued to speak as the adjutant leafed through the papers. "Here's a good example. They made a peacetime sergeant an officer. Granted, he must be good, but those medals don't mean that he's qualified to lead men."

"He seems to have made quite a record for himself," the adjutant commented.

"His platoon was the one we found in the house with all of the women in it. I know that they killed some of the women, but it would be almost impossible to prove that they did not have to. Just the same, I don't think that's the kind of thing that American soldiers should do."

"It would look like hell if the folks back home ever heard about it."

"They were all drunk, apparently. The only thing is, how can you raise hell about a platoon that fought like they did? There were more Jap bodies around that house than you could count. The platoon was almost wiped out, but they took a lot more Japs with them. They fought very well, but you can't excuse them."

The colonel turned his attention to the pile of papers in front of him. "Damn paper work," he muttered. "If I ran my business like this, I'd be broke within a month."

"I agree."

"If the Japs had any sense, they'd bomb the paper factories. If we lost them, I don't think the army could run."

"They seem to survive on it."

The colonel signed his name several times and then looked up. "The men on the range today?"

"Yes, sir."

Morris and Beecraft were frantically working on their new platoon. It was far from being as well-trained as it should be, and they and Regeic had worked harder to get their men into shape than most of the others in the camp.

The new men went about their tasks with enthusiasm. One morning, the platoon had gone out to practice defense and attack. First one squad dug in while the others attacked, and then they swapped places.

Regeic had tried to impress them with the fact that it would be real very soon. "Imagine that the blanks are real. Act like you thought they were," he had told them.

The problem was that there wasn't enough time to make them do it over and over, until each unnecessary move was ironed out. These men were fresh, and they had no idea of what the fighting would be like. All they knew was that the army and marines had been doing a good job, and a supreme attitude of confidence seemed to be with them. They did not realize that the men who had been in the Pacific before them were mostly regulars and that years of training had gone into their lives. They believed that what the others had done, they could do just as well.

When they attacked, they acted like boys playing a game. The machine guns banged with their blanks and they yelled as they ran. Overconfidence was written all over their faces. The men attacking never believed they could be killed, and the men defending knew nothing of the fear that a banzai attack could arouse.

Regeic walked down the line of men. The firing lines had been built in a clearing, with the rifle pits at the bottom of a small hill. The lines were placed at two hundred, three hundred, and five hundred yards. The targets ran up on pulleys. Each target was numbered, and a corresponding number was placed on a post on the firing line. A small red flag fluttered in the breeze and was outlined against the gently swaying palm trees.

Behind him, the range officer relayed instructions to the men on the line. In the pits, the detail men worked in two-man teams, using paper patches and paste to cover the holes that were made in the targets. Long poles with the top of a tin can on the end were used as markers. Occasionally, the red flag, Maggie's drawers, waved to indicate a miss.

Each man on the range had an instructor to help him. Some of the instructors were National Guard noncoms and knew little more about the weapon than the trainees.

For over a week, the men had "dry fired." Regeic had made every effort to shape the troops up before they went out to take their turn at dying, realizing that everything he could cram into them would make them a little better. "Squeeze that trigger, don't jerk it," he had screamed at them over and over again.

"Next line, prepare to move forward," Regeic heard the dull voice on the loud-speaker drone. He watched Ruffin move forward with the rest of the men and lie down next to Beecraft.

"All right, Ruffin," Beecraft said, "lie down and get in position. Adjust your sights for two hundred yards, three points right windage. That's right, now let's get your rifle zeroed in."

The range N.C.O. placed the field phone back in the canvas case and picked up the microphone. "Ready on the right, ready on the left, ready on the firing line. Ten rounds, ball ammunition, lock and load. The flag is up, the flag is down, ten rounds slow fire, fire at will."

Beecraft looked down at the boy, thinking that he wasn't old enough to be out here, ready to face the brutality and horror of the war. "Go ahead there, just like the practice." The boy was gritting his teeth. Trying to soothe him Beecraft placed a hand gently on the shaking shoulder. "Let's relax now."

Ruffin had forgotten everything. Roughly, he jerked at the trigger, his thumb stuck in the air. The rifle jumped in his hands, slammed into his shoulder, and the thumb hit him in the eye. In front of the target, there was a small shower of

101

dirt. His shot was low. Happily, it seemed, "Maggie's drawers" fluttered in the hot air.

Regeic walked up behind Beecraft. "He's a little shook."

"He'll be all right. You just watch his next one."

Ruffin looked up crimson-faced.

"You ever fire before?" Regeic asked the man.

"No."

"Not even in basic training?"

"Just twenty-two's."

"Oh wonderful," Regeic said, walking away.

"You've forgotten everything, ain't you?" Beecraft asked the boy.

"I'm afraid so."

"Let's try it again. Now just relax and try to remember. Real easy now, line the sights up . . . take a deep breath . . . get the thumb down this time . . . squeeze it, that's right."

*Blam!*

The marker rose from the pits and stopped on a four. The black disk showed the hit to be high, at three o'clock. "Take another one," Beecraft said. "A three at two o'clock."

Beecraft took the rifle from Ruffin and fired three shots in rapid succession. They were all in a group. "Now, what do I have to do to get the bull?" he said, handing the weapon back to Ruffin.

Ruffin's voice was unsteady. "Just a shade of windage to the left."

"Right."

Ruffin adjusted the sights and squeezed off a round. Regeic stood behind him and watched. Ruffin was not getting any bulls, but he was getting better. If there had been more of the old men to help, they could have them all hitting the bull. All afternoon, the men who had been firing with Beecraft and Morris had been getting the best scores. It had been the same way on the bayonet course.

The bayonet course was in a small clearing, and there were stuffed targets. Regeic had tried to sound vicious when he had given them instructions. "Yell like you had the devil after you," he had told them. "Run! Run! Use the butt! Knock his damn teeth down his throat . . . hit, hit! Use the butt . . . the butt! Run, dammit, run! Twist it! Sometimes, it sticks in his guts . . . if it does, blow it out."

Lantrip had been exceptionally good at the bayonet practice. Some of the others had been good too, but none had shown the promise that he had. The one man who was obviously not cut out for soldiering was Ruffin. He prayed all the time and had looked sick on the bayonet range when Regeic had yelled at him, "Scream . . . lunge, crouch, lunge up . . . tear his throat apart. Get mad, Ruffin, cuss, hit it!"

102

The three of them—Morris, Beecraft, and Regeic—had been tough and had not wasted much time in the training of their new men. The less experienced men had run the training more like a high-school initiation. One of the National Guard officers had seen a man drop a weapon on the ground. He made the man sleep with it. Another man had called his rifle a gun. He had been forced to carry it around all day yelling, "This is my rifle, this is not my gun."

Regeic had made a practice of having offenders dig foxholes. When they had to go into combat, this practice would pay off. Once, Regeic had pulled Lantrip from the ranks and slapped him. Lantrip was the biggest man in the platoon and the others let him bully them. After that, Lantrip had respected Regeic, even though he hated him.

Morris' shirt was off and he sat on the ground with his back resting against a tent pole. Regeic and Beecraft were sitting directly in front of him. For over an hour, they had been drinking a mixture of medical alcohol and grapefruit juice.

Morris lifted the canteen cup to his lips and wished that the liquid was cooler. He held the cup toward the others. "Just imagine, they have real ice back in the States. I'd give a month's pay for a cube of it right now."

"What would you do with just one cube?" Regeic laughed.

"Just let it melt in my hot mouth. I already forgot what it's like to be cool."

"Best I can remember," Beecraft said, wiping the sweat off his face with his hand, "it is one of the best feelings in the world, almost better than women."

"Ain't nothing better than that," Regeic laughed. "When I get back to the States, I may look up that girl in Texas and get married just so I'll never have to do without again. I might even chain her to the bed so I'll be sure she's there when I want her."

Morris looked up from the floor. "You sound like you're a little behind."

"I guess it's those clean-shaven kids have me all sexed up," Regeic laughed. "If they don't send me home soon, I may start acting like the navy troops."

"You're just getting horny."

"It was that damn hospital. The last time I was there, Price took me down to the officer's club for some drinks. He got drunk as hell and left, with a nurse following him. I'll bet fifty dollars he got to her too."

Beecraft snickered and wiped at the sweat that was trickling from his nose. "Hope he gets a dose."

They sat in silence for a while and drank. Regeic remembered that they had never sat in silence like that before the war. Every so often now they would sit for hours, not speaking to each other. Several canteen cups later, Morris spoke. "You know, those kids must think we're a crazy bunch."

103

"The kids think what?" Regeic laughed. "I think they're the ones that are crazy. They ain't nothing but a bunch of babies. I'll bet we're going to have to wipe their asses for them when the shooting starts. They don't even know how to shoot a rifle. The days when you could depend on every man in the outfit to do his job are long gone. From now on, we're going to have to fight the war with a bunch of half-trained little boys with runny noses."

"There sure is a difference in them. The men we had in the old days were real men. About the only man in the lot that's worth a damn is that Lantrip. He may work out if somebody doesn't kill him." Morris laughed. "He's really a no-good bastard, a bully, but sometimes he talks like a man at least. He acts like he may at least have had a woman in his life. I think he may drink too. I don't know how good he is, but at least he talks a good fight."

"Yeah," answered Beecraft, "but how do you figure that Ruffin? He's the purest kid I ever did see. About the only thing he does is talk to the chaplain. He acts like none of us are good enough for him. I'll bet he says his prayers every night. Can't you hear it now? 'Now I lay me down to sleep . . .'"

"Hell!" Regeic laughed. "I'll bet he's praying for our no-good souls right now."

"If you can't figure out that Ruffin," Beecraft said, "what do you think about that Sterner? He used to be a teacher. With all that education, you'd think he'd be an officer."

"I don't even understand half of the things he says," Morris said.

"Wait until Price gets here," Regeic said. "When he sees the men that we got he's going to have a hemorrhage."

"They not only don't look like soldiers"—Morris laughed —"they don't act like soldiers either. Beats the hell out of me how they expect us to win the war with men like them. I'm afraid that the army as we used to know it is gone."

"At least, we'll all be ready to retire by the time it's all over," Regeic said.

Each day was crowded with training, and at night the new men learned the loneliness of soldiering. Cigarettes and poker games. The same routine was repeated over and over, until the taste of tobacco and the sight of a deck of cards made them mad. Lonely men needed some diversion from the endless conversations about sex and home.

Most of the men were eating chow. At one end of the tent Ruffin sat on his bunk and looked out between the ropes. Finally he leaned back and watched the ridge pole as the tent swayed in the breeze. Melancholy swept through his body and he felt like crying.

Sterner walked into the tent. "Hi, Edward."

"Hi." Sterner was the only one of them who had seen any

combat, and Ruffin respected him. "Has everybody finished chow?"

"They'll be back soon. We had fried chicken for a change. You should have gone."

"I can't eat, it's too hot."

Sterner saw through the comment. "Are you sure you aren't just homesick?"

"Maybe a little," Ruffin admitted.

"You should get over it after a little while," Sterner said. "You never spent too much time away from home before. It's only natural that you would feel that way."

"I hope so."

Sterner sat down on the bunk and faced Ruffin. Sweat dripped down his face and fell off his nose. "There's nothing worse than being lonesome."

Ruffin tried to smile. "You don't ever seem to get lonesome."

"Sometimes I feel as if I could cry."

"Really?"

"Sure."

"It must be rough on you," Ruffin said, speaking quietly and looking down at the floor. "I mean with a wife back at home."

"War is never good. It's hard for everyone."

"Have you heard from your wife lately?"

"Sure, sure. I got some pictures yesterday. Would you like to see one?"

Ruffin took the pictures and leafed through them. Sterner's wife was very plain. "She's pretty," he said.

"Thanks."

"I've got a girl. Do you think I should write to her and ask her to marry me?"

"I couldn't tell you what to do about that. It's the kind of thing a man has to decide for himself."

"Would you like to see her picture?"

"Sure." Sterner looked at the picture. "She really is a beautiful girl."

"I guess this sounds funny to you, but I really think that if I was to lose her I'd rather get killed out here."

"Then you ought to tell her how you feel. This war will be tough for both of you, but you're going to have to make the most of it. You can't stop loving a person just because there is a war. You ought to tell her how you feel."

"I . . . I don't know."

The rest of the men were approaching the tent, and the sound of their laughter ran ahead of them. Ruffin shrank back into his shell, knowing that they would begin kidding him again. Lantrip was especially bad about it, and whenever he got close to Ruffin he never failed to push him around.

"Sterner," Lantrip called, "you ain't been keeping the deacon from his prayers, have you?"

105

"Knock that off," Sterner said. Lantrip never bothered Sterner because he was the only one of them who had seen any combat. For that reason he was respected by the others.

"Hell, I was only kidding. The deacon doesn't mind. You don't, do you, Deacon?"

"No, I guess not."

"See?" Lantrip said, turning to Sterner with a smile.

"You shouldn't kid him so much. He has a right to live the way he wants to."

"I was just kidding him."

"Hey," Gardner called. "What about this guy Regeic?"

"I don't know how any man could be meaner," Lantrip said. "I heard that they had to pull him and his friends out of a town. They were dead drunk and had even killed some women."

"That's the straight poop," Fortunado said. "I heard it from a guy that works in headquarters. He says that he heard the colonel talking about it this morning. There's supposed to be a lieutenant coming out here that's worse than Regeic. I'll bet they're all a bunch of cowards."

Sterner had never talked about his one day in combat before, but he felt called upon to speak now. "I was with them in that town and they didn't look like cowards to me."

"Tell us about it," Lantrip said.

"There isn't much to tell. We went in and lost most of the platoon. They fought all night and killed a lot of Japs."

"Were they drunk?" Fortunado asked.

"Yes," Sterner admitted. "We found some beer and they drank it. I guess they weren't too sober, but they still killed a lot of Japs."

"What about the women?"

"They tried to kill some of the men."

"Was it rough?" Gardner asked.

"It was a little bad, but I'd just as soon not talk about it. I didn't do too much except follow them around. You'll all find out how it is soon enough."

"What did you do before the war?" Gardner asked.

"I was a teacher," Sterner answered.

"I thought you might have done something like that," Lantrip said.

"It's just like any other job."

"Where did you teach?"

"High school in San Marcos."

"Well, I'll be damned. I've been there."

"Where are you from?"

"Paris."

"Nice town."

"I don't know about that. Not too much excitement."

"That depends on what you expect of a town."

Lantrip laughed. "Have you ever been to Myrtle Beach, South Carolina, in the summer?"

"No."

"Well, that's the kind of town I like. There are more women there than you can drive off. Just before I came out here, I spent a week there and there must have been a million of them looking for a man. I picked up one that had a husband out here somewhere."

"What would you do if you ran into him?"

"Her husband?"

"Yeah."

"Fat chance, there must be a million men out here named Morris. Hell, we've got one here by that name." Lantrip laughed.

"You'd better not let Morris hear you talk that way. He might kill you before he found out that it wasn't his wife you were talking about," Gardner said.

Lantrip laughed again. "This woman was a doll. No woman that nice would marry a bastard like him."

"You never can tell."

"I never thought about that. You guys just forget what I said, you hear? The first man that mentions it is going to get the hell beat out of him, understand?" Lantrip glared coldly at the men. Then he realized that only Gardner and Sterner had heard the remark. "You won't mention it, will you?" he asked them.

"You can trust us. Besides, there wouldn't be one chance in a million that it was his wife."

"I guess you're right."

Lantrip was quiet for a minute and the other conversations made the room buzz. Finally he spoke again. "Sterner?"

"Yes?"

"What made you join the army?"

"I didn't join the army; they drafted me."

"Couldn't you get a commission?"

"I might have."

"It don't make much sense to me. You've got more brains than all of us put together."

"I wouldn't say that."

"Hell, you must have learned more before you were thirteen than Regeic and those other two."

"You don't remember the important thing. I might know more about mathematics than they do, but they know about soldiering. Before I came out here I didn't know how to kill a man."

"That don't make too much sense."

"Yes, it does. That's the thing we had all better learn to do well. If we don't, none of us will live through the war."

"I could always hold my own in a fight," Lantrip said.

The sun shone like a gigantic brass ball, as Price walked down the steps of the hospital. He felt despondent and wanted to run back and see Betty again. He had almost the same feeling that his mother had given him when he had had a bad dream as a little boy. Betty had given him a sense of security while he was in the hospital. She had also given him the first real happiness he had experienced since Sandra had left him. He felt almost like a man who had been flying through the air and suddenly fallen. Fear began to come back to him and he saw the faces of the dead men. He saw Moss and Terry with his bullets tearing into them. He remembered how Choinsky had looked. The memory of Bryant as he bounced from wall to wall came back to him, and he could almost hear the screams. Each step brought the fear closer to him.

The glare of the sun was forcing him to squint while looking for the driver who was supposed to meet him. He saw the man at last. He was tall and lanky and his uniform was bleached white. There was a darker place on his sleeve that indicated he had recently been a staff sergeant. When Price approached him, the man saluted. "Lieutenant Price?"

"Yes."

"Private Hardy, sir."

"Are you the man who was sent for me?"

"Yes, sir. Colonel Thomas wanted me to bring you straight to his tent."

Price tossed his barracks bag over into the back of the jeep and climbed into the front seat. "Okay."

Almost before Price was seated, the driver had taken his seat in the jeep. He ground the gears and the jeep shot forward in a cloud of dust. The road was dirt, and a spiral of yellow dust followed them as they sped away. Every few miles, children would greet them with their fingers extended in a "V for Victory" sign. Most of them screamed after the jeep, begging for candy.

As the jeep bounced down the road, the driver spoke. "Are you a regular, sir?"

"Why did you ask that?"

"The National Guard hasn't been in enough combat to get any men in the hospital."

They bounced along the road for a long time, and neither of the men spoke. Then the camp came into view. They drove down a gentle hill and then passed the motor pool, which was filled with Negro troops.

"Sir, I don't know whether you've heard it or not, but the colonel doesn't like regulars. You'd be better off in that nigger outfit than in the National Guard. He really makes it tough for us."

"Sounds rough."

"He is."

"Is he the reason you got busted?"

The driver cast a glance at the place where his stripes had been. "Yes, sir. I was five minutes late one day."

"I'm sorry to hear about that."

"I don't mean any disrespect toward his rank because I'd salute his uniform if they hung it on a post, but I hope that colonel gets his ass shot off before he can get the whole outfit killed. I don't think he knows too much about the business."

Price thought about the remark. He secretly agreed with the man, but he said, "I think that's about enough of that kind of talk."

"Yes, sir."

They continued in silence, until the jeep rounded a corner and came to a sliding stop in front of a large tent. There was a flagpole in front of the tent. "The colonel's tent," the soldier said, as he pointed to the opening.

Price was already reaching for his gear. "Thanks."

"You can leave that stuff here if you'd like. I can wait here and take you to the company after he talks to you."

"All right." Price left his gear but tucked his records file under his arm.

He quickly jumped from the jeep and walked into the tent. "Who the hell told you to come in here?" came the high-pitched voice that belonged to the fat man in the corner. The colonel, who had a pot belly, sat on the end of a bunk, without a shirt. The perspiration was dripping off his head, and it made his face seem even pinker than it was.

Price saluted and reported. "Lieutenant Price reporting for duty, sir."

"I said," the colonel repeated, "who the hell asked you in here?" The colonel took great care to let each word sink in before he continued. "Didn't you ever learn to knock on a door?"

Price felt the anger rising in him. "Yes, sir."

"Then you get yourself out there and come in here the right way."

"Yes, sir." Price did an about-face and walked from the tent. Once outside, he could barely control his anger. The colonel had treated him as though he were a recruit. Price stood for a minute, before he turned and knocked on the pole that formed the door of the tent.

"Enter." The colonel's voice sounded as though he were enjoying a joke.

Price entered the tent and saluted. "Sir, Lieutenant Price reporting for duty, sir."

The colonel looked very satisfied. "That's better." He rose from the bed and placed himself squarely in front of Price, who was becoming red with anger.

"Yes, sir."

"We might as well understand each other right now," the colonel said. "I have the best damn outfit in the army here and I want to keep it that way. Frankly, I don't think you regulars are the kind of men I want. I want this outfit run the way I say, and I don't give a damn how you used to do it in the old army. This is the new army, and I want my men treated with respect. I doubt if you will be able to adjust to it, so the best thing you can do is to work twice as hard as anybody else to convince me that you can do the job. Is that clear?"

"Yes, sir." Price was still standing at attention and he wondered if the colonel would ever tell him to stand at ease.

"Another thing. You don't have much education compared to the other officers here. Every one of them has some college except you. I doubt if you can compare with them. You might have been a good sergeant at one time, but I don't see why they ever gave you a commission."

"Yes, sir."

"If you'll remember, I had to take my outfit into that town and save you men from being killed. When we got there, they found most of you dead drunk and apparently you'd been shacked up with some Jap women. I want it understood that there will be no more conduct like that. The fact that you managed to be lucky enough to get a chestful of ribbons doesn't mean a thing to me. Understand?"

"Keep us from being killed, sir? Wasn't it your men that scouted the town?"

The colonel almost jumped. "When I want to hear from you, Lieutenant, I'll ask."

"Yes, sir."

"Let me tell you something. I knew you regulars. I've watched you making fools out of yourselves before the war. I sincerely doubt if any of you could have made a living on the outside before the war. Even the officers you had were a sorry lot. If there had been a man among you, he would have gotten out and there would have been one less of you for the taxpayers to support."

Bastard, Price thought. "Yes, sir."

"I see from your record here," the colonel grinned, "that you're divorced. That means that you're really a no-good son of a bitch. I don't believe in divorce, and a man that can't keep his wife must not be worth a damn. What did you do, leave her for some whore?"

"Sir . . ." Price interrupted.

"I'm not through with you yet, I . . ."

"Begging the colonel's pardon, sir, but I would appreciate it if we kept my private life out of this. I don't think that my personal life has much bearing on the subject, as long as it doesn't interfere with my duties."

"Lieutenant, I will not have you talking back to me. That amounts to insubordination."

"Yes, sir."

"Then don't ever let me hear you do it again. Is that clear?"

"Yes, sir."

"Now, you've been out here a long time, and no matter

110

how stupid you may be, something must have rubbed off. You can help this command a lot by passing along some of your combat experience to the new men. We have a lot of draftees and they haven't been too well trained. I have tried to keep most of the companies together, so most of the new men have been assigned to Baker Company. You will be a platoon leader there. I've also picked out one of my best noncoms, Sergeant Higgenbotham. Higgy used to be one of my foremen, and he is a good man. He knows how to handle things the way I like, so let him do it."

"You mean I'm supposed to listen to—"

"Lieutenant, I told you about talking back to me once before."

"Yes, sir."

"Just one more thing. The general likes the idea of you combat veterans volunteering to stay out here with the new men. He made it clear to me that I had to take you people whether I liked it or not and I can't afford to fight with the general right now. That means if you ever repeat this conversation, I'll call you a liar and have you court-martialed. Is that clear?"

"Yes, sir."

"Then you can report to your CO, Captain Nuggent. He is a very fine officer and you should get along with him. He worked for me before the war, too. I intend for you to get along with him. Understand?"

"Yes, sir."

"All right. Remember what I said about repeating this conversation."

"Yes, sir." Price saluted and did an about-face.

Price silently entered the jeep and told the driver to take him to Baker Company. Neither of them spoke as they drove, until they reached the tent where the orderly room was set up. Captain Nuggent turned out to be little better than the colonel, and he did not hesitate to tell Price that he did not want him there.

By the time Price left the tent, he was boiling mad. When he found the officers' quarters, he was happy to see that they were deserted. He left his gear on an empty bunk and went to find Regeic and the others.

The platoon was doing close-order drill in the company street when Price finally found them. They seemed very young and he could not help but think that they were like lambs about to be led to the slaughter.

Price lit a cigar and stood there watching Regeic drill the men. Regeic saw him after a few minutes and halted the platoon. "Price," he called. "You old son of a bitch!" Regeic gave the platoon a rest and came running over to Price. He grasped his hand and shook it firmly.

"Regeic, it sure feels good to be back with you again."

"Don't try to snow me, I know all about you and that nurse."

"What nurse?"

"You know what nurse."

"Oh—Betty."

"Yeah, that's the one."

"Well, hell. She was a lot prettier than you."

"I don't know how you can say that," Regeic laughed.

"You haven't looked at yourself lately."

"Every morning."

"Well, you didn't improve when you shaved off the beard. Now I can see your face."

"My eyes are still bloodshot."

"A little."

"Let me get rid of this bunch of kids and we'll have a drink. Morris and Beecraft are in the tent now. I wouldn't doubt if they aren't drunk already."

"Don't you think you'd better get the troops out of the sun first?"

"Oh, yeah. I almost forgot about them."

"Wait a minute, I might as well meet them now."

Price walked over to the platoon, which was looking very surprised to see Regeic being so friendly to an officer. "I'm your new platoon leader, Lieutenant Price. I don't want to keep you out here in the sun and talk you to death, so I'll make it short.

"Regeic has probably taught you all he can and so will I. We've both been out here for a long time and we have lived through some of the toughest fighting. I want to get out of the war just as fast as I can and I'm sure that you do, too. The best way to do that is to have you men trained the best we can in a short period of time. The more you learn, the better chance we all have of getting out in one piece, or at least alive.

"Before this training is over, you're going to think that I'm a real bastard. By now you probably already think that about Regeic. Six months from now, you're going to be glad that we were.

"One more thing. An infantryman doesn't need any real close friends. You have to know people and respect them. You have to be able to depend on them, but you don't have to get to know them any better than you have to. I had a lot of good friends out here when the war first started and they're all dead now. It wasn't a good feeling watching them die. As far as I'm concerned, I don't want to know you as more than a name and serial number. That doesn't mean that I won't do everything I can for you, even with any personal problems that you may have. You don't understand that, but you will after a while out here.

"Oh yes. You may hear Regeic, Morris or Beecraft call me by my first name; but you don't. We've known each other

112

for a long time and I want it to stay that way. I'm an officer. Don't forget it."

Price's reunion with his three men was subdued and a little grave. The first night they got drunk and talked over old times. They talked about the men who had died, and Price told them about Betty. Fortunately for Price, he would have little time to think about Betty because he would be busy training the new men. The four men spent most of the evening talking about their chances of living through the war, and none of them thought they would make it through the months to come.

The four of them were lying on the cots in the tent, drinking out of the canteen cups as usual, and were already feeling the effects of the alcohol mixture that Regeic had turned up with early that evening. The platoon was now up to strength, but none of them was particularly happy about the replacements. Although none of them would admit it, they resented the men for trying to take the places of their old men. Regeic had drunkenly remarked that it would not make any difference because before long they would be dead, anyway.

Regeic put down the cup and looked around at the men. "Not too much to the new men is there?"

"What the hell do you expect?" Price said sarcastically.

"They're babies, except for that Sterner and the big one."

"You mean Lantrip?" Morris asked.

"Yes."

"He seems like he may turn out to be all right. He doesn't seem to have any fear in him and he is learning fast. Should make a good man to have around."

"We could use a lot more like him."

"Sure could."

"Well," said Beecraft thoughtfully, "at least when we want to know something, we can always find out from the teacher."

"Sterner?"

"Yeah."

"You know," Regeic commented, "the one that's going to cause the most trouble is Ruffin. He prays all the time. I think he's afraid of his shadow and uses that religion crap as a crutch."

"Probably," Beecraft laughed. "I've seen men like him before. Remember Merchant?"

"He cracked the first time we came under fire," Regeic said.

"Let's hope this one works out different."

"Yeah, let's hope."

They sat for a long time in silence, drinking, until they no longer cared if the heat was unbearable. The silence was broken at last by Regeic. "Too bad old Bryant isn't here."

113

"Yeah," muttered Beecraft.

"Yeah, too bad," whispered Price.

"Let's drink to old Bryant," Morris said, raising his cup in a toast.

"Good idea," said Beecraft.

"Good idea."

"Yeah, good idea."

They toasted Bryant, and then Choinsky, Moss and Terry, and then the rest of the older men.

"You keeping track, old buddy?" Price asked Regeic.

"Yeah, it's the fourteenth."

"We left out somebody," Price said.

"Who?"

"Can't remember."

"Me, neither."

"Can't remember, either."

"Should be able to remember."

"Yeah, should be able to remember."

"Don't seem right to forget."

"Not right."

"No, not right."

"You aren't going to start crying in your beer, are you?" Price asked.

"No."

"Not me."

"Me, neither."

"Who the hell we gonna toast now?"

"How about the colonel?"

"Thomas?"

"Not that old bastard?"

"How about Colonel Stogner?"

"Yeah, Colonel Stogner."

"Old Big Ben."

"Here's to the finest colonel that ever lived."

"Ever lived."

"How about another?"

"Yeah, one more."

"One for the road."

"Road."

"Ain't no Jap bastards going to get us, old buddy, old buddy, old buddy, buddy."

"Ain't no Jap bastards gonna get us, not us."

"Not us."

"No, sir, not us."

"No, sir, I'm gonna get a nice funeral. Ain't gonna push me in no hole with ten hundred other guys."

"Gonna get coffins and funerals."

"No mattress covers for us."

"Let 'em bury the National Guard like that."

"Not us."

"You wouldn't let 'em, would you, Ern?"

114

"You wouldn't, would you?"

"Burp."

"Let's have another drink. Might as well drink ourselves to death. We're all gonna get killed."

"Yeah, might as well."

"Sure, they're gonna shove us in a hole with a million other guys."

"Million other guys."

"Poor Roberta."

"Poor Anne."

"Don't you guys let Sandra spend the insurance; it's for Buck."

"Sure, Ern, sure, old buddy, buddy."

"Won't let her spend a nickel; we'll all haunt her."

"Yeah, haunt her."


The nights were long and the poker game that was almost always in progress continued. Lantrip held the pack of cards and smiled at the men at the table.

"Wipe that grin off your face and deal, Tex."

"Five card draw?"

"Yeah."

"Jacks or better to open."

"What about that Price? He's a real asshole."

"Never met a harder man."

"Anybody open?"

"By me."

"It's up to you, Fortunado."

"Open for a quarter."

"I'll see that."

"Cards?"

"Two."

"Three."

"I'm a damn fool, but I'll take one."

"Drawing for a straight?"

"What the hell difference does it make to you? You can see when you pay."

"Raise you two bits."

"Call and raise you back another."

"Let me see 'em."

"Three jacks."

"Crap."

"How about that son of a bitch Price."

"You think them other two bastards are any better?"

"All four of them are real diamond-plated assholes."

"Deal."

"Real assholes."

"Open for a dime."

"I'll see you."

"Somebody may put a bullet in their backs."

"Raise you a nickel."

"I fold."

"Call."

"Damn."

"Lend me a dollar."

"Okay."

The poker game continued under the light of the lamp, while Ruffin sat in the corner of the tent reading the book that his mother had sent to him. He thought about Martha, and his mind went reeling back to the night before he had left for the Pacific.

They were parked in the same place they had gone to so many times before in the last year, but that night they had felt the urgency of their last time together. Ruffin closed his eyes and could picture her as she had unbuttoned the big coat she was wearing, and tucked her legs beneath her to keep them warm.

"Edward, do you have to go?"

"I'm afraid so."

"I wish you didn't have to go. Why couldn't you stay here where you belong? I never had any other boy friends before this. What'll I do?"

"I can't have you mixed up in all this mess. I might not get back, we might change our minds—a million things could happen."

"I'm scared, Edward," she had said, her lips trembling. Small tears had trickled down her face at first, and then she began to sob.

"Martha, don't cry," he had whispered. When she went on crying, he had kissed the tears away. "You'll get over me and there will be others."

"I don't want any others," she had cried, and then fell into his arms.

"You don't know what you're letting yourself in for."

"I do," she had cried. "All I want is to be your girl."

"What will your daddy say?"

"I don't care."

They had necked for a long time. Ruffin remembered how ashamed he had felt when his hand touched her breast. It had been there for some time before either of them was aware of it. Martha had reached for his hand, and then moved her hand away, not moving his.

Ruffin had removed his hand and looked at her. "I'm sorry, Martha."

"I didn't mind, Edward. It just, well, it just made me feel funny all over. Put it back, if that's what you want. We won't go any further and it's your last night here."

"I think we had better stop."

"Just put it back for a minute, please."

"But . . ."

"Please."

116

He remembered the sensation which had gone through his body when he felt her breast, softer than anything he had ever felt before. For a long time they had continued that way, until her breathing became heavy and she moved her body tightly against his.

"Martha . . ."

"Don't talk now," she had whispered, as she held his hand over her breast, pressing it tightly. "Kiss me."

He had kissed her for a long time. "Uhmm."

"Now kiss me here," she had whispered, as she undid the buttons on her blouse.

"Martha, we'd better get back. We've never been this far before. It wouldn't be right."

"We can always stop."

He had started to protest again, but she slipped her bra strap down, and she was pressing her breast close to his face. After that, they had gone wild. He had been cruel in his haste to tear her clothes off her, and she had eagerly let her hands explore his body.

Ruffin remembered how she had looked when naked and he felt ashamed for having acted as he did. He had always felt that only married people should do those things. Both he and Martha had refused to let themselves go too far with their petting. Now, in his lonesomeness, his melancholy, he almost wished they had finished the act. If they had, he would have a memory that he could think about when the others talked about their conquests, even though he would never tell them.

Ruffin brought his thoughts back to the present, but the poker game was still going on in the tent.

"Raise you five cents."

"Raise another nickel."

"Call."

Ruffin rolled over, face down on the hard bunk, and tried to sleep.

"Mail call!"

When he heard the mail clerk announce that the mail was ready, Price walked to the tent entrance and leaned against the pole, as he watched the mail being handed out. It was always the same. Eager hands tore at their only real tie with home. The eagerness of men when they received mail never changed. He had watched it before as the men read and then reread the letters. Some of them brought hope. Others dashed hopes on the rocks.

"I got a carton of weeds."

"Cigarettes!"

"Hey, those are mine."

"Share them, dammit!"

"Sure, but let me at least get a pack for myself."

"Candy."

"Cigars."

"Wowee!"

"Christ, that cake's as hard as a brick."

"Somebody get an ax."

"Hey, a Bible. The folks at home must think I'm going to reform."

"Damn, gloves."

"Just what you'll need for the long cold nights in the Pacific."

"I'm a father, I'm a father, I'M A FATHER!"

On and on it went, the men reading the news from home. They joked about the useless gifts, and they wished they were at home.

The days slowly grew into a month, and the four old-timers became even more despondent. For the first time, they openly admitted to each other that they were afraid to go back into combat. Morris and Beecraft spent most of their time thinking about their wives. Regeic drank; while Price spent most of his free time visiting the hospital.

Late in the afternoon, they had just returned from a "short-arm inspection." The four of them sat on the bunks still dressed in their raincoats and brogans.

Regeic looked up and saw that Morris and Beecraft were becoming restless. "Have a drink."

"Thanks," said Morris. "All this walking is getting the best of me. Besides, I don't know where in the name of hell the colonel thinks we could find enough women to get V.D."

Regeic poked Price in the side. "He was probably thinking about the lover here. Price is the only man on the island that's getting it regular."

"You men just don't understand," Price protested. "Betty is different. She's always been nice to me and I know she's a hell of a lot better woman than Sandra ever was. Betty got all fouled up and took a wrong turn; that's her only trouble."

"It's a crazy world."

"Yeah, crazy."

"Have another drink."

"Thanks."

"Pour me one."

"Sure."

Morris took a large drink. "Has anybody seen that mail clerk?"

"He ought to be here soon."

Morris toyed with his cup. "I haven't heard from my wife in a month. I'd give a lot to hear from her."

"Me, too," Beecraft said.

Regeic laughed. "You married men don't know how lucky

you are to have a woman that can write to you. Price and me don't get any letters at all. At least, I don't, and the only ones that Price gets are from Sandra. All of those tell him to go to hell, so he might as well not get them."

"That's right," Price agreed.

Morris laughed. "There are a lot of times when I wish to hell I was still single. Back in the States, there were times when I wished I was out with the women I saw you two with, but now I'm glad that I've got Roberta. I never realized how much I did love her until I got out here."

"Sure," Beecraft said. "I guess there are times when any married man wishes he wasn't so tied down, but I wouldn't trade places with you two for a million dollars."

"If the truth were known," Price said, "I'd trade places fast."

"Me too," Regeic chimed in. "We have a lot of fun, but there are times when I'd give everything for a home that I could call my own."

There was a commotion outside and soon the mail clerk could be heard as he handed out the mail to the men. The four men sat in silence and waited for their own mail to be brought to them. At last, the mail clerk stepped into the tent and handed a large bundle to Regeic. Walking from man to man, Regeic passed out the mail to the men.

Regeic handed one letter to Price, who sat for a long time staring at the letter. It was from Sandra. Another letter that Price hoped would bring the news that she would reconsider. However, he knew that she would not say that. Price almost wished that he had never received the letter and he thought for a minute about throwing it away. Then he knew that he would have to read it. There was one chance that it might bring good news. He tore open the letter and began to read it.

*Dear Ernest,*

*I have been wanting to write to you for a long time, but have been terribly busy. I have been having a lot of dates lately and, with being out late and trying to take care of Buck, there isn't much time for unimportant things. I thought that you would realize that everything that can be said has been said. I do not feel any different now than I did the day I left you. I want you to stop writing the kind of letter you did last time.*

*Buck is growing fast and you will not recognize him when you get back. If you want to see him, please let me know in advance so I can arrange for the time. I will not let you see him for more than a few minutes. As you know by now, I do not want him growing up and being like you.*

*I know that you do not have too much chance to spend money out there and would like it if you sent some more money to me. Buck needs some clothes and I can't seem to make what I get go around. I am sure that you love Buck and do not want him to go without anything if it can be helped.*

*Sandra*

There it was again, another letter telling him to go to hell. She had gone out of her way to let him know that she was dating a lot. Also, the part about her letting him see his son for a few minutes made him furious.

Damned generous of her, he thought. Price cursed to himself as he read the part where she asked for more money. If she would buy clothes for Buck instead of pretty things for herself, there might be enough.

Morris and Beecraft had both received several letters and had arranged them by date so they could read the oldest first. Both of them sat with their legs crossed and began reading.

Regeic, who had received no mail, walked over to Price. "Did Sandra tell you to drop dead again?"

"Yeah."

Regeic placed his hand on Price's shoulder. "I'm sorry for you, Ern. The best thing you can do is to forget her. She just keeps hurting you. If you would forget about her, you could stay drunk with me."

"How about a big drink right now?"

Regeic poured a drink from his canteen and passed it to Price. "Here you are. Have a large cup of old Regeic's brew. It's made in the shade, stirred with a spade, and good for any old maid."

Price sat and drank the liquid as fast as he could swallow it. As he drank, the liquid began to have its effect on him and he lost some of the melancholy. He wondered if his entire life had been a failure. Surely, he thought, there must be something good in store for him.

Morris and Beecraft were still reading their letters, and happily exchanging letters and pictures. Price watched and began to feel sorry for himself. Suddenly, the smile faded from Morris' face. Price rose and walked to his side. "Something wrong?"

"It must be a joke," Morris said.

"What?"

"She says that she's pregnant," Morris almost whispered.

Beecraft laughed. "Read a little further. You know how she's always kidding. She just did that to make you jump a little."

Morris chuckled nervously. "Sure." He finished the letter and then tears formed in his eyes. "It must be true. She wasn't kidding. Says that she met a soldier and he got her drunk. The next thing she knew, she woke up in bed with him."

"I still believe she was kidding," Beecraft said.

"Do you mind if I read it?" Price asked.

"No, go ahead."

Price picked up the letter and began to read it.

*Dear James,*

*I don't know how to write this letter to you. I wish that there was some better way to say that I love you more than anything in all the world. If it had not been for our love, I do not think that life would be worth living. I know that you are the best husband in the world and that I could never live without you. Please understand that I love you very much as you read this letter.*

*You know how much I like to go to Myrtle Beach for week ends. Well, I went down there about three months ago with Agnes and Barbara. We stayed at one of the guest houses. We stayed indoors most of the time and, since all of us had husbands overseas, we were feeling a little blue.*

*We started drinking and before I knew it, I was pretty high. I tried to stop, but they insisted. The next thing I knew, it was morning and I was in bed with a strange man.*

*I swear to you, I didn't know whether we did anything or not because I was so drunk. I got out of there as fast as I could and never saw his face. I thought about telling you about it, but then decided that it might hurt you, even if you would understand, because you love me.*

*Please understand that I love you. I have missed two periods now and the doctor says that I am pregnant. I hope that you will try to understand that I love you and I couldn't bear losing you. I know that you will understand that I did not do it with him because I wanted to. It must have been after I had passed out.*

*Please write me and tell me that you understand and still love me and want me. I thought about losing the child and never telling you, but then I realized that you would understand and still love me. Please write me and tell me that everything is all right. I am so upset, I think I will die if you don't believe me.*

*Roberta*

"Do you think she's kidding?" Price asked.

"I don't think so."

"I doubt it, too. I don't believe that a woman would kid about a thing like that."

"What am I going to do?" Morris asked.

"What can you do out here?"

"I might get a leave."

"Do you want me to talk to the old man for you?"

"I don't know. Right now, I'm a little mixed up. I was reading her other letters and I was as happy as a man could be. Then I read this, and everything changed. What is a man supposed to think?"

"I don't think you should do anything until you've had a chance to think about it," Price said.

"She still might be kidding," Beecraft said.

"She wouldn't kid about that."

"I guess not, at that."

"How could she do that to me?" Morris sobbed.

"Just take it easy," Price comforted him.

"Fugg her," Morris said.

"Look," Regeic said, as he handed a cup to Morris, "have a drink. It might make you feel better."

Morris stood and walked to the entrance of the tent. "You all just leave me alone."

None of the men in the tent spoke. Each of them was feeling pity for Morris and contempt for his wife. She had sent a letter to him that could very easily cause him to give up. They had all seen a man lose the desire to come back after receiving a letter like that.

After the day Morris received the letter, he became despondent and refused to talk. He spent much of his time alone. Several times Price offered to talk to the colonel about giving him a leave, but Morris refused the help.

The training was rough and the fevers, jaundice, jungle rot and malaria kept some of the men in bed. The poker game never seemed to stop, and Ruffin spent all of his spare time in the chapel.

Several times, Colonel Thomas called Price in, to chew him out over some infraction of the rules. Captain Nuggent also called him in on several occasions. Once it was because he had used the term "officers and men" in such a way that the colonel thought it was degrading to the enlisted men. The colonel had gone into a great burst of oratory to explain that the army should be democratic. Another time it was because he had used profanity when he talked to the troops.

The division trained, and it almost died of boredom. Soon it became apparent that they would be landing on some other island, although none of them knew which one. To train the men, a tall wall was built and landing nets were hung over the sides. At the bottom, they had placed an old landing craft. The entire division practiced endlessly, until, one day, there was a sudden announcement that they would board a ship in the morning. Still, there was no indication of their destination.

When the announcement was received, the tired men trudged back to their tents and packed their gear. Most of them began to write letters back home. When Price left, Regeic and Morris were drinking and Beecraft was writing to his wife. It had been hard for Price to find a jeep, but he bribed one of the Negro drivers and was headed for the hospital just as the sun was about to set.

When he reached the hospital, Price jumped from the jeep and walked straight to the mess hall, where he thought Betty would be. She was still eating and he found a seat beside her.

"Hi, what brings the dashing lieutenant over here?"

"I wanted to see you before we left."

"Well," she drawled. "That's the nicest thing anyone ever said to me. Have you eaten?"

"Yes. I ate at the camp."

"Ern, you look sad. What's the matter?"

"I think we're leaving tomorrow."

"You mean leaving this island?"

"Yes."

"Then we'll probably leave too."

"I hope we end up on the same island."

"As long as the war has to be fought, it would be nice to fight it at the same place."

"Betty, I . . . I mean could we take a walk?"

"I'm off duty," she said. "I'd love to go with you."

"Out to our beach?"

"How would you like for me to get dressed up again?"

"I'd love it."

"Why don't you have a cup of coffee while I change. I'll come back and get you."

"Don't be long."

Much later, they were on the beach smoking. Price was lying on his back with Betty's head resting on his chest. The night was very warm and there were no clouds in the sky. Above them, the stars twinkled.

"This will be our last night," Price said quietly.

Betty's eyes shone. "Maybe not."

"It's a big war. There is no telling where I will be by this time tomorrow."

"It's not that big."

"I don't know exactly how to say what I'm thinking, so you'll have to excuse me if I sound a little silly. I'm not in love with you exactly, but I know that I would be if I had the chance. I hope you're serious about meeting me after the war. We'll have a lot of living to do."

"I'll meet you."

"You're not just kidding me, are you?"

"Ern, all women aren't like Sandra. I'll admit that most of us aren't half as good as you men think we are, but some of us do have feelings."

"Sometimes that's hard to believe. Morris' wife got herself pregnant and wrote him about it. He's almost gone out of his mind."

"Ern, I doubt if you'd understand, but she probably got lonesome. She made a mistake and did something that she's going to be sorry for all of her life. You wouldn't understand that, though."

"I think I can."

"I doubt it. No man could."

"What makes you think that men are so dumb?"

"Honey, I'm a woman. A girl that you think is sweet and innocent wears a tight-fitting sweater and you never really know why. She might even wear a low-cut dress. You know that she looks nice, but she does it for a reason. Did you ever notice how embarrassed a woman gets when she lets her dress ride up a little and you see some of her leg? Usually, it's all an act. We want you to see us because it excites you. You would be shocked if you knew how many times I've bent over in front of a man while I had on a low-cut dress just so he could see my breasts.

"Do you really think that we wear lacy slips and things so we can look at them? Most of us do it because we want to look nice when you see us in them, although we would never admit it. That's why we wear tight-fitting bathing suits, so you can see our figures. Didn't you ever notice how often a woman will accidentally brush up against you. Many times, it's no accident.

"There have been a lot of men that lost out because they stopped when a woman protested. We like it just as much as a man. If men would just keep right on, most of them would get it."

Price turned until he was looking directly into her eyes. "You sound like you think that's the only thing I came out here for tonight."

"I'm sorry," she answered in a quiet voice. "I should have talked about something else."

Price chose his words carefully. "Funny, we met under impossible conditions but you make me feel like I have found myself at last. I just wish that we could have been able to have a little more time together."

"I was thinking the same thing." Betty smiled at him.

"I think you're the finest thing that has happened to me in a long time. I don't care what kind of a woman you used to be. The only thing that matters to me is that you have been wonderful, and leaving you like this is the worst thing that I will ever have to do."

"That makes me feel good," Betty said, smiling.

"This is going to be our last night together for a long time," Price said, his voice sounding sad.

"I know," Betty said softly, and she kissed his forehead.

"What I mean is, there are a lot of things that have to be said, and I don't seem to be able to put them into words. I've been thinking about what you've meant to me, and I wish there was some way I could tell you."

"It's always like that," Betty said, trying to ease the tension. "After you have left, I will think of all the things that we should have said to each other, but it's going to be too late then."

"Too little time," Price said bitterly. "That's the story of my life."

"There is still tonight," Betty said, drawing him close to her.

"Yeah, tonight," Price said in a hushed tone.

"Just love me," Betty said, kissing him all over his face. When his hands were fumbling at her dress, Betty pushed him away gently. "Let me undress for you this last time. Please."

Price walked back to the tent area to go to the latrine. He pushed aside a clump of bushes and saw Morris standing by the slit trench. When he heard the noise, Morris turned around quickly, so his back was to Price. Price cursed Roberta silently and walked over to Morris. "Are you all right?" he asked.

"Yes," Morris whispered.

"Are you sure?"

"Yes." Morris slipped something into his pocket.

"What's in that bottle?" Price demanded.

"Nothing."

"I said what's in the bottle," Price said again.

"And I said nothing."

Price spun Morris around. "Let me see it," he said. He held out his hand and Morris began to cry. His legs practically buckled and he looked like a beaten man. Slowly he reached into his pocket and handed the bottle to Price.

"Where did you get it?" Price demanded.

"Dispensary."

"Why in the name of hell do you want to kill yourself?"

"Roberta," Morris answered flatly.

"Morris, you know that I'm your friend, don't you?"

"Yes."

"I went through almost the same thing, remember? When Sandra left me it was you and Regeic that helped me get over it. It's going to be hard, but you'll make it."

There was a noise behind them, and since Price did not want a stranger to see the bottle, he slipped it into his pocket. Beecraft stepped into view.

"I got worried about you," Beecraft said to Morris.

"He was going to kill himself," Price said. He took the bottle from his pocket and showed it to Beecraft. "He says that he got the bottle from the dispensary."

Beecraft placed his hand on Morris' shoulder. "You haven't lost your mind, have you?"

"I don't know."

"Look," Beecraft said. "It's hard now, and I don't imagine that it will get any easier for a long time, but this isn't the way to solve the problem. You can't kill yourself."

"I know you're right. I've been out here a long time trying to get up the nerve, but I couldn't do it."

"That's a relief," Price said.

"I decided that the Japs will kill me soon enough anyway."

"Let's go back to the tent and see if old Regeic has a drink for us."

Price had his arm around Morris, and he led him toward the tent. Morris followed him like a man in a dream.

## CHAPTER SIX

Price leaned heavily on the railing of the rolling ship and waited for dawn. For two days the big guns of the fleet had been banging away at the beach, causing the water to shake and tremble. With each salvo, the deck shuddered as though in protest. Price looked over the water at the island and was amazed at the beauty of the scene. The land was covered with the early morning mist, which was blue and transparent. He had trouble controlling his nerves.

Once again he was face to face with a piece of enemy-held land that would have to be taken inch by inch. A new island, and new graves to dig. The same fear had been there the last time he had stood on the deck of a ship just before an invasion, but he had been able to control himself then. This time there was no confidence. Confidence was what made a good soldier. Colonel Stogner had always used the example of a hundred men being lined up and told that ninety-nine of them would be dead. If they were soldiers they would all be feeling sorry for the ones who were going to die.

Absently, Price pulled his field glasses from their worn case and put them to his eyes. Calmly, he surveyed the beach. The steady blast of the guns shook the glasses so that he could not see too clearly. But he could see that the bombardment had done its work on the beach, and there was very little earth which did not show the effects of the shells. Price hoped that most of the Japs would be dead, but experience had taught him that they must still be there. Always before, they had seemed to crawl out of the rocks.

As he looked out over the blue water, he was filled with the beauty of the scene. It had been the same thing the day he and Regeic had looked out from the hill. That day that other island had been beautiful, but before the day was over, most of his platoon was dead.

Price looked to his right and saw that Sergeant Higgenbotham was also looking out over the water. Price frowned when he saw that Higgenbotham had not put on his life vest. He could still remember that day, early in the war, the way the men had looked in the water when their troop ship had been sunk. "Sergeant Higgenbotham, what did I tell you about that life vest. Get yours on and check the other men."

"Come off it, Lieutenant."

Price walked over to the railing where Higgenbotham was standing. "Look, Higgenbotham. I don't want to have to go around here sounding like an old maid all the time, but I've been through all this before. If you'd just listen to me you might have a better chance of coming out of this thing alive. I've seen what happens to men in the water when they don't have life vests on. Now, just get your vest and check the rest of the men. I don't want to have to tell you again."

"Yes, *sir*." Higgenbotham said the "sir" just as if it were an insult. Then he turned toward the rest of the men.

There was a tremendous roar, and Price looked up in time to see a flight of navy fighters fly overhead. They were so low that they barely missed the mast, and the red glow from their exhaust could be seen as they sped toward the beach. They began a shallow dive at the beach and pulled up in the distance. A second later, the sound of their guns could be heard, sounding weak and insufficient. They disappeared in the distance, and only the waves could be heard as they sloshed against the ship. Then the big guns sounded again and Price held to the rail for support against the concussion.

"It's almost daylight," he heard Regeic say.

"How long you been standing there?"

"Just came up from the chow house."

"Morris and Beecraft still eating?"

"Beecraft is. He's trying to get Morris to eat something, but you know how he is. He ain't been the same since he got that letter from his wife."

"Would you?"

"No, I guess not."

Price looked toward Regeic and read the same fear in his face that he felt. "It's going to be rough."

"I just hope that they knew what they were talking about at the briefing. The only thing is, none of these troops is very experienced and anything can happen."

"Just because they said that the beach had been reduced to rubble by the bombardment, doesn't mean that it's true. They know it, but does the Japanese Army? They have a habit of fighting like hell."

"You know," said Regeic thoughtfully, "I wonder why they always try to say that we're having an easy time, in the stateside papers. Hell, the Japs are good. We had a hell of a time with them every time before, and we had good troops against them. I think that on a man-for-man basis, they're probably the best troops in the world. Give one a handful of rice and he can live for a month. They never seem to get tired either. I never saw anything like them."

"Neither did I. With good equipment and some different tactics, they'd probably have pushed us off the end of the world."

"They just might."

127

Beecraft and Morris came walking over to the rail. Price half turned to face them. "How you feeling?" he asked Morris.

"Okay."

"That the best you can do?" Price laughed.

"Should I feel good?"

"Sure you should. Things can always get worse."

"I heard that before. They told me that they could always get worse, and sure enough they did."

"At least we all are still alive."

"For how long?"

"We'll get out all right."

Morris let out a nervous laugh. "With these kids, we haven't got a chance. They'll probably run right off the beach as soon as the fighting starts."

"I think they may do all right."

"I hope so, Ern," Beecraft commented, as he leaned over the rail and stared into the water.

Price looked at the three men one at a time and studied their faces. "Look, I didn't want to mention it and I don't have to, but just for the record let's try to get some of them through this. They're green so they'll have a lot to learn. I'd be lying if I tried to give you a big pep talk and and say that it's going to be easy. Frankly, I don't think that any of us will make it through many more days of fighting, but we've got to try. Those kids have a hard row to hoe and we've got to help all we can. All of us have almost cracked up before, but we have to try not to do it again. If you feel like it, try to get off by yourself, or with one of us. We can't afford to let them know."

"I just hope I don't run out of guts," Regeic said.

"You've got a canteen full of something, don't you?"

"I've got two," Regeic laughed. "One for now, and one for later. I thought you might be wanting one before we go in."

They all agreed and the canteen was passed between them. As the canteen was about to be drained, the monotone voice broke over the speaker, like a voice from another world. "First assault wave, prepare to board landing craft!"

"Wish I was a marine." Beecraft laughed.

"The only difference is that they make movies about them and they get all the publicity. Why the hell would you want your picture in all the papers?"

"At least, they get medals," Beecraft said, laughing again.

"Eighteen men to a boat!" Price called. There was a shuffle of feet as the men went to the rail. "Higgenbotham, you take the second boat, I'll go in the first." In a low voice, Price said to the three men beside him, "You go with me."

In the background, the voice of Ruffin could be heard softly praying. The landing craft bobbed on the waves below, and Price hoped that the men would remember to jump into the boats rather than climb too far down and be caught between

128

the ship and the landing craft. Price climbed down the net, careful to hold onto the vertical rope so the man above him would not step on his hands. He heard several men yell from pain, indicating that they had grabbed a horizontal rope, forgetting the many hours of practice. As he neared the the boat, Price jumped, landing in a bundle on the deck. He rose and helped the rest of the men into the craft, one at a time. As soon as the boat was full, he took his place in the front of the boat.

As he passed Lantrip, he paused for a minute and tapped the man on the shoulder. "You take care of some of the men when we hit the beach. You've shown more than most of them so far and I want to be able to count on you."

Lantrip looked up nervously. "Sure, sure," he said weakly.

The ship seemed a million miles high to Price, as he looked up at it. He realized for the first time that the sun was rising fast and the island was plainly visible, the mist gone. Other landing craft were ahead of theirs and Price looked over the side, filled with awe at the hundreds of ships and landing craft bobbing in the water. Several destroyer escorts were leading the landing craft toward the beach, and Price watched with fascination as blinker lights from the escorts signaled for the barrage to begin. There was a tremendous roar, and then the swish of shells overhead, then more blast. In the distance there was a rumbling sound, as the explosives churned the beach. As they neared the beach, the concussion became worse, and Price was aware of his body shaking violently.

Suddenly, the escort in front of them turned from its path to the beach and the shelling stopped. Price eased his head over the side and saw that they were only a hundred yards from the shore.

"Why did the big guns stop?" Lantrip moaned.

"We're getting close to the beach."

"Oh, my God," Lantrip whispered. Price looked back at the man and saw that his face was white, his skin drawn tight over the bones, and his gray lips trembling. He realized that the big man was scared. Damn, Price thought, the one man I thought I could rely on.

Suddenly there was a grinding sound and the landing craft shuddered as it came to a halt. For an instant, Price was confused, and then he realized that they had probably hit a submerged reef or something similar. He sensed panic among the troops. Then there was a water spout beside the landing craft and a gigantic roar, followed by a violent shaking of the boat.

Ruffin prayed and Lantrip whimpered. Price cursed. The Japanese were firing at them and they were a stationary target in the water. The landing craft continued to shake as shells fell all around them.

Cupping his hands, Price yelled at the coxswain, "Can you get this thing off the reef?"

129

"Don't think so."

"Then open the fugging ramp. We'll be better off in the water!" The ramp came down with a grinding sound and Price started forward. "Get the hell out of here."

The men rushed past him into the waist-deep water and splashed toward the beach. Price noticed Lantrip cowering in the corner of the landing craft. "Get up, goddammit, get UP!" Lantrip did not move. Price reached down and jerked the big man to his feet and dragged him toward the ramp. They paused at the door, and the Texan attempted to speak, his mouth moving but no sound coming out. As Lantrip's knees started to buckle, Price held the front of his fatigue jacket and shoved him into the water.

"I can't go," Lantrip finally said, in a faint voice.

Price swung the submachine gun at his rear. "You're going to die anyway, it may as well be fighting. Now move!"

"I can't."

"Let's go," Price said, pulling Lantrip through the water. Lantrip moved haltingly and Price prodded him several times with his gun.

All around him Price could see the soldiers dropping in the water. On they moved, holding their rifles over their heads and splashing forward. Behind him, the landing craft brought more men to the slaughter and dumped them in the water. In front of him a man folded over, a blot of red blood spilling out of his back, his body bobbing in the waves.

Overhead, the navy fighters roared again, sending bullets speeding toward the beach. All over the beach, billows of smoke rose high in the air. The steady whine of the bullets could be heard, and geysers of water rose in the air. Lantrip began to cry. As Price shoved him forward, another man fell and then rolled over in the water, face up. Lantrip sank into a hole under the water and Price jerked him to his feet and continued to go forward. "Come on, goddamn you," Price yelled at the man.

As soon as the water was shallow enough, Price began to run, dragging Lantrip with him until he reached the sea wall, which was approximately five feet high. Once there, he dropped the big man to the ground and sought the protection of the wall.

Looking back, he could see that the water was already full of bodies and wreckage. The Japanese were concentrating their fire on the boats which were trying to land additional troops. Geysers were rising all over the water and some of the boats were sunk by direct hits.

Price saw that Regeic, Beecraft and Morris were all about ten feet from him, and he began to inch his way toward them, keeping low as he moved. He had no idea where the rest of the platoon was, but at the moment he was more interested in survival than in finding the men.

"We thought you were hit," Regeic said, breathing hard.

"I had to drag that bastard Lantrip."

"Lantrip?"

"Yeah."

"Well, I'll be damned! Where is he now?"

Price pointed to his left. "There."

"I thought he was going to eat the Japs alive."

"Me too."

In the water the Japanese fire had become more accurate, and many of the landing craft were disappearing in gigantic clouds of smoke and water.

"They'll be hitting the beach soon," commented Regeic.

"Let's get to digging," Price gasped.

"Ern," Regeic was saying, "we can't do that. We have to move on in."

"I don't know where the platoon is."

"Damn the platoon, we got to get off the beach. You're the only officer around and it has to be you that makes the first move."

"Why is it always me?"

"Don't waste time bitching, let's get started before the Japs get after us."

"Okay. Pass the word to fix bayonets. When I give the word, over we go."

The word was passed down the line from man to man like the echo in a large canyon. All around him, the stench of death was already rising. The odor of dead men, rotting limbs and dried blood rose, as the corpses floated up onto the beach together with fish killed by the concussion of the shells. All around him were the half-dead men who had reached the beach. They were lying clutching their rifles, shaking with fear. Price hesitated to give the word that would send them forward into the interlocking lanes of fire that the Japanese had surely set up on the beach. Finally he yelled, "Charge!" For a moment he thought how silly this must have sounded, just like a cavalry movie.

Like the dead rising from their graves, the men rushed forward, screaming their defiance of the Japanese, bursting over the sea wall. The Japanese, caught off guard, were still firing at the landing craft. But before they could shift the hail of lead into the advancing men, Price had led the group of men with him into the edge of the jungle. As they reached the protection of the growth, they stopped. "Get up, keep moving, MOVE!" Price shouted. But the drive petered out. For a brief moment the men had acted like soldiers, but now they were refusing to move. Without any word being passed, the men began to dig in.

"We ain't never going to take this island," Beecraft said, breathing hard.

"We have to," Regeic puffed.

Price began to work on a hole. "We only took about fifty yards of beach. What we need are some mortars."

131

"Tonight, maybe tonight we can get some in."

"I hope so."

A few yards down the beach, Higgenbotham was hastily digging a shallow foxhole, fighting for his breath and wondering how the beach could have become so confused. To his right, Ruffin was working with his entrenching tool, praying, as he threw dirt in all directions. Suddenly there was a sharp report and a whiz as a Japanese bullet peeled bark from a nearby palm tree. Higgenbotham caught a glimpse of a running figure and fired in that direction, not really wanting to hit the man. The running figure straightened up and then fell forward. Higgenbotham and Ruffin were both on their feet, running for the man.

When they reached the spot they found a small man lying on his back, blood oozing out of two holes in his chest. His face was round and smooth, his hair cut close and seeming to grow in every direction. Quickly Higgenbotham reached down and threw the Jap's rifle about ten yards away.

"He's still alive," Higgenbotham commented.

Ruffin was staring at the man, feeling pity for him, when the little eyes opened and their eyes met. The Jap felt the hole with his hand as if he did not want to find what he knew was there. Ruffin could not help but feel that this was another man, not very different from him, a man who wished he could be somewhere else, a man whose face revealed none of the hate that Ruffin had been led to expect would be there. The Jap licked his lips, indicating that he would like a drink of water.

Without removing his eyes from the Jap, Ruffin reached for his canteen and began to uncap it. Slowly he reached down and lifted the man's head with his left hand while he tilted the canteen to his mouth with the other. The water trickled down the man's bloody mouth and he coughed, blood and water spurting out of the holes in his chest. He nodded a feeble thanks and seemed to be asking if they were going to kill him. Ruffin smiled, trying to break the language barrier and tell the man that he would not be killed. He pulled a cigarette out and after lighting it placed it between the man's lips.

As the Jap puffed, Ruffin could not take his eyes from the face below him. Suddenly the man seemed harmless, just another guy doing what he was ordered to do by a force bigger than himself, and not really wanting to do it.

The Japanese soldier was smiling now. He seemed to be trying to say, through his monkeylike chatter and sign language, that he wanted to give something to Ruffin. Slowly, he reached into his jacket. Ruffin turned back and saw both Regeic and Price running toward them.

As he reached them, Price saw that the Japanese soldier was reaching inside his jacket. Without breaking his stride, Price emptied his clip into the Jap, noticing the startled look on the faces of Higgenbotham and Ruffin.

"Lieutenant—" Higgenbotham started to say.

"What the hell's the matter with you dumb bastards? How many times do I have to tell you? Never trust a Jap. You have to kill them. They'll kill you any time they get a chance. Christ, I'm not always going to be here to take care of you."

"He wasn't hurting anybody," Ruffin said, like a child who has seen his pet run over.

Price bent over and gently pulled the Japanese soldier's hand from his jacket. A grenade came with it. He tossed the grenade at the feet of the two men and turned on his heel. "You two can stay here and get your asses shot off for all I care." Then, turning to Regeic, he said, "Let's get back."

"Damn!" muttered Higgenbotham.

"This may sound crazy as hell, but I felt sorry for the Jap. I was thinking that he was just a poor soldier like me that didn't want to die. I thought maybe he had a girl back in Japan, or a mother that wanted him back to her safely. I was helping him and he tried to kill me," Ruffin said almost in a whimper. "Why would he try that?"

"It's just the way they are," Higgenbotham answered. "Next time, I won't forget." He glanced over at Price.

Price and Regeic resumed their digging, knowing that with every second, the time was coming closer when the Japanese fire would be directed at the men on the beachhead. So far the Japanese had directed only small arms fire toward the beachhead and had concentrated on the landing craft, but soon they would be launching their banzai attacks at the troops on the beach in one last attempt to drive them into the ocean before reinforcements could arrive. Sporadic rifle fire cracked over their heads, and the men would duck every now and then when a bullet landed close to them.

Close by, Beecraft and Morris were busy digging, but Morris seemed oblivious to the rifle fire. He was making no attempt to duck. Beecraft had tried to plead with the man but it was to no avail. All Morris did was mumble something about his wife.

Price had been watching Morris for several minutes. He turned to Regeic. "Morris is trying to get himself killed. He must be out of his head."

"I wish I could get my hands on that bitch right now. She's going to be the cause of him getting killed."

"Looks like it."

They continued to dig, and the fire became heavier. Somewhere in front of him, Price heard a moan, softly at first. Then he heard it again and something stirred in his conscience. "You keep digging," he said to Regeic. "I have to go out there and get him."

"You can't, Ern. There must be a million Japs out there in the brush."

"I have to."

133

"It's crazy."

"Don't try to understand it, just keep digging and wish me luck."

Without waiting for an answer, Price rose and ran through the wall of green vegetation. The voice kept calling, and he moved toward it.

About five minutes later, he emerged into a small clearing and found a man crumpled on the ground. Cautiously, he advanced, with his finger on the trigger of his weapon. He approached slowly until he was sure that the man was an American. Then he bent over the man and rolled him over on his back. Suddenly there was a noise behind him.

Quickly Price jumped for cover behind a large bush and waited. His breathing seemed to him to be louder than usual, and he was sure that it would give him away. The sound of footsteps came closer and closer and Price found himself becoming very frightened.

Suddenly Sterner appeared.

"Sterner," he whispered.

"Lieutenant."

"Don't address me by my rank. There must be Japs all around us."

"But—"

"What brought you out here?"

"I heard a man."

"We have to get him back."

"How?"

"Can you carry him?" Price asked.

"I think so."

"All right then, you carry him and I'll cover for us."

Sterner picked up the man and Price walked behind him, alert for any movement that might indicate there would be Japs in the path. When they were almost up to the platoon, Price called out. A hail of bullets went roaring over their heads as they ran for the protection of the holes.

The soldier they had brought back was delirious. He had a large hole in his face, just to the right of his mouth. He also had shrapnel in both his legs and the blood was still running into his shoes.

Looking up at Sterner, Price could not help but smile. "Funny. That's the first time I've rescued a guy since the war started. I've heard of it, but it's the first time I ever heard anyone do it."

"Do you think he'll live?"

Price studied the man with interest. "He should. Why don't you take him on back to the aid station. Don't worry about the Jap fire. As long as they're shooting at you, you aren't going to get hit. They couldn't hit a damn thing." Without another word, Sterner picked the man up and carried him to the rear. Price fired in the general direction of the jungle to keep the Japs ducking long enough for Sterner to get to the beach.

Price slid into the hole that Regeic had finished for both of them. To his right, he could hear Lantrip moaning, and Ruffin was still praying. The attempt to get the landing craft to the shore continued, but the Japanese were hitting them with regularity now. On the beach, dead soldiers lay everywhere. The smell that rose was almost more than the newer men could stand. Occasionally, a man could be heard vomiting.

Ruffin had been mumbling a prayer for almost an hour and it was getting on Price's nerves. "Shut your damn mouth for a while, will you!" Ruffin continued to pray, sometimes in soft tones, sometimes in whimpering tones. Price crawled from his hole and slowly went to the edge of the foxhole that was occupied by Higgenbotham and Ruffin. He slammed a fist into Ruffin's face and roared, "If you don't shut your mouth I'll come back and shut it for you. What the hell are you trying to do, bring the whole Jap army down on top of us?"

The shells were still falling into the water, as Price crawled back to his hole. As he climbed into the foxhole, he turned and saw that the attempt to land troops had almost stopped. He knew that the Japanese artillery would be directed at them in a few minutes. All over the island the division had made little progress, and small groups of men were scattered all along the beach. Price hoped that the Japs had not been prepared for the invasion and that it would at least take them a day or two to bring up reinforcements.

The men lay in little clusters, leaning on their weapons, fear showing on their faces, lips trembling, waiting. Waiting, the time dragging by, it was almost as if every heart were pounding at the same time, making the earth throb in the same tense beat. Although the division was new to combat, they knew—knew with a kind of animal instinct for survival —that the Japanese would soon be coming after them. They waited and prayed, waited and cursed, waited and cried. Somewhere down the beach, a man stood and screamed and ran for the water. He fell in a hail of bullets.

Regeic was passing his canteen between Beecraft and Morris, already half drunk himself. "They're going to give us hell tonight."

"We've lost a lot of men already," Morris said, gulping down the liquid.

"They didn't know what to do. Look out there in the water at the bodies. If we had the old outfit, we'd already have taken half this island. These babies just stopped here. Couldn't even stand up to some small arms fire."

Price reached for the canteen. "It's probably best that they stopped. If we'd gone on, we would have been pretty far behind the Jap lines. All alone probably."

"It doesn't make too much difference to me," Morris said. "I don't think I'll ever get out of this damn thing alive anyway."

Price laughed. "The good always die young. You'll probably live forever."

Morris looked into the jungle. "I think there's a little yellow bastard out there that has a bullet with my name on it."

"Why don't you pray about it, or have Ruffin do it? He seems to have a good line to the man upstairs."

Morris roared with laughter. "I gave that up years ago. Everybody I ever saw that prayed got himself killed."

"I don't know about you," Regeic laughed, "but I need a drink."

Beecraft took the canteen from Regeic. "Do you think the men will run when the Japs come?"

"Probably."

"I got the area rigged with grenades and trip wires. If they try to get to us they're going to catch hell." Regeic laughed.

"Beecraft," Price said, "you go back and dig us up some flares. Regeic, you go over and get yourself dug in with Higgenbotham in the center of the perimeter. If anyone tries to run, shoot him."

As the two men left the hole, a hail of rifle fire was sent in their direction. Beecraft ran back toward the beach, bullets kicking up the dust at his feet, while Regeic lay on the ground digging.

"Pass the word down the line," Price said to the men in the next hole. "When the Japs start attacking us, Regeic has orders to shoot the first man that runs."

Late in the afternoon, Beecraft returned with the flares and dropped them off with Regeic in the center of the perimeter. Sterner had returned from the aid station and was sharing the foxhole with Price. The men glanced from their holes as they nervously ate the K-rations. Several of them had received slight wounds. The men who were hit had screamed, and it had a bad effect on the rest of the green troops.

Price was about to take his last bite, when he heard a loud roar. He jerked his head up in time to see a Japanese Zero streak past. It flew low over the water, and a navy Corsair was behind it. The navy pilot was firing at the Japanese plane, and some of the bullets were landing among the ground troops. Screams of pain rose as the two planes passed over the men. Suddenly the Japanese plane disintegrated in the air and large pieces showered down into the water.

Sterner looked into Price's face. "Will the Japanese start shelling us?"

"I don't know. I can't figure out why they haven't done it yet. The best thing I can guess is that they're running low on ammunition. It could be that we caught them unprepared for the landing and that they're bringing up troops. There

136

could be a lot of reasons why they haven't really started in on us, but I guess the only thing we can do is wait and see. I imagine they'll start on us just before dark."

"Think we can hold the beach?"

"I'm not sure. I've never been in combat with green troops before. Anything might happen. If they don't run, we might be able to hold out long enough for the navy to land more troops and some heavy stuff."

"Will Regeic really shoot the first man to run?"

"Yes."

"That's a little rough, isn't it?"

"Not the way I see it. If a man runs, he might start a panic and the first thing you know we'd all be right out in the water."

Sterner looked into Price's hard face. "How do you manage to stay so calm?"

Me calm? Price thought. Right now I'm so scared that I want to run. I ran out of guts a long time ago. After so long, your luck has to run out and I figure mine is all used up. He wanted to tell Sterner this, but he knew that it would do no good. Instead, he tried to be casual. "All you have to do is just not think about it."

Sterner had asked the question out of courtesy. He remembered the afternoon that Price had almost cracked up. He knew that Price was being casual when he was really afraid. "You didn't act very scared this afternoon, either."

"I don't know what made me go out there. It just seemed like the thing to do at the time. If I'd taken the time to think about it, I'd have left him."

"You may try to act rough, but I think it's all a defense mechanism. I doubt if you'll be like that when you get away from the front."

"I hope you're right."

Somewhere in the distance Price heard the crack of an artillery piece, and he instinctively ducked into the hole, pulling Sterner with him. Cold sweat began to form on his forehead. Over and over, he thought that it was beginning. The thought kept running through his mind until he wanted to scream. For some strange reason, he remembered that his feet were dirty. He did now want to die with dirty feet. A little laugh escaped from his tight lips. Strange that I should think about my dirty feet, he thought.

Price realized that he was still waiting for the shell to land and he knew that only a second or two had elapsed since he had heard the crack of the artillery piece. He was wondering when it would land, and wondering how he could have so many thoughts in such a short time, when the shell landed. There was a tremendous blast to the right of his hole, and the ground shook. Price tried to shrink further down into the hole to escape the hot steel that was showering down on him. A second blast sounded, and then another. Soon the ground was shaking and earth was showering down into the hole.

The first detonation knocked off Sterner's helmet as he crouched next to Price. He wondered why Price had chosen a time like this to laugh, when the second shell landed. As the ground shook more violently, Sterner wondered if he was going to die and his thoughts went back to his wife. He remembered how sad she had looked the day she had seen him off at the station. The silence had been awesome and they had stood there without saying a word. He remembered that he had actually been relieved when the train pulled out. He had left without telling her that he loved her. He had wanted to, but he had been close to tears and afraid that if he told her how he felt, he would break down. He remembered that he had just stood there and said nothing. Now that he thought he might die, he wished that he had told her how much he loved her.

With each blast, Lantrip tried to crouch lower. Tears were streaming down his face and he tried in vain to stop crying. He knew that the other men would be laughing at him when it was over. A shell burst near him and he let out a loud cry as the dirt showered in on him. I've got to get control of myself, he kept thinking. I never was scared of anything before. He kept fighting with his emotions but he thought he was going to die and he could not stop the tears.

Lantrip tried to remember Myrtle Beach and Roberta. Was she Morris' wife? If she was, what would he do when he found out? How would he find out? Another shell landed near him and new tears came. He had heard that Morris had received a letter from his wife and that she was pregnant. It couldn't be his wife, though. That kind of thing would never happen, the odds were too great.

Another shower of dirt came into his hole. What would he do to me? How many ways could he kill me? A grenade could land in my hole at night and no one would know the difference. A shot during an attack. There must be a thousand ways that he could kill me. If it was her, what would he do to me? Oh, Lord. I hope that it wasn't her. I wish I knew. Which hole is Morris in?

Ruffin was in the bottom of his hole praying. There was very little that he could do except pray that God would do as He saw fit, and, if it was His will, to spare him the agony of death. Between blasts he could hear another voice. "Holy Mary——Mother of God——pray for us sinners, now——and at——the hour——of our——death."

Then, shells careened into the beach and burst among the men, tearing bodies and trees to pieces with a cold indifference. The roar became louder, and Ruffin prayed. Further down the line, another voice prayed almost as hard. "Hail, Mary. . . ."

The barrage continued to churn over the beach, like a giant storm raging across the land. Tremendous sprays of sand and coral rock were thrown high into the air. The smell of burnt powder hung over the ground. Cold sweat ran down the faces of the men, as they tried to bury themselves in the ground. To a group of veterans, an artillery barrage is a terrifying experience, but to men going through it for the first time, the terror is almost beyond description. Each blast gave them assurance that they were still alive, but they waited for the next, knowing that it would land on top of them. Then the next one landed, and they were still alive, but they waited for the next. Then the thoughts came faster. What if it hits next to the hole and buries me alive? Every so often a man would scream and the horror would become more real. That could be me, a man would think. Some men cried, some prayed, and others cursed.

On and on, the terrible barrage lashed across the land, tearing the earth apart, whipping back and forth. Sweat mingled with the dust, and men's bodies twitched. Ruffin lay in the bottom of his hole and covered his head with his hands while he prayed. Lantrip wailed and cried. Beecraft thought about Bryant and placed his helmet over his groin.

Suddenly it was over. In contrast to the barrage, the sudden quiet was as startling as a scream. The island seemed dead. Price wiped the caked dirt off his face and looked at the mud on his hands. When he looked out of the hole he realized that the sun had gone down and it was very dark. All over the area, heads began to emerge from the holes.

Sterner was still crouched in the bottom of the hole. Price placed his hand on the man's shoulder and shook him gently. "It's all over."

Sterner looked up. His eyes had a dull film over them. He looked around incredulously, as though he could not believe he was still alive. Mud ran down his face and left streaks.

"Are you all right?" Price asked.

"Aid man!" a call rang out.

"I'm all right," Sterner answered quietly.

"Who's hit?" Ruffin called.

"Keep quiet," Regeic called.

"Somebody's hit," Ruffin called back.

"Shut your mouth," Price said harshly.

"Hadn't we better go and see who's hit?" Sterner asked.

"Can't move around in the dark."

"Oh, God," came a piercing cry from the darkness. "Help!"

Higgenbotham's voice rang out in clear, crisp tones. "Who's hit?"

"I'm going to say this once," Price called in anger across the area, "and then I don't want to hear another sound. If you hear a movement, shoot at it, and call for flares. The Japs are all around us and by now we've probably given our positions away. Don't get out of your hole for anything. Shoot anything that moves."

Price leaned back against the side of the hole and cradled his weapon in his arms. Sterner was sitting across from him, not moving. They sat for a long time, and neither of them moved.

"Sure is quiet," Sterner whispered, finally.

"Yeah."

"Night sure is still."

"Yes."

"I'd give a million dollars for a smoke."

"You can't smoke at night. The Japs can see the glow for a long way. That way, they could toss a grenade at you and you'd never know where it came from. Would you like to chew on a cigar?" Price asked.

"Chew a cigar?"

"Sure. It tastes a little bad at first but you get used to it after a while. It tastes like tobacco and gives you something to do at night."

"No, thanks. I believe I'd rather do without."

"I think I will, if it won't bother you. Regeic says it looks bad."

"No, go right ahead."

"It sure is quiet," Price whispered. "If they do like they usually do, the Japs will be coming soon."

"Do you think we will get a banzai charge?"

"They probably know that we've got a lot of green troops. The first thing they should do is to try to scare us. They'll start yelling at us. If that doesn't work, they'll call for help and try to make us think that they're Americans that are hurt. As soon as they think that they've got us unnerved, they'll attack."

"I wish they would get it over with. I think that waiting is the worst."

"I guess so. Where are you from?" Price suddenly asked.

"Texas."

"That's a fine place. I was down at Camp Maxie for a while. What town did you come from?"

"San Marcos."

"You were a teacher, weren't you?"

"Yes."

"Drafted?"

"Yes."

"Too bad. They shouldn't send a man out here like that. I was a professional soldier so I can't complain too much. I spent all my life learning to do this. I got paid to be ready to come out here, but it's different with you. I don't think it's right for them to send a man out here against his will."

"I wouldn't say that. It's a free country, but you can't live in it for nothing."

"That's a noble thought." Price chuckled.

140

"I meant it. I guess after so long it gets down to being a nasty job that has to be done. I feel that I should be here, though. I don't think I could live with myself if I had stayed home and others had gone instead."

"That's true. I guess it will be a little bad after the war. The men that didn't come out here will feel like they didn't do all that they could."

Sterner took a drink from his canteen. "Where is your home?" he asked.

"All over. The only home I have is the army. I guess I've called a lot of places home."

"I can imagine, but where are your folks?"

"Louisiana. Shreveport."

They sat in silence for a while. Somewhere in front of their position a twig snapped. Price peered into the darkness.

A voice called from the blackness, *"Yankee, you die!"*

Sterner sucked in his breath. "Christ!"

"Just lie still. This is going to be the worst part of the night."

*"Tonight you die,"* the voice called.

"Bastard!" someone shouted.

Regeic hissed at the men to be quiet, and his voice seemed to hang on the ground.

"They're just trying to rattle you and make someone shoot," Price whispered. "Just stay quiet."

*"Fugg you, G.I."* The voice was to the left.

*"Help me. I'm a G.I. Help me."* This voice seemed to be directly in front of the men.

"It's a Jap," Price said.

"Are you sure?"

"No."

*"Help me. Oh, God . . . yowee . . . help. Please, somebody help me!"*

"If you aren't sure, it might be a G.I. What if it is?"

"Then he'll have to stay out there and do the best he can."

"Don't you think we should go out there and see?"

"It's probably a Jap. They do it all the time so you'll try to help the man. When you get out there, they kill you."

"This is horrible."

Price squinted through the darkness. "Yeah."

Lantrip lay in the bottom of his hole and bit his lips to keep them from trembling. He had a desire to scream. He wanted to run, but the thought that Regeic would kill him kept him glued to the spot.

*"Yowee . . . Yowee . . . Help, please!"*

"Why doesn't somebody go out there and help him?" Lantrip said quietly.

*"The Japs got me."*

"I wonder where he is," Ruffin whispered.

"It must be terrible lying out there like that."

141

*"Aid man!"* This voice came from within the perimeter. "God help him," Ruffin said.

*"Sarge,"* the voice called again, *"please help me. I'm hurt. Please help me."*

There was a noise in front of their hole. "Who's out there?" Ruffin called quietly.

*"G.I. I'm wounded. Help me in your hole. Where are you?"*

Ruffin remembered Price's warning about not moving around at night. It could be a Jap.

*"For God's sake, help me!"* the voice called.

"Over here," Lantrip called.

"You shouldn't have done that," Ruffin said.

"The man is hurt, he needs help."

"You know what Price said."

"I don't care what he said. The man needs help and I'm not going to leave him out there to die."

"It might be a Jap."

"No Jap could speak English that good."

"But Price said . . ."

"I don't care what Price said."

*"Where are you?"* the voice called.

"Over here," Lantrip repeated.

A voice came through the night. "Quiet!"

*"Where are you? I'm hurt."*

"To your right," Lantrip whispered.

Instantly, the Jap sprang. A knife blade flashed in the darkness. Lantrip was thrown backward, the Japanese soldier on top of him. With an effort born of desperation Lantrip blocked the arm which was arching toward him and rolled away, bringing his knee up with all the strength he possessed. Dimly, he heard someone yell for a flare, as the Jap was on him again like a cat, his knife pressing down toward his throat. Then there was a blinding flash of light and he saw Ruffin standing over the Jap, hitting again and again with his bayonet. The lifeless body of the Jap fell forward, and Lantrip struggled to get out from under the body.

In the light of the flare he could see Ruffin standing straight over the body, still holding the bayonet, and looking at the man as if he could not believe that he had killed him. Quickly he stood and looked out of the hole, relieved to see that there were no more Japs in the area.

"Thanks," Lantrip mumbled.

"I killed him," Ruffin said with a shaking voice.

"You saved my life."

"I killed him."

"Ruffin!"

"I killed him." Over and over, Ruffin repeated the words, long after the flare had gone out.

Several times Lantrip made a feeble attempt to thank Ruffin. Finally he gave up and worked with the Jap's body, at last managing to get it out of the hole. Stepping on the body had made him sick and he was relieved to have it out of the hole.

The flare burst in the air a few seconds after the call had been heard. There had been a few shouts and at last the word was passed that a Jap had gotten into the hole with Lantrip and Ruffin. Price was relieved to see that the two helmets that appeared over the rim of the hole were G.I. issue. As the light faded, he hunched back into the hole.

"I never thought either of them would make it," Sterner said softly.

"You never know what a man will do when he has to."

"I wonder who killed him?"

"Have to wait until morning."

"I'll bet they're scared as hell."

"I would be, too."

The silence was around them again, so quiet that you could hear the breathing of the men, and somewhere down the line a man mumbled.

"Lieutenant?"

"Yeah?"

"Got any paper?"

"Paper?"

"Toilet paper. I got to go."

"Can't you wait?"

"I don't think so."

"Use your finger."

"Aw, come on."

"Well, what the hell you want me to do?"

"I've got to do something."

"Here," Price finally said, stretching forth his hand with the small package of paper in it. "That's one of the first things you remember to bring with you."

"Thanks. Do you think it will be safe to get out of the hole?"

"You'll have to do it there."

"How?"

"Use your helmet."

"All the comforts of home."

"It may be nasty, but it's better than getting shot."

Price tried to ignore the man, and was relieved when he emptied the contents of the helmet on the ground outside the hole.

The quiet was shattered with a loud scream. "Run . . . they've broken through our lines . . . run!" Nervous sounds were heard from around the area. "Run," the voice called again.

"Japs," Sterner whispered.

"I hope so."

"Do they keep this up all night?"

"Usually."

A shadowy figure jumped from a hole about twenty yards from Price and began to run for the rear. Regeic fired a burst over the figure's head and the shadow dropped back into the hole.

More silence, silence that ate into the entire nervous system, until a man could not think. Silence that was loud with its absence of sound. Price imagined that the quiet was so severe that the drops of sweat that were running down his face could be heard. The sweat trickled, and the silence continued.

When he first saw the flickering glow, Price was unable to move. Then it registered that it was a grenade, arching through the air toward his foxhole. He ducked, yelling at the same time, "Grenade!"

The grenade landed close by, and the hot shrapnel flew over his head. In the distance he heard the pop of the flare gun, and he raised his head and peered out into the darkness. Nothing was in view.

The light had faded, and there was the silence again. The sweat continued to flow.

*"You die tonight, G.I."*

"Why don't they start the attack?"

"Got all night."

"I'm going out of my head."

"That's what they want."

*"Fugg you, sojer."*

"Where the hell are they?"

"Who knows."

To the left, there was a crackling of fire. The night was filled with the sound of safeties being released. To the right, a flare burst in the distance, followed by another burst of fire.

*"Tonight, you die. . . . Fugg you, G.I."*

*"Help me, I'm a G.I. The Japs have me. Yeowweeeeee-eeeee! Help, for God's sake, help!"*

"Christ."

"Just take it easy. It'll be starting soon."

*"For God's sake, won't somebody help me?"*

"Why the hell don't they shut up?"

"They will . . . soon."

*"Lieutenant,"* the voice called.

Price remained silent.

"Don't you think you better answer them?"

"Jap."

*"Lieutenant."* Then there was a period of silence. *"Sarge."*

The high-pitched voice rang out again. *"For God's sake, please come and get me!"*

"What time is it?" Sterner whispered.

"Three."

"Why haven't they come after us?"

"I can't figure it. The only thing I can guess is that they don't have too many troops on this side of the island, or else

144

they've written it off as lost. The best I can figure is that they'll try one or two charges tonight and then some more tomorrow when they can get more troops."

Behind them, there was a lot of noise, indicating that there were troops landing. That would be the reserve battalion bringing the mortars and machine guns with them. I hope to hell they set up the mortars on the beach so they can give us some support when the attack comes, thought Price.

Small arms fired into the area and their crack seemed louder than usual. In the darkness, one of the grenades was tripped and a shattering explosion followed. Price knew that the Japanese were moving forward, and he thought he heard their rubber-soled shoes as they scraped across the sand. He was about to call for a flare, but he heard the *thunk* of the flare gun before he could yell. He gritted his teeth and waited for the light.

As soon as they heard the crack of the flare gun, the Japanese started their chattering. The flare burst, and Price saw a long line of Japanese soldiers advancing. A big Japanese officer led them as they struggled forward. For a second, right after the flare burst, the Japanese soldiers looked like statues. They were charging the lines in a body. Price had seen this before, but each time he saw the mass of Japanese advancing on him, he felt terror. They ran leaning forward, their legs bent in such a manner as to make them look like crabs. They were yelling like madmen.

Sterner looked over the top of the hole and gasped. He almost froze with fear, but he forced up his weapon and fired three shots into the mass in rapid succession. "God help us," he said through clenched teeth.

Wild shots were being fired from all over the area, but the mass continued to move forward. None of the Japs fell, and the fire grew more intense. Price aimed carefully at the officer and squeezed the trigger. A steady stream of fire found its way into the man. The officer was wearing glasses, and they flew from his face as the slugs hit him, but he continued to move forward. At last, he fell forward and hit the ground. The body jumped several times, as though the officer wanted to crawl forward, but at last it was still.

The firing became deafening, but none of the Japanese soldiers fell. Panic began to grip the men and they wanted to run. It seemed to them that none of the Japanese would stop. Finally, almost as though they had done it on a signal, dozens of the soldiers fell at once and large gaps appeared in the lines of advancing men.

The Japanese continued to move forward. They were yelling like lunatics. Several of them were almost on top of Price's hole when he finished slamming a new clip into his weapon. He jerked his weapon up and fired directly into them. The closest man fell like a heavy sack, his face blown away. The second man hit the ground and writhed like a wounded snake.

He writhed on the ground and looked directly at Price. He made a last feeble attempt to pick up the rifle that he had dropped and then collapsed.

There was a ping and Price realized that Sterner's rifle was empty. Price fired into the onrushing men desperately. All the men disappeared from in front of his sights except for a small soldier. He was young, and looked as if he could not have been more than sixteen. The soldier's eyes looked very small and round and there was not a trace of beard. Price aimed for the man's stomach and squeezed the trigger. A sick feeling raced through his stomach when no shot fired; his weapon was empty! Price jerked his head to the right and screamed at Sterner to use his bayonet. He was horrified as he saw the man next to him still trying to jam a clip into his rifle. He was working too fast and was all thumbs.

The bayonet on the end of the Jap's rifle looked much longer than it was, as he lunged forward with a smile of triumph on his face. It was aimed squarely at Price's stomach. Price was almost paralyzed with fear as he watched it come straight at him. Just before it reached him, he jerked to the left and swung the butt of his submachine gun at the Jap's face. Before he hit him, he saw Sterner's bayonet dig into the Jap's stomach. For a moment, the Jap hung on the end of the bayonet like a giant fish that Sterner was trying to land. The Jap screamed as he struggled, and Price swung the butt of his submachine gun at his face. It hit with a dull thud and the man slumped.

Lantrip was still trembling from the fight with the Jap who had gotten into his hole, when he heard the screams of the advancing soldiers. Almost before the flare had fully illuminated the area, he had emptied a clip into the advancing mass. Ruffin watched with a look of horror on his face.

Finally, Ruffin got control of himself and triggered the rifle.

He aimed directly at the closest Jap, but the Jap didn't fall. Ruffin fired twice more, but the Jap kept running forward. He emptied the clip and the Jap still came on. He became panic-stricken and knew that he had missed. It seemed to him that the Japanese could not be stopped. Then, to his relief, the Jap raised his arms in the air and fell face forward.

Lantrip struggled with his emotions and hoped he would not become paralyzed with fright. He forced himself to jam a fresh clip into his rifle, but it seemed to take an unusually long time. When it was in, he raised the rifle and fired into the Japanese. He looked down the sights and wondered how they could be stopped. They kept coming, although some of them were falling. They looked as though they would never stop.

When the first Japanese soldiers started falling, Ruffin

said a silent prayer and pumped the trigger at the same time. With each shot, he felt sick to his stomach, but he continued to fire. *It isn't right,* he thought, *they're men, just like me . . . I got another one . . .*

Price cast a quick look around the area after the last Jap had gone down in front of him. Horrified, he saw a Jap standing over the hole next to him. The Jap had the barrel of his long rifle pointed almost directly into Beecraft's face. Beecraft and Morris were lashing out with their bayonets when the Jap fired. The Jap was working the bolt of his rifle to fire another shot when Price sent a blast into him that almost cut him in half.

Quickly, Price jumped from his hole and leaped into the hole the Jap had fired into. Beecraft was crumpled in the bottom of the hole. Half of the right side of his head was a pulpy mass. Morris was looking down at the man with a shocked look on his face.

Price bent over Beecraft and looked at the wound.

"Is he dead?" Morris gasped.

"Not yet."

Morris sat in the bottom of the hole and cradled Beecraft's head in his lap. "Do you have a compress?"

Price didn't answer, but he reached back and pulled out the contents of his first-aid pouch. He opened the package with the compress in it and gently wrapped it around the bleeding wound.

Occasionally, Beecraft would open his eyes and look up at Morris, but then he would close them again. His breath was coming in short gasps.

"Why couldn't it have been me?" Morris cried. "He had a good wife and something to live for. Why did it have to be him?"

"I don't think anyone knows why it happens," Price answered.

"It isn't right."

The two men sat in silence for a long time. Neither of them knew what should be said. Beecraft was dying and there was nothing they could do about it. Finally, Beecraft opened his eyes.

"Anne," he called softly.

"Beecraft, it's me, Morris. Your wife isn't here."

"Anne, I want to see Anne."

"She isn't here."

"I want to see her. I can't remember what she looks like. I want to see her."

"She isn't here."

"Can't you get her for me? You're my friend. I have to tell her that I love her."

"I can't."

"I want to tell her that I'm sorry about the Japanese girl."

147

"I'll tell her for you."

Beecraft, incoherent, sucked in a great breath and died in Morris' arms. Morris and Price looked at each other. There was grief and pain on their faces.

# CHAPTER SEVEN

They had covered Beecraft's body with a blanket and gone to another hole. Price dropped off into a restless sleep after what seemed to be several hours. As he tossed and turned halfway between waking and sleeping, he tried to convince himself that he was just tired. Finally the harsh rays of the sun hit his face, and he fought his eyes open. He was shocked at the ragged appearance of Morris, and then, as he looked over into the next hole and saw the blanket-covered body of Beecraft, he remembered the night.

It seemed a little ridiculous to him that his bad dreams should be the only real peace he had been able to find. Each day was a nightmare. Price stared into the tired face next to him and frowned. "Did you ever wonder why things happen like they do?" he asked wearily.

"I gave up trying to figure life out," Morris answered in a very low voice.

"What I meant was," Price continued, "why would God let a man be born when he knew that he would be miserable all his life? Every time I remember those sweet words that the chaplain is always spouting off, I want to puke."

"If you ask me," Morris spat, "there ain't no God."

"I think you're wrong about that," Price said, rubbing his hand across his rough face. "God's in His heaven, and all's gone to hell in the world."

"I doubt it. If there was a God, he'd try to show a man the way through all this damn mess. If there is a God, he sure has handed me the dirty end of the stick." Tears were forming in Morris' eyes.

Price mumbled agreement and pulled a fresh cigar out of his pocket.

"No God," Morris continued, "good or bad, would let all this happen to His people. Look at Beecraft over there. He was the only one of us that had anything to live for. For that matter, he was probably better than the rest of us as far as religion goes. Now, he's dead and we still live on. I just can't believe that any God would let that happen. It's not right. I remember something that a preacher once said about the birds not having to worry about something to eat because God took care of them. He must have been taking a coffee break when He let them kill Beecraft. He couldn't have cared too much, because Beecraft is as dead as all hell."

"I guess that's right. A man is born and struggles like hell

148

to survive. Then all of a sudden, he's dead and someone else starts over again."

"I'll bet you a million dollars that there isn't any heaven."

Price was very grim. "If there is, none of us will get there anyway."

"No."

"You know what the worst part of it is?" Price asked.

"What?"

"I never *really* thought that it could happen to one of us. We've all been through so much hell that I just couldn't believe that any of us could get killed. Now, it seems too real for comfort."

"You should have been in the same hole. When that Jap was standing over him and pulling the trigger, I froze. If I could have got the clip into my rifle fast enough, I might have been able to get the Jap before he shot Beecraft."

"Don't blame yourself. Someone has to get killed. You couldn't help it any more than any of us. It could have been you that got killed just as well as him. If it hadn't been for Sterner, one of them would have killed me for sure."

"Ern?"

"Yeah."

"Could I take him back to the beach and bury him? I'd hate to leave him here."

"Sure. As soon as it gets a little lighter take a detail to help you. You can catch up with us later."

"Thanks."

"I thought that you might want to. You've been friends for a long time. It wouldn't be right for them to leave him here to rot in a shallow grave. When we get back to the States we can tell Anne that he has a good grave."

"She'd like that."

Price rubbed his face. "How long was I asleep?"

Morris' voice cracked. "Couple of hours."

"Did you get any sleep?"

"I tried to, but I couldn't sleep. I should be used to it by now, but every time someone I like gets killed it hurts me. I don't guess that we will ever get used to it."

"Probably not."

"The thing that gets me is that we're here because I got him drunk and we volunteered. If I hadn't gotten him drunk like that, none of us would have been here and he would be alive."

The two men sat and stared over at the body that was lying under the blanket. Another day, another body. It was a routine that had repeated itself so often that there was almost no sorrow left in the men. Beecraft had been their friend and both of them felt sorry that he was dead, but they knew that they did not feel the grief that they used to feel when a friend got killed. As a result, they sat and wondered what had happened to their feelings. Were they gone? Had they

149

ceased to be human? Had they turned into animals?

When the sun was over the tops of the trees Price stood in the hole and stretched his cramped muscles. Japanese soldiers were lying about in various poses of death. The sun glittered on the dried blood and shone out of their still-open eyes. Price's face tingled as though the blood had drained from it, and he rubbed his face with both his hands in an effort to start the circulation again.

To the rear, he could hear the preparations of the troops that had landed during the night. As soon as it was lighter, they would be moving forward, trying to take some of the island before the Japs could bring up more troops. From the noise, Price could tell that there was much confusion back there. Realizing that there would be a general advance very soon, Price cupped his hands and called out across the area. "Get ready to move out. I don't have any way to find out when, or if, they're going to use the mortars first, but stand by. As soon as the men from the beach catch up with us, move out. Don't bunch up, and try to maintain some order. Don't stop until I give the word."

Price turned to Morris, who was still sitting on the ground. He looked as though he would cry any minute. "After we've moved out, you take Regeic and get Beecraft buried."

"Won't you need Regeic with you?"

"Hell, Higgenbotham has some rank. I might as well teach him to run the outfit. In a few months we're going back to the States and then he'll have to break in some green officer. I sure would hate to think about what would happen if he had to take over now."

"I guess it would be a little ridiculous."

"Ridiculous, it would be like a blind man leading another one. The only good man we have is Sterner."

"Why don't you have him promoted?"

"Remind me when I can find the Old Man, and I will."

They sat in silence for some time and waited for the advance to start. Most of the time was spent in collecting ammunition from the dead men and in checking their weapons. There was still a strong possibility that the Japs might attack again, although it was apparent that they had made their biggest effort to stop the landing during the night. They probably had used most of their available man power and were falling back to a more favorable position.

Soon there was a rumbling sound from the beach and outgoing shells swished overhead and landed in the distance with a dull thud. It had started. A destroyer had pulled close to the beach and was firing over their heads. The shells landed several hundred yards in front of them and ran up and down the front. Solid sheets of flame rose into the air, carrying broken trees and sand high into the air. Other guns began to fire and the noise rose to a nerve-shattering intensity. The ground trembled in an ineffectual protest against the punishment that was being inflicted upon it.

Ruffin was staring around the area. He was very close to being sick. He looked at the bodies and felt responsible for all their deaths. During the attack he had counted at least three Japanese soldiers that he almost surely had killed. Love thy neighbor. Turn the other cheek. All these things were in his mind as he looked around him at the bodies. He had killed men, and this realization was in conflict with his inner beliefs. As a result, he was confused and deeply disturbed.

Ruffin had prayed as hard as he knew how that the Lord would take him away from the horror that he had faced, but nothing had happened. More Japs had come and he had fired at them. Doubt was beginning to form in his mind, and for the first time in his life he had some doubts about the power of prayer. When his prayers had apparently gone unheard, he had changed his request to "let Thy will be done," but this had seemed weak and ineffective.

The shelling continued for about thirty minutes. Then a wall of dirt and flame seemed to move in a straight line through the jungle. On the beach men came out of the shell holes, and from behind the sea wall. They came forward at a slow trot. None of them spoke or yelled, and their clean-shaven faces were very grim. Overhead, the sky was filled with the roar of navy fighters out in search of the enemy.

Price studied the faces of the advancing men and the familiar look of fear was written on them. When the troops were almost up to them, Price yelled at his men to move forward.

Price rose and looked at his men as they got out of their holes. Satisfied that they were all moving, he began to trot forward. But the effects of the heat and a practically sleepless night made his feet seem like lead weights. He took several more steps and then signaled the men to stop. He sat down and signaled Higgenbotham to come to him.

"You want me, Lieutenant?"

Price removed his helmet and banged it on the ground. His voice was filled with anger. "Damn you! How many times do I have to tell you not to address me by rank? One more time, and I'll knock the hell out of you. Is that clear?"

"All right."

"Higgenbotham, I want you to stay behind the rest of the men. Don't let any of them stop."

"Okay." Then Higgenbotham looked into Price's face. "Should we be stopped here? The other platoons have gone on without us."

"I don't want you to think that I'm being critical, Higgenbotham, but this is a disorganized mess. It's always like this. The one thing you should always remember is if you're supposed to move forward, keep moving, and if you're defend-

151

ing, don't move back. Everything can get tangled up, and then the whole success of the campaign will depend on little groups of men fighting alone and doing the best they can."

"I'll buy that. I doubt if anybody knows where we even are."

"They don't. There was a lot of confusion on the beach and nobody landed where they were supposed to. They never did get any communications started, so they don't know where anybody is."

"Don't you think I should have somebody go back and locate the CP? We can get into trouble if we move into the wrong area."

"That would be one gun less for us and we can't afford to lose it."

"I hope you're right."

"I've kept you alive so far, haven't I?"

"I guess so."

"All right then, you just do as I say and I'll do your thinking for you. You're going to have to take over this platoon some day soon, and the more you can learn the better off we'll all be."

"Okay."

From the look on his face, Price could tell that Higgenbotham resented him. He was better educated, and no doubt shared the colonel's dislike for Regular Army men. He had been promoted fast, and believed that he knew all he had to about running the platoon.

Price was about to give the word for the men to move out again when a soldier came scrambling up from the rear. He was sweating as though he had been running a long time. Several of the men pointed toward Price, and the man came running toward him. Finally he stopped in front of Price and knelt on the ground. "You in charge here?"

"Yes."

"The colonel sent me up from the beachhead. He wants to get a company back there for security. We passed a lot of Japs when the advance started and he's afraid some of them may get the supplies. He said for me to send the first three platoons back."

"I'll start back right away. Do you want to come with us?"

"Sorry, I have to find another platoon before I can start back. Be careful, though, there are a lot of Japs between here and the beach."

Price watched the man disappear through the foliage and then he passed the word for the men to start back.

The platoon trudged toward the beach and Price was at the head of the column, being very careful to watch for any movement that would indicate that there were Japanese waiting in ambush for them. The only evidence that they found that the artillery barrage had been effective was one Japanese soldier lying in the trail. He was stretched out as though he had gone to sleep.

Price approached him and stopped. He held his gun on the man's head and fired a burst at it. That way, he did not have to move the body, which might be wired. Satisfied that the man was dead, he stepped over the body and continued back. He saw that the other men were being very careful to avoid the body.

When Price got to the beach, the sun was high in the sky, scorching everything in sight. The pier that had once extended out into the water now looked like a pile of burnt matches. Some of the beams floated in the water, and they gently bobbed with each wave.

It was a breezeless day and the hot air hung close to the ground. On the beach there was a long line of wounded men waiting for the doctor to make his way toward them. They lay in agony, moaning and writhing under the blinding heat. Most of them spoke only to refuse aid and to send the medic on to a more serious case. Some prayed.

Beyond the sea wall, in the area where the attack had bogged down the day before, men lay on the ground and bled to death. All too few medics worked among them, bringing the wounded back to the beach as quickly as it was possible for so few medics to carry so many wounded.

Price surveyed the area and realized that the damage done by the Japanese artillery had been much worse than had been expected and that the casualties were many. He marveled at the raw courage of the men who littered the beach. He had thought of these unprofessional soldiers as weak, and incapable of standing up under the terrible suffering. But they did.

The stench of death was everywhere, and there was no wind to carry it away. The odor was a combination of dead fish, rotting flesh, excrement and dried blood—all rolled into one nauseating smell. The water was filled with bobbing bodies, disfigured and mangled beyond recognition. The beach area was a shambles, and each palm tree was ragged.

Several tents had been set up almost at the water's edge and they were being used as a temporary hospital. There was a great amount of confusion around each of them. At the far end of the last tent, a growing stack of dead men was being built.

Price led his men straight to a group of foxholes which had been dug along the sea wall. He had the men take up their positions and then found his way to the CP. The colonel was standing among a group of boxes. Men were unloading craft, and he was giving instructions to one of their officers.

"A runner found me and said to come back here for security."

The colonel looked very tired. Sweat was dripping off his nose, as he looked up. "Price! Of all the men for him to find!

I don't have time to explain all that I should, but have your men take up positions along the sea wall. There hasn't been any trouble in the area yet, but patrols have reported a lot of Japs that we passed. The Japs will probably try to sneak back here tonight and hit us before we can get organized. As soon as we get communications with all the units I'll have another outfit come back here and you can join your company. Take anything you need from here, especially machine guns. Set up a lot of them."

"Very well, Colonel," Price said.

The colonel nodded at Price and again turned his attention to the supplies. Price returned to the men and repeated the colonel's instructions to Higgenbotham. As soon as the other men had started digging the holes deeper, Price went to find Regeic and Morris.

Lantrip had been using his entrenching tool to enlarge the hole. He had removed his clothes and was working in his shorts. The sweat dripped off his body. Beside him, Ruffin labored heavily, handicapped by his weak frame. His face was pale. Each time he looked at the bodies, he felt sick.

Ruffin leaned the entrenching tool against his leg and wiped the sweat from his face. "It's inhuman," he mumbled under his breath.

"What?" Lantrip said.

"The way they treat those bodies back there. They stack them up like cordwood, just like they weren't human. It isn't right; they should treat them better."

Lantrip sat back on his haunches, using his helmet for a seat. "I guess it isn't much like a regular funeral and all, but there's a war going on. I don't guess they could round up a preacher and choir."

"Guess not."

"There is one good thing about all this, though."

"What's that?" Ruffin asked.

"I used to think I was pretty tough. When I was a kid I thought I could lick the world barehanded. I guess I was something of a bully. You know how I was when I came out here. I found out different when we hit the beach."

"Everything is so horrible," Ruffin said. "I never even imagined that it would be this bad. I guess you might say things look different to me, too. For the first time in my life I wish that I had been able to have sexual intercourse with a girl before I came out here."

"Well," said Lantrip, "I spent most of my time either fighting or drinking. In between, I chased all the women I could find."

"Didn't you ever think that it might be wrong?"

"Not after the first time. I guess this is about the first time I ever thought too much about it. Even if I did think it was wrong, I don't think I'd stop."

154

"Did you ever do it with a married woman? You said you did, but I mean really?"

"Sure. Back when I was in Texas I worked with this married man in a station. He ran around a lot on his wife and used to try to get me to take some of his girls out. Once, he had a new one and all he talked about was how good she was. He used to brag that she was as good as his wife. I went out with her and she was good, but not half as good as his wife. The only trouble was, he didn't have any sense of humor. When I told him his wife was better, he tried to kill me with a tire iron."

Ruffin realized that Lantrip was joking. He forced out a laugh. "I'm serious."

"Sure. Married women are the easiest. They're also the safest. If they get pregnant, their husbands never know the difference. Besides, they know what you're after, and if they go out with you you've got it made.

"I do feel a little bad about screwing a soldier's wife, though. Especially if he's out here. I got to a woman in Myrtle Beach just before I came out here, and she had a husband somewhere in the Pacific."

"I heard that Morris got quite a letter from his wife the other day."

"What happened?" Lantrip asked, his voice a little shaky.

"One of the men said that he heard she'd gotten herself knocked up."

"Isn't he from somewhere in the Carolinas?"

"I think so. Why?"

"Will you keep a secret?"

"Sure."

"Do you swear?"

"Yes."

"The girl I got to in Myrtle Beach was named Roberta Morris. You don't think that she could be his wife, do you?"

"I hope not, for your sake."

"The odds would be a million to one for that to happen. Besides, I haven't mentioned her name but once. Even if it is his wife, how could he find out if you don't tell him?"

"Morris would probably kill you if he even thought you were the one. I don't think Price would stop him, even if he could. They've been friends for a long time and he would sympathize with Morris. He might even help him shoot you."

"Hell, just don't mention it to him."

"I gave you my word, didn't I?"

"Sure."

Price found Regeic and Morris by the growing stack of dead men. The stack was growing higher and there were several layers of bodies now. Morris and Regeic were carrying them out to the pile to make room for the wounded who were still coming in. A leg stuck out in a grotesque angle here, and an arm over there.

Price walked up to Regeic. "Did you get Beecraft buried?"

Regeic had a pained look on his face. "No."

"No?"

"They wouldn't let us," Regeic said. "These damn people made us put him over there with the rest of the dead ones. That's his head down there near the end."

Price glanced at the head Regeic was pointing to. "They can't do that to him," he said, through clenched teeth.

Morris stood there and did not speak or move. He had the look of a dead man.

"They did," Regeic cursed.

"They don't have any sense. They can't get away with this," Price mumbled.

"Price, would you like a drink? I stole some alcohol from the medics. Morris and me have been drinking ever since they took Beecraft away from us."

"How the hell can they do that to him?" Price asked. Then he took two large drinks from Regeic's canteen. "It stinks here. He's got more coming to him than this. It isn't right."

Regeic pointed out a sergeant who was directing the corpsmen in placing another body on the stack. "That's the man that took him away from us."

"He must be a bastard."

"A real son of a bitch."

"One hundred per cent."

"Diamond plated."

"Bastard."

"You're an officer, Ern. Why don't you go over there and make him let us have Beecraft back so we can bury him like he deserves?"

Price swallowed hard and stared at the sergeant. Anger rose in him and his body shook with rage. Finally, he could stand it no longer and he walked fast toward him. All the way, he told himself that he would have to be calm. If he was not careful he would crack up. When he reached the sergeant, Price grabbed the front of his shirt with his filthy hand and spun him around. Placing his face only an inch from the sergeant's, he shouted, letting all the hate come out. "I want him back. I want him back right now, do you understand?"

The sergeant struggled to release himself from the iron grip, but he could do no more than move back a few inches.

"Who?"

"Beecraft."

"Who the hell is Beecraft?" the sergeant asked, frightened.

"My friend."

Still struggling, the sergeant asked, "Where is he supposed to be?"

"Over there," Price said, pointing to the bodies.

"Oh, one of them."

"God damn you, don't you call Beecraft just one of them!"

"I only . . ."

Price released the man from his grip. He knew he was losing all control of himself. It was like the time in the house when he had begun to laugh. He knew he was cracking. He shoved the sergeant to the ground, and tears streamed down his face as he yelled frantically, "You get him out right now, or I'll kill you."

The sergeant tried to rise from the ground, but Price pointed the submachine gun at his stomach and glared at him, crying. The sergeant opened his eyes wide with horror. "I can't do that."

"You'd better, damn you."

"Why?" the sergeant pleaded.

Price noted that a group of men had gathered in the area and that some of them were making an attempt to move in. Menacingly he pointed the gun in a circle. "You keep back until I'm through," he screamed. Then turning to the sergeant, he yelled. "I want to bury him like a man should be buried and you're going to get him out for me."

"Price, for God's sake forget it." It was Regeic.

"I want him."

"Price, you've got to be calm."

"Do you like to see him there with just his head stuck out?"

"No, of course not, but you can't kill the sergeant."

"I'll kill anybody I want to!" Price screamed.

A tall doctor came running out, wiping his bloody sleeves and hands with a piece of gauze. "What the hell is going on out here?"

Price turned to the doctor, his rage subsiding. He felt weak and foolish. "I'm sorry, Doctor. I guess I just lost my head for a minute. A friend is in that stack of bodies and I wanted to bury him."

"You think you'll be all right?"

"I think so."

With that, the doctor left and the sergeant rose from the ground, his jaws puffed.

"Sorry, Sergeant," Price said.

"I understand."

Price turned and walked away. "I doubt it," he whispered, "I doubt it."

The three men walked away from the bodies and passed by the tents. Due to the heat the sides were rolled up, and they looked inside as they went by. Limbs were being removed one after another and tossed into large black barrels. Blood was everywhere.

"Sure treat 'em rough," Regeic said dryly.

"I guess they have to hurry," Price said. "There must be a lot of men out here that need attention real bad."

"How about the way they treat the dead ones?" Regeic asked.

"I guess it doesn't make any difference to them now," Price answered.

"You weren't feeling that way back there with Beecraft," Regeic said quietly.

"I wasn't thinking right. I lost my head again. If they don't get me out of this damn mess pretty soon, I'm going to lose my mind. I don't think I can stand much more of this."

"We all have the same kind of trouble," Regeic said sympathetically.

"Yeah."

They continued to walk, and Morris said nothing. Finally Price turned to him.

"Are you all right?" There was no answer. "Morris?"

"Uh?"

"I asked you if you were all right?"

"Yeah, sure."

"You've been awfully quiet."

"Can't I feel bad without you asking a lot of questions?"

"Sure you can."

"Well, then leave me alone. I just can't figure out why it had to be Beecraft that got it. Me, I wanted to get killed but it was him. Why?"

"Things just happen," Regeic said.

"It ain't right."

"No, it isn't," Price said.

The three men stopped for a moment and watched the action inside another tent. The men on the tables were being sawed, hacked, hammered, and banged. The doctors wrestled with the bodies and cursed violently as they worked.

The dead piled higher and higher and the place seemed to be full of ripped intestines, torn flesh, spurting blood, and amputated limbs. Some of the men were burned to a crisp, like bacon, some of them were horribly mutilated. Some of them screamed. Possibly the worst thing was the hissing sound that came from the men with chest wounds. The sound was rising to a crescendo, and Price felt like screaming.

"Just like a butcher shop," Regeic said.

"Damned if I hadn't rather be killed outright. I don't want to ever end up in there. I never saw anything so bad. I always thought that a doctor was like a watchmaker, precision-like work and all that."

"Did you see them drop that man on the floor?" Regeic asked.

"Just like he was an animal," Price answered. He gasped as he saw them carrying a dead man out to the pile. He had apparently died on the table, because his leg was half-amputated. The bone had already been sawed through. The dripping blood left a red trail behind the medics who were carrying him.

Price turned away. He saw the chaplain coming toward them and started to go in the opposite direction. Then he thought better of it, since he wanted to be there when they buried Beecraft.

"Been a little rough out there," the chaplain said as he walked up to the men.

"A little, sir."

"I don't believe I've met you men before. Are you new?"

"No, sir."

"I don't remember seeing you in chapel."

"No, sir," Regeic said bitterly.

Price wasn't feeling good and he didn't want to talk to the chaplain about his attendance at chapel. "Don't you have something more important to do than stand here and talk to us about going to church?"

Price remembered the talks they had been forced to listen to. The chaplain had always said that God was on our side. Time after time, he had said that God was with the Americans and that He would bring about the defeat of the Japanese. "Where was God last night, Chaplain?" Price asked.

"I'm afraid I don't understand."

"What I meant was that God wasn't on our side last night. The Japs must have said better prayers than we did, or else their God is a little better than ours."

Regeic interrupted. "Tell me, Chaplain, can't you just see our God and the Japanese God having an argument over who will get the benefit of some heavenly help?" Regeic laughed wildly.

"I'm still afraid that I don't understand what this is all about."

"He's talking about all those sermons that you preached back on the other island," Price said. "He wants to know if you have seen enough to realize that God isn't on anybody's side. He's just letting all of us crazy bastards kill ourselves off."

Regeic was still laughing. "I'm sick of all this crap about praying for divine protection. A man could pray himself sick and he wouldn't get any answer. You can stand up and shout that God is in His heaven and all is right in the world until you turn blue in the face, but it isn't true. If this is right, then I'll eat your helmet. Those men are dead, can't you see that?"

"But . . ." the chaplain sputtered.

"But hell, Chaplain," Price growled. "You talk about heaven. Well, look over there at those bodies. Look at them. They're dead as they can be. Finished. It's all over for them, there isn't anything else. They're just a bunch of nothing now. There isn't any heaven, and if there is a hell it would be a relief after this. You'd better believe that if there is a heaven those men should be there. If there is a hell, I'd rather

159

go straight there and shovel coal for the rest of my life than spend one more day out here."

"Son . . ."

"Chaplain," Morris broke in, "you say that your God is a loving and just God. If He was, He wouldn't allow this to happen. No, not if He was a loving and just God, like you say. No God would do that. I'm alive," he said, pointing his finger to his chest. "Me. I'm alive and I don't have a thing to go back to. But, if you'll look right over there, you'll see the body of a man that had everything to live for. My wife is a whore and his is a wonderful woman. Did your God care what man got killed? Hell, no. If that's what your God is like then I don't want any part of Him."

"God doesn't make wars."

"Then who does? He is supposed to look after things."

"Men make wars."

"I don't know whether that is right or not, but I do know one thing," Price said. "We'll all go to hell for having any part in this. All of us, including you."

"God works in strange ways. It isn't up to us to question Him."

"Bull shit!"

The chaplain looked quickly at the ground. The men saw this and realized that they had been a little rough with him. They were about to apologize and leave, when he spoke again. "I suppose I should apologize to you because I am a failure. I've tried to get the message across to you men, but most of you don't seem to understand. You don't know how many hours I've spent in prayer over it."

"I really feel sorry for you, Chaplain," Regeic said.

"Why?"

"Because you don't have any faith either. If you did, you could say something that would make us believe."

"I think you men should come by and see me after you've had time to rest. You're just letting your emotions run away with you."

"Go see your wounded, Chaplain."

"Will I see you men later?" the chaplain asked, as he walked away.

Price called after him. "Just stay close to the dead men. We'll be in there soon enough."

Price turned to look at a detail of men digging a long ditch. Soon they were finished, and the men started taking the bodies to the edge and throwing them in. The *thunk* that each body made was sickening.

"Why do they have to do it that way?" Morris asked.

"Too many bodies. It isn't sanitary to have them lying around. They have to get rid of them, and this is about the best way."

"There ought to be another way."

160

"Seems like there should be but I'm sure the army does all it can."

Morris interrupted. "They're getting close to Beecraft. How about us putting him in?"

Morris and Regeic lifted Beecraft's body from the others and carried him to the edge of the hole. They lowered the body as gently as they could. He was lying face up on top of the other bodies, and his eyes seemed to be pleading with them to get him out of the trench. Price stared at the body and felt his nerves start to go again. Already he had tried to kill the sergeant. Next time he might not be able to recover. He took another look at Beecraft's body and then backed away from the hole. The men were placing other bodies into the trench. As he moved backward Price thought about Anne. Beecraft had been thinking about her when he had died. Price made a mental note to tell her that she was the last thing he had thought about.

Price did not look back as he moved away from the trench. He knew that he would remember the scene for the rest of his life. It was something you could not forget easily. "I want you guys to remember something."

"What's that, Ern?" Regeic asked.

"Don't ever let them put me in a hole like that. If I get killed in the jungle just bury me and leave me there."

"I feel the same way," Regeic said.

"Me too." Morris added.

When they reached the defensive area, the scene was still one of confusion. Boats were unloading supplies, and men were running in all directions. Miles of telephone lines were being run toward the jungle and that would mean that there was some order being restored. Most of the bodies had been taken out of the water. There was still no breeze and the stench hung over the beach like a fog. It was so strong that everyone was continually aware of the odor.

When they had reached the center of the area, Price left Morris and Regeic and walked over to Higgenbotham. Together, they walked around the perimeter. Price noted with satisfaction that Higgenbotham had set up a machine gun at every third hole. Further back toward the beach, he had set up several mortars. When they had made their tour, Higgenbotham looked up with satisfaction. "Does this meet with your approval?"

"How about trip wires and grenades?"

"I have them all ready to set up as soon as it gets dark. I was afraid that some of the men coming in from the front might set them off if I put them up now."

"Then you've done everything that I would have."

"Thanks."

"Don't thank me. You did a good job and that's just what you're supposed to do. As soon as I think you can handle the job I'm going to have you doing everything. I don't think you will understand it, but I'm about done in. I'd like to rest for about ten years."

"How long have you been out here?"

"Almost since the first. We've been in on everything that the army has done."

"Was it much worse then?"

"A lot."

Higgenbotham started to talk again, but Price was concerned with the men. He cupped his hands and yelled across the area. "You guys take your shoes off and leave them off tonight."

"What the hell is that for?" Higgenbotham asked.

"Keeps your feet from rotting off." Price signaled for the medic to come over. When the medic reached him, he explained what he wanted done for the men.

Price sat on the edge of his hole and pulled his shoes off. As the first one came off, a terrible smell rose and it was almost strong enough to blot out the odor of the dead men. He tugged at his socks and they came off in pieces. Price took his bayonet and began picking at the green fungus that was growing between his toes. The pain was terrific. The fungus had a good start.

The medic moved among the men with a bottle of mild acid. "Don't scrape the fungus off," he instructed them. "I'll be by to pour some of this on."

Price picked at the fungus. Once before it had started growing in his ears. He had managed to keep it out of his ears this time, but the raw places between his toes were bad. He knew that this would sap the little strength he still had. The men who were younger, or a little less battle weary, could go on with sheer courage, but his was all used up. It had been gone for a long time. He examined the fungus again and wished that the medic would hurry back to him.

"Hey," Morris called. "I hear that we already took this island."

"Where in the name of hell did you hear that?"

"One of the men on the beach said that he heard it on the radio last night. The called it a minor action, too."

Price laughed. "We should have joined the Marines. If it had been them, there would have been a dozen movies about it already."

A man came running across the area. His helmet was bouncing on his head and his breath was coming in gasps. The men around him grabbed their weapons and slid into their holes. When he saw their reaction he stopped. "Chow, hot chow!"

"Praise God for small miracles!"

"Yeoweeee!"

"Hot chow! HOT CHOW!"

There was a mad scramble as the men rose from their

holes and ran for the chow. For the first time in two days there would be hot food: spam and dehydrated potatoes. Best of all, there was plenty of hot coffee. Men opened their mess kits as they ran, and there was a great clanking sound.

"Man, this steak is great!" somebody laughed.

"How about these French fries?"

"Good."

"How about some martinis?"

"I'd like an Old-Fashioned, please."

"Straight bourbon, here."

Fortunado, the chow runner, gulped his food down in great mouthfuls. Before every bite, he had to brush the flies out of the food. Occasionally he would spit a fly out of his mouth. "These are the best bugs I ever ate." He laughed.

"Natives raise them special. They're a specialty of the house."

"I never thought that hot coffee could be so good."

"I wish these damned flies would stop stealing my food."

"Brush 'em away."

"I tried that. One of the big bastards turned around and knocked the hell out of me."

"Yeah?"

"No kidding."

The ripping sound of a Nambu sent the men into their holes. The food was quickly forgotten as they leaped for cover.

"Japs!"

Dirt flicked around the rim of the holes and the men cursed.

"Bastards!"

"Those no-good sons of bitches made me spill my coffee."

"He musta knowed that I was eating hot food for the first time in two days."

Every weapon in the area started firing into the jungle. None of the men could see a target, but the bullets were lashing into the underbrush in every direction.

Lantrip saw a shadow move and lined up his sights. "Look," he whispered to Ruffin.

"Where?"

"There."

"I don't see anything."

"Right over there by that big tree. Right there . . . see?"

"I see him."

The Jap fired again and the dirt from the bullets showered in on top of Lantrip and Ruffin. As soon as the noise stopped, both the men rose and fired in the direction of the tree where they had seen the movement. A figure toppled in the grass.

All Ruffin could think about was that the Jap had tried to kill him. Without any regard for his own safety he jumped from the hole and raced toward the spot where the figure had fallen. I'll kill the bastard, he thought. Then he was shocked at his own thought.

There was another movement near the body and he fired at a fleeing figure. It fell.

When Ruffin reached the spot where the man had fallen, he saw that the Jap's eyes were open and seemed to be staring up at the sky. There was a large hole in his chest and he was making a hissing sound. Ruffin swung the butt of his rifle into the Jap's head with a force that almost tore it from his neck. Without stopping, he raced toward the other fallen Jap. This one was hit in the head, but he ran his bayonet into the man's chest and felt the sickening halt as it hit a rib. He forced it further into the body and then cursed. "Bastard!"

Ruffin staggered back to his hole and was wiping the bloody blade on his sleeve. Lantrip looked up, intending to congratulate him. "Edward, I . . ."

"Leave me alone."

# CHAPTER EIGHT

The platoon guarded the perimeter for two days. During this time, the colonel called back three more platoons to help them, although there never was a serious threat to the beachhead. If any Japanese soldiers had been by-passed in the advance, they had already made their way back to their lines. The men had spent most of the time bathing in the surf and sunning themselves. The beach had been entirely cleared, and all the bodies had been buried. What had been a steady stream of wounded, on the first day, dwindled down to a trickle as the fighting was very light.

While they rested, the same question ranged through the minds of the men. Where would they go from there? Once again, they knew they would have to come face to face with death. Waiting was their worst enemy. It was a soldier's life to wait. Wait for the order to move, wait for the order to stop, wait for an order to come down the endless chain of command. It could be an order to stay on the beach, or an order to go back to the front. Once they were at the front, they would have to wait for the order that would bring them back to the world of the living. Then the waiting would begin all over again.

The platoon had not lost its sense of humor and the men joked through the days. There had been a change, though. Price and the other two men could not help noticing it. They were no longer boys; they were men. Even Ruffin had changed. He was smoking cigarettes now and he sounded more like a soldier when he spoke. Lantrip, who had acted like a coward, had got himself in hand and was turning out to be a good soldier. Sterner had already developed the sureness that only combat veterans attain. Each of them had been through the invasion, they had lived through a banzai attack, and they had been under heavy artillery fire. The overconfidence was gone, and in its place was a calm assurance that they could do the job. The three veterans were satisfied that the men had come through it so well that very soon they would be a fine combat outfit.

The quietest men in the platoon were Price, Regeic and Morris. When they had been pulled back to the beach, they had been given a reprieve, but it was temporary. They all had the feeling that they would die. It was always this way when they were pulled back from the front, but this time it was different. Beecraft's death had left them with the feeling that another one of them would die, then another, until they were all dead. The biggest question in their minds was, Who would be next?

Early on the third day the colonel called Price into his dugout. The colonel unfolded his maps and carefully pointed out the hill that Baker Company was dug in on. He ordered Price to take his men to the hill and relieve the stray platoon that had joined the company. He went on to explain that there would be a general advance soon. It was to be a last push to take the island.

Price returned to the area and passed on this information to the men. They took a last bath in the pounding surf and were all sitting around on the ground waiting for Price's word to move.

The sun was blinding, as the platoon moved out from their positions on the beach. The men formed a ragged line and entered the dark jungle, following a faint supply trail. When they were about fifty yards into the jungle, it seemed to close in around them. The sweat and insects made movement a torture, but the men were in a good mood and they laughed and joked as they slogged forward.

They walked for several hours. The heat became more and more unbearable. Soon the chattering stopped and there was only the sound of the jungle. Every few minutes, some man would curse and moan about the heat. Still, they went on, each man putting one sore foot in front of the other. They fought at the insects and kept moving.

Sweat poured down Price's face and fell off the bridge of his nose. Under the heavy fatigues, the sweat was making him itch. Every minute, Price would wipe the sweat away and curse at the insects. He looked over his shoulder and spoke to Regeic. "Regeic?"

"Yeah." Regeic was puffing hard for breath.

"Do you still have anything to drink?"

"Sure."

Price felt the hot metal of the canteen as Regeic pressed it into his hand. He unscrewed the top and placed the canteen to his lips. The lukewarm beverage trickled down his throat. "This is a little strong, isn't it?"

"It's just right."

"Just right for what?" Price laughed. "Are you trying to ruin my stomach? I'll bet that this damned stuff is half alcohol."

"Just about half."

"About? Have you stopped measuring it?"

"Yes. I think I'm getting good at it. I might get a job at a whiskey factory when I retire."

Price took a long drink. "I hope I live long enough to taste good whiskey again."

Regeic's voice was full of concern. "Price—" He paused. "You're drinking a lot lately, aren't you?"

"Not as much as you."

"That's true. I couldn't argue with that. What I was getting at is that I need it to keep going. You don't. I'd hate to see you get in the same shape as me. After all, you're an officer now." Regeic laughed.

"Hell, you sound like you've joined the Temperance Union."

"I haven't. Just the same, you should take it easy."

"Do you know of a better way to get control of yourself?"

"Well, it's the way I do it, but I don't recommend it. I'm not an alcoholic yet but if I keep it up much longer I may not be able to stop."

"If I want to kill myself by drinking, let me. I need something to keep my mind off things. I can't help thinking about Sandra all the time. Worse than that, I'm so nervous that I want to run every time I hear a noise."

"A drink will make you feel better. I guess I won't lecture you about it."

"Thanks." Price handed the canteen back to Regeic.

"You're always welcome. I'll give you as a reference when I apply for that job in the whiskey factory."

The platoon continued to move down the trail. They walked until they were so tired that they walked mechanically. Price was feeling sick to his stomach and Regeic was nearly drunk. Morris saw Regeic stagger once, so he had come up to Regeic's side to try to keep him from drinking any more.

Higgenbotham also had seen Regeic stagger. He ran forward and stopped at Price's side. "Regeic is drunk."

"He has a case of malaria," Price snapped.

"Malaria, hell. He's drunk."

"I said malaria. Are you calling me a liar?"

"All right. Let's say he has malaria then. Shouldn't we send him back?"

"No," Price said firmly.

"But he can't make it. He isn't in any shape to be fighting."

"Don't think so much. I told you once that I would let you

know when you could start thinking. Until then, you let me do all the thinking for both of us."

"Dammit, you don't seem to understand," Higgenbotham said in a disgusted tone. "I know that he's drunk as a lord."

"I've said about all I intend to on the subject. You just get your ass back to the rear where you belong. I'll call you when I need you."

"But—"

"Get back there!"

Higgenbotham started to protest again but thought better of it. He shrugged his shoulders and moved back. "Bastards," he muttered.

"Did you say something to me?" Sterner asked Higgenbotham.

"No, I was thinking out loud."

"I saw you talking to the lieutenant. Is something wrong?"

"No."

"Is Regeic drunk again?"

"Malaria."

"Is that what Price told you?"

"Yes."

"You don't think so, do you?"

"I know he's drunk."

"I wouldn't want to cross Price."

"Hell, he looks like he's been drinking, too."

"If I'd been out here as long as he has I'd be drinking, too," Sterner said.

They walked on, sweating and swiping at the insects. Regeic staggered and Morris steadied him. Somewhere toward the middle of the line, Ruffin cursed at each step he took. It sounded better to Price than the continual prayers.

They had just rounded a curve in the trail when they met another group of men. It was a sight that none of them would ever forget. A long winding column of young men, old before their time, came winding down the trail. They were coming back from the lines. Their faces expressed the hunger, fright and tiredness. As they passed, Price's men looked into their gaunt faces and saw the bloodshot eyes, the beards, the dirt, the pallor that came from too much fright, and the terror that showed in their tired eyes. The look of horror in their eyes seemed to be the worst. They walked along in a dazed condition, with unlighted cigarettes dangling from their trembling lips. Some of them talked to themselves and others toyed with the filthy bandages hanging from their bodies.

The shallow-faced men passed. Their hollow eyes saw nothing. The men watching them realized that they, too, might look the same way in a few days. The scene left most of them wishing they could run back to the ocean and wash off the filth.

167

Price watched the men file past him. He felt like shouting back to his own men, "Look at them. That's what you're going to look like in a week!"

"We ain't never coming back, Ern, old buddy. We ain't never going to make it back," Regeic mumbled.

"We'll get back," Price said determinedly.

"Sure we will," Morris said.

"No, we ain't. We ain't never coming back. I know."

"I'll get you back," Morris said.

"Ain't never coming back," Regeic said, as he stumbled along.

"Everything is going to be all right," said Morris.

"No sireeee. Not one of us is ever going to get out of this mess alive."

"Yes, we will, the three of us," Price said.

"Beecraft thought that too, but he's dead."

Morris looked into Regeic's face. "I'll get you back in one piece. I promise."

"You promise?"

"That's right."

"Good old Morris. Good old Price. The three musketeers. Or is it the three blind mice? Oh well, no matter. You two men are going to get me back. I'll bet the Japs don't know that. Right now, there's a Jap out there waiting for me. He's got a bullet with a name on it. It's my name. They've got one for both of you. One says Regeic, one says Morris, and one says Price. He has a pocketful of bullets marked General Delivery too, just in case he loses one of ours."

"Regeic, you've got to stop that. You'll have the whole platoon panicked. They look up to you because you're a veteran. If you go to pieces, they may get scared."

"Got to get control. Yes, I've got to. Okay, Price, I'll try."

"No more drinks."

"All right, Price."

Price walked a few more steps, and then he realized that he would have to rest. The heat was more than he could stand. He felt as though he were inside an oven. He held up his hand and halted the platoon. Then he sat by the side of the trail. He eased his pack off his shoulders and leaned back.

"Are you feeling any better?" he asked Regeic.

"Sure, sure."

"Can you make it the rest of the way?"

"I can make it anywhere you want me to go, Ern."

"I hope you make it. If the drinks last, you should be all right," Price laughed. "What the hell are you going to do when it's all gone?"

"I'll just get me some more."

"There ain't no more."

"I'll be dead by that time, anyway."

"You'll live to be a hundred." Price laughed.

"Look, Ern, there ain't none of us going to live that long. None of us."

Price laughed again. "I think I might. I want to live just long enough to tell Sandra what a horse's ass I think she is."

"I'd like to get back so I could tell Roberta the same thing," Morris commented.

"Maybe we ought to go tell them together." Price laughed.

"You're just two sad bastards," Regeic said. "I never let a woman screw up my life for me. I used to envy you married men but now I know that either way isn't worth a damn. Unless you marry a really different kind of woman, you're damned if you do, and damned if you don't. Ain't that hell?"

Price winked at Morris. "Regeic, you should have been a head doctor. You're the only man I ever heard of even trying to figure women out."

"Me? Hell no. I'm no damn good either. Right now, that girl down in Texas has my kid. I got her pregnant and then left her. That's a laugh, isn't it? Me, a father. Makes me feel real funny when I think about having a kid that's mine." Regeic paused and looked at the other two men. "You think I should have married her, don't you?"

"Of course not," Price answered.

"Yes, you do. I can tell by looking at you."

"No, we don't think that," Price answered.

"Well, I do," he insisted. "If I ever get out of this damn mess I might just do that. It ain't right for a man to let his kid grow up and be a bastard. It just ain't right. I've been thinking about it a lot, and if I ever get back I think I'll marry her. I could write, but I ain't sure of the address. I ain't sure where my own kid is, ain't that a laugh?"

"Did you ever wonder," Price asked, "why we always end up talking about women?"

"That's easy," Morris laughed. "That's the thing that we got the least of. If we didn't have any mosquitoes, we'd probably bitch because there weren't any here. Right now, I'll bet every G.I. in Alaska is bitching because there's no heat. You know what they say—a soldier isn't happy if he isn't bitching."

Sterner pulled his crooked pipe from his pack. He had just remembered it and thought he would enjoy it more than a cigarette. He filled it with tobacco and walked over to Lantrip and Ruffin. The two men were resting with their backs against a tree. "How are you two making it?"

"Fine. How about you, Teach?"

"I don't think I ever saw it so hot. Not even in Texas."

Lantrip rubbed his hands along the inside of his legs. "This heat has got some kind of rash breaking out on me. I can hardly walk."

"I'm getting a rash too," Ruffin said painfully.

"The South Pacific isn't any place for a white man to end up. It wasn't made for white men." Sterner puffed on his pipe. "The funny thing about this part of the world is that I always wanted to come out here. I had heard about some of these islands and had them pictured as a tropical paradise. Now I wish to hell they had sent me to Alaska."

"Man, I could use some of that, too," Lantrip laughed.

Ruffin had his canteen out and unscrewed the top. He took a long drink, and some of the water dripped down his chest. "I don't know about Alaska, but I wonder what it's like where we're going. Those troops that we passed a while ago looked like a walking nightmare."

"They sure looked like they went through hell," Lantrip said.

Ruffin put the canteen back in its canvas pouch and looked around at the other two men. "Have either one of you got a cigarette?"

Sterner took his pipe out of his mouth and looked directly at Ruffin. "When the hell did you start smoking?"

"He started the other night." Lantrip laughed.

"No!" Sterner laughed with mock amazement.

"Sure he did. The Deacon, here, has lost some of that religion."

"How about one of you giving me a smoke? We can discuss me and my moral life after I've got it lit."

Lantrip took a package of sweat-soaked cigarettes from his pocket and passed them to Ruffin. "Here. Don't let it ever be said that old Lantrip didn't do his part to corrupt the morals of a real churchgoing man."

"It's not you that's corrupting me, it's this damn war," Ruffin said. "I'd sure hate to end up like Price and Regeic."

"Me too."

"Don't misunderstand me. I'd give a lot to be like them in some ways. They're still more man than I'll ever be. The only thing is, they could all three be a lot happier if they had something more in their lives."

Fortunado came walking over to the men. "Are you talking about the three bastards?"

"If you mean Price, Regeic and Morris, we are," Sterner said.

"That's them. The three grim bastards."

"Price acts tough, and he is," said Sterner. "But that's his business. He's a professional soldier, and he gets paid for being able to kill Japs. Look at all the trouble he went to when he was training us. He did it because it was his job, but I'm sure that he wanted as many of us to get back as he could. They may be rougher than hell on us, but I'd rather be with them, especially Price, than against them."

"I'm not so sure I like being with him," Fortunado said.

"Me, neither," Lantrip said.

"You've got to look at it this way," Sterner said. "I don't

170

like the way he treats us any better than the rest of you. He's old army, all the way. He was an old army sergeant. That's why he acts more like a sergeant than an officer. He grew up under the theory that you rode a man until you got the most out of him, and then, when you got it, you left him alone."

"He rides us for sure." Fortunado laughed.

"In those days," Sterner spoke quietly, "the army was different. The men were taught to be rough, and Congress didn't care how the men were treated. There wasn't anything democratic, but when the time came, they knew how to fight. They did a damn good job out here, but there weren't enough of them."

"I wish there were a lot more of them, and a lot less of me." Fortunado laughed.

"Actually," Sterner said, "I imagine that he would be a hell of a swell guy if he wasn't in the army. If he worked half as hard at a civilian job as he does at the army, he would be a millionaire."

"It doesn't make any difference to me, I still don't like the way he treats us. He acts like he thinks we're a bunch of kids."

"That's what we probably seem like to him," Sterner said.

When they had waited as long as Price thought they could, he signaled the men, and they rose to their feet and started forward. Immediately, the sweat started flowing and the coarse material of their fatigues started rubbing them raw. The straps of their weapons cut deep into their shoulders, and the heat rushed up through the soles of their shoes.

They had walked for about thirty minutes when Price heard the metallic sound of a bolt being released. Then he realized that he had forgotten the sign and countersign.

"Landlubber," a voice called from behind a clump of bushes.

"Hold it a minute, we're your relief."

"Give the countersign."

"I forgot it."

"Just a minute. Don't move." Price could hear a conversation in back of the bushes and then a short man came out. He looked as though he had not slept for a long time.

"Are you our replacements?"

"Yeah."

"You must be Price."

"That's right."

The little man extended his hand. "I'm Lieutenant Collins. The captain wants you to have a look at the hill in front of us before you take over from me. If you can hold it, send a runner back and he will bring up the company."

"What hill?" Price said.

"You can see it from our position. It's almost in front of our hill."

"Damn," Price cursed. "We just walked from the beach. I'm not sure I have enough energy to get over there."

"It'll only take you another hour."

"Thanks."

"You'll have to get started pretty soon."

"Christ."

"Just try and get me relieved before night. I'd like to get some sleep."

Price did not speak to the lieutenant. He called up Morris, Regeic and Higgenbotham and explained their mission. Although he had not seen the hill, he planned to go right to it.

Price let the platoon take a thirty-minute break, and then he signaled them to their feet. He explained to them that they were to proceed to the hill and see if it was in enemy hands. If it was not, they were going to occupy it. If it was, they were either to take it, or find out how large the enemy force was. The men cursed.

Price turned to Lieutenant Collins and asked him to accompany them to the edge of his perimeter and point out the hill. The lieutenant agreed.

"Has there been much activity lately?" Price asked.

"We haven't even heard a Jap in the last twenty-four hours. My guess is that they've pulled back. The captain thinks so too."

The platoon proceeded through the area and then halted at the edge of the small hill. Lieutenant Collins explained that the rest of the company was deployed on two more hills, one platoon on each. He pointed out the hill that was directly in front of them and it was clear to Price why the company commander had wanted to take up a position on the hill. His map showed that the country flattened out on the other side of it. When the advance started, the Japs would be in a position to put up a stiff defense from it.

Price thanked the other officer and began to move forward. His senses were alert to any slight foreign sign or sound. The platoon inched forward in a long line until the hill was right in front of them. Price signaled them to take cover until he could get the lay of the land.

Regeic came up to Price and started grumbling. "I don't see why the captain couldn't have used some of his own men for this. For all we know, the Japs have cut us off from the company already."

Price was looking through his field glasses and surveying the side of the hill. "Take a look and see what you can make out."

Regeic took the glasses and looked at the terrain in front of him. "I don't see a thing moving in there."

Price studied the hill for a long moment before he spoke. "Look, you take two of the squads and stay here. I'm going to take the other one and go on ahead. If I get into any trouble, you try to flank them."

"All right. How about taking Higgenbotham with you?"

Price did not answer. Instead, he caught Higgenbotham's attention and signaled him forward. When Higgenbotham was crouching beside him, Price explained the plan.

Price picked out Morris' squad to take with him, and they cautiously worked their way up the hill, making use of all available cover. Their weapons were held at ready. Slowly, they made their way up the hill, examining each bush. A strange quiet filled the atmosphere. Finally, they were at the top of the hill and there was no evidence of any Japanese.

Price squatted on his haunches and called Morris to him. Then he noticed the footprint in the soft sand. It was from a Japanese shoe. Price rubbed the stubble on his face with the back of his hand and pointed it out to Morris, who had just come up.

"It was probably made by a Japanese patrol," Morris said.

"I hope so. Let's get on down to the bottom of the hill and see if it's clear before we send for the rest of the company."

The thirteen men made their way to the bottom of the hill. They still had not seen any sign of the Japanese. Less cautiously, they climbed back to the top for one more look. When they reached it, Price ordered a rest. He was about to send for the other two squads, and then let a runner go after the rest of the company, when he saw a movement to his right, about halfway down the hill.

Morris had seen it and nudged Price. "Look down there."

"Take cover," Price whispered.

Price made a dash for cover and tried to burrow into the ground. His breath was coming in gasps and his heart was pounding.

It was clear that the Japanese had seen them and they were deploying in the brush. Apparently there were about twenty of them and they thought they had the Americans outnumbered. Slowly, Price pushed the barrel of his submachine gun in that direction. Then he placed three grenades in front of him.

Higgenbotham had apparently not seen the Japanese and he peered over the top of a large bush. Morris yelled at him and a hail of bullets went flying into the area. Higgenbotham made his way to a rise in the ground, but Gardner, the man who was with him, let out a yelp and clutched his arm. Morris jumped up and made his way to Gardner. He hit the ground, and with bullets raining around him, he dragged the man to safety.

Morris bent over Gardner and ripped his fatigue sleeve with his knife until the wound was visible. Morris poured sulfa on the ugly wound, while Gardner gritted his teeth, his face twisting out of shape with the pain. Then he began to curse the Japs. Morris only smiled grimly when Gardner began cursing him, and he went right on with the bandaging.

The Japanese were fanning out in a great semicircle now, and Price's position was growing worse. He wanted to send for Regeic, but he knew that Regeic would undoubtedly hear the firing and come up very quickly anyway. Price could not retreat because the cover was too poor and, besides, they had a wounded man with them.

Price did not want to fire until he knew he would hit the Japanese. The rest of the men waited for his signal. The Japanese fire continued to hail around them, and it was now coming from both sides. Price realized that he could not wait much longer. Slowly he raised his weapon and began to pour fire into the brush where he thought the Japanese were. The others raised their heads long enough to fire their weapons.

Price saw a Jap raise his head and sent a flurry of shots toward him. Dirt kicked in the man's face and he disappeared into the low undergrowth. He was not sure he had hit the Jap and he cursed. Then a Jap ran from the protection of a bush and started for another one. Price fired again and the Jap fell in the road.

He was about to fire again when he saw an American helmet to his right. It must be Regeic. Frantically he called for the men to cease fire.

Suddenly there was a dull thud, and then another one. It was American hand grenades. Then there was the unmistakable explosion of M-1's. It was Regeic. Several Japanese soldiers ran out of the brush and into Price's line of fire. He made them drop with a short burst. Then there was a series of popping noises from the Japanese rifles, which was followed by more grenades.

Suddenly there was a strange quiet, followed by a scream and then a shot. The quiet continued. Then Regeic appeared about twenty yards in front of Price. He stood up and grinned.

There had been twenty-one Japanese soldiers. All of them were dead, except for one who lay wounded on the ground. Higgenbotham killed him, much to Price's surprise.

Morris walked over to Price and sat down. "Do you want me to send somebody after the rest of the company?"

"Not yet," Price answered. Then he turned toward Regeic. "Get the men spread out just below the top of the hill. The Japanese may have a lot more men near here and they may want this hill bad enough to take it back."

"Sure thing," Regeic answered, and then walked away.

Higgenbotham walked over to Price. There was a smile on his face. "I killed him." His look indicated that he was proud of his accomplishment.

"That was the right thing to do," Price said in a low voice, "but you don't have to be so damn proud. Killing a wounded man isn't the hardest thing to do."

"He wasn't hit too bad," Higgenbotham answered.

"You mean he would have lived?"

"I think so."

Price looked at Higgenbotham angrily. "Then you're a bigger fool than I ever thought you were. He might have been able to give Intelligence some good information."

"But I didn't think . . ."

"You're damn right you didn't think," Price yelled at the man. "Did you search him?"

"No."

"Then I'd suggest that you get the hell back over there and see if he has any papers on him."

"I'll go right now." Higgenbotham turned and walked toward the body.

"Price," Regeic called.

"What is it?" Price answered.

"Come up here, quick." There was urgency in Regeic's voice.

Price scrambled up the slope until he reached Regeic. Regeic was pointing to the base of the hill. There was a nervous look on his face.

The Japanese were advancing toward the hill. There were almost two hundred of them. They were marching in loose order, which indicated that they did not know their patrol had been wiped out.

"I guess we'll have to pull out," Price said to Regeic.

"Looks that way."

Ruffin glanced at Price. "You mean retreat?"

"I'm afraid so."

"You mean we did all this for nothing?"

"You'll get used to it," Regeic said bitterly. "Nothing you do in this war makes any sense anyway. You take a place, you give it back. It's all in a day's work."

"Hell of a day's work, I'd say."

"Well, it has one advantage," Regeic said.

"What's that?"

"It all counts toward twenty years."

"No, thanks, I don't think I'll stay that long."

"None of us may," Regeic said.

The Japanese were almost at the bottom of the hill and were milling around.

"Well, are you going to try and hold them?" Regeic asked.

"I don't know whether we can hold them or not. Matter of fact, I know we can't. You take a squad down to the bottom of the hill. When they come up the hill, we'll hit them as hard as we can and then come down the hill. As soon as we've cleared the top of the hill, start shooting at the crest as hard as you can. That should keep them ducking long enough for us to get down."

"Can I take Morris?"

"No, I'll get you another squad. I want him here with me."

"I'll take the squad, then, and get going. They'll be up here

175

pretty soon." Regeic disappeared and then started down the hill with a squad.

Price explained his plan to the rest of the men and placed them so they could remain hidden until the Japs were almost on top of them.

Price returned to his station and waited for the Japs. They were coming up the hill in little groups and appeared not to know that there were any Americans on the hill. Price waited until they were thirty yards from the crest of the hill and then he opened fire. The sudden burst of fire was withering and the Japs fell to the ground in clusters. The others stood for a moment and then ran to the rear in confusion.

Price barely had time to reload before the Japanese attack got under way. The Jap machine guns started hammering away and the air was thick with bullets. The figures started snaking their way up the hill and Price lined up the closest one in his sights. He fired, and the man went down. Then he swept the area with a long burst that emptied the clip.

The trunk of a small tree snapped as if it were a matchstick, and a man screamed. A bullet whizzed past Price and he tried to keep closer to the ground.

Price gave the signal when the Japs were about twenty-five yards from them, and the men began a wild flight down the hill. Gardner was in the lead and his arm seemed to give him little trouble.

They trudged into the perimeter, and Price found his way to the lieutenant. He was standing in a deep hole and smiled as Price approached. "Very many of them out there?"

"A good many."

"The old man wants to talk to you," Lieutenant Collins said, as he handed the field phone to Price.

"This is Price," he said as he took the receiver.

"Captain Nuggent," Price heard.

"Did you want me?"

"What happened out there?"

"We got a patrol of about twenty men, but they brought up what I would count as two hundred men. We shot them up real bad, but couldn't hold the hill. I'd say that they're either going to attack us, or hold the hill."

"I doubt if they'll attack. You tell Collins to go on back and take over his positions. I'll call you later."

"Okay."

Price turned to the lieutenant. "If you're ready, you can take your men and go on back. I'm not happy out here without any cover."

The other man did not speak. He crawled out of his hole. He gave a signal and the rest of his men followed. Silently they disappeared down the trail and out of view.

Price's men fell into the holes that the other men had vacated. Regeic crawled into the same hole with Price, and the

176

two men surveyed the perimeter. The hill had a long descent into the valley below, and firing lanes had been cleared. On the left, there was a straight drop of about twenty feet. The hill had been well chosen as a perfect defensive position. The Japs could attack them from only three sides and, to get at them from the right, they would have to break through another platoon.

The foxholes were dug in a rectangular form with machine guns guarding every approach. Ponchos had been hung over each of the holes to give protection from the sun and rain. Boxes were piled everywhere. Boxes of ammunition, flares and ten-in-one rations were stacked in the deep holes. Price estimated that there was enough matériel for months.

With a suddenness that is natural to the South Pacific, rain began pouring down in great sheets. It came so quickly that everyone was drenched. Price scrambled for his poncho, but was wringing wet by the time he found it. "Wouldn't you know," he said bitterly.

"Just had to rain," Regeic laughed.

"At least it'll make it cooler," Price commented.

"It'll make it wetter too."

Price slipped out of his hole and walked around the perimeter. He pulled his poncho up around his shoulders in an attempt to keep dry, but the rain poured in anyway.

"Lieutenant," Fortunado called.

Price turned toward the voice and tried to control his anger. "What the hell are you trying to do, get me killed?" he yelled at the man.

Price meant to go on, but suddenly his neck was wrenched back with a terrible force. There was a loud ringing in his ears. He felt his helmet leave his head and he fell backward, landing on his back with a splash.

Dazed, he sat up on the ground. "Shit!"

Price cast a quick look around, but all he could see was the protruding rump of the man next to him. He realized that a sniper must have hit him.

"Are you all right?" he heard Regeic ask.

"I . . . I think so."

Regeic handed Price his helmet. He turned it around in his hand and examined the dent in the side. He ran his finger around the dent. "Christ, that was close." He whistled. His jaw began to jump and he looked around. "Don't just sit there, damn your souls, shoot!"

A second of quiet followed. Then a weapon fired, and then another, until there was a continuous roar. Price jumped from his position and ran for his hole. He landed in it with a splash. Regeic followed.

"Are you all right?" Morris called.

"Yeah, I'm afraid so."

Price yelled, "Cease fire." The firing slowed down and then stopped altogether.

"That bastard Fortunado damn near got me killed," he said.

"You want me to knock the hell out of him for you?"

"I may do it myself."

Fortunado raised his head above the rim of the foxhole. He was afraid he might see a Japanese officer swinging a saber and leading a charge. The fear was so intense that he was oblivious to the rain as it beat down into his face. To his relief, he saw that there was nothing in front of him except rain. Water was dripping from the trees and dropping into great puddles on the ground.

Then he looked to one side. He spoke to Bledsoe, who was beside him. "Quiet, isn't it." There was no answer. "Bledsoe? Bledsoe? What's the matter? Have you already gone to sleep? Bledsoe?"

Fortunado turned to the man at his side and shook him. Bledsoe toppled forward and fell to the ground, face down. He was dead. Fortunado stood looking at the body, disbelief on his face. He was killed right in the hole with me, he thought, and I didn't even know it. Blood was oozing from a large hole squarely in the middle of Bledsoe's back. Fortunado looked up. "Higgenbotham, Higgenbotham!"

"What's the matter?"

Fortunado was conscious that his voice was very high. "He's dead."

"Who?"

"Bledsoe."

"Just keep calm, I'm coming over."


Price heard the conversation and climbed out of his wet hole. He slipped through the mud to Fortunado's hole. The sniper's rifle cracked again. One of the machine guns lashed out at the unseen target.

Price ducked and called to the men. "Duck every time he shoots. If he thinks he's close, he won't change his sights."

Higgenbotham already had Lantrip and Fortunado digging a shallow grave for Bledsoe. Price waded through the mud until he reached the hole and then knelt beside the men. He motioned for the two closest men to get the body out. When they had the body out, he began to go through his pockets.

The sniper fired again and the men ducked as the bullet droned past them.

Price laid out Bledsoe's articles on a poncho, and the rain continued to splash down. The rain reminded Price of movies he had seen. In them, funerals always seemed to be in the rain. Two letters addressed to Pfc. Charles J. Bledsoe were the first items that he removed from the man's pocket. The letters were rumpled and worn from many readings. For the first time, Price realized that the man had possessed a first name. He could not ever remember having heard it, but that made it easier to take. Next, he removed a pocketknife, which was rusted. A package of toilet paper, some prophylactics, and some change were the other items. He searched the other pockets and found a picture of a woman and a baby.

"Was he married?" Price asked Regeic.

The sniper fired again and they ducked.

"Beats the hell out of me," Regeic answered.

Price turned to Higgenbotham. "Was he married?"

"Yes."

"All right then, I'll keep this stuff and we can send it to his wife. I think she'll want it." A flood of sadness came over Price as he thought about the man's wife. She would be heartbroken when she got the telegram. He put the prophylactics in his pocket and then wrapped the other things in a handkerchief. He removed the man's dog tags and placed them in his own pocket. Then he let the men lower him into the grave they had dug.

The sniper fired again and the men almost dropped the body.

As they walked back to the hole, Price laughed. "I wish to hell that sniper would fall out of his tree."

"Me too."

They climbed back into the hole and were glad to be back where the sniper could not hit them. Regeic took the canteen and started to drink. He handed it to Price, who took a large gulp. When he handed the canteen back to Regeic, Price smiled. "Try and stay sober. We had to carry you halfway here."

"I'll try."

Price held out his hand. "On second thought, you let me keep that thing for you."

"Ern," Regeic pleaded.

"Let me have the canteen," Price commanded.

"I'm all right," Regeic insisted.

"If I have anything to do with it, you'll stay that way, too. Let me have it."

"Ah, Ern."

"Give it here," Price demanded.

Regeic slowly handed the canteen to Price and laughed in low tones. "I guess I will stay sober at that."

"I'll give you more than your share."

"Sure you will. I'll be lucky if you don't drink it all yourself."

The sky became light again, and the rain stopped just as the sun was setting. Even without the bright sunshine, the water turned to steam and the heat waves began to rise. The night was very still, but there was a slight breeze. The moon rose fast, and Price watched as it cast its golden beams across the wet foliage. They all were alert for a Jap attack, but about midnight Price decided they could sleep. He

179

left two men to stand guard and told the rest of them to try and sleep.

Morning came, and as usual the sleepy men were reluctant to poke their heads above the rims of their holes. A day's growth of beard was on their faces. Bayonets were used to pry off the tops of some cans and soon the men were enjoying some food. The wax paper from the wrappers drifted slowly across the area. After the meal, the men made cold coffee and sat drinking it and enjoying a smoke.

"These men are getting good," Price commented. "I never thought they would make soldiers, but they are. I think we may have been a little hard on them."

A patrol was sent out that afternoon, but nothing was seen. Price phoned the CP, which reported that there had been no activity all along the front. The rest of the afternoon was spent adjusting the ponchos and digging ditches around them to catch any water that might collect if it rained again.

Later, in the bright moonlight, Price was standing guard. He glanced around, feeling exposed and naked. As he peered over the top of the hole, he realized that the moonlight might be outlining him against the dark background of the sky and he would be a perfect target for an infiltrating Jap. The darkness was filled with silence, and seemed like a wall around Price. He strained to hear, wondering if he had suddenly become deaf. As he strained, he became aware of the ticking of his wrist watch. He breathed a sigh of relief. The sound of the regular breathing of the others came to his ears, and he wondered if he was the only man awake.

Price closed his eyes and tried to remember Sandra. He held his eyes tight shut and tried to think about how she had looked. He imagined she would be asleep now and looking like a kitten.

Her hair was tousled as she stood at the door, answering his ring. She was wearing a light brown negligee, all lace at the top. It was thin and transparent and had a bow on the bodice. Her body looked very soft as she stood in the semi-darkness of the hall. She was still more asleep than awake and she looked at him as though he were a ghost.

"Can I come in?" Price asked.

"Of course, Ern," Sandra answered.

They walked over to the green couch that was designed to look like a Victorian piece and sat down. "Sandra," Price said earnestly, "do you think we could get married again? It's all I have thought about out there. It's the only thing that keeps me going. I need you."

"Ern," she said, placing her hand on his face and tracing the outline of his eyebrow, "I'm sorry about the way I've treated you."

"You mean that we can do it?"

180

"Would you have Buck and me back again after all that's happened?"

"I told you, I need you."

"Do you still love me?" Sandra asked.

Price took her in his arms and kissed her for a long moment. "I've always loved you, Sandra. I always will."

"But I've treated you so mean."

"I still love you."

"And I love you too." She kissed him passionately and caressed his ear.

"You don't know how long I've waited to hear you say that."

"I wanted to," she answered. "The time you came by to see Buck, you don't have any idea how much I wanted you to kiss me."

"I didn't think you did."

"You should have done it anyway. Things might have worked out for us right then."

"Let's get married again right away," Price whispered.

"It's too late. We'll have to wait for two days anyway."

"I don't want to wait."

"We'll have to. Can you stay out at Maxwell so my folks won't know you're here?"

"Why?"

"Because I don't want to hurt them. I couldn't."

"That was one of our biggest problems. Can't you live your own life?"

"After we're married again. I promise that it won't be the same way after we get married. It's just that they've been so nice to me and Buck that I hate to tell them. Let's get married first."

"We can go to Mississippi and get married tonight."

"Please, Ern."

"Sandra, please. I don't want to wait. I've been out in the jungle for over a year thinking about getting you back. You just can't let me wait for two days."

"I'll have to change."

"No you don't," Price said. He took her in his arms and bent her backwards until she was lying down. His hands found her breasts and she moaned as he fitted his body to hers. Just then, someone was pulling at his shoulder.

"Get away from me, you bastard." He snapped open his eyes and was staring into Regeic's face.

"Ern, you were asleep."

"Just resting my eyes."

"Like hell."

"All right, I was asleep and I was about to have a wet dream. You would have to go and wake me up."

"If you don't stop dreaming while you're supposed to be on guard, you may never live long enough to have it."

181

"That's for sure. Do you feel like relieving me for a little?"

"Sure, Ern. Has everything been quiet?"

"Haven't heard anything at all."

"You get yourself some sleep then."

Price curled up in the bottom of the hole and was asleep immediately. He knew it was a dream and he kept telling himself to stop, but it continued as if it were something apart from him. He watched it as he would a movie. The only difference was that it involved his emotions.

This time, Sandra was standing in her living room. She was dressed in a black skirt that had little gold flakes in it. She had on a large metal belt, with a gold medallion hanging from it. Her blouse was light gold, so light that it was almost white. It fitted her large breasts snugly. Her light brown hair was brushed straight back. The light gave it almost the same color as her tanned skin. She stood in front of him, looking at him with disdain.

Price was sitting on the floor with Buck. He had taken all the change from his pocket and given it to the boy. Buck looked very healthy. Price kept trying to get him to play, but Buck did not seem to like him.

Buck stood in front of his father and placed the change in his pockets. Price laughed nervously and said, "Just like his mother."

"He already knows what money is for," she said proudly.

Price turned from her stern gaze and looked at his son. "Do you want to keep Daddy's money?"

Buck turned his large blue eyes toward his father and nodded.

Sandra coached her son, and he said thank you. Buck then ran to show the money to his grandmother. Sandra turned to Price. "Don't you think you've been here long enough?"

Price rose and walked over to her. He placed a hand on each side of her face and kissed her. She struggled and finally drew away.

"I don't think you have the right to kiss me any more," Sandra said.

"I did once."

"Ernest, can't you get it through your damned head that it's all over between us? I don't love you any more now than I did when we were married."

"I love you. Can't you understand that?"

"No," she answered firmly.

"Sandra," he said haltingly, "I don't know how to make you understand, but I've thought about having you back for a long time. All during the war, my only thought was to come back to you. It was the thing that kept me going. If it hadn't been for wanting you so bad, I'd of given up a long time ago."

182

"I can't help that. I wrote to you and told you to forget about it."

"I didn't believe you. I still don't. You have to love me, you have to."

"What am I going to have to tell you to make you understand?"

"I don't know. What am *I* going to have to tell you to make *you* understand? I still love you. Can't you understand? We've got to grow up before Buck does. This isn't the right way for him to grow up."

"I'm a good mother," she said flatly.

"Sandra," he pleaded, "I'm not stupid. I've seen a lot of the world and the things that go with it. Don't you know that every man considers a divorcée as fair game? They all try to get to a divorced woman because they know she needs tenderness and love."

"I don't appreciate that, Ern."

"It's true."

"I think I'm going to get Daddy in here."

"What's he going to do?" Price said angrily. "Chase me away?"

"Look, for once and for all. It's over. I'll never marry you again and that's final. Now I think you'd better leave."

Just like all the other dreams, Price saw himself in the sweat-soaked fatigues. "Then you tell Buck why I came out here and got killed," he screamed over and over.

"Are you all right?" Regeic said.

"Yeah."

"Dreaming about Sandra again?"

"Again," Price said disgustedly.

"I wondered when it would start again. I thought that the nurse might help, but you still love Sandra, don't you?"

"Yeah. Do you have anything left to drink?"

"You took it."

"Oh, yeah." Price bent over and felt for the canteen in the bottom of the hole. At last he found it and shook the canteen to see how much was left. "Just about two drinks," he said. Price handed the canteen to Regeic and watched as the other man took a long drink. He gave it back, and Price drained it.

"I sure wish we had some more," Regeic commented.

"It would go good right now."

Regeic leaned heavily against the side of the foxhole. "Ern, did you ever feel like you'd swallowed a glassful of vinegar?" He scratched the side of his face and frowned. "My stomach is all fouled up. My mouth tastes just like I swallowed a lot of vinegar."

"That's from being afraid all the time. I get the same way."

"It'll be over soon . . . one way or the other," Regeic told Price. "It makes a man think. That girl from Klondike, sometimes I want to go back there and marry her. Every time I think about it, I get a funny feeling in my stomach. I just can't really seem to realize that I'm a father. I wonder if I could be a good husband now?"

"I'd be a poor man to comment on that. I couldn't make a go of my marriage."

"Sandra was a bitch."

"I wasn't good enough for her, that's all."

"That ain't right. She was a no-good bitch. Haven't you noticed that all the married men feel the same way? After a while out here, they all get that feeling. That they aren't good enough for their wives. I don't know what makes them do it, but they all get that way. You're just feeling the same way."

"I guess that might be right."

"Then don't say that it was your fault. You did everything that a man could."

"If she'll have me, I'm going to marry her again."

"You know she won't. You're just going to get hurt again."

"I couldn't get hurt much worse than I am right now," Price said quietly.

"I don't know about that. Look at the way Morris got clobbered by that bitch of a wife he has."

"That was rough. I don't feel much better. I keep feeling like Sandra is in bed with some man too. Every time I think about it, I want to get sick. We may be divorced, but I don't like the idea of anyone sleeping with her. I think I would kill the bastard if I caught him with her. Just the same, I know that she must be having some men. Every divorced woman I ever knew was an easy mark if you went about it right."

"True."

A sound drifted through the night. It sounded as if something was being dragged across the ground and it seemed as loud as a clap of thunder. Electric energy seemed to flash through the two men's bodies and they strained their ears to hear it again. The quiet returned like a blanket which seemed to envelop them. Price picked up a small stone and tossed it into the hole that Morris was sleeping in. Instantly, Morris poked his head over the rim of the hole. The noise came again.

Price leaned forward in an effort to hear the sound, but thirty minutes ticked by and it did not come again. Price's nerves tingled and his ears were alert for the sound. He knew that patience was the best weapon the Japanese had. If they were out there, they would take hours to get into position. He would have to try to beat them at their own game and wait. As usual, the silence seemed to be louder than noise.

"Watch the rear," Price whispered to Morris.

"Check," came Morris' reply, so low that it could barely be heard.

Once again, Price heard the noise. This time he thought it

was clothing being scraped against a bush. The others must have heard it too because their breathing had changed and heads were beginning to appear above the rims of the foxholes. In the distance, possibly a mile away, the ripping sound of a machine gun broke the silence. Then there was another burst of barely audible fire. A flare burst in the distance. It was in the direction of the machine gun that he had heard before. It was in Charlie Company's area.

There was a muffled ringing sound as the field phone jangled. Price picked up the receiver. "Baker one," Price whispered.

A panic-stricken voice crackled. "Charlie Company is under heavy attack. There must be a thousand of them." There was a crackling sound and the line went dead.

Price cradled the phone and glanced to his right. More flares were rising in the air. The roar of the weapons indicated that the fighting was fierce. From his position, the flares seemed like matches being lit in a large room, illuminating only a small area for a moment and then going out.

The hand grenades that the Japanese used were primitive weapons. They had a cap that had to be struck on some hard object before they were aimed. The *thunk* that Price heard was the familiar sound of a Japanese grenade being hit against a helmet. "Grenade," he yelled. As he ducked, he heard the *thunk* of a flare being shoved into the barrel of a mortar. Just before the flare burst, there was a blinding explosion and showers of steel went over their heads.

There was a heavy, coarse gasp just before the flare burst. Out of the corner of his eye, Price saw a man on the ground, flopping just like a chicken that had had its neck wrung. The entire bottom half of his body was shredded and the man was rolling on the ground and screaming. A head appeared from the hole next to the man and then disappeared. All Price could see was a hand clutching at the earth. The fingers tightened and then disappeared.

The hillside became bathed in the eerie light of the flare and Price looked down his sights for a target, but the hill was deserted. The man on the ground was still groaning, his eyes rolling in their sockets and his body twitching. He gasped again and then his jaw clamped shut with a clicking sound that filled the area.

Another flare burst and bathed the area in light. Price looked intently over every inch of the hill, but he could not see any movement. "Throw grenades into the trees," Price whispered.

Price picked up a grenade and pulled the pin. He arched his arm and threw it high into the air. Then he reached for another and repeated the process. The explosions shattered the trees and lashed out in fury, shaking the ground. After he had thrown four grenades, Price picked up his weapon and emptied a clip into the brush. As Price fired, he was aware of the jarring of the thirty-caliber machine guns on either side of him. Others were emptying clips into the trees and the BAR was being fired in evenly spaced bursts.

"Cease firing!" When they had stopped firing, Price listened for the cries of the wounded, but he heard nothing. Either the heavy firing had done no damage, or all the Japanese had been killed. The only sound that Price could hear was the heavy breathing of the men around him. The firing in Charlie Company continued, and more flares burst. Then the firing started on the left flank, but it, too, was in the distance. The firing became heavier on both flanks.

The Japanese must be there, Price thought with rising horror. They're attacking all the other positions. He listened again, but he could not hear any sound in front of his position. Then he heard someone shout, "Grenade," and he ducked.

From somewhere in the brush, a hail of grenades came sputtering into the area, and they landed with a thud. Price looked up. He could see the red sputtering of the fuses as they arched in the air. Then, the area was ripped with explosions.

A grenade landed in the hole with Price and Regeic. Regeic screamed and jumped from the hole with Price right after him. They both flattened themselves on the ground just as the burst came. The noise was deafening and their ears rang from the concussion. A hail of bullets peppered the area as they leaped for their hole again.

A flare burst in the air. Price remained crouched in the bottom of the hole. Guns were firing from all over the area and the noise was so loud that Price thought they were right over his hole. He was filled with apprehension and he had the feeling that he was going to die.

Somewhere in the area, a Japanese machine gun was firing. It sent showers of sand and sparks into the hole. Price reasoned that the Japanese were using the machine gun to keep them in their holes until the Japanese soldiers could get close. Price wished he had the old platoon with him. They would have known what to do and these men might not. Quickly he pulled the pin from a grenade. He tossed it high into the air, being careful not to expose himself. Regeic was doing the same thing, and he knew that Morris would also react in the right way.

As soon as the machine gun stopped, Price rose and began to fire into the dark. A flare burst and he saw that there were something like fifty Japanese soldiers charging straight at him. They ran flatfooted, with their heads low, their bodies bent, and they seemed to be grinning. Directly in front of Price, a large Jap, who seemed to be well over six feet, was pounding forward. He had a grenade in his hand and appeared to be looking for a target. His eyes focused

186

on Price. The other Japs seemed to be looking for individual targets also, and they separated.

The big Jap kept running straight for Price. His face was twisted in a crooked smile which did not fade when Price fired a clip at his chest. Panicked, Price flicked the empty clip from his weapon and replaced it with a full one. It had turned into a contest between the two men. One or both of them would have to die, and the Japanese soldier seemed to have accepted his fate as he faced Price's bullets. Price raised his weapon and took careful aim before pulling the trigger. This time, the man fell to his knees. He raised his arm and started it in a large arch, aiming the hand grenade for Price. The next burst sent the Jap spinning backward, and he fell on his own grenade. The explosion that followed was muffled by the body.

Slightly to his right, Price saw what appeared to be at least twenty Japs fall into a wriggling heap as they ran into a cross fire from the machine guns. They were not all killed, and some of them found their way to the holes. Once Price's helmet resounded when a piece of shrapnel hit it. On the left a Japanese soldier was dancing right in front of the barrel of a machine gun. He seemed to be trying to grasp the barrel, but the blast of the weapon held him back. At that moment he looked very much like a child playing with a garden hose. The entire scene only lasted several seconds, and the soldier fell backward, his body almost cut in two.

A very small Jap, no more than five feet tall, was standing over Ruffin and aiming his rifle at his head. At the same moment, Ruffin brought up his rifle and hit the Jap squarely in the face with the butt of his weapon. There was a *thunking* sound and then a grunt. The Jap stood still for a moment, and then fell backward to the ground. Ruffin was out of the hole in an instant, and he drove his bayonet into the man's throat. Then he calmly stood and fired at the Japs around him.

Suddenly all the Japs were down except for a lone attacker. Everyone was firing at the Jap. The dust was kicking up around him. Calmly he threw a grenade into one of the machine gun positions and ran down the hill, with all the men firing at him. A man in the hole quickly picked up the grenade and threw it after him, but it was a dud. No one hit the Jap, and he disappeared into the trees at the bottom of the hill.

The last flare was fading when Price called to the men. "Anybody hurt?"

"Here," a weak voice answered.

"I'm hit," came another cry.

"Somebody that's close to the wounded men, get with them and see if you can help," Price called. "Stay alert, they may come back."

187

A man cried out, "I can't see. My God, I'm blind." The voice moaned and sounded very pitiful.

"Ern?" Regeic whispered.

"Yeah."

"Did you ever think about running?"

"Every time."

"Me too."

"What keeps you from it?"

"I guess because it's safer in the hole than out of it."

"I never thought about it that way."

"I sure wish I'd brought some more to drink with me." Regeic's lips were quivering.

"It won't be too much longer before we'll get back to the States."

"I sure hope so."

"The colonel told me that he was going to keep us out here until we were all dead, but I doubt if he can do it."

"I don't see how, Ern. He was just mad at the regulars. That was before he knew what it was like."

Suddenly Price was taken with a fit of trembling. His body shook violently and the spasm traveled down through every nerve and bone. In an effort to stop it, he sat in the bottom of the hole.

"Ern, calm down," Regeic said urgently.

"I can't help it."

"You'll be all right. Just take it easy."

"I'm sorry, Regeic."

"Just lay still for a minute, it'll pass."

## CHAPTER NINE

Dawn came rapidly, and the sun was soon burning down on the men on the hill. Ruffin crawled from his hole and stared into the face of the Japanese soldier he had bayoneted. The rays of the sun made his sparse beard look golden as he stood there, staring at the peculiarly slanted eyes of the man at his feet. The Japanese soldier still had his jaw set in determination, and Ruffin was fascinated with the way the jaw muscles bulged.

As he tried to wipe the sleep from his tired eyes, he was barely conscious of Price, who was giving orders to Sergeant Higgenbotham to get the dead men buried. He heard Higgenbotham tell Price that there had been three casualties in the platoon, and somewhere a man whimpered.

As he stared at the body at his feet again, he seemed to be several years older. As he blinked his eyes, he tried to remember what life had been like before the war, but it seemed as if that were a thousand years ago. It did not seem possible that the same boy could be standing over the body of a man he had killed. Even worse, he thought, he did not even feel sorry for the man. When he remembered how the bayonet had felt in his hands, as it bit into the Jap's flesh, he even imagined that he had enjoyed killing him.

Ruffin remembered that he had heard of men who had gone kill-crazy, and he wondered if he might be doing the same thing. During their training, he had heard the older men talk about a man named Choinsky who had gone crazy, and he hoped that it would not happen to him.

Lantrip emerged from the hole, his eyes puffed up, with large black bags under them. He shot a quick glance at Ruffin, who was staring at the Jap's body, and thought Ruffin might be feeling bad about killing the man. Hoping to make him feel better, he said, "Feeling bad about the Jap?"

"No," Ruffin said deliberately, as he slowly faced Lantrip.

"He would have killed you if he could. You had to do it," Lantrip said, trying to sound comforting.

"I didn't mind."

Lantrip smiled. "You've sure changed, Edward."

"I think I've grown up a little," Ruffin said, smiling.

"I'll say," Lantrip laughed. "You're about to be the best man in the platoon. When I first met you I thought you'd never make it."

"Thanks," Ruffin mumbled, wondering at the change that had taken place within himself.

Price was sitting, dangling his feet over the side of his fox-hole and enjoying a cigar, while Morris and Regeic sat opposite him. They had been watching Ruffin examining the body of the Japanese soldier.

"That Ruffin sure did change fast," Price commented softly, as he chewed on the cigar.

"Sure did," Regeic muttered.

Higgenbotham appeared with several packages wrapped in ponchos. He walked up to Price. "Here's what we took off the dead men."

"I'll take care of it," Price said, looking up at him. "You take care of the wounded."

Price watched Higgenbotham walk away and then turned his attention to the personal effects of the dead men. He enjoyed going through the packages since it always fascinated him to see what the dead men were carrying. Now that most of the older men were gone, it did not seem so personal. For a change, he did not even know the names of the owners of these packages. With each package, he searched until he found something with the man's name on it, and then matched the dog tags with the bundle. A key ring, some change, letters that were worn with reading, and pictures; it was always the same. As he went through the personal effects, he wondered if any of the men here on the hill would even remember the names of the dead men after a few weeks.

After all the personal effects of the dead were sorted out,

Price began to search the Japanese. He found that they had the same kinds of articles in their pockets as the Americans usually did. He fingered a picture that he removed from one of them. The picture showed a woman and several children, probably the Jap's wife and children. The picture was worn, as if the Japanese soldier had passed it among his friends many times. He could almost picture the soldier as he passed the picture around at night. His last thought was probably about his wife. He probably would rather have been at home than fighting a war.

Higgenbotham helped get the wounded from their holes and prepared them for the trip back. One man moaned that he was blind, over and over. He was able to stand but he looked dazed, like a man in a dream.

The men who had been digging the graves finished and leaned back against the ammunition cases. Most of them were stripped to the waist and their bodies glistened with sweat. They looked ridiculous in their shorts. Their chests were tanned, but their legs were white. Gently, the other men placed the bodies in the holes and shoveled the dirt on top of them.

Fortunado stood by a freshly dug grave and watched them throw the dirt on top of the small black-haired man named Hubley. They had been good friends almost since they had both entered the army. Fortunado looked for a moment as if he might say a prayer over the grave, but instead he slowly attached a bayonet to the rifle and jammed it into the ground. On the butt he hung Hubley's dog tags and his helmet.

Fortunado stood there for a long time and then walked over to Price. He placed his helmet on the ground and sat on it. Once he was sitting, he stared at Price and did not speak. Occasionally, he wiped at his face with his dirty hand, leaving little streaks of mud and sweat.

Price watched the man for several minutes, and then he became irritated. "Do you want something, Fortunado?"

"Yes."

"Well?"

"Damn you. He was a good soldier. Did you know that?" Fortunado's voice trembled.

Price could not decide what Fortunado wanted. He spoke casually. "I guess so."

"You guess!" Fortunado shouted.

"Yeah, I guess. I didn't know him very well," Price said.

"That's just the trouble with you," Fortunado shouted jumping to his feet. He was trembling and his face was red.

Price looked calmly at Fortunado. "If you've got something on your mind, speak up."

Fortunado frowned. "He was the finest man I ever knew. I went all the way through basic with him and even dropped by his house when we were on leave. You didn't give a damn about him, or any of the rest of us, for that matter. By God,

190

I want to tell you what a bastard I think you really are. You can have my ass court-martialed from here to hell and back, but that's what I think about you."

"I'm not going to court-martial anybody. You're just feeling bad about the kid," Price said sympathetically.

"You're damn right I'm feeling bad about him. How can you be so casual about a man dying?" Fortunado shouted. "How can you be so casual? I don't want to stay out here with a man like you. You must be crazy as hell to act that way."

"You'll understand after you've been out here as long as I have."

"I'll never understand a man like you, not if I stayed out here a million years."

"Look," Price said quietly. "I've been through this more times than you've been through the chow line. Don't you think I feel bad when a man gets killed? I'm not an old man, but sometimes I feel like I must be a million years old, so you just take some advice from an old hand at this. I came out here with a lot of men and they were all good friends of mine. I'd known them for a long time. They're all dead except for Morris and Regeic. Every time one of them got killed, a little of me died. You never get used to it, but you get to where you can stand it without letting it get you down. That's why you think I'm casual about it. I hated to see that guy get killed. I'd have been glad to get hit myself if I thought that would have kept him alive, but it didn't happen that way, that's all."

Fortunado stared at Price and his lips curled back in anger.

"The best thing for you to do," Price continued, "is to forget it as fast as you can. Don't make any more friends than you have to."

Fortunado balled his fist as if he intended to hit Price. When he saw that Fortunado was moving toward him, Price hooked his left foot behind the other man's leg and kicked out with the other. Fortunado was thrown backward and fell on his back. Quickly Price rose and stood over him. "I ought to knock your damn teeth out," Price said, as he stood over the man.

Fortunado looked up. There was contempt in his eyes. "Go ahead," he said.

"I think you'd better get back and help Higgenbotham with the wounded men. You can cool off that way," Price said in a calm voice.

"Is that an order?" Fortunado snarled.

"Yes."

"What happens if I don't obey it?"

"Then," said Price, "I'm going to give you a chance to see how good a man you are. After I've kicked the hell out of

191

you, I'll have Higgenbotham take you back with the wounded men."

"You no-good son of a bitch!" Fortunado snarled. Tears were streaming down his face. "Don't you have any feeling at all?"

Price's jaw muscles jumped. He was getting mad. Regeic saw this and came running over. When he reached Price, he pulled him backward. "Just forget this kid, Ern. Let's go over here and get some coffee."

"No," Fortunado said, "let him try and take me."

Regeic stepped in between the two men. "You go and get some coffee, Ern. I'll go back with the wounded men and take him with me. I want to get something to drink back there anyway."

Morris came over and walked Price back to his hole. Regeic jerked Fortunado to his feet and guided him over to the wounded.

Wearily, Price sat down on the edge of his hole. He took the cup of coffee that Morris handed him and sipped on it. Price was trying to forget what had just happened. "Looks like we had a real mess all up and down the line last night," he said. "Everybody lost a lot of men. Charlie Company lost twenty men and Able lost thirteen. We came out all right."

Morris sipped at his coffee. "The Japs are up to the same old thing. They're saving face. They don't have enough men to break us up, so they just keep hitting us in a few places." Morris assumed a very tired look. "I can't figure out why they fight so hard. Sometimes they don't have enough men or supplies, but they keep fighting their guts out. They've got more guts in one of their platoons than we have in a company. I just can't figure out why they keep fighting."

A rifle shot sounded in the distance and both men ducked.

"I can't figure out why they do it either," Price said, as he gulped at the coffee. "I do know that they're good soldiers. Their tactics aren't worth a damn, but as an individual soldier, they're probably the best in the world. The Japs are cunning and most of all, they're tough. Can you imagine an American living for a week on a handful of rice, or carrying more than his weight on his back? Look at the way they fight. As long as there's one of them left you have to kill him."

The sniper fired again and the men ducked. Price noticed that Ruffin was sitting in the open and had not ducked. "Next time he fires, you duck."

"I'll duck next time. I forgot," Ruffin said, grinning.

Price went back to his coffee. "Look at that crazy bastard."

"He sure has changed," Morris said.

Price studied Ruffin. "You know," he said, taking another drink, "I think he's going to turn out just like Choinsky did. He isn't even afraid of the sniper."

"They're all learning fast," Morris said. "I think that this is already one of the best outfits out here."

The rifle cracked again.

"I hope they learn fast enough to . . ."

An urgent cry interrupted their conversation. "I'm hit." Price turned and saw Ruffin sitting on the ground and looking at his leg in disbelief. Price rose and started over to Ruffin. "Is it bad?"

"The son of a bitch shot me," Ruffin shouted.

When Price reached Ruffin he pulled the man's hands away to examine the wound. His trousers were in the way so Price ripped them. There was a lot of blood, but Price knew at once that Ruffin's kneecap had been shattered.

"We'll have this fixed in no time," Price lied.

"It's bad, isn't it?" Ruffin asked nervously.

"I'm not much of a doctor, but I'd say that we can have you back with us in no time at all."

"Damn it, don't lie to me. I won't be able to use it again, will I?"

"I can't say for sure, but I've seen a lot worse. You're lucky. I wish to hell that I could get a wound like this. It's a one-way ticket back to the States."

"Oh, great!" Ruffin moaned.

Price had opened his first-aid pouch and was pouring the powder into the wound. It was a large wound, since the bullet had entered through the side of Ruffin's leg and blown the entire kneecap away. He tried to stop the bleeding by applying a compress where the cap had been, but the blood continued to flow. He used Ruffin's bayonet and belt to make a tourniquet. He tightened it and smiled at Ruffin.

The sniper fired again and the dirt flicked up at Price's feet. He motioned to Morris and they moved Ruffin into the nearest hole.

"That son of a bitch is trying to finish me off," Ruffin commented.

"How are you doing?" Price asked.

"I feel a little light-headed," Ruffin admitted.

"Would you like some water?"

"Please."

Price took his canteen and held it up to Ruffin's mouth. Ruffin took only a small sip and then shook his head. His eyes were becoming dilated.

"It looks like the war is already over for me, doesn't it?" Ruffin snickered.

"Ruffin," Price said quietly, "I haven't been such a good friend to you and I've given you a rough time, but I want you to know that I'm sorry to lose you. You turned out to be a hell of a fine trooper, one of the best." Price lit a cigarette and placed it in the man's mouth. "I wanted you to know that before we took you back."

"Thanks."

Price turned to Morris. "Go and get two men and make a

stretcher for him. Have them take him back to the hospital as fast as they can."

Morris smiled and left. Price turned back to Ruffin. "I meant it. You used to make me mad as hell, but you've changed a lot."

"Don't worry about how you treated me. I understand and I'm glad that I got you for a platoon leader. I might have been dead if I had gotten anybody else. I did a lot of growing up out here and you made me do most of the growing."

Price looked up and saw that Lantrip had climbed into the hole. "How are you feeling?" Lantrip asked.

"Just a little weak."

"He's going to be all right, isn't he?" Lantrip asked.

"Sure," Price said.

Ruffin closed his eyes slowly and turned his head to the side. "You sound just like two . . . two . . . two movie . . . char . . . characters."

"You just take it easy," Lantrip said.

"I think I'm going to make it all right," Ruffin said weakly. "Could I do anything for you when I get back to the States?"

"I appreciate it, but I don't guess that anybody would care about hearing from me," Lantrip said.

"You folks would."

"Well, if you get a chance, you might see them."

Ruffin closed his eyes. "I will, I will."

"I'd appreciate it."

"They might like it. Most parents worry about their kids." Ruffin coughed several times and his voice was becoming very weak. "If you'd like, I can go out and see some of your old girls. They might like to hear from you."

"Would you like for me to give you some phone numbers?" Lantrip asked.

"Yes. How about that girl in Myrtle Beach? What was her name again—Roberta?"

There was a long silence. Lantrip blanched and Price was speechless. All Price could do was look into the white face of Lantrip. He wondered if Lantrip could be the man who had gotten Morris' wife pregnant. As soon as he could regain his composure, Price glanced around and looked for Morris.

"He must be out of his head," Lantrip gasped.

"Yeah," Price mumbled. He wondered if Morris, who was coming toward them, had been close enough to hear.

The Japanese rifle cracked and Higgenbotham ducked as he leaned over the hole. "Hadn't you better keep down?"

"How many times do I have to explain to you," Price snapped. "That sniper is getting close. When they're close, don't duck. When they miss, duck. That way they never learn to change their sights."

"I'm learning, dammit."

"Not fast enough," Price said.

"I'm learning as fast as I can. One night a week for training isn't so much time. Why don't you come off that crap and let us alone for a while?"

"I've managed to keep more of you alive than any of your National Guard platoon leaders. I just hope that I can keep alive long enough to at least leave this outfit in shape to fight a little scrap. If the Japs really got rough, we'd collapse."

"We did all right last night," Higgenbotham reminded Price.

"I've seen it get a lot worse than that."

"It couldn't get worse than that."

"Look. I was fighting this damn war before you even heard about it. I won't be here forever to wet-nurse you, so you'd do better if you kept your mouth shut and your eyes open."

"I think I'd better get Ruffin back to the rear," Higgenbotham said quickly.

"That's right. I think you'd better."

Price climbed out of the hole and walked away. Behind him, he heard Higgenbotham giving the orders to take the wounded man back to the rear.

Morris stood by a small cliff and stared absently off into the distance. He was thinking about Ruffin's remark, which he had overheard. He heard Price approach and turned to meet him. "How about the water detail? We're about out."

"Pick out somebody to help you and go fill the cans."

"All right. How about Lantrip?"

For a moment Price thought about telling him to take someone else. Morris had given no sign of having heard the remark, but Price was not sure. Finally he decided to let him take Lantrip. "Be careful. The Japs are probably all around us."

Morris and Lantrip gathered all the canteens that they could hook onto their belts and carry. Then they each took a can and started down the trail. They stumbled under their heavy loads. Both of the men carried their weapons loosely in their hands, ready for immediate use.

Lantrip was making too much noise with the canteens as he scraped them against the bushes, and Morris looked back at him, to speak. "Knock off some of that noise. I could hear you clean to the next county."

"All right," Lantrip answered quietly.

Morris and Lantrip walked at a brisk pace. They both had a feeling that a Japanese rifle was aimed at their backs. Lantrip wondered if Price had mentioned what Ruffin had said, but decided that he would not do that, even though Morris was his friend.

At last, they reached the stream. Morris handed Lantrip his canteens and stood guard while Lantrip filled them. The only sound was the gurgling of the water.

"I'm all through," Lantrip announced.

Morris turned until he was facing Lantrip. He leveled the gun at Lantrip's stomach. "Throw your gun over there," he said, indicating the bank of the stream. The gun hit with a clatter. "Now, take the canteens over to the bank and set them down." Lantrip moved again, terror in his eyes.

Morris faced Lantrip squarely. "Now, what did Ruffin mean about Roberta?"

"Just a girl," Lantrip sputtered.

"I think it's my wife."

"She said that her name was Smith."

"Is that the best you can do?"

"It . . . it w-w-was Smith, that's what she said, Smith."

"Don't lie to me," Morris commanded sharply.

"I swear it's true."

"You're a liar," Morris said, advancing slowly. "I can tell, you're lying."

"No."

"Liar."

"For God's sake, you can't shoot me."

"You'd better say your prayers because that's just what I'm going to do."

"No!" the man screamed.

"I want to know before I kill you."

"You're wrong."

"Liar."

"No, please."

Morris released the safety.

"Please. For God's sake! You don't know that it was your wife."

"What did she look like?"

"About twenty."

"Liar."

"Okay. She was about twenty-eight. Brown hair, pretty."

"Her name was Morris."

"Yes."

"That's what I thought," Morris said, anger making his voice quiver. "It was my wife."

"You don't know that for sure. It could have been anybody."

"It was you."

"How can you be sure?"

"It sounds like her. It was in the right town."

"Coincidence."

"I'm going to kill you," Morris announced.

"For God's sake, don't!"

"You'll have a chance. I'm going to kill you with my bare hands."

"You can't put the gun down. What if the Japs come?"

"Then we'll both die."

"You can't."

"Ready?" Morris said, tossing the weapon aside.

196

"No," Lantrip pleaded.

Morris took off his helmet and then threw it to the ground. Next came the web belt. "Take off your helmet," Morris commanded. In slow motion, Lantrip threw away the helmet, his eyes wild with fright, like a trapped animal's.

Suddenly Lantrip leaped. He swung his large fist from knee level, aiming it at Morris' stomach. Instead of backing away from the massive arms, Morris pushed forward, swinging both hands at the big man's stomach, feeling the fists bury themselves into the muscle. There was a slight pain in his chest as a big fist drove into his body.

Morris' swift movement had caught Lantrip by surprise. Morris continued to press forward, his fist pounding away at Lantrip's mid-section. Then he aimed a fist at Lantrip's head and felt it bang home. Blood gushed from Lantrip's torn mouth. As Lantrip went down, Morris was amazed at his opponent's strength.

Almost at the same instant he hit the ground, Lantrip was springing to his feet. Morris lashed forward with a foot, catching Lantrip in the face with his heavy service shoes. Lantrip's head flew backward from the force of the blow. It was covered with blood, the nose flattened. Morris began to stomp on the man, as if he were stepping on a snake.

Desperately Lantrip rolled on the ground and at last caught Morris' foot and twisted it until Morris was on the ground with him. They were evenly matched as they rolled on the ground, thrashing wildly at each other. Lantrip wildly fought to get his thumbs in the man's eyes, but Morris caught Lantrip's wrist in his hand and bit at it, until the blood was flowing. Lantrip clutched wildly with his free hand for Morris' testicles. He finally butted Morris with his head and the two men rolled free of each other, rising slowly to their feet. Both were covered with blood.

They came at each other again. Lantrip lashed out with a wild right, knocking Morris off balance. He then turned and ran for the weapons, but Morris rose and tackled him. Together they rolled into the water. Morris landed on the big man's back and tried to push Lantrip's head under the water, but he was thrown off backward. Weakly, they rose and faced each other again, standing still for a moment. Then Morris charged again, hacking out with his fist. They fought like men who knew that one mistake could mean death. Each man was covered with blood. Their hands were raw. Morris had only one cut on his face, a large wound over his eye. Lantrip had lost some teeth, his nose was broken, and his wrist was bleeding badly.

As they circled each other, Morris lashed out with a right. Lantrip ducked, grabbing Morris' arm as it flew past and thrusting his hand between Morris' legs. With one mighty effort, he threw Morris over his shoulder. Morris landed on the back of his neck. He saw stars. When he opened his eyes.

197

Lantrip was sitting on him, his teeth buried in his neck. He could feel the blood gushing out now. Wildly he punched as the big man held tight. He pulled hair out of Lantrip's head by the handful, but Lantrip never loosened his hold.

Morris was getting faint, and he cursed himself for not shooting Lantrip. For a moment he stopped. Then, in one desperate move, he brought his knee up to Lantrip's groin. The big man held tight. Morris pounded at Lantrip's back, right over his kidneys. Then, for a second, Lantrip opened his legs just a little, and Morris brought up his knee in one last desperate attempt to free himself.

Lantrip released his grip and gasped. Morris brought up his knee again. Lantrip started to collapse. Morris turned to the side in an attempt to free himself from the weight of the other man, but lacked the strength to move. He brought his elbow around with all the force he could muster and slammed it into the big man's face. Lantrip rolled to the side.

Lantrip lay on his back, doubled up with pain, helpless. Twice Morris brought his foot forward, sending it into Lantrip's side. For a moment he stood there, sweat and blood dripping from his face, his arms hanging loosely at his sides. Slowly he raised his foot over Lantrip's testicles. Then he swiftly brought his heel down.

Still the big man seemed to be trying to rise, his body quivering. With blood streaming from his neck, Morris bent over the body. Slowly, breathing hard and wiping the blood from his eyes, he placed a foot on Lantrip's arm and pulled with his hands until he heard a loud crack. Then he broke the other arm.

Thirty minutes later, Morris still sat on the edge of the stream, trying to stop the flow of blood. He was still blowing hard and all his strength had left him. He sat looking at Lantrip, who was still on his back in the shallow water, his arms dangling as if they were not even a part of his body. "Bastard," Morris mumbled.

"Where do you want these men?" Regeic asked the corpsman.

Without looking at Regeic, the man looked at the two men who were walking. "You wait over there with the others." Then, turning to Regeic he said, "Lay them down there."

"Hudson," the doctor was saying, "you'll have to make room for some more of them."

"Getting many this morning?" Regeic asked the corpsman.

"Been coming in all morning."

The long tent was filling with the walking wounded. Silently they came in, cigarettes dangling from their lips, a shocked expression on their faces. They sat there, some semiconscious, some burning with pain, all of them waiting patiently. Some of them cried out at the pain. On the floor near the door, a row of near dead men lay on the bloody litters, in a neat line.

The doctor walked along the row of patients as if there were nothing out of the ordinary. He spoke as if he were dealing with animals. "He's dead. Tag 'em and take the bodies outside." He pulled the poncho from over one of the litters. "Good God, what the hell happened to this one?"

The corpsman looked at the doctor dispassionately. "Looks like a grenade went off right under him."

"Can't save him; move him outside."

The mangled form on the litter rolled his dilated eyes at the doctor. "You can't take me out there. I'm not dead. No!" Two of the corpsmen lifted the litter and began walking toward the tent entrance. "Noooooooooo!" the man screamed. "I'm alive. For God's sake, noooo, please!" His screams could be heard as he was carried from sight. "Oh God, please, noooo, please . . . not with the dead men, noooo!"

The doctor walked up to the next man. "Sponge," he said dryly. He wiped at the caked blood. "Hummm." He looked intently at the place where the eyes had been. "Can't save his eyes. He'll have to wait until I can get to the rest."

Fortunado, who had been standing quietly, came rushing up to the doctor. "Damn, can't you do something for him? He's my friend. Doctor, you've got to do something for him."

"There are a lot of men here that need attention before him."

"You can't just let him sit there."

"You'd better go outside, son."

Regeic began to pull Fortunado out of the tent.

At the entrance of the tent, they found the men who had brought in Ruffin. He was on a stretcher now and was screaming wildly. "What happened to him?" Regeic asked.

"He got hit in the knee."

"Bad?"

"I think so."

Regeic turned to Fortunado and told him to wait there while he went to see how bad Ruffin's wound was. He followed the stretcher bearers as they carried him inside the tent.

To his left, a man screamed. "Somebody help me!"

Regeic turned to a medic. "What happened to him?"

"Fell on top of a grenade."

"Rough."

"Yeah, he's as good as dead now."

When Regeic turned his attention back to Ruffin, the doctor had pulled back the blanket and was examining the wound. He felt Ruffin's pulse and told a medic to administer morphine. He wiped the dust from Ruffin's dog tag and looked at the blood type. Then he told a medic to get some

199

blood ready. "We're going to have to take it off just above the knee."

"No, Doc, no," Ruffin pleaded.

"Get the boy ready for amputation," the doctor said with authority.

"Can't you save it?" Ruffin pleaded.

"You should be quiet. You're going to need all your strength," the doctor warned.

"Look, Doc. Please take a little more time. I know you can save it," Ruffin wailed.

"Look, son," the doctor said. "There are a lot of men that need my attention. I don't have time to mother you. The leg is coming off and there isn't anything else I can do. I wish there was."

As he walked from the tent, Regeic listened to Ruffin pleading. "Please God, don't let them do it to me. Please. Oh God, please!" Ruffin screamed.

"Terrible, ain't it," Regeic said quietly.

"Horrible," Fortunado said.

"Somebody help me," the man on the litter screamed. "I'm not dead, I don't want to die."

"Not my leg," Ruffin wailed. "Please Lord, don't let them."

Regeic turned to the four men with him. "Let's get back to the line." Silently they started the trip back.


Price was cleaning his submachine gun when Morris appeared. He had large bleeding places all over his body and looked as though he might fall at any moment. Questioning shouts greeted him, but he made his way straight for Price. "Everybody stay in his hole," Price shouted at the other men.

"The Japs jumped us," Morris said, puffing.

"How many?"

"There must have been at least ten but I couldn't be sure. It all happened too fast. They came right up on us and I was lucky to get away."

"How about Lantrip?"

"Last time I saw him he was running into the woods."

"Are you sure?" Price said suspiciously.

"I said so, didn't I?"

Price reached into his first-aid pouch and pulled out the contents. After he dressed the wounds, he spoke in a very quiet voice. "You heard Ruffin this morning, didn't you?"

"What was I supposed to hear?" Morris said. He had tried to sound casual, but his voice had a trace of nervousness in it.

"About Roberta and Lantrip."

"What about Roberta and Lantrip?"

"You're not a very good liar, Morris. You killed him, didn't you?" Price demanded.

"He was alive when I left him," Morris said flatly.

200

"What the hell did you do to him?"

"I beat him real good. What would you have done?"

Price wrestled with his conscience. "Same thing, I guess," he finally said.

"Are you going to have me arrested?"

"What for? You couldn't help it if the Japs jumped you, could you?"

"I guess not. Thanks."

"I just hope he's able to get away before the Japs find him," Price said.

"Well, even if they do, they won't be able to do too much to him. There ain't much left."

"Jesus."

"You've seen worse out here, Ern."

"I never saw an American do that to another one."

"If it had been you, you'd have done the same thing. I was so mad that I lost my head. I've been out here thinking for so long about what I'd like to do to the son of a bitch that got her pregnant that I just went crazy when I found him."

"Are you sure that it was him?"

"I thought so at the time, but I'm not sure now. I guess I'm going to wonder about it for as long as I live. It was the first time I ever beat anybody like that. I just pray to God that it was the right man."

"I hope it was, too."

"I'm going to get one of the men to give me a picture of him. When I get back I'll ask Roberta if he was the one."

"I hope he is, for your sake."

"I'm sure," Morris said, rubbing at his sore neck.

"Don't you think you'd better go back to the aid station with that neck?" Price asked.

"I'll be all right."

Regeic appeared in the area just as Santee was finishing the ten-in-one rations. He had been bragging about his ability as a cook all morning and the men had drafted him to fix the meal. He had rummaged through the cases and come up with what he thought was a decent meal. He had built a small fire and was using several helmets for pots.

When Price saw that Regeic was close, he motioned him over. "Did you take care of the wounded?"

"They're cutting off Ruffin's leg. You should have heard him scream when the doctor told him."

"It looks like they would get enough doctors out here to save some of the limbs they cut off."

"Where the hell would they get them? They'd have to get more doctors than soldiers."

"Probably," Price said slowly.

"I think the doctor could have saved his leg if he had more time."

"It's rough."

"Yeah."

"Did you get us some medicine?" Price asked.

Regeic pulled two bottles from his jacket. "I got some."

"How about juice?"

"Three cans."

"Damn, we can get drunk again."

"Holy Jesus," Morris said. "Break it out."

Regeic noticed the wound on Morris' neck. "What the hell happened to you?"

Morris started to speak, but Price spoke first. "The Japs jumped him and Lantrip at the stream this morning. He got away, but they may have gotten Lantrip."

"Tell him the truth, Ern," Morris said.

Regeic looked up at Morris. "The truth?"

"I beat up the bastard. He was almost dead. He was the one that screwed Roberta," Morris said.

"My God!" Regeic said. "What made you think it was him?"

"He admitted it."

"Are you sure he did?"

"Yeah."

"He isn't sure," Price said.

"All right, I'm almost sure."

Regeic cast a hard look at Morris and narrowed his eyes. "Do you realize what you just did. You can't get away with this. You can't just beat a man and leave him to die and then sit here talking about it like it was nothing. What are you going to do about it, Ern?"

"Nothing."

"Ern, you can't just forget it. I'm his friend too, but you can't forget something like that. It's murder. Christ, Ern, you've got to have something done about it."

"No one else knows about it. I would have done the same thing."

"Morris," Regeic said, "have you lost your mind?"

"What would you have done?"

"Well, I don't know, but I'm sure that I wouldn't kill him."

"You'd've done the same thing I did. I didn't start out to kill him, but I got mad and lost my head. When we started fighting, he got so rough that I had to beat him good."

"I might have fought him, but I don't think that I could have killed him."

"Right or not, I guess I killed him. He was alive when I left, but I know he couldn't live. Are you going to prefer charges against me?"

"I think somebody should, but I won't do it." Regeic rubbed the back of his hand across his forehead. "A man that would get another man's wife pregnant deserves to get the hell beat out of him."

"Let's go eat then," Morris said.

The three men got their share of the food and cleaned their utensils on their jackets. The hot noodles and beef were a welcome relief from the cold rations.

"Good," Price munched.

"How about mixing us a martini?" Morris asked.

Regeic mixed the drinks and passed a little of it to each of the men. When his cup was full, Price raised it. "Here's to a quiet night."

"And many more to come," Regeic added.

The day passed very slowly for the men. Morris was troubled over his beating of Lantrip. Price and Regeic worried about what they should do. The logical course of action would have been to arrest Morris, but he was their friend. In addition, they sympathized with him and knew that they might have done much the same thing in his place. Not too long after Regeic had returned, they agreed on a course of action. A patrol was sent back for water. If they found Lantrip dead, everyone would believe Morris' story. If he was still alive, Morris could plead that he had combat fatigue. The patrol returned and said that there was no sign of Lantrip. That meant he had either crawled away or the Japanese had found him.

The night finally came and the sun disappeared below the horizon. Price was asleep, but he heard a voice and woke with a start.

"Help, for God's sake, help me!"

Price relaxed and sank back into the hole. The Japanese were at it again, he thought. Don't those bastards ever let a man get any sleep? "See anything out there?" he asked Regeic, who was standing in the hole.

Regeic strained and peered into the darkness. "Nothing."

"Price," the voice wailed.

Sitting in the hole, Price tried to rub the sleep from his eyes. He poured some water into his hands and splashed it into his eyes to jar loose the hangover that had started. His head was aching dully and his arms felt swollen. He rose to a standing position after a great effort and looked out into the darkness.

"Price," the voice wailed again.

"How do they know my name?" he mumbled.

"They probably got close enough to hear us talking this afternoon," Regeic whispered.

"Regeic!" The voice was very weak.

"That may not be a Jap," Regeic said.

"Regeic, Price, somebody help me, please!"

A voice echoed across the perimeter. "Lantrip. It's Lantrip."

"Quiet," Price whispered.

"Oh, please!" the voice answered.

"Jesus," whispered Regeic. "Do you think it could be Lantrip?"

"Not if Morris did what he said."

"It sure sounds like him."

"You know how the Japs are."

"Yeah, but that one sounds like Lantrip."

"If it was him, there's nothing that we could do about it."

"Price," Morris called, "I'm coming over."

"Hold your fire," Price said. "Morris is moving."

Morris made almost no noise and was in the hole quickly. "He's in," Price whispered to the other men.

"Price, I think that it's really him. I don't know how he managed to stay alive, but I'm sure that it's him. I can tell."

"Well, there's nothing that you can do about it tonight."

"I can go out there."

"You can't go. They'll kill you." Price saw that Morris had made up his mind. "Morris, I've never pulled rank on you, but I am now. Don't go out there."

"It's my fault that he's out there and I'm going out. Court-martial me if you want to. The only way you can stop me is to kill me. I don't want to go through life with this on my conscience."

Price realized there was no way to stop Morris. He smiled, and then cupped his hands. "Hold your fire. Morris is going out. Fire when I do and shoot high to cover him."

There was a storm of clicks as the safeties were released, and then a tremendous roar as all the weapons fired into the woods. Between muzzle flashes, Morris could be seen disappearing into the brush.

Morris reached the edge of the jungle and ran, crouching low as he moved along the edge of the wall of green to be sure that the Japs wouldn't find him if they went to the place where he had entered. After moving about twenty yards, he stopped and crouched low, his breath coming in gasps and seeming to be very loud. Morris placed his hand over his mouth as he inhaled, trying to muffle the sound of his heavy breathing.

"Oh God . . . Help!"

He waited quietly, trying to control his breathing. The voice was coming from somewhere to his left. The calls seemed to be getting weaker, but there was a pitiful urgency to the voice and Morris felt a pang of conscience as he remembered the beating he had given Lantrip. Crouching in the shadows, he cursed himself, wishing that he had not taken out his anger on Lantrip. To his right, he heard several scratching sounds moving through the wall of dark green. That would be the Japs looking for him.

Morris pulled his bayonet from the sheath, as the sound of the moving men came closer to him. Huge drops of sweat ran down his face as each sound came closer, and his stomach began to feel as though it were full of crawling insects. He felt his hands begin to tremble as he clutched at the handle of the long bayonet. Every muscle was coiled to

204

strike if the men came too close to him.

The sounds grew louder, and Morris felt as though he wanted to crawl into the ground. Strange, guttural sounds began to come from the moving green in front of him. The Japanese soldiers came into view now, two shadowy figures whispering in the dark. The men came closer, and Morris could see that they were not aware of his presence. The two small men stopped not ten feet from him, talking quietly as they surveyed the platoon's position, which was directly in front of them. The smaller of the two raised his long rifle and worked the bolt. Slowly, he raised the weapon and fired into the area.

As the Japanese soldier lowered the weapon, he laughed softly and nudged his companion in the side. Sweat was pouring down Morris' body and he tried not to breathe, afraid that the sound of his breathing would alert the Japs. Suddenly, the fear that the platoon might answer the fire, and hit him, swept through Morris. He wanted to run, but there was no place to run. If he moved, the Japs would kill him. Even if he was lucky and killed them, the others would hear the struggle and get him. Then it might be him that was lying out in the dark screaming for someone to help him.

"Price . . . Morris . . . Oh, please, somebody help me!"

The two Japanese laughed quietly and spoke to each other in the monkeylike chatter. The small man raised his rifle and fired at the hill again. There was a brilliant flash on the hill, and the machine gun fired. None of the bullets hit the brush, and Morris guessed that Price had fired the weapon high to convince the Japs that there was no American in the brush in case they had seen Morris enter. The Japanese would reason that the men on the hill would not fire into the brush unless they were sure they would not hit one of their own men.

As the machine gun chattered, Morris raised his weapon and triggered two fast bursts, one at each of the Japanese. The two men fell, but one was not dead. He was rolling on the ground. Quickly, Morris raised himself from his position and ran to the fallen Jap.

The little man's eyes were wide with fright. He already seemed to be trying to decide how he would die. The question was written on his terrified face, and Morris could almost see the man reviewing his life. Morris clamped his left hand over the Jap's mouth and drove the knife into his chest. The eyes opened wide for a second, and then the Jap relaxed.

Quickly, Morris moved back into the shadows and waited. Nothing moved in the jungle. Patience was the Japs' best weapon. He had to take his time. The Japs must have known that he had left the hill and if Price had not fooled them by firing the machine gun, they would be looking for him. Each bush could hide a lurking Jap, and Morris could not hide the feeling that there was a Japanese weapon pointed at his back.

205

The hair on the back of his neck was standing, and his flesh seemed to be crawling.

"Christ . . . Oh Christ, help!"

Morris jumped when the voice first sounded. Determined, he moved quietly, crouching low and moving very slowly. The voice was somewhere in front of him. As he moved cautiously he listened for any sign that would indicate that there might be a Jap close by. He had moved no more than ten feet when he heard it. Not too far ahead. Water trickling off a bush. It was the sound of a man urinating. A Jap. Morris crouched in a shadow and listened to the sound for a few seconds. Then there was silence. He waited, feeling his flesh crawl.

"Please, help me . . . please."

There was a shuffling sound as the Jap moved away from him. It was several minutes after the Jap had moved away before Morris began to move toward the voice. He thought there might be several Japs around the man, waiting for someone to come to his rescue. He moved steadily.

It must have been thirty minutes later, the sweat rolling off his body, when he heard the voice again. This time it was just in front of him. He crouched and waited. There was no sound for another few minutes, and it seemed to Morris that a lifetime was passing. The sweat was rolling off him. Then the voice came again. It couldn't be too far in front of him, not more than ten yards, he reasoned. Silently, Morris began to move in a circle around the voice. As he moved, the voice wailed again. When he reached the point that he had started from, he paused. There was no sound. He wondered if there were no Japs there.

He inched his way toward the place where the voice had come from. Inch by inch, he moved forward, placing his heel down quietly and then inching his toe down, feeling for any twig that might give his position away. One foot at a time, he repeated the procedure, moving no more than ten feet in five minutes. Any slip and he would be dead.

He saw Lantrip on the ground just in front of him. Lantrip was on his back, blood glistening in the moonlight that shone through the dense growth. His head was rolling from side to side. "Oh please, somebody help me!"

Morris felt around the ground for a stone or piece of bark. He threw a piece of dirt which he had finally located. The dirt landed in the brush, and Morris waited. There was no sound. Satisfied that there were no Japs close by, he inched his way to the wounded man.

He crawled the remaining few feet and placed his hand on the man's shoulder. "Lantrip," he whispered.

The big man jumped and then rolled his head to the side. Morris felt for the pulse in the broken arm. There was none. He was dead. Morris felt as if he had lost something important. Quickly he withdrew to the wall of green.

Suddenly there was a sound to his right. He crouched and waited. A tall Jap came into view. The Jap stopped in front of the man on the ground, poking him with the bayonet on the long rifle he was carrying. He grunted once and then turned and disappeared into the foliage.

There had been a long period of silence and Price was peering over the side of his hole. Sweat was dropping off his face and he wiped at it every few seconds. A swarm of insects flew around his head and he silently cursed the island.

"He's been gone a long time," Regeic whispered.

"Yeah. The jungle has been too quiet."

"Lantrip hasn't called for a long time."

"Think they got Morris?"

"I doubt it."

"He knows how to take care of himself."

"Hate to lose him."

"Me too."

Silence filled the area. The sweat ran down them, and the insects crawled over their bodies.

Price slapped at his neck. "I keep thinking that I ought to do something about Morris. He killed a man. It isn't right to just let it go, but I don't know what to do."

"You could send him back and say he had cracked."

"Would you do it?"

"I don't know. I doubt it."

"That's what I mean. After what Lantrip did to him, it seems right. I guess you just get used to all the killing, too used to it for your own good."

"All of the feelings that normal humans have seem to be a long way off right now."

"Years ago."

"I'm coming in!" The voice belonged to Morris.

Price fired a flare into the air and waited until it burst. As the flare burst in the air, Price cupped his hands. "When you see him come out, cover him."

Right after the flare burst, a shadow appeared at the edge of the jungle. Price at once aimed his weapon to the right of the figure and triggered off several rounds. The rest of the platoon fired, and the figure began to run.

Morris reached the area and dropped into the hole with Price. As soon as he was in the hole, the men ceased their firing. Almost immediately, there was a hail of answering fire from the edge of the jungle.

After the firing had ceased, the three men slowly raised their heads and peered out.

"You find him?" Price asked.

"Yeah."

"Alive?"

"He was when I got there, but he died before I could talk to him."

"Too bad."

"I would like to have apologized to him before he died. I was mad as hell this afternoon, but now, it's different. I wish I had done different."

"Too late to help now."

"I guess so."

Regeic looked at the two men. "Why don't you two get some sleep. I'll watch for a while."

Price and Morris slumped into the hole and were asleep immediately.

# CHAPTER TEN

Ruffin recovered from the operation rapidly. He had refused to talk to the other patients and spent most of his time looking out of the window. The doctors had offered to give him a leave, but he had refused. When his parents did not hear from him, they had called the doctor and he told them that although Ruffin was well enough to go home, he had refused a leave. After several weeks, the doctors had refused to listen to his excuses and ordered him to take a thirty-day leave.

Ruffin sat on the edge of his bed and looked at the stump of his leg, which protruded off of the bed at an awkward angle. He hated the sight of the still red stump and cursed it as though it was not a part of him. On crutches, he went to the dresser and very carefully laid out his underwear, socks, a clean handkerchief, a set of suntans, and a tie.

He stood with difficulty and removed his bathrobe. He smelled under his arms, made a face at the odor, and then decided to take a shower. After the shower, he shaved and put on the clean uniform. It took some time for him to roll the trousers up to the stump and pin the material. He picked up his crutches and made his slow descent to the orderly room. The first sergeant was there. He had his papers ready for him.

"Don't you wear your purple heart?" the first sergeant asked.

"I don't know," Ruffin answered absently.

"Didn't they give you one yet?"

"Yes."

"Then you're supposed to wear it."

"Sergeant," Ruffin said deliberately, "you're the first shirt and all that crap, but I don't have the slightest intention of wearing it. I didn't ask to get into this damn war, and I sure didn't ask to have this leg shot off. For all I care, the army can take their damn purple heart and shove it up their ass."

"Ruffin," the first sergeant remonstrated.

"Sergeant, I'm no good to the army now and I don't think they want to throw me in the guardhouse, so you can calm down. I just don't feel like taking any more crap from the army, or you either for that matter. I've given all that I intend to."

"Go on and get out of here," the first sergeant said calmly and then he went back to his papers. He had been through this with others and had no intention of getting mad. Most of the wounded men who warranted a discharge didn't give a damn for anything, he remembered. He had not been overseas and this made him even more reluctant to be too rough with them.

It was a long and dirty train ride for Ruffin. The women on the train had particularly bothered him. They had stared at him until he could almost hear them pitying him. A poor pathetic cripple, he could almost hear them say. After a while, he had started to look back at them with all the hate he could muster. In a small Arizona town, he had bought a bottle from a taxi driver. At first, it made him gag, but after a while he felt the effects and some of the edge started coming off.

Somewhere in New Mexico, a little old lady had chosen a seat next to him. She had not been there for long before she began to smile at him in a motherly fashion. Her voice was very sweet when she spoke. "You poor thing."

"Go to hell," he snapped.

He had to change trains in Dallas. It seemed to him as if it had been a very long time since he had started from that station. When he arrived in his home town several hours later, he took the one taxi at the station and told the driver where to take him. As he neared the street where his house was, he suddenly wanted to turn back. Texarkana would be a good place to go, he thought. He decided that he could stay there a few days before he went home. Then he knew that his parents would know he had arrived in town and would be hurt if they knew he was deliberately staying away from home.

During the periods of quiet in the Pacific, he had often thought of his home as being very wonderful, but now it was just a house, a plain ordinary house like all the others. There were the same small trees that he remembered, and the tall grass in the back of the house.

He walked onto the porch, but instead of entering, he rang the bell. There was a sound in the back and then the sound of steps coming to the door. His mother appeared in the hall and began running until she had him in her arms. She was wearing the same straw hat she had always worn when she worked in the garden, and she smelled of sweat and cologne.

"Oh," she sobbed. "Edward! You're home!" She was kissing him, and he felt repulsed and wanted to tear himself from

209

her grasp. "Jules," she called, "it's Edward. He's home."

She continued to hug him and he struggled to release himself from her grasp. His father appeared, wearing a pair of khaki pants. He was crying. He walked up and placed an arm around his son's shoulder. "It's good to have you home again, son."

They led him to the living room, and kept putting their hands on him as if he weren't real and they had to reassure themselves that it was really he. Several times Ruffin had started to speak, but each time he thought better of it and remained silent. They all seated themselves, and his father came rushing over to take the crutches.

"I can manage," Ruffin said.

"Just let me set them over here for you."

"Okay."

His father seemed very nervous and kept fidgeting in the chair. At last he lit a cigar and placed it in his mouth. Ruffin noted that he held it in almost the same manner as Price had done. At length, his father spoke. "We were about ready to come out to California and see you."

"Yeah."

"You didn't write or anything."

His mother sat on the edge of her chair and Ruffin could hear her take a breath. "Jules."

"I know."

"I'm sorry." Ruffin felt nervous.

"That's all right, son. This is your home. I understand how it was."

"Do you?"

"Look over here," his father said, as he walked to a large map of the Pacific that was filled with pins. "I've followed the whole thing on the map, son. After you've rested, you can show me where you've been."

"I'll do the best I can, sir."

"Best?"

"I don't know where I was all the time."

"You're kidding."

"No, sir."

"You mean you didn't know where you were?"

"Not all the time. I know what islands I was on, but somehow it just didn't seem too important after a while."

"We understand."

No you don't, Ruffin thought, you never will understand. It made him want to cry to see them try so hard, but he felt removed from them, not at all the same way he had felt when he had been there before the war.

"Did you carry the Bible I gave you?" his mother asked in an anxious voice.

"I'm sorry, I guess I must have lost it."

"I understand. It was hard for you to keep up with things. We can always buy you another one."

"Sure. That would be nice."

There was a long period of awkward silence. Suddenly everyone was talking at once, but nobody was saying the things they wanted to say. Ruffin felt as if he were with total strangers, and they seemed to be playing a ridiculous game.

Ruffin made several remarks about how good Beans, his dog, looked, but the dog paid no attention to him at all.

"He doesn't remember me," Ruffin said.

"You've been gone a long time. He'll get used to you again," his mother assured him.

"I guess. Say, where's Tommy?"

"He's out playing. We didn't know you were coming."

Then the conversation had reached another halt. No one knew what else to say. He knew that they wanted to hear him talk, especially about his leg. Finally, he said, "I guess you've been wondering about my leg."

"You don't have to talk about that, son," his father said.

"We understand," his mother added.

"It's all right."

"That's all that's important, son. Just that you're all right."

"Yeah," Ruffin said.

"Why don't you go on upstairs and get some rest," his mother said. "We can talk some more at supper. Besides, you must be very tired."

"Yeah."

They helped him up to his old room. It was the room he had grown up in and nothing had been changed. Just the same, he felt as though it were a strange place and he did not belong. His father stood at the door, while his mother pulled the shades.

"You have a nice nap," his mother called as she closed the door. "I'll call Martha and see if she can come for dinner."

Ruffin fell on the bed and listened to them talking in the living room. His mother broke down and began to cry and he could hear his father trying to comfort her. He buried his face in his pillow and cried softly.

Sandra Price propped her head in her hands and rested her elbows on the table. She looked into the eyes of the man seated on the other side of the table and smiled. Bob Reid was a short man, barely taller than she. He was too thin and his hair was cut short, giving his large nose a longer look. They had been dating for a long time and Sandra could tell that the man was beginning to fall in love with her.

She thought back over the months they had been dating and was satisfied that she had made a lot of progress with him. She had worked hard to make him propose to her and she knew that he would ask her very soon. She did not love him, but she knew she was not getting any younger and

211

Buck would need a father. Bob had money and would make an excellent husband.

"Bob, sometimes I think you're too good to me."

Bob smiled at her. "I like to do nice things for you. After the way your husband treated you, you deserve nice things. I want you to have all the nice things that I can get for you."

"I haven't enjoyed life too much," Sandra said quietly. "At least, not until I met you."

"I would imagine that being divorced is a hard thing on a woman."

"It is but I'm a lot better off because of it."

"I don't want to sound nosy, but you've never told me too much about it."

Sandra made wet rings on the tablecloth with her glass and looked down at the table while Bob ordered coffee. "I want you to know everything there is to know. If you're interested, that is."

"Of course I'm interested."

"Ernest drank too much for one thing," she lied. Sandra had been wondering what she would tell him and now thought that the best course of action would be to play on his sympathy. "He was an army man and it came first with him. He would rather spend the night with the men in the club than with me, and he would come home and beat me."

"No!"

"Yes," she said slowly. "There were a lot of times when he would come in drunk and hit me. He gave me a lot of bruises and once he broke my little finger." She held out her finger for him to see. It had been crooked since she was a little girl when she had broken it in the front porch swing.

Bob patted her arm. "It must have been terrible."

Sandra waited for the waitress to bring the coffee and leave, before she continued. "Oh Bob, it was. If it hadn't been for Buck, I would have left him long before I did. I loved him as much as a woman can, but he didn't care for me. It took me a long time to get over him. I guess you helped me the most of anybody."

"I'm glad you feel that way about me."

"You did help. I don't think I can ever forget how he treated me, but you've made it seem unimportant."

"I think some men should be horsewhipped," Bob said with determination.

Sandra almost smiled, but she continued to look as hurt as possible. "Don't say that."

"It's true. He's such a no-good bastard that it would do the country good if he got killed. I don't have a thing against the servicemen and I would be glad to be in myself if I could get released from my job. Just the same, it would be a good thing if some of them didn't come back."

"Oh, Bob, that sounds so terrible."

"It's true. Those men that were in the regular army before

the war were a no-good lot. They lived from drink to drink and woman to woman. Your ex-husband probably ran around on you all the time he was married to you."

A soldier who had been sitting at the table next to them rose and walked over to their table. He was deeply tanned and was wearing several ribbons which indicated he had seen a lot of action. "You're shooting your mouth off a little too much for a draft-dodger, aren't you, buddy?" the soldier said.

"Shove off, Mac," Bob said.

The soldier's face turned red and his jaw quivered. "Don't call me Mac. My friends do that, and you're not one of them."

"Look, Mac, I'm sorry. Now shove off like I asked."

"I'll move on when I get ready, and not until then," the soldier said.

Bob started to rise and was barely clear of the chair when the soldier hit him in the face. He went sprawling backward and hit the floor with a thud. The soldier spat on the floor beside Bob and then walked from the room.

Everyone in the restaurant was watching Bob and he became embarrassed. Quickly he removed his wallet and tossed several bills on the table. "Let's get out of here." He took her arm and led her from the room. Several people laughed.

Once in the car, he ground it into gear and drove out of the parking lot with a cloud of gravel behind him. They drove down Dexter Avenue, past the rows of dark houses. Only one automobile passed them. The only movement they could see was the twinkling of the street lights through the trees.

They were almost to Sandra's home before he spoke. "I would have knocked the hell out of that smart alec, but he was wounded and I didn't want to take advantage of him."

He stopped the car in front of her house and turned off the lights. She slid across the seat and sat very close to him while she caressed the back of his neck. He pulled her into his arms and kissed her. While he kissed every inch of her face, she made moaning sounds for his benefit, but was remembering the way the soldier had looked at her. She had seen contempt there. For the first time she realized that her ex-husband was fighting a war and that it was not a game.

Bob was kissing her ear now and his hands were fondling her breasts. She felt no thrill, but pretended to be very worked up for Bob's benefit. While he unbuttoned her blouse, she realized that Ernest's letters had a deep meaning. They had been full of hurt and pain. She realized that she might have done the wrong thing when she had written the last letter.

Bob was kissing her neck now and he had unhooked her brassière. She still thought about the soldier. She had seen,

213

in his eyes, the horror and terror which he had experienced. She realized that Price might look the same way, that he might have been through the same ordeal. Bob fondled her, but, his love-making meant nothing to her. Just the same, she pretended to be enjoying it, so that he would not know that her thoughts were on another man.

He ran his hands along her leg and she kissed him fiercely. Then he looked up at her. "Sandra, would you marry me?"

After months of leading him along for this moment, she was shocked to hear the words. She had been thinking about Ernest and he had asked the question when she was least prepared. She was ashamed to be in the car with this man and she felt dirty. Of course, she reasoned, he will be a good husband and I can't do anything that would lose him. She wanted to stall for time. "You're not proposing, are you?" she said lightly.

"Yes."

"Bob," she said sincerely, "you know that I love you more than anything in the world. I want to marry you, but I'm afraid. You know how my last marriage turned out and I don't want to rush into anything. Can I have a little time to get used to the idea?"

"How long do you think it will take you to say yes?"

"Not long. Can't we be engaged for a little?"

"I love you, Sandra."

Sandra snuggled a little closer to him and rested her head on his chest. "I'm a little mixed up right now, but I'll marry you. Please try to understand, though, that I want to be engaged for a month or two." She hugged him and kissed him for a long moment. "You will do that for me, won't you?"

"I'd prefer to marry you right away," he said. "I don't think I can wait for very long."

"You don't have to wait too long," she whispered passionately. "I couldn't refuse you anything."

It was several hours later when she entered the house and made her way to her son's room. Silently she tiptoed over to his bed and looked down at him. The boy was cuddled up with a Teddy bear and was sleeping soundly. She could remember seeing her ex-husband look the same way while he slept.

Sandra walked over to her bed and silently undressed. It took her several minutes to undo her brassière, since it had been hooked the wrong way. She finally was naked and walked to the shower.

After the shower, she put on an old housecoat and walked to her writing desk. For a long moment she reflected on the evening. Bob had made love twice in the car and she had felt nothing. All during it, she had been thinking about Ernest, but she had made the right noises and acted as though it were the first time for her. Apparently she had more than satisfied Bob. At length, she picked up her pencil.

*Dear Ernest,*

*I know that my last letter was a little rough and that you have been wishing that I would never write to you again. I have been doing a lot of thinking lately and I want you to know that I am terribly sorry for the way I have treated you. If you are good enough to take me and Buck back, I want to marry you again. It would make me the happiest girl in the world.*

*You must have known that I was the biggest fool in the world to ever divorce a wonderful man like you. I have never stopped loving you, but I was too busy being a fool to ever realize it. In the past few days, I have looked at our son and all I could think about was how much he was like you and how proud I was.*

*I hope that it is not too late for us to make a go of it. You were the most wonderful husband in the world. I don't think that I will ever be able to explain to you why I acted like I did, but I hope that you were telling the truth when you said that you still loved me and that you wanted me back. Please, my darling, write to me and tell me that you will have us back.*

*One of our troubles was that my parents interfered. You always said so, but I was too dumb to understand it. I know now, and I promise you that I will never let them get in our way again.*

*I know that you have been wondering about what I have been doing since we were divorced. In my last letter I told you how many dates I've been having, but really I've gone out very little, since taking care of our son is a full-time job. Of course I have kissed a few men, but it has never gone further than that. I could not let a bunch of filthy men make love to me. I never understood why until a few days ago. Then, I knew that it was because I still loved you.*

*Each time I have thought about you out there fighting in that horrible war, I have said a little prayer that God would take care of my darling. I live for the day when we can get together again.*

*Please, honey, answer this letter as soon as you get it, and tell me that you can find it in your heart to have us back. I promise you with all my heart that I will make it up to you for all the things that I did to you. You will never be sorry that you took us back.*

*All our love,*
*Sandra and Buck*

Sandra addressed the letter and then laid it aside so she could mail it in the morning. She thought that one way or another, she would have a father for Buck soon. Price was an officer now and he would be retiring soon. His pension plus a job would provide for her very well. If he had changed his mind, she could always marry Bob. She felt quite satisfied when she went to bed.

Anne Beecraft sat on an overstuffed chair with her legs crossed under her. She smoked her cigarette very slowly and watched the blue smoke curl up toward the ceiling. The night was warm and the slight breeze that blew the trees gently seemed to carry the hot air into her room. She had just written to her husband and was feeling very depressed. It had not come as a great shock to her when he had written about Morris. She had known Roberta for a long time and knew that she was not the kind of woman Morris had thought.

Once, she and Roberta had discussed their romances. Anne had been a virgin before her marriage, although she had had a hard time remaining one on a few occasions, and she had been shocked when Roberta had admitted having had several affairs. Roberta apparently had been very much in love with a married man and they had spent more than one week end together.

Anne jerked around and came back to the present when she heard a noise behind her. "I didn't frighten you, did I?" her mother asked.

"Mother," she said, as her mother seated herself in a chair by the window.

"What is it, honey?"

"He's dead, Mother. I can feel it."

"Honey," her mother said quietly, "you know better than that. It's just that you miss him. I had the same feeling about your father during the other war, and he came back. It happened almost every time I wrote to him."

Tears formed in Anne's eyes. She faced her mother and wiped at them with the back of her hand. "I had a dream last night. I saw him lying in a puddle of water and he was dead. He was face down, but I knew it was him because Price and some of the others were talking about it. Just before that, I thought I heard him calling me. It was all so real." She wiped the new tears away. "Oh, Mother, I know that something has happened to him."

"You're just tired and upset," her mother comforted her.

"I know that it sounds crazy, but I have the feeling. It's real strong. Something keeps telling me that he's dead. The end of the dream was worse. He got up out of a hole and came toward me. I was so relieved to see him that I ran to meet him. I hugged him, but he was as cold as ice and did not speak. All he ever said was, 'I had to come see you again. Poor Anne.' He just kept saying that over and over."

"It was just a dream, Anne," her mother said. "Those things just don't happen. It's normal for a woman to worry about her husband when he may be in danger. You're just lonesome,

216

that's all. Before you know it, he'll be walking through that door and you won't ever have to be away from him again."

"I never believed in those things either, Mother, but this dream was so real. When I looked at his face, it was so pitiful and hurt. I couldn't dream that. It was just too real."

"Dreams are that way sometimes."

While her mother walked to the kitchen to make some fresh coffee, Anne reflected on her life with her husband. They had been happy and she had no memory of a serious argument. What bothered her the most was that she had not always been glamorous enough. She made up her mind that if he ever got back, she would never let him see her unless she was fixed up. He had never liked to see her hair rolled up and she made up her mind that she would do that during the day and take it down for him at night. Another thing she remembered was that she had never owned a negligee. She made up her mind to buy one to wear for him when he returned.

Her mother returned with a cup of steaming coffee and placed it in her hand. "After you've had a good night's sleep," her mother said, "things will seem a lot better."

"I do hope so, Mother, but I'm so terribly afraid he's dead."

They had been moving Choinsky from one hospital to another, and the move to the new one upset him very little. He had just been checked in when they gave him a handful of pills. This time they were blue.

When he woke up, he was not shaking as badly as usual, but he still had the same tired feeling. An orderly brought him a tray of food which looked very good, but he could not get up enough appetite to eat it. He nibbled at it and then shoved the tray aside.

Shortly after lunch, a very young doctor came into the room and stopped at the foot of his bed. He looked at Choinsky and smiled. "You're looking better."

"Thanks."

"Is there anything we can get for you?"

"There damn sure is. You can get me out of this damn nut ward," Choinsky roared.

The doctor smiled. "This isn't a nut ward. Most of the men here have simply gotten too tired. That's all."

Call it a form of tiredness if you want to, Choinsky thought, but it's full of crazy people. He had become tired of listening to the raving men around him and he wanted to be released terribly. Choinsky knew that he had lost his senses back at the front and that the rest had done him good. He even realized that his nerves were still shot, but he knew that he was not as sick as the rest of the men around him. Sometimes when he thought about it, he would get so mad that he shouted abuse at the medics. Afterwards, he realized this did nothing but convince them that he was not

217

well yet. "I'm all right, Doctor. Can't you get me out of here?"

"I have some patients to see, but I'll come back again later and we can talk about it then."

It was always the same. They were always going to come back and talk about it, but they never did. He wondered if it wasn't the doctors that were crazy. Everyone seemed to have it in for him and he hated the doctors for forcing him to stay when he was able to return to the front. That was where he was supposed to be. "Sure, Doc. You come back and we can talk about it later."

That same afternoon, they took him for another physical. The doctors looked him over very carefully and even gave him a short arm. "You're a hell of a mess, Choinsky," the doctor had announced at length.

"What the hell did you expect me to look like after two years in the jungle? Mister America?" he snapped.

"That will be enough of that kind of talk," the doctor snapped. "Just remember that you're still in the army."

Several orderlies advanced on Choinsky and gave him a shot of something. Before the war, he had always been afraid of the needles and had looked the other way, but now he watched as they stuck them into his arm. He never changed expression.

"That didn't hurt, did it?" the doctor asked sweetly.

"No," Choinsky said dejectedly.

That evening, Choinsky lay in his bed and smoked. The ward was very long, and beds were lined down each side of the room. Most of the patients were quiet, and, as usual, eyed him suspiciously. He knew that the night would be the same. As soon as the night descended, there would be the scraping sounds of the patients as they scraped their slippers down the corridor. As always, there was a man who was overly religious. This ward had a man who thought he was Moses, and he was always shouting about the Ten Commandments.

Choinsky woke in the morning and was taken to an office where the young doctor was waiting behind the desk. It was the same routine. The doctor asked the same questions: "Did he like girls, did he hate his mother, did it embarrass him to take off his clothes in front of other men?" The doctor checked his reflexes and at last settled behind his desk and lit a cigarette.

"How long are you people going to keep me here with these nuts?" Choinsky asked.

"Don't you like it?"

"It don't make a rat's ass to me where I am."

"Then what difference does it make?"

"None, I guess."

After that, he was taken to the doctor's office almost every day, and they had long talks. Choinsky hated the routine, but he went along with it, and after some time, they gave him the privilege of wandering in the yard. He would spend hours sitting in the yard, enjoying the sun.

The hospital was a very quiet place most of the time, and had it not been for the fact that there were no nurses and that a big fence enclosed it, you would never have guessed that it was a nut house. Of course, it was easy to tell that it belonged to the army, because there were the usual signs. Large signs were placed over the door, and they said, "Door." Others told you that the round containers on the wall were fire extinguishers. As Choinsky thought about this, he wondered if the people running the hospital were not crazy too. Of course there were the usual signs telling you to keep off the grass, and the patients had to salute the officers.

When Christmas came, there were trees in the corridors and the chaplain came by. He even had the men sing carols, until one of the patients went out of his head and started screaming. Then, the man who thought he was Moses started on the Ten Commandments.

The army was obviously trying to make things up to the shattered men in the hospital. Every day, there were fresh eggs, real milk, and even steaks. In the mess hall, the K.P.'s even sold them whiskey, and Choinsky was consuming almost a pint a day.

Every evening, there were old movies, and the U.S.O. sent shows in frequently. The personnel of the hospital did everything they could to pamper the men. Most of the men relaxed a little, but some still wandered around in a daze, the horror of the war written on their faces.

Occasionally they would change doctors. The new ones would come in and inspect the wards, and scream at the men to stand at attention. Almost always the new doctors would tell them it was against regulations to smoke. Of course, they soon learned that the men did not care and when the men refused to obey, the doctors became frustrated, finally giving up on the patients.

The hospital was run on a rigid routine that never varied. The patients were assigned to companies, and doctors were assigned to patients. Most of the men in Choinsky's ward were broken in spirit, rather than in body. Most of the time, Choinsky stayed to himself and refused to have anything to do with the other men. He thought they were all crazy.

He had regained his memory and knew that he was in much better shape than the others. It depressed him to be thought of as crazy. At times, when he was in the yard, he felt ashamed when people looked at him. He reasoned that they had no way of knowing that he was in the section for the men with combat fatigue, but he was never sure. Several times, a passer-by had laughed and, although he knew that it was not at him, he could not help wondering if they knew.

Choinsky's doctor was a large-boned man named Grim. He had raw features, and Choinsky always thought of him as looking like Abraham Lincoln. One day the doctor came in and caught Choinsky smoking in the bed.

"You'll burn the place down if you're not careful," the doctor said. He was not at all like the others and seemed to have little regard for military discipline. This made Choinsky dislike him because he thought the doctor should enforce the regulations. After all, he was an officer.

"I'll put it out, sir."

"That's all right. Just be sure you don't go to sleep with that thing in your hand." The doctor smiled. Then he sat on the edge of the bed. When he was settled, he pulled out a cigarette and lit it. "You'll be going home on a leave soon."

"I'm going to be able to stay in the army? You won't have them discharge me, will you?"

"I don't know about that. We'll have to see how you are when you report back from the leave."

"How in the name of hell can I make you people believe that I'm all right? I just had a little breakdown. Lots of men do it."

"We'll see."

The doctor made several other comments, but Choinsky only nodded his head. Finally, the doctor gave up and left. Several hours passed and the shadows that were forming made the room look like the jungle. Choinsky watched the shadows creep across the room and he thought about the war. Soon, he could hear the jungle sounds. The more he thought about it, the more convinced he became that he *was* in the jungle. He slipped from the bed and crawled on the floor so the Japs would not see him. He felt the familiar feeling of fear eating at his stomach.

An orderly came by to make his nightly check, but to Choinsky, it was a Jap. He crouched and waited for the Jap to come closer. He searched for his submachine gun, but he couldn't find it. Then he looked for his bayonet, but that was not there either. In desperation, he decided to kill the Jap with his hands.

A dark form appeared at the door and Choinsky sprang at it. The Jap went down and called for help, but he closed his hands around the Jap's throat. Choinsky screamed for Price to help him but the Jap started to overpower him.

Finally, the orderly succeeded in knocking Choinsky off and he pinned him to the floor while some of the other orderlies came to his rescue.

"Snap out of it," the orderly shouted at Choinsky.

"You're a Jap. You son of a bitch, you can't fool me, you're going to kill me."

The orderly fought to keep Choinsky on the floor. "There aren't any Japs here."

They gave him a shot of morphine and strapped him to the bed.

Polly Bryant sat in the coffee shop and slowly sipped at the coffee in front of her, thinking that the time would never pass. Ten minutes until visiting hours and already she was a nervous wreck. For weeks she had been wondering what she would say to her husband when they came face to face.

Several weeks ago, she had talked to the doctor, and the shock had been almost more than she could stand. Polly had tried to get her husband to tell her what his injury was, but he avoided the subject. When he had first reached the States, she had attempted to see him, but he refused. In desperation she had talked to his doctor, and he had broken the suspense. At first, the horror of the wound had repulsed her and she was glad that she did not have to face her husband.

The doctor had taken a lot of time explaining to her that the wound would probably mean no more than that they could never have any children. He had patiently explained to her that Bryant was faced with a very serious adjustment, and that she would have to be very patient with him.

Polly took another sip of the hot coffee and then glanced at her watch. She suddenly felt sick when she realized it was time to see him. Her hand was shaking, as she fished in her crowded pocketbook for the correct change. Picking up the check, she hesitated a minute and took a deep breath before walking to the cashier's desk.

Several times, as she walked down the long corridor, she wanted to turn and leave, but she continued to walk down the hall. When she had reached the correct door, she took another deep breath and then said a silent prayer, hoping to find the courage to act happy with him. Finally, she knocked. There was no answer, but she knew that he was in the room, probably afraid to face her.

At length, after knocking several times more, she slowly opened the door and entered the room, managing a smile. Her husband was in bed, his back turned to her. For a long moment she stood there not knowing what she should do. Slowly she began to walk to the bed. When she reached the side of the bed, she reached out with all the tenderness of a wife and softly called to him.

Bryant finally turned over in the bed, fear written on his face. They both stared at each other, tears in their eyes, and neither of them spoke. Polly could not help but notice that he looked older. He had flecks of gray in his hair and he had deep wrinkles.

Bryant was the first to speak, his voice very low and the words coming jerkily. "You didn't have to come."

221

Polly wiped at a tear and reached out to stroke his forehead. "Honey, I love you. You're my husband, I want to be with you and get you well."

Bryant looked at her for a moment before he spoke. "Didn't they tell you what happened?"

"Of course they did. Do you think that a thing like this would make any difference to me? The only thing that matters is that you came back and that we can be together again. I love you, and you love me. That is the most important thing in the world to me." As she spoke, Polly wondered if she really meant it, or if the words were empty. Every time she thought about having to look at the wound, she wondered if she would be able to stand it.

"Polly," he said feebly, "it does make a difference. I'm not even a man any more. We might not even be able to have intercourse again and you're young. That wouldn't be right for you."

"Sex isn't the most important thing in the world," she assured him. Polly really didn't feel that way at all. She wanted to scream.

"Even so," he continued, "women need to have children, and I can't be a father."

"Honey," she said stroking his forehead, "the doctor told me that we can live a normal life in all probability. If we can't have children, we can always adopt one."

"You will be the laughingstock of the town. Don't you know all the other women will make fun of you for having to live with a man like me?"

"I don't care about that," she lied. "The only thing I want is to have you with me again."

"Why don't you go away somewhere and let me alone for a while," Bryant suddenly said.

"You don't really mean that," she almost cried.

"I do," he growled. "I'm not even sure if I love you any more. I've got to have some time to think things through."

"Please don't talk that way, honey," she pleaded.

"Please leave," he insisted.

Polly realized that he was serious and sobbed into her hands. "Please."

"I don't like to hurt you," Bryant said, "but please leave me alone. You can come back next week. Just try and understand."

Polly did not understand and she was deeply hurt. She tried to understand what he must have gone through, but after so long an absence, she could not understand anything at all. "Do you really want me to go?" she asked.

"Please."

Polly leaned over the bed and kissed him tenderly. Then she left the room, the tears streaming down her face. She could not decide whether the emotion that she felt was pity or love. Maybe both.

Heddy Person was waiting for her date. She had received a letter from Regeic that afternoon. He said he wanted to marry her and raise his child. She was confused and hurt. Since she had given birth to the baby, she had managed to live a fairly normal life. Her mind took her back over the events of the previous years.

When she had found out that she was pregnant, she had written to Regeic and told him, but he had not bothered to answer. She was lonely and afraid. Heddy had kept her secret until it was no longer possible. Her mother and father had been furious at first, but they had both been wonderful about it. After the initial shock, they had discussed her having an abortion or going away to have the baby. Her parents had been in favor of an abortion, but in the end, she had decided against it.

Heddy had gone to Dallas, where she gave birth to a boy. She had left it with a relative to keep for a while, in hopes that Regeic would marry her. After a year of waiting, she had the child adopted. Her parents had explained to the neighbors that she had gone to work in Houston, and no one had ever found out her secret. After a year she had returned to her home and had lived a normal life since then. She had dated the same boy since that time and he was very serious about her. The shock of having a child had been great, and she had never allowed herself to become involved even in slight petting since then.

The boy, Cleveland Joiner, was a clean-cut type and he had never pushed her. Several times, they had become excited during a kiss but had mutually drawn the line. He was coming to pick her up tonight, and they were going to drive to Paris to see a movie. She had decided to tell him the whole story.

The problem should not be serious because she felt he would understand and still want her. Still, her problem was that she did not know for sure if she loved him. She had thought so, until the letter had come. Now, she wondered how she could be sure. She wanted to see Regeic again before she made a decision. Besides, Regeic might not want her if he found out that he could not get the child back. He might have written out of a sense of shame. She decided that this was probably the reason, since he was not the type of man who would marry. She decided that she would write to him and tell him that she would marry him when he came back, if she still loved him, and if he accepted the fact that he could not get his child back.

She heard Cleveland at the door and went to meet him. Right away, he saw that something was wrong and asked her about it. Since her parents were not home, she decided to tell him there. She seated him and told him the whole story.

Cleveland was shocked. His jaw hung open. He had listened to her story and made no comment. Finally he turned and stared at her for a long time. She felt crushed and could not meet his eyes. "Do you think that I'm horrible?"

"I don't know what to think. It's such a shock to me. I always thought that you were such a nice girl."

That hurt her. She wondered how he felt now. "Do you think you could ever forgive me for it?"

"I don't know. Like I said, it's such a shock to me. I just don't know what to say."

"Cleveland, honey. I could have waited until after we were married to tell you. Then I might not have let you know about it. I could have gone on and let you think I was sweet and pure and you wouldn't have known the difference. I'm not really bad. I made a mistake and I've paid for it a million times. Please don't turn against me."

"Do you still love him?"

"I don't know. If he hadn't written, I would have been glad to marry you. I've been dreaming about the day when you would ask me. Now I'm not sure and I have to wait until I can see him. I could have married you anyway, but it wouldn't be fair to you."

"I think that's best," Cleveland said at last. "I have to have some time to think about it and that will give me some. Does anybody else know?"

"No."

"Well, let's not mention it to anybody."

Heddy placed her arms around him and kissed him passionately on the lips. "I knew that you'd understand."

Cleveland kissed her. He reached up and turned off the table lamp. This left only the soft glow of the hall light. He took her in his arms and kissed her again. They stayed in a tight embrace for some time and he became more passionate. His lips went over her face and neck until she had trouble breathing. Heddy knew she was getting more excited than she had been since Regeic had gotten her pregnant. She thought about stopping Cleveland there, but she decided against it. He was hurt and the best thing she could do was to love him. He would stop before they got too excited.

Cleveland pulled her backward until he was on top of her and she could feel him against her. When he started his hand toward her breast, she became panic-stricken. She tried to struggle free, but he forced his body down on her and she could not move. She tried to keep her legs straight, but he kept working his body against her until, in excitement, she spread her legs for an instant. He pushed against her and his body was between her legs. Although they were clothed, he ground his body into hers and she felt her dress working up. She fought at his hands.

"Please don't," she whispered.

Cleveland paid no attention to her but continued to grind his body against her. Soon, little sparks of pleasure were shooting through her, but she was afraid. She had done this

224

with one other man and had gotten pregnant. What if it happened again? She began to cry and plead but he continued. Her arms grew tired of fighting him off and she finally gave up. He worked swiftly and soon she was bare from the waist up. She sobbed, but his hands and body kept at her until she could stand it no longer.

"I can't make you stop. I'll have to let you do what you want to, but please don't," she pleaded. She felt a strange mixture of pleasure and fear.

"Please stop," she pleaded. Then she felt his hands against her and let out a gasp of pleasure. "What if I get pregnant again?" she whispered in a panic-stricken gasp.

"Then, I'll marry you."

He continued to caress her and she had trouble thinking. She wanted him terribly and knew that he would not stop. With a great effort, she tried to get from under him, making sure that she pressed herself even harder against his fingers. She knew that he would do it, but she had to make him think she was struggling to the last. When she was completely naked, she cried and tried to cover her face.

Cleveland looked down at Heddy and knew that she would never be his wife. Every time he thought about her doing this with the soldier, he wanted to spit in her face. "I love you," he whispered.

"Please don't," she begged.

"I love you. I've stood it as long as I can. I have to have you."

"Can't I stop you?" she panted.

"No."

"Please, for God's sake! Please! Nooooooo!"

The light came on suddenly. Evidently both of them had exhausted themselves and they were asleep. Her mother and father stood in the room. Her mother cried and her father grew red in the face.

"You're no better than a whore!"

She jumped up and started toward her father with tears streaming down her face. Halfway across the room she realized that she was naked and she stopped. Cleveland was on the corner of the couch, trying to cover himself.

"Get your clothes and get out," her father told Cleveland. Both her mother and father stood and watched while Cleveland dressed. No one spoke as he left. Then, her father gave her a hard look and left the room, taking his wife with him. She had hurt them twice and she knew that she could not stay. Cleveland would never have her now. Still naked, she sat on the couch and cried. Her last hope would be Regeic. What if she was pregnant again? she thought in panic.

# CHAPTER ELEVEN

As month after weary month passed, the Japanese were slowly beaten. The remnants of the enemy army were driven back into the hills, where they starved to death. Price's battalion had been left to clear the island while the engineers built a giant airstrip. The Japanese seldom showed themselves. The only action occurred when an occasional patrol went after some Japs that someone had spotted. Usually the patrol would return without having seen any of the Japanese.

A great change had come over Higgenbotham and the other men. They were no longer boys playing at a man's game. They had become hardened veterans, and though Price hated to admit it, they were good soldiers. Price watched them with silent pride, and even the colonel had been forced to admit that they were the best platoon on the island. Although he had fought it, Price became friendly with most of them, and they relaxed together. Most of the new men could count Price as a good friend, something that they would not have even dreamed of several months before.

Malaria ran through the battalion and there was also a virus that none of the medics had been able to diagnose. The battalion's strength had been reduced to almost half. The only diversion from the talk of women and the poker games was an occasional movie. The men grew restless.

Word came down that the older men would be sent back to the States. It was a few days before Christmas when the word reached Price's platoon. They greeted the news with enthusiasm at first and went on a two-day drunk. It was Morris who had thrown cold water on the party when he commented that they had better wait until they were on the way before they celebrated. He reminded them that they had heard this rumor before and had always ended up on a new island. All they had left after that was a headache and a deflated morale.

The day before Christmas found the battalion in worse spirits than ever before. No one spoke more than was absolutely necessary, not even to his close friends. Most of them had never spent a Christmas away from home before. Everyone was touchy, and they all sat around drinking quietly. Even the jokers were quiet. Nothing lifted the gloomy spirits of the men, not even the meal that the cooks had prepared.

Price trudged to the tent, carrying a can of juice and a pint of gin that he had bought from a naval officer. Regeic had been suffering terribly from fever and the juice was supposed to be good for him. Price had accepted the doctor's theory about the juice being good for Regeic, but it was his opinion that the gin would do more for him.

When Price entered the tent, Regeic was lying with his

back to the entrance. Price walked straight to the cot and sat down on the edge of it. This brought only a moan from Regeic. Regeic had wasted away to a skeleton after the long siege of malaria, and his eyes were ringed with black circles. His skin had turned yellow and was drawn tightly about his face. The tight skin and the heavy growth of beard gave his eyes a hollow appearance.

Regeic turned over. "How are you doing today, Ern?"

"Just fine, and so will you when you see what I've brought you!"

"My fever is gone," Regeic said.

"I brought you something to drink," Price said jubilantly.

"I'm afraid that I'd puke it up."

"Have you been eating anything?"

"I still can't hold anything in my stomach."

"You must have eaten something, while we were out on patrol."

"Very little."

One of the medics, looking very tired, trudged into the tent and nodded to Price as he bent over Regeic. The medic had been working almost around the clock looking after the sick men, and wearily bent over Regeic, sticking a thermometer into his mouth.

"How is the gold brick today?" he asked.

Regeic started to answer, but the medic frowned at him and pointed to the thermometer. After some time, he removed the thermometer and read it. "Good."

Regeic looked up with pain in his face. "Gone?"

"Yeah. If you'd just eat something and drink the juice I bring in, you'd get better pretty soon."

"Makes me puke."

"How is he?" Price asked.

"Gold-bricking." The medic turned and walked from the tent, and Price followed.

"Isn't there anything you can do for him?"

"His fever has gone. If he'd just eat, he'd be all right in a week or so."

Morris came walking up with a mess kit full of Christmas food—turkey, sweet potatoes, peas, cranberry sauce, real ice cream, and a cup of what looked like eggnog.

"Is that eggnog?"

"Sure is."

Price reached for the food. "You wouldn't mind if I ranked you out of the food, would you? The doc says that Regeic hasn't been eating too good since we been gone and I want to feed him."

Morris handed the food to Price. "I'll go get us some and bring it back here. We'll eat with him."

"Thanks." Price took the food and entered the tent again.

Price was smiling as he walked to the cot. "You no-good son of a bitch, I brought you some chow, and if you don't eat it

227

I'm going to kick you in the ass."

Regeic looked at Price through slitted eyes and managed a feeble smile. "I don't want any."

"I meant it."

"I'll puke, Ern."

"If you do, I'm going to get some more and do it all over again until I can get some down. Even if it takes all week."

Price propped Regeic up and sat with one arm supporting him. For two hours he fed Regeic nibble by nibble until the mess kit was completely empty. Finally Regeic leaned back and rubbed his stomach.

"I hope it stays."

"It better."

"Got a smoke?"

Price pulled a package from his shirt and lit a cigarette for Regeic.

Morris and Higgenbotham returned with mess kits filled to the brim and entered the tent. Morris approached the bed and set a mess kit on the cot for Price. "That was the longest damn line I ever stood in."

"Thanks."

Higgenbotham laughed. "Did that no-good old sergeant eat anything?"

"Just a little."

Price ate the chow, and afterward lit a cigar. As he blew the smoke into the air, he wondered. Last year it had been K-rations in a hole on another island. This year it was turkey on still another island. Where would next Christmas find him? Who would he be with? Price looked out over the water, and the ocean seemed very large. With each day the States seemed to be a million miles further away from him.

As he sat smoking, he reflected on the States and remembered how his son had looked as he crawled across the floor a million years ago. He felt like crying. Desperately, he tried to picture the scene in Montgomery, to transplant himself into the living room as Buck came in and saw the tree.

*"Silent night, holy night. All is calm, all is bright."*

Price's thoughts were suddenly snatched back to the present, as the sound of the rough voices drifted through the night.

*"Sleep in heavenly peace . . ."* Tired soldiers from all over the camp lifted their voices in the familiar Christmas carol. The voices were rough and raspy, and they were far from the carolers that could be heard on the streets at home, but it was Christmas eve in the islands, and the homesick soldiers were trying to keep up their spirits.

Fortunado and another man came reeling into the tent, each holding a canteen full of the mixture of juice and alcohol, singing the carol. Without breaking the song, they sat on the floor.

"Merry Christmas, Price," they shouted.

"Merry Christmas."

"Have a Christmas drink?"

"Sure," Price answered, reaching for the canteen.

Suddenly the tent was filled with the sound of singing. " 'Hark the herald angels sing . . .' " It was Regeic. The others looked up and began to sing with him, and the drinks were passed among them.

"This your first Christmas away from home?" Price asked as he turned to face Higgenbotham, who was sitting on the floor.

"It's the first one that I ever missed. As a kid I was at home with my folks, and since then I've always been with my wife and kids."

"You're a lucky man."

"I never thought much about it. At least not until I got out here. Always before, Christmas came, and we celebrated it and that was all. All of a sudden"—he paused—"I find out that Christmas is one of the best times of the year for a family to be together. It's a family time and right now I want to be with my wife and kids more than anything in the world."

"You know, I have a kid, too."

"I heard."

"Well, I wish I could be with him right now. Suddenly it seems like I've been robbed of the best experience that a man can have."

"Lieutenant, I'm sorry for you."

"Yeah."

"No, really. If we ever get back, you can come and spend every Christmas with me and the wife."

"Thanks."

Morris laughed loudly. "He won't have to. When I get back to the States I'm going to kill the hell out of my wife, or at least get rid of her some way, and all of us single bastards can get together each Christmas. Old Ern and Regeic and me will go out and have us a ball."

Price sat on the floor next to Higgenbotham. "You don't understand, Morris. I'm sick to death of being with men. I want a family. Kids and a wife to be with. There must be something more to Christmas than getting drunk and giving out gifts. God knows I'm about the worst reprobate that ever was, and I don't really think I'll ever change, but this is supposed to be Christ's birthday. Did you ever think about it that way?"

"Well I'll be damned!" Higgenbotham muttered.

"I don't guess many people think about that, do they," Morris said, quite seriously.

"Merry Christmas!" Sterner shouted, as he weaved into the tent.

"Here's the professor," Higgenbotham shouted.

229

"Peace on earth," Sterner laughed. "Peace on earth."

Price looked up at the man. "You're drunk."

"You're damned right I'm drunk. If you had the most wonderful wife in the world you'd be drunk too. If I thought I could swim that damned ocean there I'd jump in and try to make it, but I know I can't, so I get drunk."

"I know how it is," Price said. "I guess all of us have some place we want to be right now. Even the war can't take first place over Christmas."

"I'll bet it does," Fortunado said. "Some place out there a man is getting killed right now."

"Sure he is," Price said. "I've spent the last two Christmases out here and was in the line both times. Even then we made trees out of bushes and empty shell cases. Men got killed then, too."

Turning to Price, Morris spoke. "It was last Christmas that Kincaid got killed, wasn't it?"

"Yeah."

"Damn good man."

"The best."

"Hey, you gold-bricking bastard," Price said to Regeic, "you get yourself well enough to drink a toast to old Larry Kincaid?"

"Sure, here's to old Larry."

"Old Larry."

After the toast had been drunk, Higgenbotham spoke. "Ain't this a bitch? If the folks at home could see us celebrating Christmas now they wouldn't believe it. Can you imagine how it would look if they saw Regeic there, starved to death and with a month's growth of beard?"

"Yeah, and listen to that singing. Did you ever hear anything worse?"

"Never."

"It sounds good, though," Sterner commented.

"How about that peace-on-earth stuff?" Regeic asked.

"How about that?" Higgenbotham laughed. "We believe in it, but do the Japs?"

"Don't you think they feel something when we seal a caveful of them up without even asking them to give up?" Price said.

"They won't ever give up."

"That's because they're good soldiers. I don't hate the Japs as individuals, but I have to kill them, and I do it the best way I can. They must feel the same way about us. For all I know, they told them we started the war.

"I do know that they're crowded on the Japanese islands and needed room to expand. They had people starving to death for the lack of land. Sure they took the wrong way to do it, but what other answer was there. Do you have any idea what we would have told them if they had said to Roosevelt, 'Let us have California so we can feed our people?' We would have told them to go to hell, that's what."

Higgenbotham laughed. "Peace on earth. Do you think there ever will be any?"

"Probably not."

"Brotherhood, that's the answer," Fortunado said.

"Brotherhood?"

"Sure. Me, I'm from the North and I guess that makes me a little prejudiced, but look at the way the Negroes are treated in the South. Look at the way they're treated in the army."

"Look at the way they're treated in the North, too," Price said.

"Don't you see that they're American citizens and should have all the privileges that go with it?"

"I didn't say they weren't. I want to see them get all the good things in life, too. I've been in the army for so long that I can live with anything, but I don't think all the people back home feel that way.

"Right or wrong, it's the way things are," Price continued. "Anybody that tries to rush the thing is just calling for trouble. Do you have any idea what would happen if they tried to get them into the schools?"

"No."

"They would have a lot of trouble. Besides, it isn't just the South. The army is run by Congress, and we have segregation here. Look at the cities in the North. They do the same thing. The only difference is that they don't make it legal. If you ask me, the Negro is better off when he knows where he stands than he is in the North where he never knows what will happen."

"Well, that may be true."

"Sure it is."

"Ain't no nigger going to school with my kid," Regeic said weakly.

"You ain't got no kids," Morris snapped.

"Like hell I don't. You remember the girl I got knocked up down in Texas? Well, I wrote a letter to her and told her I would marry her when I got back. I'll have a kid for sure."

"You lost your mind?" Price asked.

"Hell, no. I've done a lot of thinking since I been out here and I know that a man has to do at least one decent thing in all his life. The kid is mine and damned if the least I can't do is to give it my name."

"A hell of a thing that is," Sterner said. "When we all came to this outfit, you old men were like animals to us. I never even thought you had any feelings at all. Now, we're getting like you used to be, and you're getting sentimental. I guess the cycle has run its course. It's a good thing you're going home or you'd be out there having a tea party with the Japs instead of fighting them. Price is already feeling sorry for them."

231

"After you've been out here as long as we have, you'll feel different about a lot of things. Mostly you learn not to feel about anything at all that's real. Mostly I think about my ex-wife, although I know that nothing will ever get us together again. Regeic thinks about that girl in Texas, and Morris hates his wife. I know I'll never get with Sandra again; Morris won't do anything about his wife; and Regeic will never marry the girl in Texas. But at least it gives us something to think about."

"Strange how a man's mind works, isn't it?"

"That's the way the army makes a man."

Higgenbotham scratched his stomach and glanced around nervously. "I've never mentioned this before, but I was the leader of the patrol that scouted the town where your outfit got so shot up. I know you must have wondered who did that to you. I made a lot of mistakes that day because I didn't know how to do my job."

"If you'd told me that a month ago," Price said, "I think I might have killed you."

"How do you feel now?"

"It seems like it was a million years ago and I don't give a rat's ass."

"How about you, Regeic?"

"Me, neither."

"Morris?"

"I ain't cared about nothing in months."

"I'm glad you can take it that way," Higgenbotham said with relief.

Price passed a full canteen cup to Higgenbotham. "It's Christmas and, besides, we've been through a lot together since then. Just don't let it worry you. If I worried about all the men I've killed because of a mistake I've made, I'd lose my mind."

"Thanks, Price."

"Merry Christmas."

"And an alcoholic New Year to you too," Higgenbotham said, as he raised the cup.

The tent became quiet. Most of the men were in a drunken stupor. Price sat on the edge of the cot and wiped at Regeic's forehead with a wet cloth, trying to make him more comfortable.

"You're better to me than my own mother," Regeic said.

"Blow it out."

"You should have been born a woman," Regeic smiled.

"Why don't you just go to sleep?"

"I'm not sleepy, but you must be tired of taking care of me."

"No."

"Don't lie to me."

"You just get some sleep."

"Why don't you?"

"I don't want to leave you by yourself. You might have a bad dream in the dark." Price laughed.

"I'm a big boy now."

"Then you're too young to drink this."

Regeic grabbed the cup from Price and took a large drink. "Thanks," he said, as he handed it back.

"Did you really write to that girl, Regeic?"

"I said I did."

"Really?"

"I said I did."

"You really going to marry her when you get back?"

"I don't think so. I feel about the same way about her that you do about Sandra. I like to think about it, but I don't know what I would do if the time came."

"I'd marry Sandra again."

"That's what I meant to say. You would, but you and I both know that she wouldn't have you again anyway."

"I guess you're right."

"Sure I am. We both know that we don't really want to go home. Our lives have been such a mess that we'd just as soon get it over with right now. I used to think that a man that committed suicide was a coward, but now I realize that he has to have more courage to pull the trigger than I have.

"We could have gotten home before now if we'd really bitched and kept it up. The only reason we stayed is that we got nothing to go back to. We know that we'll get killed as sure as hell, but we stay anyway.

"In one sense, you're killing yourself over Sandra. Morris is doing the same thing over Roberta, and I'm doing it because I've never had anybody at all. When I get back I'm going to be an old man, all used up and not worth a damn. I don't think I can stand the thought of living in a barracks all the rest of my life."

"Three no-goods, aren't we?"

"That's right, Mother."

"Mother?"

"Sure, look at the way you're wiping at my head."

"Kiss my ass."

"Is that any way for a mother to talk?"

A week after New Year's day, orders were passed down for the platoon to hike to the far end of the island. Intelligence reported that there were Japs living in a small village. If they could be caught, most of the harassing would come to an end. According to the colonel, they were half-starved and could not have much ammunition left.

The rain began to come down almost before they could get out of the company area. There was a mad scramble for the ponchos. Each man broke out his own, and the man right behind him would help him on with the clumsy rubber garment.

233

Looking backward, the line of men looked like so many hunchbacks, as they sloshed along.

The men had been out only an hour when the rain began to pour down in great sheets. Price passed the word for the men to quicken their pace. A forceful wind blew the rain into their faces in drops sharp as needles. Ponchos flapped in the breeze and the water ran down them into the men's shoes. The morning was dark as night. Wringing wet from the rain and heat, the platoon plodded along without stopping.

Price felt the water swish in his shoes and knew that his wool socks were soaked. He hoped that the men had brought clean socks with them because wet feet in this part of the world led to jungle rot.

One rest, then another, and still another, each more miserable than the last. The heat and rain became more unbearable every time they halted. The rain was so heavy that the men could not even light a cigarette.

A little after noon, the platoon left the trail to eat chow. Price directed the men off the small trail, and they took shelter in the heavy foliage. The men labored with their packs, trying to keep them and their remaining clothing dry. Most of the men stacked them and covered the piles of equipment with shelter halves. Too tired even to bitch, the men worked with the cans of beans and wieners. It was impossible to heat the coffee, so it was mixed, and the men gulped it down cold.

After the break for chow, the men staggered back to the trail. The short rest had given their bodies time to begin to ache. Most of the men were already getting blisters, although they had thick layers of calluses leathered into their feet through the months of walking.

The rain poured down, and it was almost impossible to shift the weight of the packs or move the straps to ease the sore spots that the pack straps and belts were making. They slogged down the trail, the rain blinding them. Soon the numbness set in. It was all they could do to keep walking, each man riveting his attention on the back of the man in front of him and cursing the rain.

The day seemed as though it would never end and the column pushed on, mile after mile, the only sound being the swishing of the water in their shoes. Numb, each man picked up one foot and placed it in front of the other. Occasionally turning around, Price saw that the column had the same hunchbacked look, and the rifles made a strange hump under the ponchos.

Finally Price called a halt. The men again went into the dense jungle growth for the protection that it offered, trying to anchor shelter halves in the wet ground.

Price made the rounds of the area in a stupor, so tired that he could barely move. Slowly, he crawled into the shelter half that he shared with Regeic and buttoned it down. The semi-

234

dryness was a welcome relief. Noting that Regeic was already asleep, he pulled off his wet shoes and rubbed his feet dry. A sharp pain warned him that the blisters were there, and he cursed to himself. He fell to the ground and was asleep before he knew it.

The heat was already becoming unbearable when Price struggled awake the next morning, sweat running down his body. Slowly he crawled from the hole, scratching his stomach and then stretching. His body responding, he bent and kicked Regeic's foot until the man was awake.

Regeic busied himself with getting the men on their feet and packing their gear. Groggy and bitter, the men gathered their equipment and were once again on the trail. They kept up a steady pace all morning. Price staggered like a punch-drunk fighter as he reeled down the road. Most of the men were limping from the blisters on their feet. Price had been too tired to talk as he lunged forward, and as far as he could tell, not a man had spoken. Only the grunts of the men could be heard as they slogged onward.

It was late in the afternoon when Price saw the small stream ahead. This meant that the village was just ahead of them, about three hours' march. He signaled for the column of men to stop and he sat on the ground wearily.

"How much further do we have to go?" Regeic said, puffing.

"Three hours."

"Think the Japs have spotted us?"

"I doubt it. They don't think we know about this place yet and probably aren't expecting any trouble."

"Hadn't we better post a guard?"

"I hate like hell to do it, but you'd better have the men dig some holes tonight. I think one man per squad is enough to stand guard, don't you?"

"It'd better be. I don't think the men can stand too much more. We've done a lot of walking."

"Tell them to get a good sleep tonight. No smoking and no more talking. We don't want the Japs to find us if we can help it."

"How early are we pulling out in the morning?"

"As soon as it's light."

"I'll pass the word."

The men had rested well, and they walked for three hours without any visible signs of being tired. When he thought they were close to the village, Price halted the column and signaled for Regeic to come with him.

It only took them fifteen minutes to find the village. It was just inside the jungle wall, fifty yards from the water's edge. Silently, Price and Regeic crept to the edge of the vegetation and surveyed the village.

All of the structures were made of bamboo with leaves

235

woven together for a roof. In all, there were no more than ten houses. A few Japanese soldiers could be seen moving in and out of the largest structure. Apparently, they were storing supplies that had been brought in from small boats or submarines. They did not act as if they suspected there might be any Americans in the area.

"They don't know we're here," Regeic whispered.

"Good."

"What do you intend to do?"

"Watch for a while and see what they're doing. I'd like to catch as many of them as we can when we go in."

"We going to just bust in?"

"I'd like to get about three men on the other side with a machine gun before we come in. That way, if any run, the machine gun can cut them down. We can attack from here and back in the jungle."

"Don't you think we'd better get started?"

"Let's get back to the men first."

Price sent the men to their stations. Higgenbotham took two men and a thirty-caliber machine gun and started for the far side of the village. Morris took a squad and disappeared into the jungle. Price took the rest of the platoon and returned to the point from which he and Regeic had been watching the village. The plan called for an all-out attack at Price's order. When the first shot was fired, both Price and Morris would advance and Higgenbotham would cut off any retreat. No prisoners would be taken and any supplies found would be destroyed.

While they waited, Regeic whispered. "You know, I was wondering. If we take the town and then wait, we might be able to get the boat that's bringing in the supplies."

"Good idea."

It was late afternoon when the Japanese soldiers began to assemble in a large building. Some of them seemed to be carrying mess gear, and it seemed to Price that they must be eating their evening meal.

He turned to Regeic. "What do you think?"

"Good a time as any."

"They won't know what hit them."

"Ready?"

"Let's go."

Price signaled the men to fix their bayonets and waited for them to obey. Satisfied that they were ready, he silently moved forward.

Moving forward, Price felt that the Japs must see him, but he continued. He was almost twenty yards from the jungle before the first Jap turned. The man stood, his mouth open for what seemed like a full minute before he yelled. Price triggered the submachine gun and the man was slammed backward by the force of the slugs.

The platoon began to run forward, firing at all the Japs

236

who appeared. They were almost to the first building before there was a shot fired from the Japanese.

As they reached the first building, several Japs raced through the door, firing as they came. Price fired at them, and he thought several men behind him had also fired. The ground seemed to erupt around the Japanese, who fell in a squirming mass. Someone had thrown a grenade into the house, which almost disintegrated from the force.

There was a burst of fire from the other side of the village and Price thought some of the Japs might have tried to escape past Higgenbotham. When he looked up, three Japs were running toward the water. They had lost their weapons, or left them, in their haste to run. Price triggered his weapon and the three men went down. Two were hit in the face and the blood gushed from them. The other seemed to be hit in the midsection and fell backward into a sitting position. Regeic trotted toward the man who was staring up at him, fear engraved on his face. When he was in range, Regeic sent a heavy barrage into the Jap's face, almost tearing it from his neck.

Suddenly, about thirty Japs, some of them not armed, came rushing at Price in a headlong charge, screaming, "BANZAI." Every weapon opened up at them and they began falling in clusters.

A Japanese officer was charging at Price, swinging his saber in a wide arc. Price triggered his weapon and felt it buck in his hand.

Regeic saw the saber slice into Price's stomach and fired a burst directly into the Jap's face, sending the man to the ground. Quickly he turned his attention to Price, who was trying to crawl forward. His body was writhing, his arms flailing away, his eyes popping, and foam coming from his mouth. At last he lay still, as though he were dead, only his burning eyes giving any evidence that he was alive.

As Regeic bent over Price, he saw that the wound was bad, a large gash cut into his stomach. Quickly he ripped away the filthy fatigue jacket and poured the contents of the sulfa package into the bloody crease in Price's stomach. The saber had cut a gash into the skin so deep that the intestine could be clearly seen. At last Regeic had the wound bandaged.

Price looked up into Regeic's face. "Is it bad?"

"Should get you to the States."

"You wouldn't lie to me?"

"You know better than that."

"Like hell."

"We'll get you back."

"Back to where?"

"Camp."

"You mean to the grave diggers, don't you, Regeic?"

"Come on, you got a trip to the States—how lucky do you want to be?"

Price started to answer Regeic, but his head started to spin

237

and he could not see. When he opened his eyes again there was no noise, and the face of Regeic was above him, tears running down his face. "There you are," he whispered.

"I'm here."

"What the hell are you bawling about?"

Regeic turned his head away. "I'm not crying."

"Like hell," Price said. "Tell me, how bad is it really?"

There were several faces over him now. "Get the hell away from me!" he shouted. Then he remembered that Regeic had not answered his question. "Is it bad?"

"No."

Price tried to move, but he couldn't make it. He felt blood running from his mouth and down his chin. Pain was everywhere, but mostly in his stomach and chest. He groaned and closed his eyes.

"We'll get you back."

"I don't want to go back."

"I'd like to be going with you."

"Where to?"

"Home, where else?"

"Where the hell is home for us?"

"What the hell do you mean by that?"

"Do you know where your home is?"

"Of course."

"Tell me then."

"Well . . ."

"Well, hell! Home is a barracks for us. We got no home except the army. For people like us there isn't any home, not any."

"You're not making any sense."

"You just don't understand."

Price saw Morris bending over him. "How you doing?" Morris asked.

"I'm dying."

"You'll be all right, Ern."

"I've been through all that with Regeic. I know I'm dying and I don't give a damn."

"Thirsty?" Regeic asked.

"Don't waste the water on me."

"Have some," Regeic pleaded, tears streaming down his face.

"I thought I told you not to bawl like that. You're the ranking man. You have to get the platoon back."

"I'll get you back too."

"I told you, I don't want to go back. I don't want to be buried in a damn ditch like they did with Beecraft."

"But, Ern—"

"I want to be buried under one of those big trees back there," Price said.

"You ain't going to die," Morris said reassuringly.

"Don't hand me that shit."

238

"I wouldn't lie to you."

"That's what you told Beecraft. So did I."

There was a long silence, and it was then that the full realization struck Price that he was going to die. "You know how we used to feel about dying?"

"Yeah."

"Remember the day we talked to the chaplain?"

"Yeah."

"This is going to sound silly to you, and I don't expect you to understand, but right now I wish I had lived a different life. Not that I'd probably do anything different if I had it to do over again. Matter of fact, I know I'd probably do all the same things over even if I knew it was wrong. I guess I'm just a no-good bastard at heart, but I can see where I did a lot of things wrong. You two guys should do a little reforming. I'm serious. You still have time, and I don't."

Tears were streaming down Regeic's face. "Sure, Ern. I'm going to start by marrying that girl in Texas. I heard from her and she said she would marry me."

"And I think I'm going to try to make up with Roberta. After all, I ran around on her," Morris said in a choked voice.

"I know you two guys think I'm crazy as hell, don't you?" Price said, coughing blood.

"No, Ern, I think you're right," Regeic said, as he wiped the tears from his eyes. "I think you're the greatest friend that a man could have."

Pain seemed to be in every nerve now, and Price was seized with a fit of coughing. Blood flowed down his chin, and each cough seemed to make it worse. "Regeic?"

"Yeah."

"I don't have much time, but I want to get a promise from you."

"What is it, Ern?"

"Will you tell him for me?"

"Who?"

"Buck."

"Sure, Ern. What do you want me to tell him?"

"You tell my son"—Price coughed again—"that I was not the bastard that his mother has taught him I was."

"I'll tell him."

"Is that a promise?"

"I wouldn't lie to you about that. I'll go to see him before I do anything else, and I'll see to it that he gets taken care of."

"Morris?"

"Yes."

"Will you go with him?"

"I'll go with him, Ern."

"And be sure to tell Sandra that I still loved her. Even when I died."

"I'll tell her," Regeic said. Tears were flowing freely down his face.

"I would have given a million dollars if I could have seen Sandra and Buck before I died. If she'd just sent me one good letter, I'd feel a lot better about dying."

"I'll tell her, Ern."

Price tried to see them, but his body seemed to be getting lighter as the blood flowed out of it. He felt like a feather floating in the air. He seemed to be in a dark tunnel and floating toward a great light. Then he thought he could see Sandra holding Buck in her arms.

"Sandra, Sandra," he whispered.

Morris and Regeic watched as Price's body twitched.

Price was dead and Regeic bent over him to remove the dog tags, tears streaming down his face. He removed them and placed them in his pocket. His fingers struck an envelope and he pulled it out. "The clerk gave me this from Sandra," he said, "and I forgot to give it to Price."

Morris looked very tired and there were tears in his eyes. "She just wrote to tell him to go to hell again. I'm glad he didn't read it."

"Probably," Regeic said. He tore the letter into pieces. "When I see her I'm going to tell her how bad he wanted to see her and how much he wanted to get a nice letter from her. That ought to make her feel great."

Sterner stood with the others and watched while they dug a deep grave near the trees. Tears were streaming down Morris' and Regeic's faces when they put him in the hole. Sterner walked over and silently dropped a green sprig that he had taken from a tree. It fell on Price's chest. Then he walked back to the other men.

"He's dead," Sterner said, "and I doubt if too many people will remember him, but his kind will always make the army great."

"Amen," Higgenbotham said.

Regeic tried to say a prayer over the grave, but all that came out was a choking sound. Finally he looked up at the sky. "Take good care of him; he was a great guy." Tears were still running down his face. He made a motion with his arm and started to lead the platoon back. But he turned for a last look at the grave.